Skulduggery Pleasant
THE DYING OF THE LIGHT

DEREK LANDY

HarperCollins *Children's Books*

First published in hardback in Great Britain by HarperCollins *Children's Books* 2014
HarperCollins *Children's Books* is a division of
HarperCollins*Publishers* Ltd
77-85 Fulham Palace Road, Hammersmith, London W6 8JB

Visit Skulduggery Pleasant at www.skulduggerypleasant.co.uk

Derek Landy blogs under duress at www.dereklandy.blogspot.com

1

HB ISBN: 978-0-00-748925-1
TPB ISBN: 978-0-00-748926-8
Black Edition ISBN: 978-0-00-810615-7

Typeset in Baskerville MT by
Palimpsest Book Production Ltd, Falkirk, Stirlingshire

Printed and bound in England by
Clays Ltd, St Ives plc

This book is dedicated to me.

Derek, without you, I would not be where I am today.

Words cannot convey how much I owe you for the guidance you've shown me – for your wisdom, your wit, your keen insight and your keener intelligence, your taste, your strength, your integrity and your humility. I won't mention the charity work you do, or the political activism you're involved in, or the ecological work you've spearheaded. And it's not just because you won't talk about it – it's because no one else does, either.

You have taught me how to be a better person.

Nay – you have taught us all.

Do not go gentle into that good night,

Old age should burn and rave at close of day;

Rage, rage against the dying of the light.

Dylan Thomas

1

MEEK RIDGE

Five in the morning and Danny is up, rolling slowly out of bed, eyes half open as his bare feet touch the floorboards. Getting up this early is worse in the winter, when the cold threatens to push him back under the covers. Colorado winters are something to behold, as his dear departed dad would say, and Danny isn't one to argue with his dear departed dad. But the summers are warm, and so he sits on the edge of his bed without shivering, and after a dull minute he forces his eyes open wide, stands up and dresses.

He goes downstairs, puts the coffee on while he opens the store. Five thirty every morning except Sundays, the General Store is open and ready for business. It was that way when Danny was a boy and his folks ran the place, and it's that way now that Danny is twenty-seven and his folks are cold and quiet and lying side by side in the ground. On his more maudlin days, Danny also likes to think his dreams are buried down there with them too, but he knows this is unfair. He tried to be a musician; he moved to LA and formed a band and when it didn't all happen the way he wanted he scampered back home to take over the family business.

He quit, and there's no one to blame but himself.

By six, the town of Meek Ridge is awake. People stop by on the way to work, and he speaks to them with none of that easy patter his mom had been famous for. Back when she was alive, she'd talk the hind legs off a donkey, and she'd always be quick to crinkle up her eyes and laugh. His dad was more measured, more reserved, but people around here still liked him well enough. Danny doesn't know what they think of him, the wannabe rock star who lit out as soon as he finished school and skulked back with his tail between his legs years later. Probably just as well.

Early morning grows into mid-morning, and mid-morning sprouts wings and becomes a hot, sun-blasted afternoon. Unless there's a customer perusing the shelves, Danny stands at the door, cold bottle of Coke in his hand, watching the cars pass on Main Street and the people walk by, everyone seeming like they have things to do and places to go. By around three, business has picked up, same as it always does, and that keeps him busy and away from the sunshine, until finally he raises his head and it's coming up to seven in the evening and his favourite time of the week.

He takes out the list even though he doesn't need it, just to make sure he hasn't missed anything. When he's done, he's filled two large grocery bags – the reusable canvas kind, not paper or plastic. He locks up, puts the bags on to the passenger seat of his dented old Ford and drives out of Meek Ridge with the window down, his busted AC not doing a whole lot to dispel the trapped heat. By the time the road gets narrower, he's already sweating a little, and as he follows the twisting dust trail, he can feel the first trickle of perspiration running between his shoulder blades.

Finally, he comes to the locked gate and waits there, the engine idling. He doesn't get out and hit the intercom button. Same time every week, he's here and she knows it. Hidden somewhere in the trees or the bushes, a camera is focused on his face. He's stopped trying to spot it. He just knows it's there. The gate clicks, opens slowly, and he drives through.

The previous owner of this farm died when Danny was a teenager, and the buildings fell into disrepair and the fields, hundreds of acres of them, got overgrown with weeds and such. Now the fields are meadows, lush and vast and green, and the buildings have either been salvaged or rebuilt from scratch. A fence encircles the property, too tall to climb over, too sturdy to break. There are hidden cameras everywhere, and every last thing is rigged with alarms. Stories of the farm's new owner swept through Meek Ridge like a tidal wave when she first moved in, and ever since the waters have been unsettled.

There are those say she's an actress who's had a breakdown, or an heiress who rejected her family's lavish lifestyle. Others reckon she's in Witness Protection, or the widowed wife of a European gangster. The tidal wave has left behind it pools and streams of gossip in which rumours and stories and outright lies ebb and flow, and Danny doubts any of them even remotely touch upon the truth. Not that he knows what the truth is. The farm's new owner is almost as much a mystery to him as to anyone else in town. Only difference between them is that he gets to meet her once a week.

He pulls up to the farmhouse. She's sitting in a rocking chair, an actual rocking chair, in the shade on the porch, something she likes to do most warm evenings with her dog curled up beside her. He takes the grocery bags, one in each arm, and walks up the steps as she puts down the book she's reading and stands. She looks to be nineteen or thereabouts, with dark hair and dark eyes, but she's been living here for over five years and she hasn't changed a bit, so he reckons she's somewhere around twenty-four or so.

Pretty. Real pretty. She has a single dimple when she smiles, which isn't quite so much a rare sight any more. Her legs are long and strong, tanned in cut-off jeans, scuffed hiking boots on her feet. This evening she wears a sleeveless T-shirt, the name of some band he's never heard of emblazoned across it. She has a tattoo on her left arm, from the shoulder to the elbow. Some kind of tribal thing, maybe. Weird symbols that almost look like hieroglyphics.

"Hi there," he says.

Xena, the German shepherd who never leaves her side, growls at him, showing teeth.

"Xena, hold," she says, talking quietly but with an edge to her voice. Xena stops growling, but those eyes never leave Danny's throat. "You're early," she says, focusing on him at last.

Danny shrugs. "Slow day. Decided to give myself some time off. That's one of the advantages of being your own boss, you know?"

She doesn't respond. For a girl who lives up here with only a dog for company, she isn't someone who embraces the gentle art of conversation.

She pulls open the screen door, then the door beyond, beckons him through. He brings the groceries inside, Xena padding behind him like an armed escort. The farmhouse is big and old and bright and clean. Lots of wood. Everything is heavy and solid, the kind of solid you'd grab on to to stop yourself from floating away. Danny feels like that sometimes, as if one of these days, he'd just float away and no one would notice.

He puts the groceries on the kitchen table, looks up to say something, realises he's alone in here with the dog. Xena sits on her haunches, ears pricked, tail flat and still, staring at him.

"Hi there," he says softly.

Xena growls.

"Here," she says from right beside him and Danny jumps, spins quickly to the dog in case she mistakes his sudden movement for aggressiveness. But Xena just sits there, no longer growling, looking entirely innocent and not unamused.

Danny smiles self-consciously, takes the money he's offered. "Sorry," he says. "I always forget how quietly you walk. You're like a ghost."

Something in the way she looks at him makes him regret his choice of words, but before he can try to make things better she's already unpacking the bags.

He stands awkwardly and tells himself to keep quiet. He knows the routine by now. As she busies herself with packing away the groceries, she will ask, in the most casual of tones—

"How are things in town?"

"Good," Danny says, because that's what he always says. "Things are quiet, but good. There's gonna be a Starbucks opening on Main Street. Etta, she owns the coffee shop on the corner, she's not too happy, and she tried to have a town meeting to stop it from happening. But no one went. People want Starbucks, I think. And they don't really like Etta."

She nods like she cares, and then she asks, just as he knew she would, "Any new faces?"

"Just the usual number of people passing through."

"No one asking about me?"

Danny shakes his head. "No one."

She doesn't respond. Doesn't smile or sigh or look disappointed. It's just a question she needs answered, a fact she needs confirmed. He's never asked who she's waiting for, or who she's expecting, or if someone asking about her would be a good thing or a bad thing. He doesn't ask because he knows she wouldn't tell him.

She closes the kitchen cabinet, folds one of the canvas bags into the other, hands them both back to Danny.

"Could you bring some eggs next time?" Stephanie asks. "I think I'll be in the mood for an omelette."

He smiles. "Sure," he says. He's always been a sucker for the Irish accent.

2

LIVING IN THE SHADOW

The flickering lights of the trashed supermarket threw deep shadows from dark places, and Stephanie stepped through it all with one hand wrapped tightly round the golden Sceptre. Rows of shelves lay toppled against each other in a domino-sprawl of scattered food tins and ketchup bottles. She caught the scent of a small ocean of spilled vinegar and glanced to her right in time to catch a flash of pinstripe. Then she was alone again in this half-collapsed maze, the only sound the gentle hum from the freezers.

She edged into the darkness and out again into the light. Slow steps and quiet ones and once more the darkness swallowed her in its cold hunger. The maze opened before her. A man hovered there, a metre off the ground, as if he were lying on an invisible bed. His hands were clasped on his belly, and his eyes were closed.

Stephanie raised the Sceptre.

One thought would be all it'd take for a bolt of black lightning to turn him to dust. One simple command that, less than a year ago, she wouldn't have even hesitated to give. Ferrente Rhadaman was a threat. He was a danger to her and to others. He had stepped into the Accelerator and the boost to his powers had turned him violent. Unstable. Sooner or later, he was going to

14

kill someone in full view of the public and, just like that, magic would be revealed to a world that wasn't ready for it. He was now the enemy. The enemy deserved to die.

And yet... she hesitated.

She was not one to second-guess herself. She was not prone to introspection. For the majority of her existence, Stephanie had been all surface. She was the reflection, the stand-in, the copy. While Valkyrie Cain had been out playing hero, Stephanie had gone to school, sat at the dinner table, carried on with normal life. People viewed her as an unfeeling object. She had been an *it*.

But now that she was a *she*, things were murkier. Less defined. Now that she was a person, now that she was actually alive, she found that she didn't want to deprive any other living thing of that same opportunity – not if she could help it. Which was, she openly admitted, hugely inconvenient.

Wearing a scowl as dark as her hair, she stepped out from cover and advanced on Rhadaman slowly. She took a pair of shackles from the bag on her back, made sure the chain didn't jingle. She kept the Sceptre pointed at him – she didn't want to kill anyone if she could help it, but she wasn't stupid – and chose her steps carefully. The floor was littered with supermarket debris. She was halfway there and still Rhadaman hadn't opened his eyes.

The closer she got, the louder her pulse sounded in her head. She felt sure he was going to hear her heartbeat. If not her heartbeat then at the very least her ridiculously loud breathing. When had she started breathing so loud? Had she always breathed this loud? She would have thought someone might have mentioned it.

Three steps away Stephanie paused, looked around, watching for pinstripes. Nothing. Why hadn't she waited? Why did she have to do this on her own? Did she really have that much to prove? Probably, now that she thought about it. So would capturing Rhadaman single-handedly make her a worthy partner? Would that justify her continued existence?

She wasn't used to all these conflicting thoughts ricocheting around in her head.

Three more steps and she reached out, shackles ready.

Rhadaman's eyes snapped open.

He stared at her. She stared at him.

"Um... This is a dream?" she tried, and a wave of energy threw her back.

She went tumbling, realised in some dim part of her mind that her hands were empty, and when she came to a stop she looked up and Rhadaman was standing there holding the Sceptre.

"I've seen this in books," he said. He was American. "It's the real thing, isn't it? The Ancients actually used this to kill the Faceless Ones, to drive them out of this reality. The original God-Killer." He pointed it at her as she stood, then frowned. "It doesn't work."

"Must be broken," said Stephanie. "Could I have it back?"

She held out her hand. He looked at her a moment longer, and his eyes widened. "You're her."

"No," she said.

He dropped the Sceptre and his hands started glowing. "You're her!"

"I am not!" she said, before he could attack. "You think I'm Darquesse, but I'm not! I'm her reflection! I'm perfectly normal!"

"You killed my friends!"

"Stop!" she said, pointing at him. "Stop right there! If I were Darquesse, I could kill you right now, yes? I wouldn't need shackles to restrain you. Listen to me. Valkyrie Cain had a reflection. That's me. Valkyrie Cain went off and turned evil and became Darquesse, but I'm still here. So I am not Darquesse and I did not kill your friends."

Rhadaman's bottom lip trembled. "You're not a reflection."

"I am. Or I was. I evolved. My name is Stephanie. How do you do?"

"This is a trick."

"No," said Stephanie. "A trick would be much cleverer than this."

"I should... I should kill you."

"Why would you want to do that? I'm working with the Sanctuary. The war's over, right? You do remember that? We're all back on the same side, although you guys kind of lost and we're in charge. So, if I tell you to surrender, you have to surrender. Agreed?"

"No one gives me orders any more," said Rhadaman.

"Ferrente, you don't want to do something you'll regret. The Accelerator boosted your magic, but it made you unstable. We need to take you back and monitor your condition until you return to normal. You're not thinking clearly right now."

"I'm thinking very clearly. Killing you may not bring my friends back, but it'll sure as hell make me smile."

"Now that," Skulduggery Pleasant said, pressing the barrel of his gun to Rhadaman's temple as he stepped up beside him, "is just disturbingly unhealthy."

Rhadaman froze, his eyes wide. Skulduggery stood there in all his pinstriped glory, his hat at a rakish angle, his skull catching the light.

"I don't want you getting any ideas," Skulduggery said. "You're powerful, but not powerful enough to walk away from a bullet to the head. You're under arrest."

"You'll never take me alive."

"I really think you should examine what you say before you say it. You're not sounding altogether sane. Stephanie, you seem to have dropped your shackles. Would you mind picking them up and placing them on—"

Rhadaman moved faster than Stephanie was expecting. Faster even than Skulduggery was expecting. In the blink of an eye, Skulduggery's gun was sliding along the floor and Skulduggery himself was leaping away from Rhadaman's grasping hands.

"You can't stop me!" Rhadaman screeched.

Skulduggery's tie was crooked. He straightened it, his movements short and sharp. "We wanted to take you in without violence, Ferrente. Do not make this any harder than it has to be."

"You have no idea what it's like to have this kind of power," Rhadaman said, anger flashing in his eyes. "And you want me to give it up? To go back to being how I was before?"

"This power level isn't going to last," Skulduggery said. "You know that. It's already starting to dip, isn't it? In fifteen days, there'll be more dips than peaks, and by the end of the month you'll be back to normal. It's inevitable, Ferrente. So, do yourself a favour. Give up before you do any serious damage. We'll get you the help you need, and when it's all over, you'll return to your old life. The alternative is to keep going until you hurt someone. If you do that, your future will be a prison cell."

"You're scared of my power."

"As you should be."

"Why should I be scared? This is the greatest thing that's ever happened to me."

"This?" Skulduggery said. "Really? Look around, Ferrente. We're in the middle of a supermarket. The greatest thing that's ever happened to you and you choose to trash a supermarket? Are you really that limited?"

Rhadaman smiled. "This? Oh, I didn't do *this*."

"No? Who did?"

"My friends."

Stephanie couldn't help herself – she had to look around.

"And where are your friends now?" Skulduggery asked.

Rhadaman shrugged. "Close by. They don't wander off too far. There were loads of them around after the various battles, and I found a group and adopted them. They don't say a whole lot."

Stephanie picked up a faint whiff in the air. "Hollow Men?"

"I've given them names," Rhadaman told her. "And I've

dressed them in clothes. I've called them after my friends, the ones Darquesse killed. I think they like having names, not that they'd ever show it."

"Hollow Men don't like anything," Stephanie responded. "They don't think. They don't feel."

"Reflections aren't supposed to feel, either," Rhadaman said. "But you say you do. What makes you any different to them?"

"Because I'm a real person."

"Or you just think you are."

"If you surrender," Skulduggery said, "I promise we'll take your friends in and treat them well. Once the effects of the Accelerator wear off, they'll be returned to you. Do we have a deal?"

"You know what they *do* enjoy?" Rhadaman asked, as if he hadn't even heard Skulduggery. "They enjoy beating people to a pulp. They enjoy watching the blood splatter. They love the feel of bones breaking beneath their fists. That's what my friends enjoy. That's what will make them happy."

"You don't want to do this," Skulduggery said.

Rhadaman smiled, curled his lip and gave a short shriek of a whistle.

Skulduggery flicked his wrist as he ran at Rhadaman, sending the Sceptre flying into Stephanie's hands. Rhadaman caught him, threw him and leaped after him, and before she could run to help, the Hollow Men came at her, stumbling through a mountain of cereal boxes. Hollow Men dressed in clothes, ridiculous in badly-fitting suits, ludicrous in flowing floral dresses.

Black lightning flashed from the crystal set into the Sceptre, turning three of them to dust without even a sound. Lightning flashed again, and again, but they kept coming, and there were more Hollow Men behind her, and they were closing in. They had that knack. They were slow and clumsy and stupid, but it was when they were underestimated that they were at their most dangerous.

Stephanie darted right, clearing a path for herself, ducking under the heavy hands that reached for her. She led them down a narrow aisle, big heavy freezers on both sides, turned to them and backed away as they gave lurching chase. Numbers mean nothing if the enemy can be corralled. Skulduggery had taught her that. It's all about choosing where to fight.

The black crystal spat crackling energy. If it could kill insane gods whose very appearance drove people mad, then artificial beings with skin of leathery paper and not one brain cell between them didn't stand much of a chance. They exploded into dust that drifted to the floor and was trodden on by their unthinking brethren. They didn't stop. Of course they didn't. They didn't know fear. They had no sense of self. They were poor imitations of life, much like Stephanie herself had been. Once upon a time.

But now Valkyrie Cain was gone, and Stephanie Edgley was all that was left.

From elsewhere in the supermarket, she heard a crash as Skulduggery fought Rhadaman. She wasn't worried. He could take care of himself.

The shadows moved beside her and a fist came down on her arm. Her fingers sprang open and the Sceptre went spinning beneath an overturned shelf. Stephanie ducked back, cursing. Her only other weapon was the carved shock stick across her back, which had a limited charge and was useless against anything without a nervous system. She ran by a shelf of microwaves and blenders, past pots and pans. She grabbed a stainless-steel ladle that felt unsurprisingly unsatisfying in her hand, and immediately dropped it when she saw the one remaining box of kitchen knives. She dragged it from the shelf, threw it straight into the face of the nearest Hollow Man. The box fell, knives scattering across the floor.

Stephanie snatched up the two biggest ones and swung, the blades slicing through the Hollow Man's neck. Green gas billowed like air from a punctured tyre. Even as she ran on, she could taste the sting of the gas in the back of her throat.

Two Hollow Men ahead of her, one in a shirt and tie and no trousers and the other in a silk dressing gown.

She dropped to her knees, sliding between them, cutting into their legs as she passed, and even as they were starting to deflate she was already on her feet again, stabbing the filleting knife into the chest of a Hollow Man wearing pyjamas. She spun away from the blast of gas, coughing, her eyes filling with tears. Something blurred in front of her and she hacked at it, shoved it away, her vision worsening, her lungs burning. Her stomach roiled. She tasted bile. She slipped on something. Fell. Lost one of the knives.

A hand grabbed her hair, pulled her back and she cried out. She tried slashing at it with the second knife, but the blade got tangled in her jacket and then it too was lost. She reached up, dug her nails into rough skin, tried to tear through. Her hair was released. Something crunched into her face. The world flashed and spun. She was hit again. She covered up, her arm doing its best to soak up the heavy punches, her head rattling with each impact. If she'd had magic, she'd have set the Hollow Man on fire by now or sent her shadows in to tear it apart. But she didn't have magic. She didn't have such a luxury to fall back on, to get her out of trouble. She wasn't Valkyrie Cain. She didn't *need* magic.

Stephanie brought her knees in and spun on her back. The Hollow Man loomed over her, little more than a black shape. Its fist came down on to her belly like a wrecking ball, would have emptied her lungs were it not for her armoured clothes. She braced her feet against its legs and pushed herself back out of range, rolling backwards into a crouch, the Hollow Man stumbling slightly. She plunged her hand into the display stand next to her, scrabbling for a weapon, fingers curling round a mop. The Hollow Man came at her and Stephanie rose, swinging the mop like a baseball bat.

She missed wooden mops. Wooden mops had a little weight to them – whereas the plastic one in her hands merely bounced lightly off the Hollow Man's head.

She flipped it, drove the other end into its mouth, pushed until she'd sent it staggering and then she let go, turned and ran back the way she'd come. Her eyes were clearing. She no longer wanted to puke. A Hollow Man turned to her and she dodged round it, tripped and fell and saw the Sceptre. She threw herself forward, plunged her hand under the fallen shelf, her fingers closing round its reassuring weight. The Hollow Man reached for her. She turned it to dust.

She got up, disintegrated the next one, and the one after that. Three more trundled into view and she dispatched them with equal ease. Then the only sounds in the place were coming from Skulduggery.

She hurried back to the open area, in time to see Rhadaman pull Skulduggery's arm from its socket.

Skulduggery screamed as his bones clattered to the floor. A blast of energy took him off his feet, and Rhadaman closed in, ready to deliver the killing blow.

"Freeze!" Stephanie yelled, the Sceptre aimed right at his chest.

He looked at her and laughed. "That doesn't work, remember?"

She shifted her aim, turned the door behind him to dust. "It only works for its owner, moron. Now, unless you want your remains to be swept into a dustpan, you'll shackle yourself." She kicked the shackles across the floor at him. They hit his feet, but he didn't move.

"I know what you're thinking," she said. "You're thinking, 'Can I kill this girl before she fires?' Well, seeing as how this is the Sceptre of the Ancients, the most powerful God-Killer in the world, and it can turn you to dust with a single thought, you've got to ask yourself—"

Skulduggery swung the butt of his gun into Rhadaman's jaw and Rhadaman spun in a semicircle and collapsed.

Stephanie stared. "Seriously?"

Skulduggery nudged Rhadaman with his foot, making sure he was unconscious.

"I was in the middle of something," Stephanie said. "I had him, and I was in the middle of something. I was doing a bit. You don't interrupt someone when they're doing a bit."

"Cuff him," Skulduggery said. He holstered the gun and picked up his arm, started to thread it through his sleeve.

"I'd almost got to the best line and you... fine." Stephanie shoved the Sceptre into the bag on her back, walked over and cuffed Rhadaman's hands tight. She stood as Skulduggery's arm clicked back into its socket.

"Ouch," he muttered, then looked at her. "Sorry? You were saying something?"

"I was being cool," she said.

"I doubt that."

"I was being really cool and I was quoting from a really cool movie and you totally ruined it for me."

"Oh," he said. "Sorry."

"No you're not. You just can't stand it when other people get to say cool stuff while you're too busy screaming, can you?"

"He did pull my arm off."

"Your arms get pulled off all the time. I rarely get to say anything cool, and usually there's no one else around to hear it anyway."

"I apologise," Skulduggery said. "Please, continue."

"Well, I'm not going to say it *now*."

"Why not? It obviously means a lot to you."

"No. There's no point. He's already in shackles. Also, he's unconscious."

"It might make you feel better."

"I'd feel stupid," said Stephanie. "I can't say cool things to an unconscious person."

"This isn't about him. It's about you."

"No. Forget it. You'd just laugh at me."

"I promise I won't."

"Forget it, I said."

He shrugged. "OK. If you don't want to finish it, you don't have to. But it might make you feel better."

"No."

"OK then."

He stood there, looking at her. She glared back, opened her mouth to continue the conversation, but he suddenly turned, walked away, like he'd just remembered that she may look and sound and talk like Valkyrie Cain, but she *wasn't* Valkyrie Cain.

And she never would be.

3

THROWING DOWN THE GAUNTLET

Roarhaven was a young city – barely more than three weeks old. It had grown from its humble beginnings as a small town beside a dead lake to a wonder of architectural brilliance in the blink of an eye. Constructed in a parallel reality and then shunted into this one, it overlaid the old town seamlessly. Roarhaven's narrow streets were now wide, its meagre dwellings now lavish. Its border was immense, proclaimed with authority by the protective wall that encircled it, a wall that used tricks and science and magic to shield it from prying, mortal eyes. At the city's centre was the Sanctuary, a palace by any other name, resplendent with steeples and towers and quite the envy of the magical communities around the world.

This was to have been the first magical city of the New World Order. Others would follow, as per Ravel's plan. When the Warlocks started killing mortals and the mortals needed saviours, the sorcerers would swoop in, beat back the horde and be hailed as heroes. They would prove themselves invaluable allies against the newly-discovered forces of darkness. Sorcerer and mortal would stand united. And then, slowly and subtly, the sorcerers would nudge the mortals to one side, and the world would be theirs. But what was that quote Valkyrie Cain had heard once, that Stephanie now remembered?

No plan survives first contact with the enemy.

The Warlocks had come in numbers far greater than expected. They took down the shield, smashed the wall and breached the gate. To even the odds, Erskine Ravel sent Accelerator-boosted sorcerers to fight them – but these supercharged operatives proved to be as much a threat to their own side as to the enemy. And then Darquesse appeared.

In the chaos that followed, many more people died. The Warlocks, having seen their leader killed, scattered and withdrew, nineteen supercharged sorcerers fled, and Darquesse inflicted the punishment of all punishments upon Erskine Ravel.

Roarhaven survived, but the dream had been broken.

Now, sixteen days after the battle had ended, only a fraction of its lavish buildings were occupied. Its streets were quiet and its people humbled and scared and ashamed. They had been promised glory and dominion; they were told they were going to claim their birthright as conquering heroes of the world. What a shock it must have been to discover that they were the villains of this little story.

Stephanie had no sympathy for them, however. They may have seen themselves as lions, but they flocked like lambs.

She hadn't made up her mind about the city, though. Yes, it was impressive and in places beautiful, and the emptiness of it all added a certain eerie quality she found she liked, but it took the Bentley eight minutes to get from the city gates to the Sanctuary. And that wasn't because of traffic – there was barely any to speak of – but because of the ridiculous grid system they'd used to arrange the streets. It would have been fine if those eight minutes were filled with conversation, but this morning Skulduggery was in one of his quiet moods, so Stephanie sat in silence.

They got to the Sanctuary – or to the palace that the Sanctuary had become – and took the ramp down below street level, where they parked and rode the elevator up to the lobby. No expense had been spared to remind visitors that this was where the power lay. The lobby was a vision of statues and paintings, white marble and deepest obsidian. Grey-suited Cleavers stood guard, their scythes gleaming wickedly.

The Administrator walked to meet them. "Detective Pleasant," Tipstaff said, "Miss Edgley, Grand Mage Sorrows will be ready to receive you shortly."

Skulduggery nodded as Tipstaff walked away, already checking his clipboard for the next item on his to-do list. Skulduggery waited with his hands in his pockets, standing as still as any of the statues around him. Stephanie wasn't nearly so patient, so off she went, glad for the chance to get away from him. He had his moments of levity, moments when the old Skulduggery would emerge, but they were few and short-lived. His mind was on other things. His mind was on Valkyrie Cain.

She didn't need to be around him when he was thinking about her.

She left the marble and the brightly-lit corridors and entered the area that had become known as the Old Sanctuary, what remained of the original building with its concrete walls and flickering lights and dancing shadows. Not many sorcerers bothered coming down here, and that's why Stephanie liked it. Those other sorcerers looked at her uneasily. To them, she was the reflection of the world-breaker, the cheap copy of the girl who was going to kill them all. They didn't trust her. They didn't like her. They certainly didn't value her.

She stepped into the Accelerator Room.

"Hi," she said.

The Engineer turned. The smiley face that Clarabelle had drawn on to its smooth metal head was still there, and gave the robot an endearingly cheerful expression. Parts were missing from its sigil-covered body, and in those gaps a blue-white light pulsed gently, almost hypnotically.

"Hello, Stephanie," the Engineer said. "How are you today?"

She shrugged. The Accelerator stood in the middle of the room like an open vase, the uppermost tips of its wall almost scraping the ceiling. Circuitry ran beneath the surface of its skin, crackling brightly. It drew its power from a rift between this world and the source of all magic, a rift the size of a pinprick that the machinery had been built around.

"It's getting brighter," she said.

"Yes it is," said the Engineer. "Every time the power loops, it grows."

It had originally given them twenty-three days, eight hours, three minutes and twelve seconds until the Accelerator overloaded. Tasked with extending that deadline if at all possible, it had tinkered with the machine, re-routing its power flow and usage, until seven more days had been added to the countdown. But that brief moment of breathing space had been swallowed up as time marched onwards.

"How long left before it all goes *kaboom*?" Stephanie asked.

"Fourteen days, seven hours and two minutes," the Engineer said. "Although the sound it makes will not be *kaboom*. If and when the Accelerator overloads, the sound will more than likely be a very loud *fizz*. Possibly a *whump*."

"Right. So not very impressive, then."

"Indeed. The effects, however, will be most impressive."

"Yeah," Stephanie said. "Every sorcerer in the world boosted to twenty times their normal level of power and driven insane in the process, effectively dooming the entire planet. That's damned impressive, all right."

"Sarcasm is your forte, Miss Edgley."

She smiled. "So nice of you to say, Engineer. So, has anyone come forward yet to offer their soul in exchange for shutting it down?"

"Not yet."

"They're probably busy."

"That is what I have surmised."

"We have two weeks left. I'm sure there'll be a queue of volunteers once word gets out."

"Undoubtedly."

She laughed. "You're a cool robot, you know that?"

"Possibly the coolest. You are damaged?"

"Sorry?"

"Your face. It is bruised."

"Oh," she said, "it's nothing. Just another perk of the job."

"Does it hurt?"

"No. Not really. Only when I poke it."

"Seeing as how pain is not generally sought after, why would you poke it?"

"Exactly what I was thinking." Stephanie grinned, then the grin faded. "Can I ask you a question? It's about the symbols you have on you. One of the things they do is make sure you can't be seen by mortals, right?"

"Essentially."

"But I'm mortal, and I can see you."

"But you are different."

"How? I mean, I'm not magic."

"But you come from magic," the Engineer said. "You are a thing born from magic, as am I. But, unlike me, you have surpassed your original purpose. You have become a person – much like Pinocchio in the old fable."

"Pinocchio," Stephanie said. "Huh. I hadn't looked at it like that."

"My creator, Doctor Rote, would read to me at night. That was his favourite story. It is now my favourite also."

"Aw, that's actually sweet. You want to be human?"

"Oh, no, not at all," said the Engineer. "I want to be a puppet."

She found Skulduggery in the Medical Wing, talking with Reverie Synecdoche. She didn't get too close. Synecdoche was a nice enough doctor, but she was way too fascinated by Stephanie's independent existence for it to be anything other than unnerving. Stephanie let Skulduggery talk and hung back, out of the way.

The Medical Wing was adjacent to the Science Wing, and everyone in this part of the Sanctuary was serious and industrious and at all times busy. Apart from Clarabelle. Stephanie watched her work – or at least do something that could be misconstrued as work. She moved with none of the energy of the people around her and carried an empty clipboard, but the look of concentration on her face was fierce, and double that of anyone else. She had bright green hair today.

"Hi, Clarabelle," said Stephanie.

Clarabelle stopped walking, but didn't lose that look. "Hi, Valkyrie."

Stephanie shook her head. "It's still Stephanie, I'm afraid."

"Why are you afraid? Did you do something wrong?"

"That's very likely," said Stephanie. "You look busy."

"I know. I'm practising. None of the doctors will let me do anything until I've proven myself, so I'm pretending to be busy so that they'll see I'm really good at it."

"Do you think that'll work?"

"I'm fairly confident," said Clarabelle. "It's how I got Professor Grouse to hire me. He told me afterwards that he immediately regretted his decision, but by then I'd already moved my stuff in. The doctors here aren't as much fun. There's one who looks like a toadstool. You'd imagine someone who looks like a toadstool would be fun to hang around with, but he isn't. He also doesn't appreciate being called a toadstool. Even Doctor Nye was more fun than Toadstool-head. Where is Doctor Nye?"

"Prison."

"When is it getting out?"

"Not for a long time."

Clarabelle pursed her lips for a moment, then nodded. "That's probably a good idea. Doctor Nye isn't very nice. It likes experimenting on things. I heard it once combined the top half of a centaur with the bottom half of a minotaur and the creature escaped, and you can hear it sometimes, roaming the woods at night, howling at the full moon..."

"I'm not sure any of that is true."

"Still, though," Clarabelle said, walking away, "it makes you think, doesn't it?"

"Stephanie," Doctor Synecdoche called, and waved her over.

Stephanie stifled a groan, and joined them without much enthusiasm.

"I have something for you," said Synecdoche, rooting around in a desk. "I don't approve of it, personally, as I'm in the habit of saving lives rather than taking them. But an item was recently discovered buried in the backrooms of the Old Sanctuary, and I was considering your situation and I thought that... let me just find it..."

"My situation?" Stephanie asked.

"Not having magic," said Skulduggery. "The shock stick is useful, but limited if you can't recharge it yourself. The Sceptre is unstoppable but, in its own way, also limited. You may not have the space to aim and fire."

"So I saw something," Synecdoche said, "and thought of you. Ah, here we are. What do you think?"

She held out a gauntlet made of black metal.

Stephanie's eyes widened, and even Skulduggery stiffened.

Synecdoche couldn't help but notice the reaction. "Is something wrong?"

"This is the gauntlet I wear in the vision," Stephanie said.

"So it would seem," murmured Skulduggery.

"You've seen this in a vision?" Synecdoche asked. "But I just came across it yesterday. I thought you might want it as a last-resort weapon."

Stephanie frowned. "What does it do?"

Synecdoche hesitated. "The Old Sanctuary was built by a more

31

ruthless breed of sorcerer. This belonged to one of them. It's called a Deathtouch Gauntlet. When it's activated, one touch will take someone's life. Ordinarily I'd have had it destroyed immediately, but considering what you're going up against, I thought you could use all the help you can get. You said Mevolent pulled Darquesse's head off and she reattached it, yes? She managed to use her last few seconds of thought to heal herself. With the Deathtouch Gauntlet, there are no last thoughts. Physical death and brain death are instantaneous, so, provided Darquesse doesn't know what's coming, she won't even have the *chance* to survive."

Stephanie looked at Skulduggery. "If I don't wear it, will the future we've seen be averted?"

"Not wearing the gauntlet will more than likely have no impact whatsoever on the vision coming true," Skulduggery said. "We've seen details of the vision change, but the result is always the same."

"Well, I'm not wearing it," said Stephanie. "There. I've decided. Can we go see Cassandra? Check if the vision still ends the same way?"

Skulduggery nodded, his voice suddenly brighter. "I'll tell Cassandra to expect us. Doctor, thank you for your efforts, but it appears we won't be taking the gauntlet."

"OK," said Synecdoche. "But I'll put it aside for you, Stephanie, just in case."

"Don't bother," Stephanie said, already moving away. "I'll never wear it."

4

FRIENDS AND FOE

hina Sorrows was waiting for them when they entered the Room of Prisms. Thin pillars of angled glass stretched from floor to ceiling, and in the centre of the room sat the Grand Mage herself, elegant in a flowing powder-blue dress, a brooch on her breast signifying her elevated status. Stephanie had heard people say she'd chosen this room to receive visitors because it had more angles with which to reflect her unnatural beauty – her raven hair, her eyes like ice, her perfect features – but Stephanie knew better. China had chosen this room so that she could see anyone trying to sneak up behind her. China was a cut-throat, and only cut-throats know how cut-throats work.

Behind China's throne – for that's what it was   the Black Cleaver stood with silent menace.

"Here they come," China said, smiling. "The only two people who ever bring me any good news. Do you know how depressing that can be? If I were delicate, I'd surely faint with the pressure."

"You wanted the job," said Skulduggery.

"I wanted the title, the power, and all those lovely books. The stress I could do without. I think I'm close to getting a worry line on my forehead."

"How dreadful," said Skulduggery.

"See? You understand. And so here you are, with good news. Congratulations, by the way, on taking down Ferrente Rhadaman without alerting one single member of the public. Scrutinous and Random have been working overtime to cover up some very sloppy displays. I'm amazed we're not splashed all over the news. Did Rhadaman have any information on the remaining renegade sorcerers?"

"He didn't have specifics, but he did say they're grouping together."

"Because there is safety in numbers?"

Skulduggery shook his head. "He said someone has been in contact with them. Sounds like a refuge is being offered."

"I don't like the sound of that. Do you mean another Sanctuary?"

"I have no more information."

China sat back, and said nothing for a few moments. "If it's another Sanctuary offering them asylum, we have to find out which one it is. Since the War of the Sanctuaries, international relations are... precarious. The last thing we need is one of them going rogue and upsetting everyone else."

The door opened, and Tipstaff walked in. He whispered in China's ear, and she nodded. When he left, she glanced at Skulduggery and Stephanie.

"Bear with me one minute," she said.

A man walked in. Tall and lean, unshaven, with dark hair that needed a cut and faded jeans that needed a wash. He exuded an air of menace that was as natural to him as breathing.

"Mr Foe," said China. "I was beginning to wonder if you would ever get here."

Vincent Foe looked at them all warily. "Apologies, Grand Mage. I was working on my bike."

"Well," said China, smiling, "if your motorcycle has broken down the next time I call for you, I expect you to catch the next available bus."

Foe's lip curled at the thought.

China continued. "You would do well to remember that, on a whim, I could have the Cleavers round you up and throw you in a cell and nobody, and I do mean nobody, would raise a single objection."

Foe brushed the hair out of his eyes. "That kind of strikes me as a potential abuse of power."

China's smile deepened. "As I always say, what's the point of power if you can't abuse it? You owe me, Mr Foe, and until your debt is paid, you are mine. Do you understand?"

"Yeah."

"I'm sorry?"

Foe cleared his throat. "Yes. I understand. And how, I wonder, will I know when the debt has been paid?"

"Oh, I'll be sure to tell you."

Foe smiled thinly, then looked over at Skulduggery and Stephanie. "You're OK with this, are you? This is how tyrants are created."

"What do you care?" Stephanie asked. "You're a nihilist."

He shrugged. "Just pointing it out."

"Mr Foe," said China, "I'm not done abusing my power."

Foe gave a little bow. "Once again, my apologies. What enemy is in your sights, may I ask?"

"An old one," said China. "Eliza Scorn has her Church of the Faceless up and running. I've watched her take it over, gather support, build it up, and I've waited for the perfect moment to tear it all down. I want to do it properly – not just here in Ireland, but around the world. So I need access to every little secret she has."

"You want us to break in somewhere, steal her files?"

"I said I wanted this done properly. Above board. No breaking, no stealing. I need a reason to confiscate every last scrap of paper that woman has."

"So?" Foe asked.

"She wants you to join the Church," Skulduggery said.

Foe frowned. "But we don't worship the Faceless Ones."

"That doesn't matter," said China. "One of the rules that were set down when the Church was given official status was that no one with a criminal background could be a member."

"Ah," said Foe. "And me and my little gang are all ex-cons."

"Precisely. You join, we swoop. Eliza loses it all."

"And then we're square?"

China laughed. "Mr Foe, you tried to kill me. We are a long way from being square. Leave."

Foe hesitated, then nodded and walked out.

When he was gone, Skulduggery spoke. "It would be a mistake to trust that man."

"Just as it would be a mistake for him to cross me," China responded. "Now where were we? Oh, yes, congratulating you on taking Ferrente Rhadaman into custody. Very good work, both of you. Of course, it's not the work you *should* have been doing. I assigned Dexter Vex and Saracen Rue to track down these renegades with the aid of the Monster Hunters."

"And they're doing very well," said Skulduggery. "Out of the nineteen, we've taken down one, they've caught six, two more have burned out all by themselves, and various Sanctuaries around the world have dealt with a further four. Which leaves us with six renegades still at large."

"And you're wilfully missing the point," said China. "Rounding up the renegades is hugely important, I accept this. But I assigned the two of you to the task of finding and stopping Darquesse. I've given you access to whatever resources you need to get this done, as it remains our number-one priority. If the renegades are not corralled, they will alert the world to our existence. But if *Darquesse* is not stopped, there will be no world to alert. So tell me, how are things progressing on *that* front?"

"As expected," said Skulduggery.

"Really? We expected no progress?"

"Just because we have no results doesn't mean we've made no

progress. We're looking for one person who could be literally anywhere in the world. At this early stage, it's a process of elimination."

"I see," said China. "And where have you eliminated so far?"

Skulduggery looked around. "Here. Darquesse is not here, therefore this room can be eliminated from the list of places she could be. Unless she enters this room after we've gone, in which case, we'd be foolish to rule it out completely."

China sighed. "So what you're saying is that it's impossible to track her down."

"No, not at all. In fact, we have two ways of finding out where she is. The first is quite simple – we bring her to us."

"And how do we do that?"

"She's punishing Erskine Ravel for the murders of Anton and Ghastly. For twenty-three hours of every day, he's subjected to unimaginable agony. If the doctors try to alleviate his suffering, the pain increases. If he grows somewhat tolerant, the pain increases. This link between them is something we can exploit. If we shunt Ravel into another reality, the link could break."

"And how does this help us?"

"Once the link is severed, Darquesse will come looking for answers. When we bring Ravel back, he'll be her first target. Naturally, we'll have to be ready, because we're only going to get one shot at luring her in."

China pursed her lips. "Risky."

"Oh, yes," said Skulduggery. "Hugely risky. Possibly suicidal. But we should probably get started on finding a reality to shunt him into."

China sighed. "Very well. And the second way?"

"That's a little trickier, but it's also more straightforward. We don't have to track her – we just have to track the people with her."

"You mean Tanith Low."

Skulduggery nodded. "Yes I do. Tanith Low and Billy Ray Sanguine."

5

TO WATCH THE
WORLD BURN

He watched her standing in the air, her eyes closed, hovering just above the wooden floor. She was wrapped in darkness, from each individual toe right up to her jawline, a darkness so tight he could see the muscles in her legs, the tightness of her belly. She'd been like that for days. Hadn't opened her eyes, or said one word. Just hovered there.

Sanguine took off his coat, dumped it on a straight-backed chair, the only piece of furniture in the room. It was cold outside, but hot in here, all that heat generated from the eighteen-year-old girl slowing rotating in mid-air. What was going on inside her mind, he had no idea. Were they human thoughts she was thinking, or something else? Something beyond human?

Someone that powerful, he reckoned, would only take a short while to start thinking thoughts that had no place in a human head.

A whisper of leather behind him, but he didn't turn. Tanith Low was quiet when she did her patrol of this little house in this little ghost estate. Were he to glance out of that window, he'd see a dozen identical houses to this one, but all hollow and empty. Years back, they were set to be sold to the affluent Irish and the lucky immigrants who came here for a better life. Then the money went away and immigrants sought better lives elsewhere, took a good chunk of the Irish with them.

Sanguine was tired of Ireland. It was coming to the tail end of winter, but the winds were still bitter and the rain was still mean. He wanted to go home, back to the heat of East Texas. He was sick of living the life of an outlaw. He wanted to sit on the porch in the evenings and not have to worry about the world ending, or how to play his part in it.

He watched Tanith slip out of the window and walk up the outside wall towards the roof. She had binoculars up there she could use to sweep the full 360. She hadn't said much since they'd arrived here, and she barely slept. The Remnant inside her kept her going, kept her strong and alert. Sometimes he'd catch her looking at him and wonder if today was the day she'd kill him.

Because she had to kill him. He knew that much.

Darquesse, that god-in-a-girl's-body that had once been known as Valkyrie Cain, was the Remnant's messiah, destined to decimate the earth and reduce civilisation to cinders for some reason yet to be discovered. When Darquesse had asked Tanith to look after her while she "hibernated" – her words – Tanith had been overjoyed. Sanguine had tagged along, of course he had. Tanith was his fiancée, after all. He loved her. But no matter how much he loved Tanith, Darquesse had never been his messiah, and he had no wish to see the world burn.

Tanith knew that, given enough time, he'd go on to do something drastic to avert that apocalypse, and the only reason she hadn't killed him yet was because she obviously didn't think he'd be up to it. But even now there was a dagger tucked into his belt, one of four God-Killer weapons he'd hidden away from her that were more than capable of ending this god-girl's life. He'd heard what Darquesse could do. He'd heard her head had once been pulled off, and she'd put herself back together in those last few moments before brain death.

Yet Darquesse was killable. Darquesse was very killable. But in order to kill her, he needed to plunge this dagger into her before she had a chance to formulate any thoughts on the matter. He could do it now. Tanith was on the roof, Darquesse had her eyes closed, and here he was, standing with one hand already sneaking round behind his back to the dagger. He lifted it from his belt with great care, and when he held it he pointed it down and away from his body. These weapons killed whatever they nicked, and if they could kill a god they could certainly kill Momma Sanguine's favourite son.

The dagger felt good in his hand. Well-balanced. Three steps and he'd be next to her, then all he'd have to do would be to reach up, drive the blade through her skull. It'd be the easiest kill of his life, and the most important. Hell, he'd be saving the damn world. How many other hitmen could say that? Course, by killing Darquesse he'd be destroying the dreams of Tanith Low, the only woman he'd ever loved, and in doing that he'd be inciting her rage to the point where he'd have to kill her before she killed him.

Darquesse hovered there, head down and eyes closed, turning ever so slowly, and Sanguine put the dagger back in his belt. He reckoned he could allow his warm and fuzzy feelings to stay alive a little longer.

6

MY NORMAL LIFE

Home.

It always made her smile to go home. Those awkward days filled with awkward silences and occasional, maddening bursts of friendship were made bearable by the fact that Stephanie had a home to go to at the end of it all. The smile began when she got out of the Bentley, and it broadened to a grin when she pushed open the front door.

Comfort.

No, more than comfort. Belonging.

Her dad was in the living room, her mum moving round the house, and at this time of night Alice was already in bed. Her whole family, alive and safe. Shoving the knowledge of their possible fates into a dark corner of her mind, Stephanie went up to her room, changed into jeans and a hoody, and stowed the Sceptre and the stick under her bed. In her bare feet, she crept into Alice's room, looked down at her as she slept.

"Hey there," she whispered. "Sorry I didn't get to play with you today. Doing important stuff. When it's all done, I'll be able to play with you every single day, I promise."

Alice lay there, eyes closed and mouth open, looking beautiful. Stephanie felt such an overwhelming sense of love and, not for the first time, sheer thrilling excitement that this was her life now. She had a family. Parents and a sister. She was a normal girl living a normal life. Or it would be a normal life, just as soon as she escaped all the weirdness.

She crept back out and went downstairs. Her first stop was the kitchen. She'd been starving for hours, but hadn't bothered to tell Skulduggery. She'd started to feel that these biological needs of hers – to eat, to pee – were complications he could do without knowing about. Things were fraught enough between them as it was – she didn't want to annoy him any further.

She heated some leftovers in the microwave and washed them down with a glass of cold milk. Her belly no longer rumbling, she cleaned the plate and took her glass into the living room. Her dad didn't even glance up from the TV.

"Muh," he said, waving a hand.

"Hi, Dad. Whatcha watching?"

"TV."

"What's on?"

"Film."

"What's it called?"

He didn't answer.

"Dad? What's it called?"

"*Three Days of the Condor.*"

"Is it good?"

"Mm-hmm."

"Is it complicated?"

"Very."

"What's it about?"

"Not sure," he said. "I think it's about a bird."

Stephanie left him to his movie, and picked up a sealed envelope from the side table. Someone had written *Edgleys* across it, in handwriting she didn't recognise. Something slid around inside. She dug a fingertip in, ripped it open, and a memory stick fell out on to her palm.

"What's this?" she asked.

"What's what?"

She turned, showed him.

"Oh, that," he said, looking back at the TV. "I don't know what that is."

"It's a memory stick," she said.

"If you knew, why did you ask?"

"It was in an envelope addressed to us."

"Was it?" her dad asked. "That's odd. That's very odd. Well, it's sort of odd, but not really." He paused the movie. "I have no idea what's going on in this film."

"Who sent the envelope?"

"Hmm? Oh, someone knocked on the door, handed it over, said something and walked away. The strangest thing I've ever seen except, again, it wasn't really."

"Who was it?" said Stephanie.

"Haven't the foggiest."

"What did he say?"

"Can't really remember. It was weeks ago. He stood there and I remember thinking, *This is unusual*. It looked like he was about to cry, or hug me, or both. I think he said something like, *It's an honour to meet you*. Which, of course, it is, though most people don't usually say it out loud."

"And you didn't open the envelope?"

"I was going to," said her dad, "but I got bored. Is that the only thing in it? It didn't come with a covering note?"

"Just this."

"Are you going to see what's on it?" he asked. "I don't know if that's wise. It might be a virus, or an artificial intelligence like Skynet who just wants to usher in nuclear war so that our robot overlords can take over. I don't know if I'd like the responsibility of setting all that in motion. I mean, I probably would, because at least then I'd be famous, but seeing as how it would lead to everyone dying... I don't know. I'm conflicted."

"I doubt it would usher in Armageddon."

"But you can't be sure, can you? I'm not equipped to survive Armageddon, Steph. Maybe once upon a time I could have led the resistance, but I've gone soft. I've lost my edge. I wear slippers now. I never used to wear slippers."

"What's this about slippers?" Stephanie's mum said, walking in.

"Dad's just saying he could never lead the resistance against a robot army because he wears slippers."

"This is very true," her mum said.

"Then it's decided," Stephanie's father said. "When the robot army makes itself known, I will be one of the first traitors to sell out the human race."

"Wow," said Stephanie.

"Now that's an about-turn," said her mum.

"It's the only way," said her dad. "I have to make sure my family survives. The two of you and that other one, the smaller one—"

"Alice."

"That's her. You're all that matter to me. You're all I care about. I will betray the human race so that the robot army spares you. And then later, I will betray you so that the robot army spares me. It's a dangerous ploy, but someone has to be willing to take the big risks, and I'll be damned if I'm about to let anyone else gamble with my family's future."

"You're so brave," Stephanie's mum said.

"I know," said her dad, and then, quieter, "I know."

Stephanie grinned, left the memory stick on the side table and went to the couch, sank into it and curled her feet up under her. They all watched the rest of *Three Days of the Condor* and then Stephanie and her mum explained the plot to her dad. When he was satisfied, they said goodnight and Stephanie went up to bed. She climbed beneath the covers and closed her eyes, and a few seconds later her phone beeped. She read the text, sent back an answer and turned on her bedside lamp as she sat up, holding the covers close.

Fletcher Renn emerged from thin air in the middle of her room. "Hi," he whispered.

"Hey."

He sat on the bed. He looked good and strong and healthy. He looked tanned. His hair was awesome. He leaned in and they kissed.

"You taste yummy," she said.

"I've just been in New Zealand, eating strawberries. Do you want some? We could pop over...?"

"I'm in bed," Stephanie said, smiling. "It's bedtime now. And Skulduggery's picking me up early to drive over to Cassandra Pharos, so no quick jaunts for me."

"You're no fun."

"Were you in New Zealand with the Monster Hunters or just for the strawberries?"

"Strawberries," said Fletcher. "There's a little shop in Wellington that I love. They always have the best strawberries, for some reason."

She leaned back against the headboard. "So how is life as a big, bad Monster Hunter? Is it official yet?"

He grinned. "It is, and I'm actually enjoying it. Donegan and Gracious are pretty cool. Gracious is such an unbelievable geek, though. It's like everything he's ever loved is now on a T-shirt. They asked Dai Maybury to join, too, did you hear that? He said he couldn't, he was too much of a lone wolf – those were his exact words – but he agreed to be an Emergency Monster Hunter, to be called on only when needed. And now he just won't go away."

Stephanie laughed softly. "Sounds like you're all getting on well."

"We are," said Fletcher, nodding. "It's nice to be a part of something that... changes things, you know? We go after the renegade sorcerers with all their supercharged powers, and we beat them, we shackle them, we throw them in a cell. We stop them from killing innocent people, we stop them from exposing magic, and we move on to the next one. It's just... it's a wonderful feeling. To be useful."

"Look at that," Stephanie said. "My boyfriend is taking pride in his work."

"Boyfriend, am I?" he said, raising an eyebrow.

Her smile vanished. "Aren't you?"

"I don't know. Do you want me to be?"

"Well... yes."

He leaned closer. "OK. Then I suppose I'm your boyfriend. Are you my girlfriend?"

"That's usually how these things go."

He kissed her again. "Good."

7

VISIONS

kulduggery was at the pier on time the next morning, because Skulduggery was always at the pier on time. Stephanie was always a few minutes late. Valkyrie had rarely been late, but then Valkyrie had enjoyed this stuff a lot more.

"Sorry," Stephanie said, buckling her seatbelt. "Dad wouldn't get out of the shower."

Skulduggery nodded, didn't answer, and they pulled out on to the road. Stephanie sat back in her seat. Great. Another one of those days.

Cassandra Pharos was ready for them when they arrived. The door to her cottage was open, and Skulduggery led the way inside. They went down into the cellar, where the coals beneath the floor grille were already glowing orange, filling the chamber with a close, muggy heat. Cassandra sat on the chair, umbrella open and held comfortably over her head. Her lined face, framed by a cascade of grey hair, broke into a smile when she saw them.

"Hello there," she said brightly.

Stephanie liked Cassandra. She was one of the only people who didn't treat her like a poor replacement for a real person.

"There have been a few changes to the last vision I showed

you," she said. "Skulduggery, be a dear and turn the water on, would you? Now, while it's still fresh in my mind."

Skulduggery turned the valve on the wall, and water sprinkled from the pipes in the ceiling. The coals hissed and steam billowed. Skulduggery waited until Cassandra was lost to sight, then turned the water off.

The first time Valkyrie had come down here, she'd witnessed Cassandra's vision of the future. The second time had revealed greater detail, and yet there were some aspects that were different. Knowledge of the future changes the future, Cassandra had said. The second time, the vision had begun with Erskine Ravel in his Elder robes, his hands shackled, screaming in agony. That future had already come to pass with two tiny differences – Ravel hadn't been wearing his robes, and the room in which it occurred wasn't the room in the vision.

This time, with Stephanie down here instead of Valkyrie, the vision was different again. It didn't start with Ghastly running by. It started with Tanith staggering through the fog, one hand at a wound in her belly, the other gripping her sword. It wasn't a ruined city that materialised around her this time, but one of the Sanctuary corridors. She stumbled against a wall, waited there a moment to catch her breath.

"Suppose it's fitting," she said, looking up at someone just over Stephanie's shoulder, "that it comes down to you and me, after all this time."

A figure walked right through Stephanie and she jumped back, disrupting the steam.

Tanith did her best to stand upright. "Come and have a go..." she said, but her words faded along with her image, and the steam swirled and Stephanie saw herself standing in the city.

Because that's who it was. It was *Stephanie*. When Valkyrie had seen this, she hadn't been able to understand how there could be a Valkyrie Cain and a Darquesse in the vision at the same time. But of course there had never been a Valkyrie Cain. It had always been Stephanie and Darquesse. From the very beginning, that's how it was meant to be.

The Stephanie in the vision wore a torn and bloody T-shirt, black like her trousers. No jacket. The Deathtouch Gauntlet was on her right forearm, and on her left arm she had a tattoo. There was a bag on her back, the strap slung across her chest, the same bag Stephanie was wearing now to carry the Sceptre.

"I've seen this," her future self said, looking up to stare directly into Stephanie's eyes. "I was watching from... there. Hi. This is where it happens, but then you know that, right? At least you think you do. You think this is where I let them die."

"Stephanie!"

The voice was so real and so sharp that Stephanie forgot for a moment that it came from the vision, and instead looked around for her father, her heart lurching. The panic passed as suddenly as it had arrived – it wasn't real, not yet – and she watched her parents, her mother carrying Alice, searching the ruins.

Her future self shook her head. "I don't want to see this. Please. I don't want this to happen. Let me stop it. Please let me stop it." She took something from her pocket and looked at it, tears streaming. "Please work. Please let me save them."

Stephanie's future self was lost in a fresh swirl of billowing steam that rippled through the images of her parents, but failed to disperse them.

"Stephanie!" her father shouted. "We're here! Steph!"

Darquesse landed behind them, cracking the pavement. Her shadowskin covered her from toe to jawline, and she smiled as Stephanie's dad positioned himself in front of his wife and child.

"Give our daughter back to us," he said.

Darquesse didn't say anything. She just smiled.

"Give her back!" Desmond Edgley roared, and in the next instant he was enveloped in black flame.

Stephanie had known it was coming, but it still hit her like a fist. She sagged, made a sound like a wounded dog, and thankfully the steam billowed and took the image away. It was replaced with a new one, of a black hat lying on a cracked street. A breeze tried to play with it, tried to roll and flip it, but the hat proved resistant and eventually the breeze gave up. A gloved hand reached down, plucked the hat off the ground and brushed the dust from it. Skulduggery, dressed in black, returning the hat to his head, angling the brim and looking good while he did so.

They were coming to the end now, Stephanie knew. The only thing left was for Darquesse to...

...and here she was now.

Darquesse walked up behind Skulduggery and he turned, unhurried. He reloaded his gun.

"My favourite little toy," said Darquesse, her voice echoing slightly in the chamber.

"Are you referring to my gun or to me?" Skulduggery asked.

Darquesse laughed. "You know you're going to die now, don't you? And still you make jokes."

Skulduggery looked up slightly. "I made a promise."

Darquesse nodded. "Until the end."

"That's right," said Skulduggery. "Until the end."

He walked forward, firing the gun. He'd taken three steps before the pistol fell to the ground, followed quickly by his glove. Stephanie glanced at the real Skulduggery, wishing he had a face she could read while he watched his future self come apart, limbs falling, bones scattering. The Skulduggery in the vision collapsed and Darquesse picked up his head.

She kissed his teeth, then dropped the skull, and as the steam billowed and the last dregs of the vision were swept away, she turned, looked straight into Stephanie's eyes, and smiled.

8

CURIOSITY

He didn't want to do it. There were a ton of things he'd have preferred to do right at that moment. Leave it alone, for one thing. Walk away, for another. Take a vacation, somewhere hot and lazy, and let other people sort this out. But he couldn't just abandon everything. Not yet. Not until he knew for sure that there was someone out there who could stop her. So Sanguine put down the beer he'd barely touched, and went to investigate the scream.

He pushed open the door to the spare room. It hit something on the other side, something that rolled, then came to a lazy stop as the door swung wider. A head. Male. Sanguine didn't recognise the face. Nor did he recognise the other faces he saw in the room, twisted as they were in frozen snapshots of terror. How many were in here was impossible to judge. Body parts were grouped in piles, with the heads in the near corner. The floorboards were red and sodden. Blood splattered the walls and dripped from the ceiling. In the centre of the room crouched Darquesse, her fingers digging into what remained of a torso. She'd woken up from her hibernation, and she'd woken up curious. She looked up at him, her face calm.

Sanguine had no problems with taking a human life. He didn't even have a problem with taking an innocent life, provided he was paid for it or had sufficient personal reasons. He was a killer. When he slept, his victims didn't haunt his dreams, and so he was a good killer. All these things he recognised and acknowledged when he said, with some horror, "What have you done?"

Darquesse dug her fingers in a little more. The blood didn't show on her shadowskin. "I'm investigating," she said.

Words, he felt, needed to be chosen with care. "Who were they?"

"I'm sorry?"

"The people... the bodies."

Darquesse stood. "Their names, you mean? I don't know. I didn't ask. I think that one's name is Daisy, because it says Daisy on her badge. She works in a supermarket."

"I see. And why did you kill Daisy?"

"I didn't."

"You didn't kill her? Then who did all this?"

Darquesse looked around, then back at him. "I did."

"Then you *did* kill her."

"No. Well, I stopped her heart beating and her brain functioning, if that's what you're asking."

"That's what I'm asking."

"But I didn't *kill* her. She's still here. They're all still here, Billy-Ray. I wouldn't just kill them. How cruel would that be?"

"Yeah," he said. "That'd be pretty cruel, all right. So when you say they're still here, what exactly are you talking about?"

Darquesse fluttered her fingers. "They're still here. Around us."

"You mean like ghosts?"

"In a way," Darquesse said, smiling. "I mean their energy. Can't you feel it?"

"Have to be honest with you, Darquesse, I cannot feel that. That must be one of your special abilities, because to me, it looks like you just killed a whole bunch of people for no reason."

"Oh," said Darquesse. "That's so sad."

"It's a little depressing, yeah. So is that what you're investigating, this energy?"

"I'm seeing how it works."

"Found out much?"

"A fair bit. I might need to talk to some experts, though. Maybe scientists. I need to know how things work before I can play with them, you know?"

"That makes sense," said Sanguine carefully.

"You know what'd be handy? Remnants. Lots of them. They take over the experts, the experts tell me what I want to know. Doesn't that sound handy?"

"Uh, it sounds more trouble than it's worth..."

"Nonsense," said Darquesse. "The Remnants are lovely. Aren't you engaged to one, after all?"

"Tanith's a special case, though. And how are you even gonna find them? The Receptacle has been hidden away—"

"No it hasn't," Darquesse said happily. "There were plans to relocate it. Great plans. Plans that got sidetracked. Forgotten about. Quietly abandoned. The Receptacle is still in the MacGillycuddy's Reeks, guarded by a few sorcerers and a squad of Cleavers. No problem."

"You really think this is a good idea? Last time those Remnants were loose, you killed a whole bunch of them. Remnants have long memories."

"You don't think they'll like me?" Darquesse asked, and frowned. "Maybe we should ask Tanith."

She walked out and Sanguine hesitated, then followed. They found Tanith in the kitchen, sipping from a mug of coffee.

"I'm going to set the Remnants free," Darquesse said. "What do you think about that?"

Tanith paused, then took another sip and shrugged. "Don't really care one way or the other, to be honest. Some of them will be happy to see you. Some won't."

"Want to come with me? Say hi?"

"Sure," said Tanith. "Let me drink this and I'll meet you on the roof."

Darquesse grinned, went to the window and flew out.

Tanith watched Sanguine for a moment. "You look like you have something to say."

He kept his voice low. "You know she killed some people just to look at their energy, whatever the hell that means? She's killing people, but not *seeing* it like killing people. Tanith, that ain't safe. She's tipping over the edge."

"Of what? Sanity? Billy-Ray, what does sanity mean to someone like her? How does it apply?"

"She could kill us just as easily as anyone else."

"No," Tanith said. "She won't kill us. Not till right before the end."

"She can do no wrong in your eyes, can she?"

"Actually," said Tanith, "she's doing plenty wrong. She's wasting time, for a start. I mean, what's the problem? She has enough power to turn the world into a blackened, charred husk."

"Is that what you want?"

"You know that's what I want."

"I know that's what you *wanted*," said Sanguine. "But that was before you talked to that guy who'd learned to control the Remnant inside him."

"His name is Moribund. And he doesn't control the Remnant, OK? How many times do I have to say it? After a few days, the Remnant stops being a separate entity."

"OK, sorry, but my point remains. He said you didn't have to be this way. He said you could rebuild your conscience if you worked at it."

"Why would I want to?" said Tanith. "I'm happy being me."

"No you're not."

Tanith laughed, put the coffee down. "Oh, really? You're the expert on how I feel and what I think, are you?"

"I saw you working alongside Valkyrie and the Monster Hunters and the Dead Men. You were having fun, sure, but it was more than that. You were where you belonged."

"Why don't you just admit it? You don't want Darquesse to destroy the world, do you?"

Now it was Sanguine's turn to laugh. "Of course I don't."

"Then why are you helping us?"

"Because I love you and I wanna be there when you realise you're wrong, because on that day you'll need someone to have your back."

"That's the stupidest thing I've ever heard."

"Love makes a fool of us all."

"Will you please stop saying that word?"

"Why? It making you uncomfortable? Maybe the more you hear it, the more you'll remember it. Maybe that's the problem here."

"There is no problem," said Tanith. "I just want Darquesse to hurry up and kill everything."

"You want the world to end now because the longer it takes, the more time you have to think, and doubt, and question yourself. See, you're coming off a wonderful certainty, where you knew for sure that you wanted the world to end. But you don't have that certainty any more, and that scares you."

Tanith shot him a glare, and walked to the window. Right before she climbed out she looked back and said, "You don't know me half as well as you think you do."

"That's right," said Sanguine, "I don't. But hell, Tanith, you don't know yourself, either."

9

SIGNATE

Back to Roarhaven, and not a word spoken in the car. Stephanie replayed the vision over and over in her head. Details changed, but the facts remained the same. Stephanie, standing there with a tattoo and that gauntlet. Darquesse, murdering her family. Skulduggery's skull plucked from his spine. That smile. Those things didn't change. Those things wouldn't change.

They drove by the elderly sorcerer whose job it was to turn back any mortal who strayed too close. He nodded to them, and a few moments later the road narrowed and they passed through the illusion of emptiness that protected Roarhaven from mortal eyes. The city loomed, its huge gates open. The Bentley slid through the streets, parked below ground. Stephanie followed Skulduggery into the Sanctuary corridors and they went deeper. They walked without speaking. Stephanie wondered if Skulduggery even remembered she was there.

They got to the cells. Skulduggery spoke with the man in charge, told him what he needed. Moments later, they were in the interview room. Skulduggery sat at the table. Stephanie walked slowly from one wall to the other and back again, her hands in her pockets. She looked round when the door opened, and a small, neat man stepped in. Creyfon Signate was dressed in an orange prison jumpsuit, and his hands were shackled before him.

"Finally!" he said, once he saw who had summoned him. He walked forward, dropping into the empty chair.

Skulduggery tilted his head. "I'm sorry?"

"I've been asking to speak to someone in charge ever since I was arrested," said Signate. "I've been locked up here for *weeks!*"

"Erskine Ravel orchestrated a war in which hundreds of sorcerers were killed," said Stephanie, "and you played a huge part in that. Of course you were locked up. You're lucky we kept you here instead of shipping you out to an actual gaol."

Signate shook his head. "I had nothing whatsoever to do with the war. I was brought in to do a job, to oversee the construction of a city in a hospitable dimension and then to shunt the people and the city itself back to this one. The city we built had to overlay the town of Roarhaven exactly. It took pinpoint planning, an absurd attention to detail, and it required my full attention. Do you really think I had time to plot and conspire with Ravel and the Children of the Spider, even if I'd wanted to?"

"So you're entirely innocent?" Skulduggery said. "You were just doing your job?"

"I believed in what Ravel tried to do. I believed in his vision. But having an unpopular ideology is not a crime, and yet here I sit. In shackles."

"You're not in shackles for the ideology part," said Stephanie. "You're in shackles for everything else you did."

"But I didn't do anything! I didn't kill anyone, I didn't hurt anyone. I didn't even lie to anyone. All I did was obey the Grand Mage."

"Construction on the city started long before Ravel became Grand Mage," said Skulduggery. "You can't use that as an excuse."

"It's not an excuse, Detective. I was just doing my job, and breaking no laws while I did it. Bring in your Sensitives, have them read my mind. They'll tell you I'm innocent."

"They'll tell us you *believe* you're innocent," Skulduggery said. "That's not the same thing."

"Then allow me a trial. We can still have one of those, can't we? They haven't been rendered *completely* obsolete? Allow me to be judged by my peers, based on evidence and testimony. Let them weigh up the facts and deliver their verdict."

"No," said Skulduggery.

"This is preposterous! You cannot keep me in prison! I deserve a chance to prove my innocence!"

"Mr Signate," Skulduggery said, his voice calm, "you won't require a trial because we're here to offer you a deal."

Signate's fury vanished. "You are?"

"Darquesse poses a threat like virtually nothing we've ever seen. While we do have a way of fighting her, we don't have a way of *finding* her. She could be anywhere. That's why we need you."

"I don't understand how I could be of use."

"You're one of the best Shunters alive, Mr Signate. We're going to require someone of your skill to do what needs to be done."

"I... I still don't see what—"

"If you're interested," Skulduggery said, interrupting him, "and you agree to help us, then you walk free this very afternoon. You'll be working with the Sanctuary and all your previous misdeeds will be forgotten. Are you interested?"

"I... I am," Signate said. "What do you need me to do?"

"Before she vanished, Darquesse punished Erskine Ravel for everything he'd done. In particular, the murder of Ghastly Bespoke. She took that personally. You may have heard that Ravel is allowed one hour free of agony every day. The other twenty-three hours are spent screaming. No sedatives or painkillers can help him, no Sensitive can calm him. On his hour off, he has taken to begging. He wants to die. He wants the pain to end. Obviously, I won't let that happen. I took Ghastly's murder personally, too."

"I didn't know Ravel was planning to... to kill Elder Bespoke," Signate said, fear in his eyes for the first time. Stephanie believed him.

"The human body adapts," Skulduggery said, ignoring Signate's distress. "If constant pain is inflicted, it raises its threshold. Ravel has been denied this luxury. Every time he gets used to the pain, the pain intensifies. The only way this is possible, we think, is if Darquesse has formed a direct link to Ravel. She's turning the dial on his agony herself."

Signate looked at Skulduggery for a few moments. "You want me to shunt Ravel into another dimension," he said.

Skulduggery nodded. "Doing so should sever the link between them, catching Darquesse's attention. Then, when you bring Ravel back, she should come for him."

"And you'll be waiting."

"Yes. You'll take a team of Cleavers with you when you shunt to keep Ravel in check."

"It's a good plan," said Signate. "But there's a problem. I have access to four dimensions. Three of them are inhospitable at this time of year. The fourth is where we built the city."

"So that's where you'll be shunting."

"I'm afraid not. There are creatures in that reality that we barely managed to hold back with the city's walls. Some of these creatures are as big as elephants. Some are the size of large dogs. They're all predators, and now that there are no walls to keep them at bay, we would be shunting straight into a feeding frenzy."

"So you need a new dimension to shunt into," Skulduggery said, and went silent for a moment. "Tell me, Mr Signate, do you know Silas Nadir?"

Signate's lip curled in distaste. "I know him. Haven't spoken to him in over sixty years. If you're hoping I know where to find him, I'm afraid I can't help you. I try not to associate with serial killers."

"We don't need you to find him. We've come close to it in the past, and one of these days we'll catch him and make sure he never kills again. But you're aware of the dimension he found?"

"I am, of course," said Signate. "A reality where Mevolent rules the world. Not somewhere I'd ever be interested in visiting, mind you, but... oh."

"Do you think you can find it? I'm aware that every dimension has its own frequency and there's an infinite number of realities, but—"

"Once a frequency has been found," said Signate, seizing his own opportunity to interrupt, "it's out there, open, waiting. It becomes noticeable, if you're of a particular skill level. And of course I am. It would help me greatly if there was something I could draw a reading from, though. Did you happen to bring back any souvenirs?"

"We have this," said Stephanie, taking the Sceptre from her backpack.

Signate's eyes widened. "Oh, my... That's the Sceptre of the Ancients, isn't it? That's a piece of history. It's... magnificent."

"It's not ours," Stephanie said. "Our Sceptre was destroyed. This one belongs in the other dimension. We kind of liberated it."

"Can I... Can I touch it?" Signate asked. "It won't go off, will it?"

"It's Deadlocked," she told him. "It's bonded to me, so I'm the only one it'll work for. Can you get a reading from it?"

With slightly trembling hands, Signate reached out, fingertips brushing the Sceptre. He closed his eyes and bit his lip. His fingertips tapped lightly. Then he withdrew his hands, and looked up. "That is tremendously helpful. It would have taken me months to find the proper frequency – now it will only take weeks."

"You have days," said Skulduggery. "Do you think you can do it?"

Signate smiled for the first time. "I have always appreciated a challenge."

Skulduggery stood. "You'll be out in an hour. Report directly to Administrator Tipstaff. You're working with us now, Creyfon. Do not disappoint me."

They left him there and walked back. The silence was beginning to get to Stephanie. It was a peculiar sort of silence. It was sharp. It had angles. It jostled between them, its edges cutting into her. But she kept her mouth shut. Attempting to start a conversation, trying for small talk, would be a defeat. If Skulduggery didn't want to talk to her, then she didn't want to talk to Skulduggery.

Even though she did. Badly.

10

GIRLS' NIGHT OUT

Deep within the mountain, Cleavers came and Cleavers died, their bodies crumpling while their energies burst free of their earthly bonds and soared upwards into the heavens. It was a beautiful thing to behold, amid the spray of blood and the mangled limbs, and Darquesse found she could appreciate it on a whole new, artistic level. The squalor and the splendour of existence, displayed before her like a grand diorama.

Tanith wasn't appreciating it, unfortunately. She leaped and dodged and fought and killed in the shadow of the giant Receptacle that housed all of her fellow Remnants, and she did so with the same look of intense focus on her face that she always had. She wasn't even smiling. She rarely smiled any more, now that Darquesse thought about it. Curious.

Darquesse wondered what Tanith was making of the grand diorama of existence she was seeing. She had become so pragmatic lately that she would probably dismiss it. That almost made Darquesse sad. If only everyone could see things the way she did. She reckoned people would be a lot happier. She grinned as she stepped between two Cleavers, dodging every move they made. "Did you know that Cleavers fight naked?" she asked as she ducked a scythe blade.

Tanith beheaded a downed opponent. "I did."

Darquesse nodded, leaned away from a kick, and immediately spun to avoid a grab. "Deep within every training area in every Sanctuary, they have a Combat Circle. They step in there, strip off every item of clothing, and fight."

The Cleavers kept attacking – not slowing up, and yet not allowing their frustration to show. Impressive. "It's a huge honour to step into the circle, apparently. It is a challenge that cannot be refused. That's where they prove themselves, without armour or protection."

"I know all this," said Tanith. "I was the one who told you. Years ago."

Darquesse happily ignored her. "These guys would all have fought naked, at some point. Wouldn't that have been something to see?"

She suddenly lunged, driving her hand through the chest of the Cleaver nearest to her. The last two closed in, but their scythe blades exploded into rust before they got close. Darquesse flicked her wrists and their necks snapped.

"That was fun," she said.

"Was it?"

She turned to Tanith. "You didn't think so?"

"You could have killed them all with a wave of your hand," Tanith said. "We didn't have to fight."

"But you like fighting."

"Fighting without a reason to fight is stupid. And having someone like you around just takes the fun out of it."

"Oh," said Darquesse. "I didn't know that."

Tanith put away her sword. She looked up at the Receptacle, a globe 100 metres in diameter, set into a cradle of metal with thick wooden struts. Within the globe, blackness swirled. "You're really going to let them all out, then?"

"I am," said Darquesse. She trailed her fingers along the side. "All these thousands of Remnants, your brothers and sisters...

They've been cooped up in this thing, deprived of even a change of scenery. You remember what it was like to be trapped in that room in the Midnight Hotel, don't you?"

"Yes I do," said Tanith. "And I didn't like it one little bit."

Darquesse gave her a wicked smile. "You want to be the one to let them out?"

Tanith hesitated. "I don't know. The longer the Remnant is inside me, the longer I'm *me*, the less I care about other Remnants. I want to free them, but I don't... *need* to. It's something I wanted to do, once upon a time. But now..."

"Personally," said Darquesse, "I think it's important to hang on to things like that. That's why I'm so determined to keep punishing Ravel. It's what I wanted to do, once upon a time, and I remember that feeling of satisfaction when he first started to scream. I liked that feeling. I want to preserve it."

"So you think I should let them out?"

Darquesse shrugged. "Only if you want to."

"Well... freeing them would be advantageous. We could set them loose to distract Skulduggery and the others while you..."

"While I what?" Darquesse said. "What is it you think I'm doing?"

"I've seen the future. I've seen what you do to the world. You destroy everything."

"And that's what you want, is it? Even now? You want a world where everyone is dead? But then there'd be no people to possess, and no trouble to get into. And we both know how much Remnants love getting into trouble."

"Darquesse, looking into the future, seeing what you do... it was the most beautiful thing I'd ever seen."

"That was then. What about now?"

"I haven't changed my mind, if that's what you're asking. If you doubt my loyalty—"

"This isn't about loyalty, Tanith. You're a different person to who you were."

"Well, what about you? Only a few days ago you were insisting you had no intention of killing every living thing on the planet. But I notice you've stopped correcting me when I say it."

Darquesse shrugged. "I'm still figuring this all out, and I reserve the right to change my mind. As you should."

Tanith looked her dead in the eye. "You can count on me."

Darquesse smiled. "Of course I can. I know that. Pick up our friend, would you? He's regained consciousness but trying to hide it."

One of the two last remaining sorcerers in the place heard her, but amusingly he stayed where he was, slumped in the corner where Tanith had knocked him out and shackled him. Now Tanith grabbed his hair, pulled him to his feet. He cried out in pain, and stumbled after her as she presented him to Darquesse.

"And what is your name?" Darquesse asked.

"Maksy," the sorcerer said, tears in his eyes. "Please don't kill me."

"Like we've killed all these other sorcerers, you mean? And all these Cleavers? Like we've killed just about everyone who was assigned to guard the Receptacle?"

"Yes," said Maksy. "Please don't kill me."

"I'm not going to kill you," Darquesse said. "I have other plans for you."

She pressed her hand against the Receptacle. The globe looked like glass but wasn't – it was a solid energy field, a giant version of a Soul Catcher. She pushed her arm through, and the shadows on the other side stirred into a frenzy.

"Ooh," she said. "Tickles."

She pulled her arm out, a Remnant in her grip. It twisted and writhed, but couldn't squirm free. Darquesse noticed Tanith's lip curling in distaste. "Something wrong?" she asked.

"No," Tanith said quickly. "Nothing."

"Don't make me ask twice."

A hesitation. "I don't know, I... I once thought that Remnants were slivers of pure evil. But they're not, are they? They're just nasty little unfinished *things*. The creature you're holding is nothing but a bundle of sickness that needs a host to become whole. They're not evil. They're desperate and pathetic. I've seen evil. I know what evil looks like now, and that isn't it."

"So what does evil look like?" Darquesse asked.

Tanith glanced at her and said nothing.

Darquesse shrugged, and turned to Maksy. "Open wide."

He shook his head. He was pale, sweating. Terrified. "No. Please. I have a newborn son. Please. I need to be there for him."

"Don't be afraid," Tanith said. "You can still be you, even when you have a Remnant inside. It won't even be in there that long. We'll just need you to carry it around for a day or two, and then it'll be gone, and you won't remember any of it."

"My family—"

"We won't let you near them," said Tanith. "You won't hurt anyone. I promise."

Maksy tried to pull back as Darquesse approached, but Tanith dug her fingers into his arm, and he reluctantly opened his mouth. The Remnant reached for him, gained purchase, and Darquesse let go and it squirmed in. Maksy staggered and Tanith let him go. His throat bulged for an instant, and then he sagged. Ever so slowly, he rolled his head back, his lips darkening, black veins running under his skin.

He opened his eyes and smiled. "The first thing I see through human eyes in years, and it is two beautiful women. It's almost worth the captivity, it really is." He took a moment to breathe in, and then slowly out. "Physical form," he muttered. "It's so nice. It's like coming home. Although this one... Before we release the others, can I go get another host? Someone better looking? Some Remnants go for hosts with power, but I've always found that power comes to good-looking people anyway, and... Here, which one of you gorgeous girls is going to help me out of these shackles?"

Tanith hit him and he dropped, unconscious, to the floor.

"You haven't changed, eh?" Darquesse said, a small smile on her lips. "So, when you were nice to him just now, assuring him that everything will be all right, that was you... what? Being mean and uncaring?"

Tanith ignored the mocking tone. "I just remember what it was like to fear the Remnants," she said. "There's no harm in telling someone he's not going to kill his family if we know he's not going to kill his family, is there?"

"Harm?" said Darquesse. "No. No harm at all."

Tanith shrugged. "Then what's the big deal? We have another captive that we can put a Remnant into and take around with us, and then we can release the others and get out of here while they cause their usual amount of chaos and panic. Job done, right?"

"Job done," said Darquesse. "I'm glad we got to do this, Tanith. We needed a girls' night out, didn't we? This was fun."

"Yeah," said Tanith. "This was a hoot."

11

HONEY, I'M HOME

Life as a woman had its ups and downs.

Ups: people listened to him a lot more. When he had been a man, Vaurien Scapegrace had found it somewhat difficult to be taken seriously. But once his brain had been transferred into the red-haired woman's statuesque body, everyone seemed to find a lot more time for him. This was good for pub business.

Downs: sometimes he felt as though people weren't *really* listening to him. Sometimes he felt as though they'd laugh at any feeble joke he made, just so long as the joke emerged from his new, plump, incredibly soft lips. He also didn't like the way all those eyes would follow him as he went to fetch a patron's drinks. It was unnerving.

Walking down the street was unnerving, too. He felt far too self-conscious to be comfortable. He'd left Roarhaven and gone into Dublin the previous week, and that was even worse. All that time spent living apart from the mortal world had made him forget what mortals were like. They didn't even try to hide their staring. A few of them – random people he passed on the street – had even made comments about his appearance.

And this was *acceptable*?

He'd seen a lot, had Scapegrace. In his time as the self-deluded Killer Supreme, he'd surrounded himself with murderers and low lifes and religious psychopaths. In his time as the self-deluded Zombie King, he'd surrounded himself with rot and evil and decay and corruption. He had seen a lot of bad things happen. He had encountered a lot of bad people. But these were, in a way, *professionally* bad people. They were insane or twisted or downright evil, but they carried that air of professionalism with them wherever they went. And they certainly didn't make catcalls or wolf whistles whenever they saw a passing female whose form they appreciated.

When he'd got back to Roarhaven, he vowed to never again leave unless it was an absolute necessity, because at least in Roarhaven he had a sanctuary. And it wasn't the huge palace in the middle of the city, either. It wasn't the one surrounded by Cleavers and ruled by China Sorrows. Scapegrace's sanctuary was a small house, tucked away in the corner of the south district, and it was here he returned to at the end of another long night in the pub.

He walked through his front door, hung his coat on a hook and went through to the kitchen. He sagged. It had been Clarabelle's turn to clean, but Clarabelle had a unique way of doing things that made sense only to her. Her way of cleaning, for example, entailed taking everything that was messy and moving it to another side of the room. It took as much time as cleaning would actually take, but the end result was far less useful.

Light footsteps came down the stairs. Clad in a fluffy pink bathrobe and wearing fluffy pink slippers, on which swayed twin ping-pong balls painted like eyes, Clarabelle's hair was a furious shade of green. "Hello," she said.

She didn't launch into a full-blown babble, which was unusual. Very unusual.

"What did you do?" Scapegrace asked.

A series of expressions flitted across Clarabelle's face. First, there was indignation, then there was resignation, followed by hope, chased by confusion, and finally knocked down and sat upon by innocence. "Nothing."

"Did you set fire to something again?"

She shook her head.

"Are you sure?"

She frowned, then nodded.

"Where were you just now?"

"Up in my room," she said. "I was sorting through my favourite socks. I have seven. Snow White had seven dwarves, did you know that? I have seven socks. In a way, I'm kind of like Snow White."

"Snow White cleaned the kitchen every once in a while."

"She had little birds and squirrels to help her. All I could find was a hedgehog, but he was useless. I had to do everything myself."

"Moving things is not cleaning them."

"Do you want to know what I did wrong?"

He sighed. "Yes."

Clarabelle scrunched up her mouth, like she did when she was figuring out the best way to say something. Before she could confess, the front door opened and Thrasher walked in.

"I'm home!" he called, even though he could see them both standing in the kitchen.

"Gerald!" Clarabelle said, bounding over to him. Thrasher hugged Clarabelle, wrapping her in his massive, muscular arms. "Did you have a good day? Did anything fun happen?"

"Every day is a fun day when you're doing what you love," Thrasher said, and flashed an eager smile at Scapegrace. Scapegrace ignored him, walked to the fridge and left them to their chit-chat. He poured himself a glass of milk, leaned his hip against the cooker and drank.

It was sad how quickly he'd got used to normal things again. Life as the Zombie King, as self-deluded as he'd been, meant that magic had sustained him and his steadily-rotting body. But after Doctor Nye had placed his brain into its new home, he'd had to deal with the gradual reawakening of natural bodily functions. Normal things like eating and drinking had become astonishing adventures in sensation. A glass of milk was a delight. But now? Now it was a glass of milk again. How quickly it had lost its thrill.

Thrasher and Clarabelle came into the kitchen, still talking. He ignored them. He did that a lot lately. He just couldn't summon the anger he used to direct Thrasher's way. It was... gone. It had slowly evaporated these past few weeks. Thrasher had noticed, of course. Thrasher always noticed things like that. But where he had assumed that it was as a result of living a normal life, maybe even of a softening of attitudes and a growing fondness, Scapegrace knew better. The anger was gone because the anger was beaten. There was no point to it any more. It had lost.

Scapegrace was living in the suburbs of a city full of sorcerers. He was no longer deluded enough to call himself the Killer Supreme. No longer dead enough to call himself the Zombie King. He was just another citizen, just a regular guy who'd had his brain transplanted into the body of a beautiful woman. He was normal. He was average. And this was his life.

"Master?" Thrasher said.

Scapegrace brushed his luxurious hair from his face and looked up. "Hmm? What?"

Thrasher and Clarabelle looked at him with real concern in their eyes. The old Scapegrace would have heaped scorn upon them. The new Scapegrace didn't see the point.

"I was saying that I washed the floor in the pub, just like you asked," Thrasher continued.

"And I was saying you shouldn't get Gerald to do that every time," said Clarabelle. "He's not your slave."

"I don't mind, really," Thrasher said, blushing.

"You should mind," said Clarabelle. "Scapey, it's just not nice, the way you treat Gerald. He's your best friend in the whole entire world and you two are *my* best friends in the whole entire world and best friends shouldn't treat each other like that."

71

It had been a long day. All Scapegrace wanted to do was have a shower and go to bed. "You're right," he said. "I'm sorry."

They stood there and blinked at him.

"You're sorry?" Thrasher asked.

Irritation flared in the back of Scapegrace's mind, then sputtered out. "Yes. I'm sorry."

"You... you've never said that to me before," Thrasher said, tears in his eyes. Dear lord, he was going to cry.

"Then I'm not sorry," Scapegrace said hastily, in an effort to hold off an embarrassing display of emotion. "Does that make you feel better?"

Thrasher's hands went to his mouth as tears spilled down his perfect cheekbones. "You've never cared about how I feel before."

Scapegrace went to roll his eyes, but lost his enthusiasm halfway through and ended up looking at the ceiling.

"Are you feeling OK?" Clarabelle asked.

For the second time in the last few minutes, Scapegrace sighed. "I'm fine."

"But are you *really*?"

"Of course. The pub is doing good business. We have a loyal customer base. Most of them are in every night. What's to complain about?"

"I don't know," said Clarabelle. With natural grace, she sprang on to the kitchen table and sat there, cross-legged, while the dishes she'd knocked off crashed to the floor around her. "You tell me."

Scapegrace hesitated. He'd always viewed himself as an old-fashioned type of guy, not the kind to talk about whatever was troubling him. But circumstances, he supposed, had changed. One glance at his reflection in the window proved that.

"I always wanted to do something important," he said. "I wanted to be someone important. I wanted to make a difference."

"You make a difference to me," said Thrasher.

The old Scapegrace would have thrown something at him for that. The new Scapegrace didn't bother.

"I never wanted to be normal," he continued. "But here, normal is all I am. In Roarhaven, I'm... unexceptional."

Clarabelle frowned. "Do you want to leave?"

"No. Nothing like that..."

"But if you do leave," Clarabelle said, "do you promise to take me with you?"

"I'm not leaving."

"OK," Clarabelle said happily. "Just don't decide to leave one morning before I get up. Then I'll get up and you'll be gone and Gerald will be gone and I'll be all alone in this house and I'll have no friends."

Thrasher wrapped his gigantic arm round her shoulders. "We're not going anywhere."

She nodded. "Because I have trouble making friends. People think I'm weird, just because sometimes I see things that aren't really there, and just because I say things they don't understand. They don't want to be my friends. But you guys don't care about things like that. You two are really nice."

"I'm not leaving," Scapegrace said. "I'm just feeling sorry for myself, that's all."

"Why?"

"I don't know, I... I suppose I can just see myself living out the rest of my life as an ordinary person."

"You're not ordinary," Clarabelle said. "None of us are."

"I get sad, too," Thrasher said. "I don't like to bother anyone with it, but... I mean, my new body is very nice. It really is. But every time I look in the mirror, I see someone that isn't me. I don't think that feeling is ever going to go away."

Scapegrace nodded. "You're always looking into the face of a stranger."

"That gets to you," said Thrasher. "After a while, the novelty wears off and you just want to see your own face again."

"You forget where you came from," Scapegrace said softly. "You forget who you are."

Clarabelle leaned forward. "Would it make you feel better to remember?"

"It would."

She smiled. "Then the news I have is *good* news. I went exploring today. I've never been to the left side of the Medical Wing before because, when I walk in the door, I always turn to the right."

Scapegrace frowned. "Why?"

"I don't know. I've always wanted to turn left, but I never do. I think I turned left once in a previous life and I was beheaded or something, so I've never even wanted to walk down that side. But today was different. I was playing with a Cleaver and we were both taking it in turns to spin around really fast. I was winning, because he kept forgetting to spin, and he just stood there and I spun and spun and spun, and by the end of the game I was really dizzy and I think I threw up on him a little bit. Just on to his coat, though. I don't think he minded much. He just stayed standing there. He probably thought we were playing musical statues."

She hesitated. "Maybe we were. Oh, I think we were. If we were, then he won, because statues aren't supposed to spin around. Anyway, I was dizzy, and when I walked into the Medical Wing I started to fall. It took me ages to fall, and I knocked over a few people along the way, but when the dizziness went away I was in the left corner of the Medical Wing. It was amazing! The sights that were on show... You know the way tables seem really different if you look at them from a different angle?"

"Clarabelle," said Scapegrace, "it's been a long day. Could you get to the point?"

"Right, sorry. Anyway, there are all these rooms in the Medical Wing, so I went into a few of them. And in one of them there was a big glass tank full of green water, and there were two people floating in that tank. It was you. It was the two of you."

Scapegrace frowned. "What?"

"Your old bodies," she said. "They still have your old bodies."

12

THE CAULDRON

The lead came in a little after seven that evening. A sorcerer named Midnight Blue had turned it up, found a link to one of Billy-Ray Sanguine's old friends, a gentleman called Axle. It was tenuous, this lead, but while they waited for Signate to shunt Ravel away and break the connection to Darquesse, tracking down Sanguine and Tanith was the only course of action open to them. The good news was that Axle lived right here in Roarhaven. So then it was back into the Bentley for Stephanie, and another quiet car ride through the streets.

They got to Axle's house. Stephanie went round the back while Skulduggery knocked on the door. Sometimes people with dodgy pasts liked to sneak out of windows. She cupped her hands, blew on them. It was chilly out. Roarhaven was as dark and as quiet as ever. She heard the low murmur of Skulduggery's voice. No alarm raised, no windows opening, no one trying to run.

She heard the front door close, and walked back to the Bentley. Skulduggery was already behind the wheel. They didn't speak as they pulled away from the kerb. They drove for a few minutes, stopped outside a dingy little pub called The Cauldron.

Skulduggery led the way into the chatter and the laughter.

Stephanie didn't have his skills. She couldn't glance at a room and notice every single thing, catalogue every single face, in one go. It took her a few seconds to notice the man sitting at the bar with an empty stool beside him. His work boots were dirty, his clothes not much better. He sat with his head down, shoulders slumped unevenly, staring into his drink. They walked up to him and for a few moments he didn't notice them. He had a small cut on his jawline, another on his neck. There was a larger abrasion on his right hand and across his thick knuckles, and a plaster was wrapped clumsily round the thumb of his left.

"Mr Axle," Skulduggery said, and Axle looked up sharply. He paled when he saw them, and when he finally spoke he could only manage one word.

"What?"

"Mr Axle, you know who we are, yes? We don't need to introduce ourselves, or tell you what we do. From the look on your face, you know all that."

Axle swallowed. "So? What do you want with me?"

"When we walked in this door, all we wanted was the location of a friend of yours – Billy-Ray Sanguine."

"Sanguine's no friend of mine," said Axle. "I know him, that's all. Haven't seen him in months. Maybe over a year. We're not friends. Can't help you."

The bartender wandered over, and Axle went back to hunching over his beer.

"Can I get you folks something?" the bartender asked.

"I'm a skeleton," said Skulduggery, "and she doesn't drink."

Stephanie frowned at him. "How do you know I don't drink? I'm eighteen. I can drink if I want to."

"Do you want to?"

She kept frowning. "Shut up."

The bartender shrugged and wandered away again, and Axle watched him go.

"We're looking for where Sanguine might go if he were in

76

trouble," Skulduggery said. "A safe house, something like that."

Axle straightened with a pained expression, and shook his head. "Didn't know him that well. Ask someone else. I haven't even been in this dimension all that much over the last few years."

The clothes, the cuts, the rough hands... construction work. "You helped build this city?" Stephanie asked.

He looked at her. "Helped build it? I practically built it myself. None of those other foremen could have done what I did. My crew built the best and we built the fastest. It's because of us, because of me, that the city was ready to be unveiled by Grand Mage Ravel. Just in time for those bloody Warlocks to wreck half of it."

"How's the rebuilding going?"

Axle snorted. "You'd be surprised how a simple job can get complicated once you introduce a little red tape. When we were working in that other reality, we were below the radar. We were working in secret. Things got done. But now that it's all out in the open you have committees and safety inspections and what have you, and immediately you're behind schedule and waiting for approval and blah blah blah..."

Skulduggery tilted his head at the empty stool. "Waiting for someone?"

Axle stiffened again. "Yeah," he said. "A friend of mine."

"Is he late?"

"He is, yeah. He'll be here, though."

"Is this a regular thing? Going for a drink after work?"

Axle nodded. "End of a long day, yeah, it's good to relax. That a crime?"

"No, it isn't," said Skulduggery. "Murder is, however."

Stephanie raised an eyebrow, but left the question for Axle to ask.

"What the hell are you talking about?"

Skulduggery took a pair of light handcuffs from his jacket and laid them on the bar. "What started the argument? Was it about work? Was the pressure getting to you?"

Axle gave a sharp, dry laugh. "What murder? Who's dead?"

"Your friend."

"You're talking nonsense. He's not dead. He's just late."

"What's his name?"

"There! See? That's how ridiculous this is! You don't even know who he is and you're saying he's dead!"

"What's your friend's name, Mr Axle?"

Axle stared at Skulduggery. "Brock."

"You're incredulous, and yet you're keeping your voice down. You're scared of meeting the barman's gaze, but you don't want to take your eyes off him. You're worried that he might have seen something last night – maybe he overheard your argument with Brock. You're scared he'll mention something about it in front of us."

"This is ridiculous. I don't have to sit here and listen to—"

He went to slide off his stool, but Stephanie stepped up close to him, blocking his way. Skulduggery leaned in from the other side.

"You have muddy water dried into the left leg and the right knee of your trousers. Also the left side of your jacket. It wasn't raining last night, but it was the night before, and there are still puddles out the back of this pub, aren't there? You had too much to drink, you got out there, the argument turned physical. You hit him. That's when you cut your knuckles. He went down and you went down with him. You started strangling him. He managed to turn you over, and you fell on to your left side, into a puddle. But you pushed back, got on top, straddled him, hence the stain on your other knee. He clawed at your hands, leaving those scratches. And you choked him until he died."

Axle shook his head quickly.

"You're having trouble sitting up straight," Skulduggery continued. "Did you do something to your back? Maybe as you were carrying his body through the back streets and alleys? You couldn't have supported his weight for too long, not in your inebriated state, but you would have needed to take him somewhere you knew well, and somewhere you knew would be deserted. The construction site you're working on isn't too far away from here, is it? That's where you dumped his body – probably in a pit scheduled to be filled in this morning.

"But you couldn't leave – you couldn't risk someone coming in early and discovering your crime. So you stayed. When your co-workers arrived, you poured in the concrete yourself – hastily, by the state of your boots. After that, you had to act as if nothing was wrong, so you put in a day's work. A sloppy day's work, judging by the more recent cuts on your hands. You had to stick to your routine, so you rushed home to shave, not bothering to change clothes, and then came here."

Stephanie frowned. "Why did he shave?"

"From what I can see, Brock was an Elemental. He tried to shove a handful of fire into Mr Axle's face. He only barely missed, too. See how the skin is slightly paler around the cheeks and chin? You had a beard up until a few hours ago, didn't you, Mr Axle? But you shaved it off. Nicked yourself a few times, but that didn't matter. What mattered was getting rid of the singed beard. You even had to cut your own hair in a few places. You missed your left eyebrow, though."

"You don't know what you're—"

"I'm arresting you for murder, Mr Axle. Please stand up and put your hands behind your back."

"I didn't do anything," Axle said, but stood just the same.

"We'll let the Sensitives take a peek inside your mind. Maybe they'll see something that'll get you a reduced sentence."

"No," said Axle, backing away, "please. I'll help you. I'll tell you everything I know about Sanguine. Do you know about his family home, in Texas?"

"The Americans are keeping an eye on that," Skulduggery said. "He hasn't visited."

"I know others," said Axle. "There's a house in Dublin. I think it's his. An ex-girlfriend of mine told me about it. He took her there once."

"Where?" Stephanie asked.

"Stoneybatter, just off Norseman Place. That's worth something, isn't it? I didn't mean to do it. I didn't mean to kill him. It was a stupid argument. I didn't know what I was doing."

"We'll see you're treated fairly," Skulduggery said, reaching for him.

"No!" Axle shouted, snapping his palms out. The air rippled and Stephanie flew backwards, getting tangled up with Skulduggery. Tables and chairs scattered and people cursed and cried out, and she glimpsed Axle running out.

Skulduggery hauled her to her feet. "Outside," he said. "I'll lead him to you."

And then he was off in pursuit.

Stephanie barged through the stunned patrons, forcing her way outside. She ran down the alley, her boots splashing in puddles. No sign of Axle. She went to double back and the window above her exploded. She cursed as Skulduggery and Axle landed beside her in a shower of broken glass. Axle staggered, his eyes wide and terrified, his hands already shackled. He fell to his knees.

Stephanie glared at Skulduggery. "What was wrong with the door? You could have just come down the stairs and walked out the door. Why did you have to jump out the window?"

"You know why," Skulduggery said, walking away.

Axle looked up, tears streaming from his eyes. "Why did he do that? Why?"

Stephanie glowered. "Because doors are for people with no imagination," she said, and led Axle to the car.

13

MY FRIEND. MY FURNITURE.

Sanguine moved through the wall, stepping into the quiet kitchen. A man sat at the table. His name was Levitt. The chatty one, Maksy, was missing. That could mean one of two things – either Tanith had killed him out of sheer irritation, or Darquesse had needed Maksy's Remnant to inhabit someone she wanted to talk to. Sanguine didn't know what would have become of Maksy after that. Darquesse had probably killed him.

He moved on. The safe house was quickly becoming his least favourite place to be. Sure, it had its upsides. It was where Tanith was, so that was nice, even if she'd barely spoken to him the entire time they'd been hiding out there. But it was enough to be close to her, he reckoned. And once they were married, all this awkward tension would just drain away and leave them with the rest of their lives to get on with. Assuming the rest of their lives meant anything longer than a week.

And then there was the downside.

Darquesse.

Every time he returned to the place, he had to steel himself before he saw her. It was a good thing she usually stayed in the spare room these days, conducting her terrifying little experiments.

Sanguine didn't think he'd be able to handle it if she took to roaming about the—

Goddamn.

Darquesse was in the living room, sitting in the armchair with her legs crossed. The man on the sofa across from her would have looked like a normal, middle-aged college professor were it not for the black lips and all those black veins that he wasn't bothering to hide.

"Billy-Ray," Darquesse said, smiling brightly. "Allow me to introduce Nestor Tarry, my new best friend. Nestor was just telling me about his work in quantum mechanics."

"That so?" said Sanguine, leaning against the doorframe, trying to appear casual and not at all intimidated. "Just your average, ordinary, everyday conversation about quantum mechanics, huh? You managing to keep up?"

"Actually," Tarry said, "Darquesse is quite well versed in quantum theory."

"I read a lot," Darquesse said, shrugging, "and absorb information instantly. It's a talent."

Tarry smiled. "One of many, it seems. But I have taken you as far as I am able. The answers you seek are, I'm afraid, beyond me."

"So who takes me further?"

"I could give you a list of names – but it would be a short list, made even shorter by events over the last few years. Actually, I think your next port of call is a book, not a person. The *Hessian Grimoire* is a collection of, essentially, theories about the next stages of magic. Where we can go from here, how we can expand our knowledge, the ways in which we can use what we know to delve deeper into the source of all magic. I don't know who is currently in possession of the book, unfortunately, but if you can find it, I think it could help you."

"The *Hessian Grimoire*," Darquesse said, nodding. "OK then, sounds good. And after that? The list of names you were going to give me?"

Tarry raised his chin and moved his head from side to side, acknowledging the request, but see-sawing between options. "There are two or three people left alive who could help you. Really, the person who could have helped you the most would have been Walden D'Essai."

"Argeddion."

Tarry nodded. "His work was just... it was far beyond any of his contemporaries. I never liked the man, I was always far too jealous of his accomplishments. That's something I could never have admitted without this Remnant inside me, by the way." He chuckled, and didn't seem to notice when Darquesse didn't join in. "But his mind was an astonishing thing. His work, his research... Even the questions he posed in his field outshone the answers I got in mine. If you truly wanted to master this thing called magic, if you truly wanted to touch infinity... I would have said talk to D'Essai. Talk to Argeddion. But, of course, now it's too late."

"Argeddion is alive," said Darquesse.

Tarry frowned. "No. He's dead. Skulduggery Pleasant killed him when—"

Darquesse spoke over him, her words calm. "Officially, Argeddion died following the confrontation with those super-powered hooligans he'd created. Skulduggery finished him off. That's the story that was circulated."

Tarry sat forward. "It's a lie?"

"They couldn't kill him," Darquesse said. "They didn't know how. So they rewrote his personality, convinced him he was normal, and hid him away. Even I don't know where he is now."

Tarry was quiet for a moment. "The *Hessian Grimoire*," he said. "That should help you find him."

"How?"

"You have a deep understanding of energy, Darquesse. Your understanding might even surpass my own."

"Oh," said Darquesse, "it does."

A faint flicker of irritation crossed Tarry's features. Sanguine noticed it. And if Sanguine noticed it, then Darquesse certainly did. That faint flicker of irritation had most likely just signed Mr Tarry's death warrant.

"But once you read that book," Tarry continued, "you will know how to detect and track energy. Argeddion found out his true name, the same as you. For all intents and purposes, he is lit up like a beacon – providing you know how to look for him."

"The *Hessian Grimoire* sounds like the answer to all my prayers," Darquesse said. "Thank you, Nestor. You have been most helpful."

Tarry stood, but wavered. Finally, he plucked up the courage to ask, "Can I come with you? When you find Argeddion, I mean. You'll need a Remnant to possess him, won't you? So he'll talk? I would do anything for the opportunity to peek inside his mind. He is... astonishing."

"He is," said Darquesse. "But I'll just have to use my other Remnant to possess him. I've kind of grown bored with you."

Tarry paled, making his black veins stand out even more. "What?"

"You've just rubbed me up the wrong way," Darquesse explained.

"I... I'm sorry. I apologise. I didn't mean to—"

"It's not your fault," said Darquesse as she got to her feet. "It's mine. I'm probably just overly sensitive. I've only been studying quantum mechanics for a few days, and... I don't know. Any kind of criticism or – what's the word? – *irritation* shown is just... it's more than I'm prepared to accept right now."

Tarry backed away. "I wasn't irritated. I wasn't, I swear. And I would never criticise you. Never. The amount you've learned in such a short space of time is hugely, *hugely* impressive."

Darquesse narrowed her eyes. "Oh, I do not like being patronised."

She raised her hand and Tarry exploded into nothingness.

Sanguine jerked back in astonishment. No blood, no meat, no bones. Nothing.

"There," Darquesse said, a smile on her face once again. "I feel so much better now."

"What did you do to him?" Sanguine asked. "Where is he?"

"He's still here," said Darquesse, her fingers playing lightly against the air. "His atoms are spread out around the room. It's funny, isn't it? Group all those atoms together and Nestor has a body. Separate them, and you have to ask where he's gone. I can put him back together, if you'd like."

"You could do that?"

"Sure. I think. Putting things back together is a lot harder than pulling them apart, but I'll do my best."

Darquesse chewed her bottom lip as she focused. A moment passed, and she closed her fist, and Tarry reappeared, blurring into existence. He staggered, eyes glassy, and dropped to his knees.

"He's in shock," said Darquesse. "Either that or he's a vegetable. The brain is tricky. I can see how the body reassembles, how the nervous system fits, but the brain will take a little more practice. Want a seat?"

Sanguine looked at her. "Sorry?"

"A seat," she said. "You want one? You look tired."

Before he could answer, she had splayed her hand and Tarry exploded into nothingness once more. This time when she closed her fist, however, a chair blurred into being.

"There," Darquesse said.

"Did you... did you just turn him into a chair?"

"Yes I did," said Darquesse, grinning. "Atoms are atoms. It's all about what you do with them and how you arrange them. Man gets turned into a chair. Chair gets turned into a glass of water. It's still Nestor, though. He's still there. I haven't killed him."

"You turned him into furniture."

"It's just another form to take."

"I'm gonna have to disagree with you on that one, Darquesse. He's dead. You killed him. Where are his memories? His personality? Where are all the things that define him?"

Darquesse tilted her head. "None of that stuff defines us, Billy-Ray. Memories can be lost. Personalities can be changed. Who we are, our true essence, is our energy. If I wanted to kill him, I'd just do it."

She clicked her fingers and the chair was incinerated in a burst of black flame.

"There," said Darquesse. "Happy now? Nestor is dead. Every last trace of him. His atoms, his energy – gone. He can't be brought back now. That's how you kill someone, Billy-Ray. You wipe them from existence. Stopping a heart from beating, cutting off thoughts, turning some*one* into some*thing*... that doesn't mean anything. Consciousness doesn't mean anything. Are you any more valuable than a rock, just because you have sentience? No you're not."

"But you're still punishing Erskine Ravel for killing Ghastly Bespoke."

"That's different," said Darquesse. "I'm punishing him out of anger."

"So what about your friends?" Sanguine said. "Tanith, or China Sorrows, or Skulduggery Pleasant? You've formed attachments to them, right? You value them more than you'd value a rock."

Darquesse shrugged. "Not really. That was my old way of looking at things. Personalities are fun for a while, but when you think about it, and I mean really think about it, they're just side effects of brain function. I don't mean I don't value them at *all*, it's just not so much of a big deal to me any more."

"So... so you'd turn them into furniture, too?"

"Sure. I could turn you into a cushion, if you want."

"Please don't. I don't wanna be a cushion."

She laughed. "If you were a cushion, you wouldn't know any better. What would you miss? Your thoughts? Cushions don't sit there missing their thoughts, Billy-Ray. Your thoughts seem important to you now, but I'm here to tell you... they don't mean anything."

"They mean something to me."

"Well, now you're just being silly. What you're saying, basically, is that your thoughts mean something to your thoughts. It's a loop of nonsense. Go off and think about it, OK? It took me a while to come to terms with all this, too. But I've learned so much. And not just about how to mix and match atoms and particles and molecules and stuff. Other things. Fun things. You know the God-Killers?"

"Uh... yeah, like the Sceptre..."

"Actually, no, I'm talking about the sword and the dagger and the stuff you and Tanith stole."

Sanguine felt the blood drain from his face. She knew. Oh, God, she knew. And he didn't even have the dagger with him. He'd been worried that she'd notice it under his jacket. Why the *hell* hadn't he just brought it anyway? "Sure, right," he said. "What about them?"

"Do you know how they were made?" Darquesse asked. "Those four? Other God-Killers were made in different ways, of course. The Sceptre was forged by the Faceless Ones somewhere, but these four weapons started out as ordinary objects. Nothing special about them. But then they were left in this pool of water, deep inside the caves under Gordon Edgley's house. Whatever qualities that water had, it made the weapons soak up magic, made them acquire the ability to kill a god. Isn't that fascinating? It goes against everything we've been told about how magic works. I'd love to find that pool. Don't you think that's fascinating?"

"Yeah," he said. "Pretty fascinating."

"Billy-Ray?"

"Yes?"

"You look nervous."

"Yeah. I guess I am."

"You think I'm going to turn you into a cushion, even though I told you it wouldn't matter if I did?"

"That's why I'm nervous, Darquesse."

She chuckled. "You're funny. I don't know how I didn't see that when Valkyrie was in charge."

"Maybe my humour is an acquired taste."

"Maybe."

"I just popped by to make sure everything was, y'know, hunky-dory. I'm actually heading out again."

"Oh? Where are you going?"

"Just out. Just headed out. Errands to run. I'll be back later, so... OK, well, I gotta go."

"See you soon," Darquesse said, smiling, and Sanguine smiled back. He walked out and immediately sank into the ground.

He turned, moving deeper through the darkness. The familiar rumble of shifting rocks filled his ears. It used to make him feel safe. There were only a handful of people in the world who could do what he did – even fewer now, after what had transpired during the War of the Sanctuaries – and that little fact had transformed the dark and the cold into a refuge. Down here, he couldn't be touched. Down here, he couldn't even be found.

But Darquesse could find him. There would be no escape from her down here, not if she were coming after him.

He piled on the speed.

He didn't pay attention to how fast he was going. Sometimes he liked to time himself. Not tonight. He got to his place in Dublin, rose up through the cracking, crumbling floorboards. The first blush of dawn brightened the house, not that he needed light to see. There weren't even any bulbs in this small house on this quiet street. No one knew about this place. Not even Tanith. The only people he'd brought back here were—

"Move and I shoot."

Sanguine yelled and spun.

Skulduggery Pleasant was sitting in Sanguine's favourite armchair, the one in the corner. His hand was on the armrest. In his hand was a gun.

14

A COMMON ENEMY

"Technically," the skeleton said, "I should have shot you for that. But let's start over. Move *again* and I really will shoot."

Sanguine stayed perfectly still. He was too busy getting over the fact that there was someone in his house to even think about trying something sneaky.

The girl walked in. The reflection, Stephanie. She walked right by Sanguine like she didn't have a care in the world. For a moment, she was close enough for him to grab, maybe use as a shield. But she knew that. She was testing him. They both were. He wasn't going to fall for it.

She went to the couch. Sat. Looked at him like she was bored. He started to feel that maybe now was the time to start speaking.

"I'm real glad you're here," he said.

Stephanie laughed and Pleasant tilted his head.

"I'm serious," Sanguine continued. "I was coming to talk to you, actually. I just stopped off here on my way to Roarhaven to, y'know, collect my thoughts. And a few other things."

"Where is she?" Pleasant asked.

"Darquesse is with Tanith."

"And where is Tanith?" Stephanie asked.

"With Darquesse."

"I don't have to shoot anything important," Pleasant said, pointing the gun at his legs. "I can just shoot something painful."

"I don't want you to shoot anything, but I'm not gonna tell you where they are. You really think Darquesse won't be able to sense a strike team if they get in close? And then who'll she blame for telling you where to find her? Momma Sanguine's favourite boy, that's who."

"Then if you weren't going to tell us where she is," Stephanie said, "why were you coming to see us? Unless, of course, you were fibbing about that."

"Stephanie, I'm insulted. I would never fib to you. I can't tell you where she is, but I can help you stop her. Would you be interested in such a deal?"

Pleasant's head moved slightly, casting a deeper shadow over his jaw. "What could you possibly offer us?"

Sanguine gave him a smile. "Gifts. Gifts that you would find very useful indeed."

"Oh," said Pleasant. "You mean the God-Killers."

Sanguine's smile faded. "What?"

And now Sanguine noticed the blanket on the couch beside Stephanie. She pulled it back, revealing the sword, the dagger, the spear and the bow.

"You found them."

"Yes we did," said Pleasant. "Very good hiding places, by the way. Took me all of six minutes to find all four. These are your gifts, I presume? You're gifting these to us?"

"Uh, yeah. Kinda. They weren't easy to keep a hold of, let me tell you. See, the weapons I told Tanith I was melting down were—"

"Forgeries," Pleasant said. "Yes, we figured that out, thank you."

"No problem," said Sanguine. "However, I'm just gifting you with *three* of these weapons. I'm actually keepin' the dagger for my—"

Sanguine made to take a step towards the sofa and all at once Pleasant was on his feet and across the room with the barrel of the gun pressing very firmly against Sanguine's forehead.

"Woah."

"I told you not to move," Pleasant said, his voice dangerously quiet.

Sanguine licked his lips. "I thought we were over that. I thought we'd moved on to being buddies. Compadres. We got a common enemy, after all."

Stephanie hadn't budged from where she was sitting. "Do you always treat your enemies like they're your boss?"

"I don't have a boss. I'm a free agent, dammit."

"You're a lackey. Just like Tanith."

Sanguine went to shake his head, then thought better of it. "We ain't lackeys. She's following Darquesse because she's had this notion for a while now that Darquesse is her messiah, and I'm following Tanith because we're in love and we're gonna get married. But be that as it may, I am a practical man, and I see only advantages in my fiancée's messiah getting killed, so... common enemy."

"How romantic."

"I take it," said Pleasant, "that Tanith doesn't know that the God-Killers haven't been destroyed."

"No, sir, she doesn't. She'd likely kill me if she found out. And while you may think I'm saying this just because you have a gun to my head, these weapons really are for you. Let's be straight about this – I wish I didn't have to give them to you. I was counting on you to figure out a way of taking down Darquesse on your own, but I guess I overestimated your competence, now didn't I? So here I am, riding in to the rescue, a cavalry of one."

Pleasant lowered the gun, and Sanguine took a step backwards.

"If you want Darquesse dead, why don't you do it yourself?"

Sanguine grinned. "Because I ain't the hero in this scenario. The hero does dumb things like go up against the pretty girl-god, and is liable to get himself killed in the process. Me, I have every intention of surviving the next few days. If I see an opportunity, sure, I'll take it, but I'm not gonna go looking for it. That's your job."

"What are her plans?" asked Skulduggery. "Where will she be?"

"You think I'm privy to those details? To Darquesse, I'm the hired help she hasn't even hired. She won't even tell Tanith what her plans are. Seems she thinks Tanith's faith ain't what it used to be."

"Is that true?" Stephanie asked.

"To talk to her, my fiancée is just as determined to bring about the end of days as she ever was. But I don't know. Closer it gets, the more the doubts seep in. Cold feet, as it were. Of course, when she finds out that I betrayed her, she's gonna want to kill me. So I'm keeping the dagger."

"You think so, do you?" Pleasant asked.

"Oh, I know it," Sanguine said. "You know it, too. From this point on, I'm your man on the inside. Because of that, I need some way to defend myself. So the dagger stays with me."

A moment passed, and Sanguine thought he had overplayed his hand, but Pleasant motioned to Stephanie and she stood up, held the dagger out for him. Sanguine took it, but not by the blade. He kept his hands well away from the blade.

"The Remnants are out, by the way," he said, once the dagger was back in his possession.

Pleasant tilted his head. "When?"

"Yesterday morning."

"No. We would have heard something. The news would be full of reports of disturbances and violence."

"Even more than it already is? Naw, Darquesse gave them an order, so Tanith said. She told them to behave. Guess they're obeying."

"Why'd she do it?" Stephanie asked.

"For one thing, she wants an army should she need it. Another, she's using Remnants to get all these scientist guys to talk to her about magic and quantum mechanics and whatnot. She's expanding her knowledge in a big way. Last guy she talked to, a guy she turned into a damn chair not a half-hour ago, told her to read something called the *Hessian Grimoire*. I were a betting man, I'd say that's where she's going next."

15

FINBAR'S DREAM

"**G**ood morning," the Administrator said when Stephanie and Skulduggery walked by. Tipstaff fell into step beside them. "Finbar Wrong is here to see you. I asked him to wait in the lobby."

"Did he say why he was here?" Skulduggery asked.

"He did not. I pressed him, but he seems to believe he has information best delivered personally. I told him you were scheduled to brief Grand Mage Sorrows on your investigation, and when you were finished, if you were so inclined, you would perhaps speak with him."

"That's fine," Skulduggery said.

"Mr Wrong is a most unusual man," Tipstaff continued, frowning slightly. "He tried to convince me to allow him to give me a tattoo."

Stephanie grinned at the idea. "And you said no?"

"I did," said Tipstaff. "I simply don't have room for another one. Miss Sorrows will be joining you in the Room of Prisms shortly. Have a good day." He gave them a nod and veered into another corridor, leaving them to continue on on their own.

"What do you think he wants?" Stephanie asked.

"I don't know," Skulduggery said.

End of conversation.

Stephanie came to an abrupt halt. "I'm sick of this."

Skulduggery stopped and looked back. "This?"

"This," she said, pointing between them. "You and me. The awkwardness. The silences. That uncomfortable feeling."

He tilted his head.

"I'm not her," Stephanie said. "But you seem to think that I'm trying to be. Even though I've told you a hundred times that I have no interest whatsoever in replacing Valkyrie. I'm helping you because you asked for my help. You came to me and you asked. For *my* help. Not the other way around. I'm not the annoying little girl tagging along."

"I know that."

Anger flashed. *"So stop treating me like I am."*

Skulduggery went quiet for a moment. "I see."

"Do you? Because I don't think you do. You're caught up in our mission and that's fine. You're in mourning for Valkyrie, and that's fine, too. That's understandable. But don't punish me for everything that's happened."

"I don't want to punish you, Stephanie."

"Then stop making me feel like this."

"I'll... try."

All at once, her anger vanished. She felt bad. His best friend had, essentially, died, and she was berating him for not being his usual cheerful self.

"I'm sorry," she said. "I didn't mean that."

"Yes you did. And there's nothing wrong with that. There's nothing wrong with you, either. You're a good person, Stephanie. Or you've become one, anyway. You've proven yourself. And I appreciate how difficult it must have been to say that just now. Thank you."

"You're welcome," she mumbled.

He swept his hand before him. "Shall we continue on? We don't want to keep the Grand Mage waiting."

Stephanie smiled, and they resumed walking. She opened her mouth to speak, but Skulduggery held up a finger to silence her. He tilted his head at the look on her face, took her arm gently and led her down an adjoining corridor. She began to hear a raised voice. Female.

They got to the corner, saw Eliza Scorn standing toe to toe with China. It looked like Scorn would have thrown a punch if the Black Cleaver hadn't been standing at China's shoulder.

"Why don't you just admit it?" Scorn snarled. "You sent Vincent Foe and his gang of degenerates over to the Church to join us. I want a Sensitive down here right now to pick the truth from the filthy recesses of your mind."

"That's hardly necessary," China said, the epitome of calm. "Even if I did do that, which I did, the fact is your weasel-faced little man didn't know any better, and he allowed it to happen. So the raid you're here to lodge a complaint against was entirely justified."

"You set us up!"

"And your man fell for it and, in doing so, broke the terms of your Church's agreement with this Sanctuary. This is all very regrettable, though it isn't really, and I wish to assure you that I, in no way, derive any personal satisfaction from any of this, even though I so obviously do. If you feel the need to vent any more of your frustration, please feel free to do so, as I intend to build a collage of this moment and I'd like some more amusing anecdotes to go along with it."

Scorn jabbed a finger at her. "This isn't over."

"I dare say you're right," China said, and smiled as Scorn stormed away. She waited a moment, then turned her blue eyes on Stephanie and Skulduggery. "Good morning. I take it you heard all that?"

"We did," Skulduggery said.

"Was I as marvellous as I thought I was?"

"You were supremely aggravating and terrifically smug."

"Oh!" said China. "The perfect combination! Come walk with me. Tell me good news."

They took up positions on either side of her and moved down the corridor, the Black Cleaver a silent shadow behind them.

"I'm afraid good news is in short supply," Skulduggery said. "Darquesse has freed the Remnants."

"She did *what?*"

"We sent people to the Receptacle to check. Most of the guards there are dead or injured. Two are missing, probably possessed."

For a heartbeat, it looked like China might narrow her eyes in anger, but she took a deep breath, exhaled, and calm was restored. "Where have they struck first?"

"That's just it," Skulduggery said. "They haven't struck anywhere."

China frowned. "So where are they?"

"We don't know," said Stephanie. "There's been nothing on the police scanners or news reports, either."

"This is just what we need," China said. "Darquesse, the renegades, and now the Remnants. Do you think they'd be nice enough to stay out of trouble while we deal with the first two?"

"It's always possible," said Skulduggery.

A pair of sorcerers passed, nodding respectfully to China, and Skulduggery waited till they were out of earshot before continuing.

"The Remnants, in their natural form, are very hard to control. It's only when they've possessed a host that they can take orders. Darquesse may think she has herself an army, and she may well be right, but there's a chance that she's overestimated her control over them."

"I don't like relying on *chance*," said China. "The remaining renegades are still lying low, aren't they? Well, until they resurface, tell Vex and Rue to take the Monster Hunters and track down the Remnants. Once we know where they are, we'll take care of them once and for all. If the renegades poke their heads up in the mean time, we'll take care of them, too. No more half-measures. From this point on, when we solve a problem, it stays solved. No matter what. You two, meanwhile, keep your sights on Darquesse. Have there been any developments on that side of things?"

"We've spoken to Billy-Ray Sanguine."

"You have him?"

"We spoke to him."

"You let him go?"

"Sanguine finds Darquesse's long-term goals objectionable," Skulduggery said. "In his own way, he seems to be on our side."

"He's been on our side before, and he's betrayed us."

"He's given us three God-Killers as a show of faith. The ones he destroyed were forgeries."

"I see. Did he tell you where to find Darquesse?"

"He told us her next move. She's looking for the *Hessian Grimoire*."

China frowned again. "The *Hessian*? But that... that's all theory. There's nothing at all practical within those pages. I could name a hundred grimoires that would be more useful than the *Hessian*."

"The *Hessian Grimoire* contains *knowledge*," Skulduggery said. "That's what she's after. The only reason most of those theories remain theories is because there's been no one powerful enough to test them. Until now. If she gets her hands on that... it's all over. The one advantage we have is that we know where the grimoire is being stored, and Darquesse doesn't."

"It won't take her long to find out," China said. "You need to get to it before she does."

"Agreed," said Skulduggery. "I was thinking we go and get it tonight, actually."

"What a coincidence," said China. "So was I."

They walked to the lobby and found Finbar Wrong asleep on one of the chairs. His tattered denim jacket was covering him like a blanket and his Doc Martens were off.

"Finbar," Stephanie said, shaking him gently.

"Mmm."

"Finbar, wake up."

He opened his eyes slowly, blinked up at her and grinned sleepily. "Oh, hello. Mmm. Sorry. Where am I?"

"Roarhaven," Skulduggery said. "You have something for us?"

"I'm in Roarhaven?"

"You are."

"How did I get here?"

"We don't know."

"Maybe I drove. I think I drove. I probably drove. Can I drive?"

"Tipstaff said you had information for us."

"Who's Tipstaff?"

"The Administrator. The man you were talking to about tattoos."

"That's Tipstaff? I was calling him Kevin. Aw, man, that's so embarrassing."

He held up his hands and Stephanie pulled him out of the chair.

"You're not used to early mornings, are you?"

He shook his head. "Early mornings were invented by the system to keep the people occupied. But not me. I'm on to them. They're not gonna catch me napping. Metaphorically, like. Obviously, they can catch me physically napping like, four or five times a day, but, metaphorically, I am so far beyond their reach."

"Finbar," Skulduggery said.

"Hey, Skul-man."

"Hello, Finbar. You told Tipstaff you had information you could only pass on to us personally. So here we are."

"There you are," Finbar said, his eyes narrowing as he looked around. "Can we trust the others?"

"There's no one else here," Stephanie said.

"Oh. But aren't we being monitored or something?"

"Nope."

"Oh. Well, OK then, though I'd seriously look into planting a few microphones around here. You never know what people might be whispering about."

"Finbar."

"Right. Yeah. Something big has happened. Something huge. Last night, while I was asleep? I had a dream about Valkyrie."

Stephanie looked at him. "So?"

"So, um, so I had a dream about her."

"So what?"

"No, no," said Finbar. "I don't mean I just had a dream and Valkyrie was in it. Although, yeah, I do. But what I also mean is that Valkyrie came to me in a dream."

"What do you mean, she came to you?" asked Stephanie.

Skulduggery tilted his head. "What happened?"

"I was in some vast city," said Finbar, "full of neon lights and skyscrapers. I was a Power Ranger. I don't know why I was a Power Ranger, but I was. I was the Red Ranger. Sharon was dressed up like Princess – y'know, from G-Force? Anyway, we had to rescue our son, who was this weird turtle thing, from all these kaiju – Godzilla and Mothra and Rodan, and for some reason King Kong was there as well, but I don't think that's relevant."

Stephanie blinked. "You don't think *that's* relevant?"

"He's not a kaiju, is he? Not technically. He's just a giant ape."

"Where does Valkyrie enter into all this?" Skulduggery asked.

"Ah, yeah, right, OK, so there we were, me and Sharon, and we were fighting these people made from broccoli, which I'm pretty sure was a dream nod to a Warren Ellis comic, and then Rodan came thundering towards us and it all looked bad, it looked like we were about to die, and then the ground, like, exploded, and there was this... this thing... with all these tentacles, bursting up and grabbing Rodan, and it threw him away, over the skyscrapers. And then it turned to me, and I couldn't see a face, but I heard its voice, and it was Valkyrie. She called my name and said, 'Help me.' And then I woke up."

"That's it?" Stephanie asked, frowning.

"Well," Finbar said, "there was a bit more action with the Fiery Phoenix and some mechs, but I don't think you'd be interested in any of that unless you're a big anime fan. Are you?"

"I meant," Stephanie said, "is that it as far as Valkyrie's concerned?"

"Oh," Finbar said. "Yeah, it is."

"Then I must be missing something. You had a dream where you were fighting Godzilla and you heard Valkyrie talking. You're not saying it's a premonition, are you? Because there's no such thing as Godzilla, and you're not a Power Ranger."

"Not a premonition, no. But I think Valkyrie was trying to communicate with me."

"How do you know it wasn't just another part of the dream?" asked Stephanie.

Finbar answered her frown with one of his own. "Because I'm a psychic. I know the difference. I usually know the difference. Sometimes I know the difference. I'm sure it was her, that's what I'm trying to say."

"But Valkyrie's gone," said Stephanie. "If you heard her voice, that was Darquesse."

"But why would Darquesse be asking for my help?"

"That's exactly what I'm saying," said Stephanie. "Maybe it was just part of the dream."

"It *was* part of the dream," Finbar said. "And it was also Valkyrie trying to communicate."

"How sure are you?" Skulduggery asked.

"Relatively," Finbar said.

Skulduggery took Finbar's arm. "Come with me," he said, leading him out of the lobby.

"But my Doc Martens..."

"You can pick them up in a minute." Skulduggery pushed open a door, made sure the room was empty, and closed it once

Finbar and Stephanie were both inside. He pulled out his phone, dialled and put it on speaker.

Cassandra Pharos answered. "You just can't stay away from me, can you?"

"Be warned, Cassandra, you're on speaker."

"Oh, phooey."

"I'm here with Stephanie and Finbar."

"Good morning, Steph. Finbar, what has you up this early on a weekday?"

Finbar frowned. "It's a weekday?"

"Valkyrie came to him in a dream," Skulduggery said. "She said 'help me' and disappeared."

"I see," Cassandra said. "Finbar, it was really a communication? You're not getting confused again, are you?"

"I'm sure," Finbar said. "The TV wasn't even on this time." He glanced at Stephanie. "Last time I thought someone was contacting me, it was William Shatner." He looked back at the phone. "But this time I'm sure, Cassie. It was her. It was Valkyrie."

"How would Valkyrie even *know* how to possess someone?" Stephanie asked. "If the dream was real, how do we know it's not someone pretending to be her? Either a Sensitive or Darquesse herself? Maybe they want to lie to us or distract us or just spy on us. We don't know it's Valkyrie. Valkyrie's gone."

"I'm not entirely convinced of that," said Cassandra. "There is a possibility that Valkyrie could merely be subdued, in the same way that Darquesse was when Valkyrie was in control. If that's the case, it's entirely reasonable to assume that she's diverting some of Darquesse's power to contact us without Darquesse even being aware of it."

"But Valkyrie doesn't know how," Stephanie said.

"She knows everything Darquesse knows," said Skulduggery. "And Darquesse learns, adapts, and acquires new abilities at a remarkable rate."

"Is this what you think," Stephanie asked, "or what you hope?

You're all acting like Valkyrie is still there to be saved. I'm here to tell you, as the only one who could possibly know, that there *is* no Valkyrie any more. I know how strong Darquesse is. She would have swallowed Valkyrie whole."

"Is that what you think or what you hope?" Skulduggery murmured. She glared at him as he spoke into the phone. "If it is Valkyrie, and I'm not saying it is, how do we use that to help her?"

"I don't know," said Cassandra. "There are two distinct viewpoints within her mind, and yet they're the *same* personality. Theoretically we could push one aspect down, suppress it, using some of the techniques we employed with Argeddion. But we'd need some very powerful Sensitives to do it."

"This is insane," said Stephanie. "If we go after her with the intention of subduing her, she'll kill us. We agreed on this, Skulduggery. We agreed that if I had the shot, I'd take it."

"If we have no other choice."

"We don't."

"We have this," he said. "This is a choice. If that *is* Valkyrie, she's reaching out to us."

"You're putting the world in danger for someone who's already gone."

"I'm not giving up on her unless I absolutely have to."

"Even if it works, what then? Darquesse is pushed back down into the dark corners of Valkyrie's mind. So what? She'll rise to the top. She'll emerge. She'll take over. Just like she's done before. If she can be saved, then the only way to do it would be to do what was done to Argeddion. Push everything down. Repress everything, and rewrite her personality. Give her a new mortal identity and send her away where she'll never bother anyone ever again."

"She could be right," Cassandra said quietly. "That might be the only way to save Valkyrie's life."

Skulduggery didn't answer.

16

THE NATIONAL BLACK BELT REVIEW BOARD

Life as a Monster Hunter was not without its perks. There was the opportunity to travel, for one – though as a Teleporter, travel was pretty much Fletcher's thing anyway. But then there were other perks, too, like being part of an internationally recognised and respected team of adventurers. Although they weren't quite as recognised and respected as Fletcher had been led to believe. Most of the sorcerers they spoke to around the world had only a passing notion of who they actually were, being more familiar, in fact, with the books they wrote than their actual real-life escapades.

Gracious O'Callahan – the short, strong one with the muscles and the T-shirts – and Donegan Bane – the tall, dapper one with the skinny jeans and the skinny ties – spent most of their time signing autographs and posing for photos while Dai Maybury stroked his beard and looked on with envy and Fletcher was ignored altogether.

The reason they'd got as far as they had in their search for the renegade sorcerers had nothing to do with the Monster Hunters at all, and everything to do with the two men who accompanied them. Dexter Vex, he of the chiselled abs and the scuffed boots, and Saracen Rue, of the winning smile and the designer suits, had a reputation that all but guaranteed straight answers to their many questions. The Dead Men were taken seriously wherever they went.

And now they were back in a small town in Ireland with a new set of targets – the Remnants. Even Gracious had looked apprehensive at the idea of taking on those sneaky little bodysnatchers. Vex and Saracen, of course, hadn't batted an eyelid, and gradually their sense of calm had spread throughout the group, and the casual nature of the team returned. Unfortunately.

"I remember *my* first girlfriend," said Gracious as they prowled the town's quiet back streets.

"Stephanie is not my first," Fletcher responded.

Gracious ignored him. "A farmer's daughter, she was, though back then nearly every girl was a farmer's daughter. Or a farmer. She had hair as long as rope, and a nose. All her eyes were blue and she had a smile like a radiant hole in the ground, with teeth. God, she was beautiful."

"She sounds terrifying," said Donegan.

"Hush, you. I will hear no bad word spoken of your sister."

"Stephanie is not my first," Fletcher repeated. "I really don't need any advice."

"Lads," said Gracious, "any words of wisdom for Fletcher here?"

The others closed in.

"Honesty is, honestly, the best policy," said Saracen. "But when honesty doesn't work, lie, and lie convincingly."

"Treat her right and with respect," said Vex from up ahead. "Even when it ends, you want to remain friends."

Donegan pondered. "My advice would be to go for someone better than you are. Stops you from getting complacent."

"Grow a beard," said Dai.

Fletcher frowned back at him. "Sorry?"

"A beard," Dai said. "Women love beards. Grow one like mine. Mine is a manly beard."

"I suppose it is kind of... manly."

"I've had it since I was twelve."

"You must have been a very hairy child."

"The hairiest."

"Hold on a second," said Donegan, waving around a forked branch. "My divining rod is picking up something."

"It's not a divining rod," Saracen said. "It's a twig. You broke it off a tree."

"It does work, though," Gracious said. "It's not one hundred percent accurate, it doesn't lead you straight to the source of magic, but it gets you into the general area."

"This way." Donegan led them down a narrow alley. "Something's close. Very close."

"How sure are you?" Vex asked.

"Pretty sure," Donegan called back. "This isn't an exact science."

"It's not even *remotely* a science," said Saracen.

"Aha!" Gracious said, picking up speed and passing Donegan. He pointed to two chocolate bar wrappers as they skipped along on the breeze.

"I'm missing something," said Fletcher.

"One of the strongest urges a Remnant has once it takes a new host is to sate its appetites," Vex told him. "It needs sensation. It needs to experience pleasure or pain. Food is an instant source of pleasure."

"So all these sweet wrappers..."

"Classic signs of a Remnant possession. Look. More."

They followed the trail to a loose pile of wrappers beneath an open window. Fletcher peered in. A small office with a single desk and cheap trophies on a shelf.

"A dojo," said Saracen.

Fletcher looked back. "What?"

"A martial arts school. Looks like our Remnant might be an instructor."

They walked round the corner to the street entrance. It was an unimpressive building with a cheap sign showing a badly-drawn man executing a flying kick. Fletcher followed the others inside. They passed a framed photograph of a man with a ponytail in a black karate uniform. The name under it was Noonan.

They pushed through another set of doors, entered the hall. Parents sat at one end while their kids stood to attention in the main space. The uniforms they wore were black and red. Only the man in charge, the one called Noonan, had a black belt around his waist.

A teenaged student hurried to the top of the class and faced him. The student settled into a fighting stance, and at Noonan's nod he stepped in with a right punch. Noonan moved, blocking with a quick exhalation, and then he pivoted, shouting out a "*Ki-yah!*" as his fist sank into the student's side. The student dropped to his knees, wheezing.

Noonan swung round to address the students and their parents. "A basic defence against a straight punch!" he announced. "Now I will demonstrate a defence against a knife attack!"

He gestured to another student, and Fletcher saw the trepidation in the girl's eyes as she picked up a rubber training knife and approached the mat. Noonan said a few words to her, the student nodded, and Noonan readied himself.

A curt nod to the student, who stepped in with a wild slash. Noonan dodged back and kicked, his foot connecting with the student's wrist. The knife went flying, and Noonan continued the technique with a series of whirling kicks that sent the student slamming back into the wall.

"Is this guy always so rough?" Saracen whispered to a parent.

The parent glowered. "Every time. He's a bully and a thug."

"Questions?" Noonan said loudly. "No? No one? Our system speaks for itself, doesn't it?" He laughed. There were a few uneasy

107

chuckles from his students. "But anyone can do it, regardless of age or fitness level. I can teach any student to defend themselves and their loved ones. Would one of the parents like to volunteer for a demonstration? No? Are you a little nervous of being shown up in front of your kids?" He laughed again.

Vex walked forward.

"A volunteer!" Noonan said. "Give this brave soul a round of applause, ladies and gentlemen!"

Everyone clapped. Fletcher joined in.

"I'm just going to demonstrate some simple defences against a right punch," Noonan told him. "I'll go easy on you, don't worry! Just take your shoes off and – no, just remove your shoes. Take your shoes off when you're on the mat. Take them—"

Vex strolled across the mat, his boots still on. Noonan's smile became a little strained.

"OK then," he said. "Shoes staying on, are they? Well, seeing as how this is your first time, I can forgive that." The anger in his eyes suggested otherwise. "Now then, sir, this defence is against a right punch, so—"

Vex strolled by him and his left fist flashed out, struck Noonan right on the nose. Noonan stepped back, hands at his face, and Vex circled him unhurriedly.

"Ow!" said Noonan. "No! I didn't say begin! You can't just begin without me being ready! Is it bleeding? Am I bleeding?"

He took his hands away from his nose to show Vex, and Vex hit him again.

"Ow! What are you doing? We weren't doing the technique that time! Oh, God, I'm bleeding now, amn't I? Now I'm bleeding!" Noonan wiped the blood from his nose and sniffled. "And they weren't even right punches. Those were left jabs you threw. Stop walking. Stop walking, for God's sake!"

Vex stopped walking.

"Thank you," Noonan said, seething. "Now then, you're going to throw a right punch, so put your left leg forward, and step through with the punch when I say begin, OK? Do you understand? Am I being clear?"

Vex stomped on Noonan's bare foot, and Noonan screeched.

"You can't do that! You can't do that!"

He hopped, clutching his foot, then lost his balance and toppled over. He glared up. "I see. You're here to prove yourself, are you? You're a tough guy, and you want to cheat? Any other night, I'd throw you out right now. But tonight is different. Tonight, I'm different. So, if you want to freestyle..." Noonan stood up. "Let's freestyle."

Noonan started moving, bouncing on his toes, shifting his weight, weaving from side to side and forward and back. His right fist was up at his chin, his left lower and out in front. A classic fighting stance.

Vex just stood there.

Noonan snapped out a kick, whirled with another, jumped and spun with a third. All three of them were well out of range, though, and Vex just kept standing there. The unimpressed look on his face seemed to agitate Noonan almost as much as the foot stomp. Black veins started to rise as he lunged with a punch.

Vex covered up and went to meet him, arms up and elbows out. Noonan's fist crunched against one of those elbows and he howled. Vex grabbed him, drove him backwards, smacked his head against the wall. The crowd gave a horrified "oooh" and Noonan staggered. The black veins had vanished as quickly as they'd risen. Vex gripped the back of his neck with one hand, and led him into the office.

Saracen stepped forward, turning to smile at the onlookers. "Ladies and gentlemen, we are inspectors from the National Black Belt Review Board, and we need to talk to Mr Noonan about his teaching methods. I'm afraid tonight's class will have to be cut short. Thanks very much for your attention, and safe home."

Saracen bowed, then turned on his heel and walked after Vex. The Monster Hunters followed as the students and parents murmured among themselves and began to file out. Fletcher was the last one into the office, and he closed the door behind him. Noonan was sitting in his chair, his hands shackled, while some very intimidating men looked down at him.

"Where are the others?" Vex asked.

"Other what?" said Noonan. "I don't know what you're talking about. I need some ice for my head. I think my hand is broken. And my foot. And maybe my nose."

Saracen sat on the edge of the desk. "Do you like being him? This man you've hijacked? He seems a tad petty, doesn't he? I bet you've inhabited far more interesting people over the years than *this* loser."

Noonan glowered. "I'm not a loser."

"You're a pudgy martial arts instructor with a quick temper and no control. You regularly hurt your students in order to show off and boost your own ego. You're a loser, my friend."

"Take these cuffs off and I'll show you who the real loser is."

"Don't make this any more difficult for yourself," said Vex. "Listen, we've seen worse Remnants. Some of them, they possess a body and their first instinct is to kill. To cause damage. But you? Your first instinct was to eat junk food. To *experience*. It looks like you really wanted to make this work."

Noonan nodded. "I did. I do."

"You're probably tired of being hunted, right? Tired of being caught and locked away?"

"Exactly!" said Noonan. "I just want to fit in now. I want to live."

"Like this?" Saracen asked. "Like a loser?"

"I am not a loser!"

"You really think you could keep this up? We know what you're like. You're a Remnant. You have no conscience. Sooner or later, you'd kill someone."

"No! Not this time! This time I'm going to have a proper life!"

Saracen laughed. "I swear to God, I'd almost believe this guy."

"I'm telling the truth!" Noonan insisted. He looked to Vex. "I'm not going to kill anyone. Yeah, fine, I don't have a conscience, but so what? Most of the really successful business people in the world are technically psychopaths. They don't kill people, do they? I don't have to, either. Let me prove it. Let me stay in this body, and let me prove it."

Vex frowned. "What? You want us to just walk away? We came here to track you Remnants down and lock you up again."

"Please," said Noonan. "I can help you. The others aren't here. They've gone on. If you leave me alone, I'll tell you where."

"And how do we know you're telling the truth?"

"Have you seen any other Remnants? You haven't, have you? You said it yourself, most of them start to kill people pretty soon after taking a new host. There haven't been any murders in the area because they're not here. Things are different this time."

"Different how?"

Noonan hesitated.

"I'm your only chance of getting what you want," said Vex. "You either talk to me now, tell me what you know, or we take out the Soul Catcher and lock you away."

"Darquesse released us," said Noonan. "She wants an army, ready to swoop in at her command. Only... only things have changed. We don't think of her in the same way any more."

"Does she know this?" Saracen asked.

"No," said Noonan. "I don't think so anyway. But she ordered us to lie low until, you know, she needs us. So they all went off."

"Except for you."

"We passed this town. I saw all the people. I couldn't resist. I took a body. I realised, yes, I actually want a life without looking over my shoulder the whole time. So I took another body, and then I took this one."

Saracen frowned. "This loser is the best you could find?"

"I am not a loser! I am a martial arts instructor! I am respected in my community!"

"Calm down," said Vex. "Look at me. You have one chance to stay in this body. Where are they headed? The other Remnants?"

"East."

"That's it?" Gracious asked. "East? That's the best you can do?"

"They're looking for a town small enough to take over," Noonan said. "Then they'll settle down and wait."

"But you don't know where? There are a lot of towns east of here. You want us to check every single one of them?"

"I'm really sorry. I don't know. Please... what are you going to do with me?"

"You're possessing a body without permission," said Vex. "I'm afraid you have to come out."

"No. No, please, you said I could stay! You said it!"

Dai took something that looked like an empty snow globe from his coat, and Noonan jerked away.

"This is a new and improved Soul Catcher," Saracen said. "China Sorrows herself etched a few sigils into it. Can you feel the pull? You can, can't you? You can feel it dragging you in."

Noonan shook his head. He was sweating badly now. "No. Nope. No."

Dai pushed the Soul Catcher closer, and Noonan screamed.

His throat bulged. Fletcher glimpsed darkness – dark claws, snapping jaws – rise up in Noonan's open mouth. The Remnant tried to burst free, to dart towards Gracious, but it was caught in the globe's gravity and sucked into it. The globe instantly turned black.

Noonan collapsed in his chair. He began snoring.

Vex lifted the Soul Catcher and peered into it. "At least we know China's improvements work," he said. "Now all we need is another few thousand of these and we're set."

17

A VOICE FROM THE DARKNESS

"Hold hands," Cassandra said, and Stephanie scowled.

This was ridiculous. Sitting round a table, holding hands, staring into a flickering candle. This was a bad seance in a bad TV show. She had Skulduggery on one side and Cassandra on the other, and across from her was the placid face of Finbar Wrong.

She wondered how long they'd have to sit like this.

After a few minutes, Finbar's chin dropped to his chest. He was asleep. Again.

Stephanie bit back the ridicule. If she said something and interrupted whatever the hell was happening, they'd probably have to start again. The best thing she could do was wait until everyone else at this table realised the stupidity of what they were—

"Valkyrie?" said Cassandra. "Can you hear me?"

Stephanie took a cautious look around. She wasn't quite sure what to expect. Valkyrie's ghost to appear, perhaps?

"Valkyrie," Cassandra said again. "If you can hear me, give me a sign."

Nothing. No ghost. No lightning strike. The candle didn't blow out. Not one thing. Just as she'd thought.

"I can hear you," Finbar mumbled, without raising his head.

Stephanie frowned. She was about to point out that Cassandra wasn't talking to him when he muttered something else, then said, "Skulduggery? Where's Skulduggery?"

"I'm here," Skulduggery said. "I was beginning to think you were lost to us."

Finbar's mouth twitched into a brief smile. "Sorry. You're not going to get rid of me so easily."

Stephanie's eyes widened. *No way*.

"Valkyrie, what can you tell us about where you are?" Cassandra asked.

"It... it's dark here," Finbar said. "Cold. Finbar is like... his mind is at the far end of a bridge, and you're just beyond that. You're this dim light..."

"Do you know where you are physically?" Skulduggery asked. "Where is Darquesse right now? What's she doing?"

Finbar's frown deepened. "Experimenting," he said. "Experimenting with magic. Expanding her abilities. When she's like this, I can... I can talk, and she won't notice."

"Hold on there," Stephanie said. "Wait a second. How can we be sure that you're really Valkyrie?"

"*You* don't get to speak to me," Finbar said, his voice sharpening. "Last time I saw you, you tried to kill me. Skulduggery, why is she here?"

"Stephanie's helping," Skulduggery said.

"You can't trust her."

"He can't trust *you*," said Stephanie, the anger rising.

Finbar pointed a finger straight into Stephanie's face. "Shut. Up." His arm collapsed back on to the table. "Fine. Whatever. I'll deal with her when I'm back in control. So how do I do that?"

Cassandra sat forward. "Valkyrie, we're going to need you to focus."

"I'm focused."

"Not now. We need you to prepare yourself, psychically, for what we have to do."

"Uh," said Finbar, "how do I do that?"

"By listening, and understanding. I've been speaking to every Sensitive worth talking to and, while the chances are slim, we think there *is* a way to force Darquesse from your body, at least theoretically."

"*Theoretically* fails to fill me with hope," Finbar said.

Cassandra gave a soft smile. "Deacon Maybury has the ability to rewrite personalities. To do this, he builds up psychic walls, constructs corridors for thoughts, and shuts off aspects of the personality that need to be kept hidden. He fundamentally redesigns the architecture of the mind. Not even Argeddion, who also knows his own true name, has broken through these walls."

"But we don't want to suppress Darquesse," Finbar said. "We want to get rid of her. And the only reason Argeddion hasn't broken through is because he's unaware of his situation. Darquesse knows what Deacon Maybury can do."

Cassandra nodded. "Getting rid of her is still the goal, don't worry. Essentially, what Deacon's redesign does is to split the original personality in two, creating a pocket personality that is then sequestered off to one side. Working with some friends of mine, I believe I can isolate this part and remove it from your mind."

Stephanie frowned. "And put it where exactly?"

Skulduggery set a glass orb on the table. "A Soul Catcher will trap Darquesse's essence just as effectively as a Remnant. What we do with her after that is a conversation for another time. Valkyrie, the only thing you have to concern yourself with is preparing to hold on with everything you've got once the Sensitives start their work."

"I can do that," said Finbar.

"It won't be easy," said Cassandra.

"Dammit," said Finbar.

"You'll feel your thoughts splitting," Cassandra said. "You'll find it difficult to concentrate, difficult to remember. But you must.

You have to focus on something, a word, a phrase, something to latch on to while we're pulling Darquesse away from you."

"The sparrow flies south for winter," Finbar said immediately.

Stephanie heard the amusement in Skulduggery's voice. He was talking a little faster now, with a little more life to his words. "Yes. Good. When Cassandra and the other Sensitives are doing their thing, I'll be with you, and that phrase will bind us together. The moment you hear me say it, you focus on it, repeat it, pour everything you've got into those six words."

"I don't know how long the process will take," said Cassandra. "It might be minutes. It might be days. You have to be ready for anything."

"So when do we do it?" Finbar asked.

"Soon," said Skulduggery. "I don't want to tell you exactly when. I don't want Darquesse to pick up on anything unusual. But be ready."

"OK," said Finbar. "I can do this. OK. I mean, it's risky, though. What if she figures out what I'm up to?"

"You just have to hope she doesn't," said Skulduggery.

"And we just have to hope that you're really Valkyrie," said Stephanie. "Otherwise we're the ones who'll be walking into a trap."

Finbar paused, then said, "I really don't like you." He frowned. "I have to go. I've talked to you for too long."

Skulduggery squeezed Finbar's hand. "I'll see you soon, Valkyrie."

Finbar managed a smile, and then his face went blank. A moment later, he snorted, raised his head and opened his eyes, looked around. "Well? Did it work?"

Stephanie pulled her hands back, and folded her arms.

"Oh, it worked," said Skulduggery.

He was insufferable. Stephanie walked beside him as they made their way through the Sanctuary's corridors, and Skulduggery would not shut up. He cracked jokes, he told stories, he was by turns smug, arrogant and whimsical and, worst of all, he was paying attention to her.

"I thought you wanted me to talk more," he said when he noticed her silence. "Can't have it both ways, Stephanie. I can't be quiet when you want to sulk and chatty when you want to chat. That's not how it works. That's not how *I* work."

"I'm not sulking."

"Well, you're doing something with your face that *resembles* sulking. Are you glowering? You might be glowering. Glowering is like sulking only scarier."

They stepped into the elevator, and Skulduggery thumbed the button for the top floor. The doors slid closed.

"You're definitely frowning, though," he continued as they started to move. "Do you know how many muscles it takes to frown, as opposed to the muscles it takes to smile? I don't. I doubt anyone does. What constitutes a smile anyway? Is it just the movement of the mouth, or are the eyes involved? And to what extent is each muscle utilised? The old homily about how frowning uses more muscles than smiling is entirely redundant unless, of course, you're talking about the underlying message, and as a message, it's a wonderful, life-affirming thing that bypasses anything so pedantic as actual, provable facts."

"Could we go back to the awkward silences, please?"

"We've moved beyond the silences, Stephanie. We're on new ground now."

"I hate new ground."

"Do you want a hug?" asked Skulduggery.

"God, no."

"You're probably right. I should probably save my hugs for later."

The elevator stopped and they got out. They approached a set of double doors guarded by the Black Cleaver.

Skulduggery knocked, then nodded to the Cleaver. "Hi."

The Black Cleaver didn't acknowledge him.

"I meant to say, I like the new look," Skulduggery continued. "It's moody. It's edgy. It doesn't really leave a whole lot of scope for anything further down the line, though. That would be my only criticism. You've gone from grey to white and now to black and, really, what's left? You could go multicoloured, I suppose. You could show your support for the gay, lesbian and transgender communities. The Rainbow Cleaver, perhaps? No? Too much? That's not your thing? Ah, that's a pity."

Skulduggery stopped talking. The Black Cleaver didn't move a millimetre.

Skulduggery resumed talking. "I don't know if you know this, you probably do, but people here have been around for a few hundred years and, well, things happen. You stop being so fixated on things that don't matter. The pursuit of happiness, that's what it's all about. That's all I'm saying on the subject. It's OK to be different, because we're all different in our own ways. There. Sermon over. Would you like a hug?"

The doors opened. "Are you giving out hugs?" China asked.

"Only to those who need them," Skulduggery said, leading the way in.

China raised an eyebrow. "Someone's in a good mood."

"He won't shut up," Stephanie muttered.

China's apartment was on the top floor of the highest tower in the Sanctuary. White walls and high ceilings. It was a celebration of taste – of art, of culture, of history, of magic. Of power.

China closed the doors behind them. "Should I take it that this good mood means you were successful in communicating with Valkyrie?"

Skulduggery walked up to the floor-to-ceiling windows and looked out over Roarhaven. "You should," he said.

"And she agreed to Cassandra's plan?"

"She did."

China smiled. "Well, that *is* good news."

For some reason, seeing recent events brighten China's mood was even more annoying than Skulduggery's chirpiness. At least Stephanie had *expected* Skulduggery's chirpiness. Some of it anyway.

"In order for the Sensitives to do their part," Stephanie said, "we'll need to hold Darquesse in one place for a period of time, right? Have we figured out just how we're going to do this, or are we simply hoping she trips over and knocks herself out?"

"Such attitude," said China. "I dare say this one is even more sarcastic than the original. She lacks a certain warmth, though, a quality that made Valkyrie so endearing."

"I'm not here to be warm or to be liked," said Stephanie. "I'm here to stop Darquesse and go home. Are you going to help us with that or aren't you?"

The corner of China's mouth curved slightly upwards. "But of course, my dear. I do apologise for wasting time with small talk. I believe I may be of some assistance, yes."

She led them to a large table filled with open books. On a clear space by the edge was a journal, in which was drawn a circle of symbols. Notes were scrawled in different coloured inks, linked by arrows and underlined for effect. Measurements spilled out on to the adjoining page, like an idea that couldn't be contained.

"For the last few weeks, I have been spending my precious time designing traps," said China. "This design you see before you is the culmination of my work. It should take a sorcerer's power and throw it back at her. Once Darquesse enters this circle, her own strength will loop back and stun her, incapacitating her for between five and ten seconds. Because Stephanie is the only one of us without magic, and so the only one who will not be affected by the trap, I suggest she act as bait. Fletcher Renn will be waiting with the Sensitives in a secure location, and when Darquesse is stunned Stephanie can deactivate the trap, the Sensitives can teleport in, and the day can be saved. Can we be certain that Darquesse won't recover while they work?"

"Cassandra seems confident," said Skulduggery.

"Splendid. Our entire existence rests on the assurances of a hippy."

"She hasn't let me down yet. My main concern is this trap of yours and whether or not it'll work on someone of Darquesse's power."

China smiled. "Oh, my dear, you wound me. Have I ever let you down?"

"Numerous times."

"I meant today."

"Then, no. You haven't. That I know of."

"So we have our trap," Stephanie said, cutting across them both, "but we don't have any way of luring Darquesse into it. Creyfon Signate is still trying to find Mevolent's alternate reality and until we have that, Ravel can't be our bait."

"We don't need him to be," Skulduggery said. "Darquesse is after the *Hessian Grimoire*. All we have to do is break into the Vault and get to it before she does."

"The Vault?" said Stephanie. "Beneath the Dublin Art Gallery? The one with the vampire security guards?"

"The very same. Security has been tightened since Valkyrie and I broke in six years ago, but it's nothing we won't be able to handle."

Stephanie frowned. "But why do we have to break in? We're the Sanctuary now. Why don't we just set up the trap in the gallery, Darquesse will walk in, and we'll have her. What's the problem?"

"The Sanctuary has no jurisdiction over the Vault," said China. "They won't let us set up the trap, and we can't force anyone to open those doors for us. Also, the man who owns this particular grimoire is unlikely to loan it out."

"We'll just explain that we need it to save the world," Stephanie said. "Who's going to say no to that?"

China smiled. "I've been trying to get my hands on that book for centuries as a private collector. He may see this request as simply an attempt to use my newfound position of authority to snatch up all the little trinkets I've had my eye on – something I would never, ever admit to. So a little bit of crime is in order."

"We break in and steal the grimoire before Darquesse has a chance to," said Skulduggery. "We set up the trap nearby. When Darquesse arrives, Stephanie takes the grimoire and leads her into the circle. The Sensitives separate Valkyrie from Darquesse and Darquesse is pulled into the Soul Catcher. No one gets hurt, no one gets killed, and Darquesse is locked away forever. Questions?"

Stephanie raised her hand. "How do I deactivate the trap?"

"It's easy," said China. "NJ will show you."

"NJ? Not you?"

"Unfortunately, I will not be attending," China said. "But I am sending NJ and another two of my best students and, believe me, they will have detailed instructions on what to do. I would go myself, but I haven't had a chance to test the trap yet, so I don't know if it'll work, and I don't want to be killed if it doesn't. Any more questions? No? Wonderful. I have a good feeling about tonight. This is a good plan. Nothing can possibly, *possibly* go wrong." She smiled again. "At all."

18

BROGUES AND BURRS

inter's come, and it's a slow day, and cold, and Danny is in the backroom strumming on his guitar, a battered old six-string he's had since he was fourteen. Inspired by Stephanie, he's singing 'Spancil Hill' by the Dubliners.

He's playing softly enough to listen out for the bell over the door, and when it tinkles he puts down the guitar and walks out to greet his prospective customer. Two of them, actually. There's a tall old man over by the magazine rack, his back to Danny, and a younger, shorter, fatter man waiting at the counter. He has a black goatee beard that is failing in its attempt to hide twin moles, one on his upper lip, one on his chin. His thinning hair is long, pulled tight into a ponytail. He looks like he'd be more comfortable in a grubby Black Sabbath T-shirt, but here he is, stuffed into his shirt and tie like a sulky schoolboy forced to dress up for church.

"Do you sell rat poison?" is the first thing he says.

"Afraid not," says Danny, "but we do have some rat repellers that work on an ultrasonic frequency if you have a rodent problem."

The fat man considers this by chewing his lip. "You sell knives?"

"Penknives, yes."

"Hunting knives?"

"No."

"OK. You sell hammers?"

"We have a few," says Danny. "Other side of the shelf behind you."

The fat man doesn't even glance over his shoulder. Usually this kind of time-wasting is done by kids to distract Danny from shoplifting going on elsewhere, but the only other person in the store is the old man, and he stays in plain sight.

"You sell guns?" the fat man asks.

"No," says Danny, the hairs on the back of his neck starting to prickle.

"Pity," says the fat man. "I like guns."

He doesn't say it in a threatening manner – in fact, he says it wistfully, almost like a sigh – but a feeling starts to grow in the hinterland of Danny's mind, and it grows fast and it grows big.

The fat man has a Boston accent. A long way to travel for a hammer and some rat poison. With just the counter between them, Danny can examine the unhealthy pallor of the man's skin and pick out the different stains on the badly-knotted tie, fixed so tight it makes thick rolls of flesh bulge out at his shirt collar.

"Anything else I can help you with?" Danny asks, meaning *you can leave my store any time now, thank you very much*, but the fat man doesn't take the hint, and he stays where he is, eyes moving sluggishly over the racks of stuff on the wall before he comes to something that snags his interest.

"You sell padlocks."

"Yes we do," says Danny. "You want one?"

The fat man shakes his head. "We have all we need. Chains, too. I was just remarking on the fact that you have them, that's all. Doesn't mean I intend to buy any."

"Right."

For the first time, the fat man's eyes meet Danny's. It isn't a pleasant experience. "You shouldn't be so quick to try to sell me things. That's the problem with this country, you know. That's the problem with America. Everyone is out for number one. Everyone's out for themselves. So eager to part me from my money. If I keeled over of a heart attack this very moment, you probably wouldn't think twice about rifling through my wallet before calling for an ambulance, would you?"

"I'm sorry," Danny says. "You pointed out the padlocks. I took that to mean you were interested in buying one."

"Didn't I just say I have enough padlocks? What are you, stupid?"

The last of Danny's politeness washes away. "I'm going to have to ask you to leave my store."

The fat man's eyes bug. "What? You're the one started this! You're the one trying to take my money! Customer's always right, you ever heard that? *The customer is always right.* You were being stupid and dumb and selfish, and what, I'm not allowed to call you on it? I'm not allowed to stand up for ordinary, decent values?"

"Leave or I'll call the police."

"*Police?*" the fat man screeches, his face going a deep red. "You're the one in the wrong! I'm the victim here! Call the police! Go on, do it! We'll let *them* decide who here is the aggrieved party! Oh, not so cocksure now, are you, now that I've called your bluff?"

"Are you going to leave, or not?"

The fat man's lip curls unattractively. "What's wrong – you don't want me to make a scene in front of all these customers?"

"What are you talking about? The only other person in here is your friend."

"Who, him?" says the fat man. "I've never seen that gentleman before in my life."

On cue, the old man turns, smiling. His face is a fascinating map of lines and wrinkles clustered round the landmarks of his features. A large nose, small, bright eyes, a thin, wide mouth. His hair is white and trails from his mottled scalp in wisps. There is something of the vulture about him.

He marches forward, moving surprisingly smoothly for someone so elderly, his gnarled hands held at his sides. "Pardon me ever so," he says, "but I couldn't help but overhear this lively debate from where I stood, perusing the magazine stall. If I may interject, in the spirit of an impartial observer and a stranger to you both, I would offer the opinion that a simple misunderstanding is at the root of this current discord. May I enquire as to your names, kind sirs, so as to better sow the seeds of calmness and brotherhood?"

"My name is Jeremiah Wallow," says the fat man, standing a little straighter. "I hail from Boston, in Massachusetts, which is in the region known as New England."

"It is a singular pleasure to meet you, Jeremiah Wallow," says the old man. "And may I say what an unusual last name you have. My last name, Gant, is somewhat of a rarity also. Originally I came from a small town in a small country in Europe, but as you can probably tell by my accent I have long since made my home in the Midwest, specifically in St Louis, and that is in Missouri. And you, young man? May I inquire as to your details?"

Danny looks at them both. "I'm Danny," he says.

They wait, but he offers nothing more. The old man, Gant, widens his smile. "And where do you hail from, Danny? Are you a native of Meek Ridge?"

"I am."

"That must have been marvellous, to have been raised in such beauteous surroundings. I myself cannot remember a town with such natural charm. Can you, Mr Wallow?"

"I cannot," says Jeremiah.

"You have lived here all your life, then?" Gant asks Danny. "You have watched the comings and goings of your friends and neighbours? And this being, in fact, the General Store, situated as it is on the main thoroughfare, I doubt there is anything, or indeed anyone, that escapes your notice for very long, now is there?"

Danny waits for him to get to the point.

"I dare say you hear an awful lot of accents, do you not?" Gant says. "Accents and dialects and brogues and burrs. What's your favourite? Do you have one? I personally have always been partial to the Scots accent. It's the way they roll their r's. Do you have a preference, Danny my boy?"

"Not really."

"No? No favourite? What about you, Mr Wallow? Or may I call you Jeremiah?"

"I insist on it," says Jeremiah. "And I would say, if asked, which you have, that out of all the accents in all the world, Irish is my favourite, what with me being a Boston boy."

Gant claps his hands. "Irish! Yes! Oh, those beautiful lilts and those soft t's, every word an event unto itself. I knew an Irishman once – he could charm the birds out of a bush, as the saying goes, and it was all down to that accent. What do you think of the Irish accent, Danny?"

Danny works very hard to keep his expression neutral. "Don't have much of an opinion on it."

"You don't?" says Gant. "Well, my boy, in that case, you need to listen to an Irish person speak in order to form one. What are we without our opinions, after all? When was the last time you heard an Irish person speak?"

Gant looks at him, all smiles, while Jeremiah's eyebrows are raised in a gently quizzical manner.

"Guess it was the last time I saw a Liam Neeson movie," Danny says.

Gant waves his hand dismissively. "Movies hardly count. Real life, now that is the only experience worth having. When was the last time you heard an Irish person speak in real life?"

"Years ago," Danny says. "Probably when I was in LA. Don't really remember."

Gant's smile fades a little. "I see."

"No Irish around here?" Jeremiah asks.

Danny shakes his head.

"No Irish girls?" Jeremiah says. "Irish women? You sure?"

"Meek Ridge doesn't have a whole lot to offer," says Danny. "We don't get many people moving in. We usually get people moving out."

"And you say," presses Gant, "no Irish?"

"Nope."

"Well... that is odd."

"You were expecting some?" asks Danny.

"Expecting one," says Gant. "Friend of mine. Niece, actually. Dark hair. Tall. Pretty. Kind of girl you'd remember."

"What's her name?"

Gant smiles again. "Thank you for your time, Danny, but I must be going. Jeremiah, might I offer you a lift?"

"That would be most kind," says Jeremiah, trailing after the old man as he walks from the store.

They leave, and the bell tinkles, and silence rushes in.

19

ME AND HER

tephanie dripped ice cream on to her T-shirt and made a face. "Aww."

"Should have got you a bib," Skulduggery muttered, leaning out past her to take another look through the café window at the Dublin Art Gallery. The face he wore was good-looking and clean shaven. Out there, through the window, Dublin City was in full night-time mode, with people spilling out of one bar and piling into the next. Nobody was paying attention to the sleek, gleaming art gallery and its tastefully minimalist garden protected by a high wrought-iron fence. The fence was new.

"I probably shouldn't have got an ice cream," Stephanie said after a moment. "Technically, it's still winter. Why is this place even *selling* ice-cream cones in winter?"

"Because there are people like you who will buy them presumably."

The café was warm and quiet. A bored girl sat behind the till, reading a magazine. It was nearly closing time. Stephanie got up, dumped the ice cream in the bin, and used a napkin to dab her T-shirt. She'd also got some on her jacket, but she didn't mind that. One wipe and it came right off.

She headed back to the table, but stopped, looking out through the glass partition in the door. "You're about to get a ticket," she said.

Immediately, Skulduggery was on his feet, putting his hat on and stalking outside. Grinning, Stephanie followed him over to the man standing by the Bentley.

The traffic warden looked up. "This your car?"

"It is," said Skulduggery.

The traffic warden nodded. "Very nice, very nice. But you can't park here, day or night."

"I wasn't aware of that."

"There's a sign right over there."

"I didn't think it applied to me."

"Why wouldn't it have applied to you?"

Skulduggery tilted his head. "Because I'm special."

"Don't care how special you think you are, you're parked in a no parking area and as such you're—"

"We're here on official police business."

The traffic warden narrowed his eyes. "You're Garda? I'm going to need to see some identification."

"We're undercover," said Skulduggery. "This is a very important undercover operation which you are endangering just by talking to us." He opened his jacket. "Look, I have a gun. I am Detective Inspector Me. This is my partner, Detective Her."

The traffic warden frowned. "Her?"

"Me," said Stephanie.

"Him?"

"Not me," said Skulduggery. "Her."

"Me," said Stephanie.

"You?" said the traffic warden.

"Yes," said Stephanie.

"I'm sorry, who are you?"

Stephanie looked at him. "I'm Her, he's Me. Got it? Good. You better get out of here before you blow our cover. They've got snipers."

The traffic warden swung round, scanning rooftops. "*Snipers?*"

"Don't look!" Stephanie whispered. "You want to get us killed? Get out of here! Run, but don't make it *look* like you're running!"

Eyes bulging, the traffic warden hurried away, alternating between speed-walking and panicked jogging.

"Nicely done," said Skulduggery.

"Thank you," said Stephanie. "So can we break in yet?"

Skulduggery checked the time on his pocket watch. "Since you're so eager... I don't see why not. Come along."

They walked to the iron fence and looked around, made sure no one was looking.

"Keep watch," Skulduggery said, and lifted off the ground.

Stephanie stuffed her hands in her pockets, tried her best to look casual. She had the reassuring weight of the Sceptre in her backpack to ease her anxiety about what they were about to do. It helped. A lot.

A minute later, a gust of wind took her off her feet. She passed over the fence, landed on the grass beside Skulduggery.

"I've disabled the cameras and the external motion sensors," Skulduggery said as she followed him across the garden area to the gallery wall, where the shadows merged.

"So how are we getting in?" Stephanie asked. Last time it had been through a skylight.

"We're taking a leaf out of Billy-Ray Sanguine's book," Skulduggery said as he placed both hands flat against the wall.

Stephanie frowned. "Seriously? You're going to try to—"

The wall cracked, a thousand little fissures opening up and spreading downwards.

"Now then," Skulduggery muttered, "this is either going to be very cool or very stupid..." He pushed one hand into the wall, and kept going until he was in up to his elbow.

"Well?" Stephanie asked.

He looked back at her. "I'm still in one piece. Grab on."

Stephanie's left eyebrow arched all on its own. "Uh, no, I don't think so."

"We don't have time to argue."

"Who's arguing? I'm asking relevant questions. Is this your first time doing this?"

"I've actually been developing this aspect of the Elemental discipline for a while now. Sanguine's ability is merely a focus on earth magic, after all, so I thought to myself, why couldn't I achieve the same results with a little bit of work?"

"Yeah, that's all very interesting, but is this the first time you've tried to move through a wall?"

He hesitated. "No, actually."

"You've tried it before?"

"Yes."

"Did you succeed?"

"Strictly speaking?" Another hesitation. "No. I kind of got stuck."

"You got stuck in a wall?" she said. "For how long?"

"A few minutes. Half an hour. An hour at the most. Maybe two. Or a day. Remember that day I called Valkyrie and told her to take the afternoon off? Yeah, I was stuck in a wall. But I got out of it, and I've been working on it ever since. So grab on, Stephanie."

"I'll wait out here, thank you very much."

"He who dares wins."

"Fools rush in."

"Valkyrie would trust me."

She glared as he held out his free hand, then sighed. "If you get me stuck in a wall, I will be seriously annoyed with you."

"Duly noted."

She took his hand and he pulled her close. She screwed her eyes shut and then she was passing through something cold, something jagged. Sharp corners prodded her all over at once. The pain was bearable. The rumbling was loud, like great slabs of rock scraping against each other.

And then she was out, stumbling into empty space. Her eyes opened to the dim surroundings of the gallery after closing time.

"There," Skulduggery whispered, "told you I could do it."

"You sound surprised," she whispered back.

"Actually, I'm astonished," he said, and moved on.

They passed through a room of paintings, Skulduggery manipulating the air so as to mute their footsteps. When they got to the corner, he peeked out first, then turned to her and raised a finger to his lips. She nodded.

He peeked again, and motioned her to join him. She inched forward. There was movement in the darkness at the far end of the wide room that adjoined this one. She glimpsed alabaster skin. A person, a thing, almost on all fours. Bald. Naked. Big black eyes. A mouth that couldn't close properly due to the mass of jutting, irregular fangs contained within.

Skulduggery's hand closed round Stephanie's wrist, and she saw another vampire, and another. The place was crawling with them. She and Skulduggery backed away, out of earshot.

"Looks like they've hired more security since we were here last," he said softly. "This might be a tad trickier than I'd anticipated."

They chose another route and moved up a set of stairs silently, Skulduggery taking the lead, reading the air around them. They got to the dark café, passed chairs stacked upon tables in the gloom. To the left of the tables was the balcony overlooking the exhibits in the room below.

They looked over. The Vault was down a narrow corridor marked Staff Only. Stephanie could see the sign from where they stood. Skulduggery nodded to her and she threw one leg over the balcony, then the other, and perched there, ready to jump. Skulduggery merely rose into the air, floated over the balcony, and descended until Stephanie could wrap her arms round his neck. Then they drifted low, skimming over the exhibits, and landed gently by the Staff Only sign.

Down this corridor was a wooden door criss-crossed by metal. Skulduggery picked the lock while Stephanie kept watch. No vampires passed. She sneaked back to Skulduggery when the last tumbler fell, and they passed through. Skulduggery closed the door behind them, as gently as he could, and clicked his fingers. Guided by his light, she followed him down the steps. It was cold down here. Cold and creepy. They passed half a dozen doors, each etched with a unique shield.

"Are you ever going to reclaim your family crest?" she asked, keeping her voice down.

"Now is not the time, Stephanie."

"I think you should. Reclaim it, I mean. You've saved the world, for God's sake. That has to make up for all the bad stuff you've done."

"That's the thing about redemption," said Skulduggery. "If you're looking for it, the chances are you'll never find it."

"Well, I think your family would be proud of you, and I think they'd be even prouder if you took back your crest."

"This is the one we're looking for," Skulduggery said. The crest on this door was a tree and a lightning strike.

"You're changing the subject."

"Imagine that," he said, and held up both hands. Air moved down narrow spaces she couldn't see, but she heard tiny sounds, like mice skittering behind skirting boards. There was a click, and the door opened.

They hurried in, Skulduggery closing the door behind them, and the light flickered on. It was a narrow room, with two walls, floor to ceiling, of safety-deposit boxes, each one with a sigil over the lock. Skulduggery didn't say anything for a few moments. When he finally did, it wasn't very encouraging.

"Dammit."

Stephanie walked forward. "There are a lot of boxes here. Ten down and, how many is that, fifty across? Five hundred boxes on each side at least. Do we have time to open them all?"

"The time it'd take is suddenly irrelevant," Skulduggery said. "These locks can't be picked. Even if they could, each box has an alarm that'd alert the vampires the moment we tried to tamper with it. I have to be honest here. I did not expect this."

Stephanie said, "They hired more vampire security guards after the last time you broke in. Kind of makes sense that the security *inside* the Vault would be heightened, too. Every action has a consequence, right? Stuff you did when you first met Valkyrie is coming back at you now, six years later. Kind of makes you wonder what repercussions our actions today will have, six years down the line."

"If we don't get the grimoire, I doubt we'll need to worry about that." Skulduggery rapped his knuckles against one of the boxes. "OK then. We wanted to do this quietly so that no one would notice. That's no longer an option. So we go loud."

"What do you suggest?"

"I suggest," said Skulduggery, "that you point the Sceptre at the boxes and blow them open. As many and as quickly as you can."

Stephanie grinned, and took the Sceptre from its bag.

"Just don't aim right at them," said Skulduggery. "Aim at an angle. A point-blank shot would probably fry everything inside the boxes, not just the surface."

Stephanie nodded. "I'll try my best."

"The alarms will draw in the vampires," Skulduggery said. "When we have the grimoire, you make a hole in the far wall. If I'm not mistaken, that should take us into the manuscript room. Try not to damage anything in there, it's all very valuable. The door to our right will take us back to the main exhibits. We'll want to go up, on to the roof."

"Last time you were here, Valkyrie had to jump from that roof."

"But I couldn't fly back then. I can now, so we'll be fine."

"You sure about that?" asked Stephanie. "Vampires are fast."

"Vampires are overrated."

"You once called them the most efficient killing machines on the planet."

"Ah, they're not so tough. Ready to go?"

She exhaled. "Why the hell not?"

"That's the spirit."

Stephanie took the Sceptre from her backpack.

"Now," said Skulduggery.

Black lightning turned a patch of steel boxes to dust, and an alarm wailed while Skulduggery waved his hand. The dust blew into the corner of the room and Skulduggery checked the contents.

"Keep going!" he shouted.

Stephanie fired again and again, keeping her angle shallow, to avoid destroying the contents of the boxes. Dust swirled in the narrow room, and behind the alarm, Stephanie could hear the frantic scrabbling outside the door.

"Got it!" Skulduggery called, pulling a thick, leatherbound tome from the crumbling dust. Stephanie turned so that he could slip it into the bag on her back, then fired at the wall opposite. Skulduggery went first and she came after, coughing, stumbling into a glass case displaying three curling, aged pages. Skulduggery took her wrist and they ran, up some steps, back into the gallery proper.

A snarl, from somewhere to their right. Stephanie was about to shout a warning when a gust of wind took her off her feet, sent her hurtling up over the balcony. She caught her foot on the edge and went tumbling, snatching a glimpse of Skulduggery turning to face the onrushing vampire. Then she hit the ground, badly, and cursed to herself as she rolled. She got to her feet. If the alarm were raised, if they were separated, the plan was for Stephanie to get to the roof.

Well, OK then. She just had to find the stairs leading up, and she'd be—

The hairs on the back her neck stood up. There was something behind her.

Stephanie broke into a run a moment before the vampire launched itself at her. She twisted as she ran, firing the Sceptre, but the vampire was moving too fast. It streaked through the shadows, knocking tables and chairs out of its way. Stephanie stopped trying to aim at it and instead fired ahead of her, black lightning turning a section of the wall to dust. She ran through, took a short cut through the next wall as well, and the next, and then she was running up stairs, disintegrating the steps behind her. She reached the top before the whole thing collapsed, and it was like the entire building was roaring at her. She glanced back, daring to hope that the falling debris had trapped the vampire, but it sprang from the billowing clouds of dust, caught sight of her again and snarled.

Stephanie ran on, found the door, burst out on to the roof. The vampire followed.

She backed away, missed with every shot she took, and the vampire jumped and she leaped backwards, fired at the section of roof she'd just been standing on. The vampire fell through, vanished from sight, and Stephanie collapsed on to her back, taking a moment to catch her breath and gather her strength.

She sat up, pushed herself to her feet and shook the dust from her hair. She looked at the hole in the roof and went cold. The vampire's claws were clinging to the edge.

It shot up, out of the hole, and Stephanie spun and ran for the edge of the building. She leaped and fell towards a tree, steeling herself for the impact, but something slammed into her, hands clutching her, and she was lifted – twirling – into the sky and over the city, the streets becoming blurred streams of light beneath her. The arms that held her were warm and strong – flesh and blood arms, not bone. Not Skulduggery. She looked up into a bright smile.

"Hello, you," said Darquesse, and threw her.

20

HOME DELIVERY

After Gant and Jeremiah leave the store, Danny counts to sixty, then steps out into the cold air and looks up and down the street. He can't see them. He returns to the warmth of the store, and stands behind the counter. He gives himself a half-hour of standing there, then fills two grocery bags. He hopes Stephanie won't mind getting her delivery on a Wednesday instead of a Thursday. He decides she won't, not when he tells her his real reason for being there.

He closes up early, puts the bags on the passenger seat of his car and pulls out into traffic. If anyone tries following him, they'll find themselves lost in the school run. Hopefully. It starts to snow, and he realises how cold it is. He puts the heater on full blast and leaves town, heading north, part of a loose convoy of cars and pickups. One by one they turn off the narrowing roads, until there's just Danny with one other car in his rear-view. It's dark by this stage, and Danny swings smoothly round a bend and picks up speed on the straight, but when there are no headlights behind him he slows a little and drives on, the wipers sweeping the snowflakes into little triangles on his windshield.

He doesn't know what he'd expected when he imagined

someone actually asking about her. He'd expected journalists, maybe photographers, or cops. Maybe the FBI or the Marshals Service or someone. He hadn't expected an old man and a fat man. He hadn't expected the menace they brought with them. Not for the first time, he wonders about Stephanie, about who she is and what she's done. Maybe today's the day she'll tell him. He hopes she won't have to kill him afterwards.

Approaching the turn-off for her farm, Danny happens to glance in his wing mirror and catches a glint of something behind him in the snow, something polished and dark. He curses, once and loudly, and tugs at the wheel, fishtailing slightly before getting the car back under control. He passes the turn to Stephanie's place, his palms sweaty, his throat dry. They had turned their headlights off. That's all they'd done. They'd turned their headlights off and he'd almost led them straight to her. Almost.

Danny keeps driving, his mind a frozen blank. What happens now? Is he going to drive until he runs out of gas? Out of road? What will happen once they realise he's been driving aimlessly? Will they pull him over? What will they do to him? What are they capable of? Will they hurt him?

He doesn't know, he can't know, but he feels it. He feels sure they'll hurt him. An old man and a fat man. He's young, in better condition than either of them, but he's never been in a fight in his life. Not even at school. He isn't built for physical confrontation. He has no idea what to do. He digs in his pocket, yanks out his phone. No signal. He curses again, but this one is quiet, like he doesn't want them to hear.

Will they have weapons? The fat one, Jeremiah, he'd been asking about hunting knives and guns. *I like guns.* Danny doesn't have a gun. There's probably a tyre iron in the trunk, but as far as weapons go, that's it. There's nothing but maps in the glove box and an empty coffee container in the cup holder. In the grocery bags there are a few steaks, chicken breasts and some celery and soft drinks and a dozen other useless items. He could possibly throw the grocery bags at them when they run at him, but he doesn't think it'll do much good.

Then an idea occurs to him.

He drives on for another few minutes, slowing as he reaches a turn. He takes a smaller road left, trying to drive casual, the car jolting every time it hits a pothole. After a minute or two, he pulls up outside an old cabin, gets out and grabs the grocery bags from the passenger seat. He takes his time, waits until he sees, out of the corner of his eye, the black car crawling up through the swirling snow and patches of darkness. Once he feels sure they can see him, Danny walks up to the cabin door and knocks.

He knocks again.

Oh, God, please be home please be home please be—

The door opens. Eddie Sullivan peers up at him suspiciously. It takes a few moments for the old man to recognise Danny outside of the store.

"Hello, Mr Sullivan," Danny says, smiling brightly. "I thought you might be having a little trouble getting into town with the snow and all, so I figured I'd come up here and deliver a few essentials."

Eddie peers at the bags. "I didn't order nothing."

"I know," says Danny. "Just being neighbourly."

Eddie chews his lip. "I didn't order it, so I ain't paying for it."

Danny nods. "Sounds reasonable. May I come in?"

Eddie grunts, but shuffles sideways and allows Danny to step in out of the snow. Danny puts the bags on the table and immediately goes to the window, makes sure not to disturb the curtains as he peers out. The black car crawls by, headlights still off. It's an old model, a Cadillac by the look of it. He sees a flash of Jeremiah's pale, fleshy face pressed up against the passenger window, staring at the cabin, before the Cadillac does a U-turn and goes back the way it came.

"This gonna be a regular thing, then?" Eddie asks. "You running a delivery service?"

Danny turns, watches him root through the bags. "I'm just trying it out, seeing how it works. Think of it as a one-off kind of thing, then—"

"I'll take it," says Eddie. "The delivery service. But next time don't bring so much damn celery or feminine hygiene products."

"Right. Yeah."

"Stay there. I'll make out a list for you. Add more beers."

It takes Eddie Sullivan ten minutes to scrawl out a messy list on the back of a crumpled receipt, and then Danny is back in his rapidly cooling car. He puts the heat on again, cruises slowly back towards civilisation, but this time he keeps his headlights off. No sign of the black Cadillac. He takes the turn for Stephanie's farm, stops at the gate and jumps out, runs to the intercom. He presses it and waits, standing in clear view so that the camera, wherever it is, can see him. After a few moments, the gate opens, and he drives through.

Stephanie is waiting for him when he pulls up, standing in the warm light of her front door. She's dressed in jeans, boots and a heavy, oversized sweater. Her hair is pulled back. Danny gets out of the car, jogs up to her.

"Hope you don't mind your groceries coming a day early," he says.

"I wouldn't," she responds, "if you'd brought them."

He looks down at his empty arms. "Oh, yeah. I gave them away, actually. To Eddie Sullivan. Sorry."

"Don't worry about it. I'm sure he'll enjoy the hygiene products. Come in out of the snow."

He hurries in and she closes the door and Xena raises her head from where she lies by the crackling fire. When she sees it's only Danny, she puts her head down and goes back to sleep. On the armchair beside her there's a blanket tossed to one side, and an open paperback lying on a cushion.

"Everything OK?" Stephanie asks.

"Not really," says Danny, turning to her. "Two men came into the store looking for you."

No widening of eyes or dropping of jaw. Stephanie doesn't go pale or stagger back. She just stands there and nods, waits a moment and then asks, "What did they say?"

"They came in, pretended they didn't know each other. They had this, this... routine worked out. An overweight man with a ponytail, said his name was Jeremiah Wallow, and an old man who said his name was Gant."

"Never heard of them," says Stephanie. "Go on."

"They came in, and Jeremiah started asking if I sell rat poison or hunting knives or guns. He said something about already having padlocks and chains. Then Gant came over and they started talking about where they were from, and their favourite accents, and they asked if I'd heard any Irish accents recently and if I knew any Irish women in town. I said no."

"Thank you."

"They seemed surprised. I waited a bit, then came up here, but they followed me."

"That's why you went to Sullivan," Stephanie says. "You gave him my groceries to throw them off the scent. Clever."

"If I was clever, I wouldn't have led them up here in the first place."

"You're sure they didn't follow you here?"

"Pretty sure."

Stephanie looks away, considering the situation, then she turns and walks into another room. Danny hesitates, and follows slowly, clearing his throat to announce his presence. He finds her in a room lit up by a bank of security monitors that show images of entry points all around the property. Not only is there a camera at the gate, like he's always known, but there's also one at the turn on to the road. Both screens show lightly swirling snow, but no sign of Gant or Wallow.

"They were driving a black Cadillac," says Danny.

Stephanie takes another moment to cast her eyes over the monitors. "Well, it looks like you lost them."

"Who are they? If you don't mind me asking."

"Don't know," says Stephanie. "I don't recognise their names or their descriptions."

"Why do they want you?"

"I'm afraid I can't tell you that."

"Are you in trouble? Maybe you should call the cops or something. Nothing these two did was threatening *exactly*, but... I kinda got the feeling they'd be dangerous if, you know..."

Stephanie smiles, showing her dimple. "I'll be fine, really. I can take care of myself. And I have Xena here. She'll protect me."

Danny glances at the dog, who is whimpering softly in her sleep, her hind legs kicking out as she chases some poor unfortunate rabbit through her dreams.

"Yeah," he says. "But listen, if I give you my number, would you call me if they turn up, or if you need help or you just get, I dunno, nervous out here on your own?"

"Sure," says Stephanie. "Give me your number and I'll call you if any of those things happen."

He writes his number on a pad and she doesn't even glance at it.

"Thank you for coming out," she says. "I do appreciate it. If you see them again, just stick to your story that there are no Irish people living around here. They're probably on their way to the next town already, using the same routine and asking the same questions."

"You're not worried that they'll find you?"

Stephanie looks at him, and he sees something in her smile. "I can take care of myself," she says.

21

THE EVICTION

Hurtling towards the wall of glass, Stephanie only had time to cover her head and close her eyes before she felt the impact and heard the world break around her. She landed amid the shards and rolled into darkness, eventually slowing into a sprawl. Her clothes had protected her body, but the backs of her hands were cut, sliced open. Blood ran freely, trickling around to her palms, dripping to the floor as she got to her knees.

She looked at her bloody hands, frowning, noticing how empty they seemed. It took another moment to realise she'd lost the Sceptre, but by then Darquesse was already floating in through the broken window.

"You get prettier every time I see you," Darquesse said, touching down. Her body drank in the shadows around her, her pitch-black silhouette stark against the orange-tinged sky of the city at night.

Stephanie stood, the pain in her hands forgotten. They were in a store, a department store, surrounded by mannequins in frozen poses. No alarm sounded. She wasn't surprised. Not many department store security systems expected people to crash through their top-floor windows.

"What were you doing in the Vault?" Darquesse asked, walking forward slowly. "Did Finbar have a vision? Did he know I was going after the *Hessian Grimoire*? Were you trying to foil my insidious plan?"

She chuckled. It was soft, and mocking, and filled with menace.

Stephanie backed away. She was sure she'd been holding the Sceptre when she hit the window. She was sure she'd brought it in with her. She thought. She hoped. So it was here. Somewhere around her, it was here. It was just lying on the floor, waiting for her to find it, to grab it and use it to turn Darquesse to dust.

"You won't kill me," Stephanie said. She stopped backing away. She stood her ground.

"Oh no?"

"If you kill me, it'll destroy Mum and Dad. You don't want to hurt them, right? That's what you said? If you do *anything* to me, they'll—"

"They'll get over it," said Darquesse. "In the grand scheme of things, my little reflection, what does one life matter? What do a million lives matter? A billion? Not much is the answer. We're all just energy."

Darquesse stood right in front of her now. Stephanie's boots gave her a slight height advantage over Darquesse's bare feet.

There. The Sceptre, on the ground right behind Darquesse's heel.

"Fine," said Stephanie. "You want to kill me? Kill me. But not before I break your nose."

Darquesse laughed. "By all means. Give it your best shot."

Stephanie grimaced. This was going to hurt.

She swung a punch and her fist connected. Darquesse's nose smashed, but her head didn't move back, and Stephanie's knuckles crumpled under the impact. As Darquesse healed herself, Stephanie cried out, clutched her hand and fell to her knees.

"I hope you think it was worth it," Darquesse said.

Stephanie grabbed the Sceptre with her left hand and Darquesse cursed and jerked back as black lightning streaked by her face, turning a mannequin to a cloud of dust.

Darquesse lunged sideways as Stephanie fired again, and Stephanie stood, trying to get a fix, but Darquesse was impossible to see in the dark, dodging between racks of suit jackets and disappearing behind partitions. Then Stephanie glimpsed movement, spun and fired and this time Darquesse dropped back, stumbled, turned to run and launched herself at the wall. She flew straight through it, leaving a gaping hole.

The Sceptre held in a hand slick with sweat and blood, Stephanie turned in a slow circle. Her right hand throbbed so badly it made her want to scream. Movement by the window outside and she jumped. Nothing there now. A glimpse out of the corner of her eye and she spun. Saw nothing.

She heard laughter.

There was a knock behind her, knuckles on glass, so loud and so sudden that Stephanie barked out a cry of surprise as she whirled.

Another knock on another window.

And another.

Knock after knock, Stephanie turning with each one, faster and faster, catching the briefest of glimpses of something blacker than night blurring by outside, and that laughter, that cruel, confident laughter. Stephanie raised the Sceptre, fired, again and again, trying to catch Darquesse as she passed, trying to anticipate, trying to match her speed, the black lightning disintegrating walls and windows and sections of floor and ceiling. A whole display cabinet full of ties went up in dust.

Stephanie spun one more time and stopped, her head buzzing, adrenaline snapping at her fingertips, fear biting at the corners of her mind. The window before her was in one piece. She saw her own reflection in the glass. She looked pale. She looked small and weak and terrified. She looked like a victim. Like prey.

Then she realised there was a face behind the face of her reflection, and it was smiling.

Darquesse burst through the window and her hand closed round Stephanie's throat. Stephanie was lifted off her feet and she felt the fingers tighten and there was nothing she could do and she was going to die. Then the hand released her and she fell. She hit a display stand, scattering shoes as she rolled off. She rubbed her throat, gasping for breath, looked up as Skulduggery and Darquesse spun through the air and slammed into a wall.

Darquesse started to say something, managed to get out, "Now do you really think this was a good ide—" before Skulduggery headbutted her. Her head smashed back into the wall and Skulduggery headbutted her again and again, crunching bone, caving in her skull.

Not that a caved-in skull would stop Darquesse, of course. She ducked under Skulduggery's arm and got behind him, wrapping her legs around his waist. She grabbed his head, went to twist it off, and Skulduggery flew backwards. Even before they hit the ground and separated, Darquesse's face was already healed.

Skulduggery clicked his fingers.

"Stephanie," he said. "*Run.*"

He raised his hands and twin streams of flame enveloped Darquesse, and her laughter filled the air as Stephanie ran for the stairs. She shouldered the door open and jumped, the steps hurtling beneath her. She landed heavily, grunted, slammed against the wall and rebounded. She ran to the next set of stairs and jumped again. She nearly twisted her ankle when she landed this time, but she sprang up, stumbling, and jumped the third set of stairs. Her foot hit the last step and she went sprawling. She bit her tongue and banged her head and dropped the Sceptre.

Stephanie lay there for a moment, stunned, before a *crash* from above kick-started her brain. She got up, stuck the Sceptre under her arm and took the stairs three at a time with her left hand firmly on the banister.

She reached ground level. Black lightning dissolved a fire door and she was out on the street. She jammed the Sceptre

146

into her backpack with the grimoire and sprinted on, barging past late-night revellers. Suddenly realising she had no idea where she was going, she dug out her phone, opened up Maps to figure out the quickest route back to the gallery. She found it. Five minutes away, at a run. She stuffed the phone in her pocket, started to move, then stopped at the sound of screeching car brakes. She turned slowly.

A taxi driver had come to an emergency stop, his headlights catching Darquesse in full glare as she walked slowly across the road. He slammed his hand down on the horn and Darquesse turned her head to him.

Stephanie ran.

There was a crash and a shriek of metal and then the driver was screaming and Stephanie ran and she ran and she ran. She forgot about the pain in her broken hand. She forgot about her burnings lungs, her tired legs, her aching muscles, the cuts and the bruises and the blood. She ran, because to do anything else would get her killed. She ran until she was alone. She ran until she came to a blue door, and then she staggered to a stop. She sucked in air and looked behind her. No more screams. Sirens, though. More than one.

Darquesse stepped out of the shadows beside her. "How far did you think you'd get?"

Stephanie stumbled, flattened herself against the door. She panted, sweating and panicked, while Darquesse stood there, calm and smiling.

"Skulduggery?" Stephanie managed to get out.

"I pulled his legs off," said Darquesse. "Nothing too traumatic. I would have taken my time, but I didn't want you to get too far with my little book. I've heard it's quite a page-turner." She held out her hand. When Stephanie didn't move, she laughed. "Come on now. Do you really want me to take it from you? Wouldn't it be easier for you to just give up, and hand it over?"

"You're going to kill me anyway."

"You all keep using that word. *Kill*. I'm not killing you. I'm changing you back to your natural form."

"Whatever you call it, you're going to do it whether I give you the grimoire or not."

"True," said Darquesse. "But this way, you have a few more moments of awareness before I snuff you out. Isn't that worth a little surrendering? Maybe even a little grovelling?"

"You... you want me to grovel?"

Darquesse's smile grew wider. "I want you on your knees."

"I don't beg."

"Just because you don't like begging doesn't mean you're not going to. Give me the grimoire, get on your knees, and beg for mercy."

Stephanie reached her hand behind her, fumbling against the backpack.

"Friendly warning," said Darquesse. "If you go for the Sceptre, I'll make your death go on for days."

Stephanie paused, then resumed her fumbling, much slower. Darquesse laughed softly.

Stephanie grabbed the door handle, twisted it and it swung open behind her. She staggered back, fell, scrambled up, but Darquesse was already walking in behind her, starting to say something, not noticing the circle of symbols painted on the floor.

The circle flashed with a blinding light as Darquesse got her power reflected back at her. The force spun her around and she staggered, her eyes unfocused, and fell to her knees. She dropped on to her hands, her movements heavy. Stephanie crouched by the symbol in the centre, ran her finger along it just like NJ had shown her, and the circle stopped glowing. She stood, yanked the Sceptre from the backpack with her left hand and pointed it at Darquesse's head.

One command. That's all she had to do. Just think that one command and the crystal would fire out that black lightning and Darquesse would turn to dust. There'd be no coming back from that. Darquesse would be dead, Valkyrie would be gone forever, and Stephanie could live a normal life.

Just one simple command.

Scowling, Stephanie banged the heel of her broken hand against the triangular piece of metal on her belt, and a moment later Fletcher teleported in with Cassandra and Finbar and Deacon Maybury. Deacon saw Darquesse and his courage deserted him, but Cassandra grabbed him, pushed him forward. Panicking, Deacon immediately clasped Darquesse's head between his hands and the others formed a circle of their own, their hands linked, and Darquesse gasped and snapped her head up.

Her eyes were wide. Unfocused. She didn't try to rise.

"We have her," Finbar whispered.

Skulduggery charged in, slamming the door behind him. He didn't even look at Stephanie. He crossed to where Darquesse knelt, and crouched in front of her, took her hands and held them.

"The sparrow flies south for winter," he said. "The sparrow flies south for winter."

Fletcher stood beside Stephanie, his hand touching hers. In his other hand he held up the Soul Catcher. It started to glow, lit up from the inside with swirling light. Darquesse threw her head back and screamed, her whole body shaking. Skulduggery gripped her arms, keeping her sitting upright.

"The sparrow flies south for winter," he said loudly. "The sparrow flies south for winter."

The Soul Catcher shone so brightly Stephanie was almost forced to look away, but then a deep blue spread over its surface, locking the light inside, and the Sensitives stepped away, their link broken.

"We have her," Cassandra said, taking the Soul Catcher from Fletcher and holding it like it was a bomb about to go off.

Stephanie moved round so she could take a better look at Darquesse. No, not Darquesse. Not any more. Valkyrie.

Valkyrie's shadowskin went into spasm and she scrambled away from Skulduggery, away from everyone, scampering backwards into the corner. Her eyes were wide, uncomprehending and terrified.

Skulduggery rose, his hands up. "Valkyrie," he said. "It's me. It's Skulduggery. You're OK. You're safe. Listen to me, listen to my voice. Your name is Valkyrie Cain. You're in control."

The darkness that covered Valkyrie's body twisted and writhed, its sudden movements seeming to scare her more than anything. Skulduggery took a thick necklace from his pocket, on which hung a heavy amulet. He tossed it on to the ground beside Valkyrie and the shadows latched on, started flowing into it. Then Skulduggery whipped off his jacket and rushed forward, covering Valkyrie as the amulet absorbed the last of her Necromancy power.

"Valkyrie?" Skulduggery said softly.

Valkyrie blinked, looked up at him. For a long time she didn't speak, and then, "You... you're a skeleton."

Skulduggery tilted his head. "Yes I am. I have been one for a few years now."

Valkyrie nodded. "I like skeletons," she said, and closed her eyes, and Skulduggery scooped her up into his arms.

22

THE RETURN OF
VALKYRIE CAIN

Stephanie went shopping.

While everyone was still fussing over Valkyrie's return the previous night, she took a walk through Roarhaven's shopping district. A few of the stores were obviously beginning to struggle, denied as they were the promised influx of sorcerers eager to part with their cash, but they were all still open, at least. She found one that sold armoured clothes – not as effective as Ghastly Bespoke's, and certainly not as finely tailored, they nevertheless did the job they were supposed to do. She bought a whole outfit, paid at the till, and while she waited for her change the lady behind the counter positively radiated hatred. But Stephanie was used to it.

It wasn't her fault she looked like Darquesse.

She walked back to the Sanctuary, taking her time, enjoying the solitude. The sun was out and it was pretty warm considering how early in the year it was. She passed a few people. They hated her, too. She let them.

She climbed the steps to the Sanctuary. The Cleavers standing guard were the only people to have ignored her presence in the last two hours. She prepared herself for a lot more of that, and entered the grand lobby. Lots of excited sorcerers walking by.

Darquesse was defeated. Darquesse was done. The crisis was over. No need for panic, no need for worry. No need for Stephanie.

She found an empty room in which to change her clothes. She hadn't gone for black. She wasn't Valkyrie Cain. She was Stephanie, and Stephanie had always loved the coat that Ghastly had once made with the arms of burnished red. She dressed in trousers and a jacket of that same colour, a tight but flattering fit that made her look like she was covered in rusted blood. She grinned at her reflection, then put the black clothes Ghastly had made into the bag and went wandering. She found herself in the Accelerator Room.

"Hello, Stephanie," the Engineer said. "How are you today?"

"Grand," she said. "Great, I mean. Or I should be great anyway. Don't really know why I'm not."

The Engineer nodded. "Human emotions are difficult to navigate."

"They are," she agreed. "So how long do we have?"

"The Accelerator will overload in eleven days, four hours and eight minutes."

"Right."

"Would you like to use your soul to deactivate it?"

"Even if I wanted to, I doubt it'd work."

"And why is that?"

"I'm a reflection," said Stephanie. "I wasn't born. I'm not natural. I'm a malfunction. I wasn't given life – I took it. I don't think I even *have* a soul."

"In that case, step into the Accelerator, on to the dais, and I will attempt to extract your soul. If you truly believe that you do not possess a soul, you will not be harmed, so what is there to be scared about?"

"I'm not... I'm not *scared*, I'm..."

"If, however, there is a part of you that dares to hope that with all life there comes a soul, in whatever form, then I would advise you to decline my kind offer."

Stephanie narrowed her eyes. "You've got a sneaky way of helping people."

The Engineer made a movement that could have been a shrug. "I like people. I have helped many on my travels."

"Why did you walk away in the first place? You were built to look after the Accelerator. That was your whole purpose. That was why you existed."

"I stood here for decades. I grew bored."

"No, I get that, it's just... Maybe what I'm asking is how? How did you decide to ignore your original purpose and, you know, take on this new one?"

"It was easy," the Engineer said. "The thought occurred to me that I was master of my own destiny. Once I realised I could exist, and I mean that on a purely intrinsic level, the world opened up for me. I defined my own purpose."

"But you're right back here, where you started."

"Because I am needed. When I am no longer needed, I will redefine my purpose again. Why do you ask?"

"I... I don't know. I suppose I'm wondering what my purpose is. A few days ago, everything was clear. Do the job, have a normal life. But now I'm... I don't know if I'm going to get that."

Footsteps outside and Stephanie turned as Fletcher peeked in.

"Thought I'd find you here," he said. "Hi, Engineer."

"Hello, Fletcher. Would you like to use your soul to deactivate the Accelerator?"

"Cheers, but no," he said, walking in. "I'm here to see Stephanie, actually."

Stephanie forced a smile on to her face. "So how is Valkyrie?"

"She's doing good," he said. "Doctor Synecdoche is running a few tests, and apart from being hungry, she seems fine. Apparently Darquesse moved beyond the need to consume food."

"Good for her," Stephanie said. "So why aren't you with Skulduggery, huddled round Valkyrie's bedside, giving thanks that she's returned to us alive and well?"

Fletcher looked at her. "What are you worried about?"

"Me? I'm not worried about anything. I'm good. I'm great. I'm—"

"Steph..."

"We were meant to kill her!" Stephanie blurted. Immediately, she reddened. "I mean... not Valkyrie. Darquesse. That was the plan. That's why I agreed to help in the first place. We kill Darquesse, we all go home. Instead, what have we got? Darquesse is in a snow globe, Valkyrie's in a hospital bed, and where am I? What's my place now? Just like that," she snapped her fingers, "I'm dropped as Skulduggery's partner. Just like that the original is back, the real one, and once again I'm the scary reflection nobody can trust."

"I trust you," said Fletcher.

"You? The moment Valkyrie bats her eyelashes at you, you'll forget all about—"

His hand went to her face and he turned her head and kissed her and took the rest of her words.

When they broke apart, he looked into her eyes. "You're my girlfriend," he said. "You. Not her."

"But she's—"

"You, Steph. Got that?"

Stephanie nodded.

Fletcher smiled. "Love the outfit, by the way."

They went upstairs to the Medical Wing.

Valkyrie had her own room. Of course she did. Only the best for Valkyrie Cain. Stephanie and Fletcher walked in, and Skulduggery and Valkyrie looked up.

"Hi," said Stephanie.

"Hi," said Valkyrie.

A moment passed.

"Well, at least this isn't awkward," Fletcher said brightly.

High heels on polished floor and Stephanie stepped aside as

China swept in, going straight to the patient. The Black Cleaver stayed at the door.

"Welcome back, my dear," China said, kissing Valkyrie's cheeks. "Out of all of the outcomes possible, your not dying last night is probably one of the best."

"That means a lot," said Valkyrie, "coming from a Grand Mage. How did you manage that little manoeuvre?"

China waved a hand airily. "Scared and desperate people do scared and desperate things. But enough about the election process. Where is Darquesse?"

Skulduggery brought out the Soul Catcher, holding it up for China to peer at.

"And that will hold her?" she asked.

"We have no reason to think otherwise," Skulduggery said. "We'll reinforce it. Make sure there's no chance of her ever escaping."

China tapped the glass. "Then it's done. It's over. It *is* over, yes?"

Skulduggery nodded. "It's over."

China straightened up. "A celebration is in order, I think. This could have gone horribly wrong, but look at us now. The threat averted, the villain trapped, and we even have Valkyrie back. Tipstaff!"

Tipstaff appeared in the doorway. "Yes, Grand Mage?"

"Organise a party, would you? Something celebratory – extravagant without being indulgent."

"Extravagant but not indulgent, of course," Tipstaff nodded. "Will there be anything else?"

China looked at the others. "Requests? Anything you'd like to see at this party? Balloons? A trapeze act? Elephants? We have to make a big deal out of this. People need reassurances that things are getting back on track. We'll invite every Council from every Sanctuary around the world. It will be wonderful. It will be fabulous." Her eyes settled on Skulduggery. "And you will deliver the invitation to Zafira Kerias personally."

Skulduggery's head tilted. "I was wondering how long this respite would last."

China waved her hand again, and Tipstaff went away. "We had three problems," she said. "Darquesse was the first, but she's no longer a threat. You've saved us all and you have our thanks. But we still have two problems left – the renegades and the Remnants. Fortunately for us, I've been keeping my ear to the ground, and the latest reports suggest that the American Sanctuary is hiding the renegades. You've solved the first problem – now I want you to take Vex and Rue and the Monster Hunters, and solve the second problem. When the renegades are in shackles, you'll tackle the third."

"When you say you've kept your ear to the ground…"

China smiled. "This information came to me from a confidential source."

"One of your spies from the old days?"

"Precisely. Their information has always been accurate, and I see no reason why it should be any different now."

"Fletcher," said Skulduggery, "you're teleporting back to Dexter in a few minutes, aren't you?"

"Now, actually," Fletcher said. "I want to help them search the next town on our list. Shouldn't take more than an hour or so."

Skulduggery nodded. "Good. When it's done, we'll all pay Grand Mage Kerias a visit."

"I'll tell them," Fletcher said. He gave Stephanie's hand another squeeze before dropping it and disappearing.

China turned to Valkyrie. "Now that all that pesky business is taken care of, it really is good to have you back with us. How are you feeling?"

Valkyrie smiled grimly. "Tired. I'm not entirely sure what's been happening, but… but I'm OK. I'm quite surprised to see you making house calls, though. I thought they weren't your style."

"I felt I could break that rule for you. You saved my life, you know. Do you remember that?"

"I remember you burning up."

China nodded. "You could have let me die. Darquesse could have let me die. But she didn't. There was enough of you left in her to save me. I won't forget that."

"I'm just glad I was stopped before I could hurt anyone else."

"We've all done things we're not proud of. We've all done questionable things. Some of us have even done terrible things. But you're back with you now, and you're safe and you're well, and you're going to get better." She looked round as Synecdoche walked in. "Isn't that right, Doctor?"

Synecdoche read the monitors. "Absolutely," she muttered. Then she looked up. "Yes. Perfect health. There's no reason why Valkyrie can't walk out of here in the next few minutes. May I see the Soul Catcher, please?"

Skulduggery held it out, and Synecdoche ran her hand round the glass. Her hand glowed. Even from where she stood, Stephanie could feel the radiating warmth and the welcoming comfort.

"What are you looking for?" Skulduggery asked.

"Energy readings," the doctor said. "Erskine Ravel is still being tortured. With Darquesse shut away like she is, that link should have been broken. I don't understand why he's still in pain."

"You think the link is still active?" China asked.

"It looks that way," Synecdoche said. "Although I can find no traces of it here."

"Maybe we'll need to reinforce the Soul Catcher before the link will break."

Synecdoche murmured something, then nodded. "Yes. Maybe. We'll need to isolate the Soul Catcher, though. If the link is still active, Darquesse may still have some other tricks up her sleeve. May I take it?"

Skulduggery handed it over. "Try not to drop it. It contains a god."

"I'll do my best."

China watched Synecdoche walk off, carrying the Soul Catcher in both hands, and she said, with only a hint of malice, "I do

157

hope Tanith Low isn't too distraught at losing her messiah. Are we any closer to finding her, by the way?"

"We've sent Cleavers to the safe house Valkyrie told us about," said Skulduggery, "but there was no sign."

China looked at Valkyrie. "Do you have any idea where she might be headed?"

"I don't know," Valkyrie said. "Now that Darquesse is gone, she'll be desperate. Maybe..." She faltered.

"Yes?"

"She might go after Argeddion," Valkyrie said, sitting up straighter. "Darquesse wanted to use the grimoire to track him down – she reckoned peeking inside his brain would be a shortcut to fulfilling her potential. If Tanith finds him, she could use him as a hostage, remind him who he really is unless we hand over Darquesse."

"Darquesse will not be exchanged for anything," said China. "Even so, Argeddion is in too fragile a state to withstand someone as annoying as Tanith Low. One word from her could snap him out of the illusion he's under, the consequences of which would be... disastrous."

"Then we make sure Tanith never gets to him," said Skulduggery. "Who knows where he is?"

"As far as I am aware," said China, "only Erskine Ravel and Deacon Maybury know anything of Argeddion's new life. We'll protect Maybury, and Ravel is too busy with his agony to say anything about it, so I think we're reasonably safe for now. In the mean time, I need you to take care of this renegade problem."

"I'll call Dexter now for an update," said Skulduggery. He looked at Stephanie. "What are your plans?"

Stephanie blinked. "What do you mean?"

"You've held up your end of the deal. You helped us stop Darquesse. We could get someone to drive you home."

Yes. She wanted to say yes. She wanted to say yes and walk out of here and never look back. Only...

Only Valkyrie was sitting right there, and Stephanie felt something twist in her gut when she thought about walking away from a situation that Valkyrie was happy to walk into. Ego. That's what it was. Pride and ego.

"I'll stay until we take care of the renegades," she said. "I've got the most powerful weapon, after all. I'll help you one last time, then I'm gone."

"Your help is appreciated," Skulduggery said, turning to leave. Stephanie started to follow and Valkyrie went to get out of bed, but he glanced back at them. "Stay here, both of you."

"What?" Stephanie said. "I said I'd help."

"You are not leaving me out of this," said Valkyrie

"I don't intend to," Skulduggery said, "but I don't want you two arguing the whole time."

Stephanie frowned. "We've only said one word to each other!"

"Exactly. I want you to talk. You have a lot to sort out, and the faster you do it, the more use to me you'll be. We'll be teleporting to America in an hour. I expect you to be friends by then."

He left, China by his side. The Black Cleaver followed.

Stephanie looked at Valkyrie. Seconds dragged by. "So what's going to happen now?" she asked.

"I don't know," said Valkyrie. "Maybe—"

"I'll tell you what's going to happen now. You went away. You gave in, and you gave up everything you were born into. They're my family now."

Valkyrie's eyes narrowed. "We could have sorted this out, you know. You didn't have to attack me. You didn't have to try and kill me. We could have *talked*."

"You wouldn't have talked," Stephanie said. "You wouldn't have even considered a compromise."

"So let's compromise. I'm still going to need a reflection to—"

"I'm not your reflection."

Valkyrie held up her hands. "Sorry, sorry, I didn't mean it like that. I meant, now that I'm back, I'm still going to be heading off with Skulduggery every day, so I can't do without you. I need you to keep doing what you're doing. I think we should share my – our – family. When I'm at home, you spend the night somewhere else, and for the rest of the time, you're there."

Stephanie shook her head. "It'd never work, not without the mirror. What if we get different haircuts? Or one of us gets a pimple? What if you put on weight?"

Valkyrie frowned. "How come I'm the one who gets fat in this scenario?"

"Without the mirror, this won't work. And there is no mirror any more. And even if there were, I wouldn't get back into it."

"It'll be a learning process," said Valkyrie. "We'll settle into a routine. We'll come up with ways to work round problems. Does that sound agreeable?"

Stephanie grunted. "Maybe."

"We can co-exist, you know."

Stephanie grunted again, and put the bag she was holding on the bed. "Here are your clothes."

Valkyrie looked surprised. She opened the bag, peered in. "You don't want them?"

"I don't want people mistaking me for you. I have my own outfit now anyway. The shock stick's in there, too. You can keep it. It doesn't recharge for me, and I have the Sceptre."

"OK. Well... thanks, I suppose."

"So, are we friends now? Can I leave you alone without Skulduggery berating me for it when he gets back?"

"I won't tell him if you won't."

Stephanie shrugged. "Suits me," she said, walking to

23

the door, and then she left, and the room was quiet. All the tests had been run, and the Sensitives had been in, and the questions had been asked, and Darquesse had fooled them all.

She got off the bed and dressed. Black trousers – tight. Black jacket – zipped. Black boots – awesome. She'd missed these, the clothes Ghastly had made for her. Well, for Valkyrie really, but what was the difference?

She caught herself, and laughed. Actually, now there *was* a difference. Now that Valkyrie was trapped in that Soul Catcher, Darquesse was alone in her own head for once.

It felt good.

She just needed to remember how Valkyrie behaved. She needed to remember the things Valkyrie cared about. Family. Friends. Hitting people. She didn't know how long she could keep up the act, but she didn't need an exorbitant amount of time. Just long enough to find out who and where Argeddion was, and to take a look at the *Hessian Grimoire*, and maybe have a little mischievous fun while she was at it.

She left the Medical Wing, and went for a walk.

The Sanctuary had changed since she'd been here last. It

reminded her of Mevolent's Palace in that alternate dimension. In fact, Roarhaven itself now resembled that entire city, even down to the great wall protecting its borders. She wondered if this little coincidence bothered Skulduggery. It probably did.

Mevolent. Now he had been fun. He had been a challenge. He hadn't even discovered his true name, and yet he'd stood toe to toe with her and very nearly beat her.

She looked forward to the rematch.

She wandered the corridors, smiling at everyone she passed, until she glimpsed Deacon Maybury rounding a corner. She followed, hanging back whenever he was around other people. When he was finally alone, she stepped into the room behind him.

"Hi there," she said.

Deacon looked up. She could see the surprise on his face. He was used to being despised – especially by Valkyrie. He wasn't expecting a smile.

Darquesse wandered in, all casual. "Looks like I've got you to thank for pulling Darquesse out of my head."

Deacon blinked a few times before answering. "I suppose," he said. "I mean... there was a team of us..."

"But you were the key ingredient, weren't you? No one else could have separated our personalities like that? No one else has the skill? At least that's what China said."

"She said that? Well, yeah, I mean..."

Darquesse laughed. "You're just being modest."

He laughed along with her. "That's not something I'm used to."

She let his little joke turn her laugh into something more heartfelt, and saw how much he beamed at her reaction. That beaming smile told her everything she needed to know. Poor little Deacon Maybury – all he'd ever wanted was for someone to show him a bit of affection.

"Thank you," she said. "Genuinely, I mean that. You don't

know what it was like, to be in here and not able to control anything, not even able to speak. Then I felt your hands on my head and I heard Skulduggery's voice and I focused, just like they told me to. And I hung on while she was dragged out, kicking and screaming..."

"It must have been awful."

"But it was worth it. Now I'm free of her, and it's all thanks to you."

"Well, like I said, there was a team of us, but..."

"But it was mostly you," she finished, and he laughed again.

"So what was harder," she asked, "separating me from Darquesse or rewriting Argeddion's personality?"

Deacon bobbed his head from side to side, weighing up the answer. "They each had their challenges," he said at last. "With you, the problem was isolating two sets of thoughts, and setting it up so that the other Sensitives could pull one set out. I'd never done that before. No one had. The problem we faced wasn't exactly a common affliction. With Argeddion, it was a complete personality overhaul, with false memories and a false identity thrown in. But even though I'm more familiar with that kind of work, it still took some doing."

"Did you at least give him a cool identity? A rock star or a billionaire or something?" she asked.

"That's what I wanted to do! But they wouldn't let me. They were right, of course. If we're lucky, this overhaul will last his whole life. The key to ensuring Argeddion never resurfaces is to make him boring, and give him a boring existence. Don't include anything that could set him off."

"So what is he?"

"A secondary school teacher."

Darquesse laughed. "You honestly think that's the best career for him? Every teacher I've ever met has been stressed and overworked! If anything is going to set him off, it's being in a class full of insolent teenagers!"

163

Deacon grinned. "I never thought of that. It was a choice between a teacher and a librarian, but at the rate libraries are closing down he'd probably be out of a job already and that would certainly have kicked something off."

"Why a teacher or librarian?"

He blinked. "They were the most boring jobs I could think of. I wasn't going to turn him into a cop or a firefighter or a jet pilot or—"

"Yeah. Fair enough. But what about, like, an office worker or something?"

"What kind of office?"

"Who cares? Give him a desk and a stapler and a meaningless, inconsequential career with zero responsibility and no stress."

"Oh, yeah," said Deacon. "I didn't really think of jobs like that. Maybe I should have."

Darquesse shook her head, amused. "Please tell me he's teaching at a good school, at least."

"I don't know, actually," Deacon said. "The details were filled in later by Grand Mage – or ex-Grand Mage – Ravel. He picked where Argeddion worked and where he lived. Don't think he told anyone else. It's like Witness Protection, you know? The fewer people know about it, the safer it is."

Darquesse nodded. "So you don't even know whereabouts he's living?"

Deacon chuckled. "I don't even know his last name!"

"Ah. Right then. Suppose I should kill you now, so..."

The chuckle dried up. "I'm sorry?"

"Well, not *kill*, exactly. I mean, yes, I'm going to end your life and this, this *person* I see before me will not exist any more, but I wouldn't worry about it. Physical death means nothing. We're all just energy, after all, aren't we? Poor little Deacon Maybury. One of six identical brothers, only two of which remain alive. How did the others die, Deacon? Remind me?"

"I don't... Valkyrie, what's going on? Why are you—"

164

"Davit locked himself into a room, but forgot to provide ventilation, I know that much. Dafydd fell into a wood-chipper. That one's my favourite. How did the other two die?"

Deacon backed away slowly. "Intestinal distress and rabid goat."

Darquesse clapped her hands. "Eaten by a rabid goat, that's right! I think that might be my new favourite, to be honest. So now there's just Dai and you left alive."

"You're not... you're not Valkyrie..."

Darquesse gave him a smile. "No I'm not. So, how am I going to kill you, Deacon? What is the amusing fashion in which you'll die? It is a family tradition, after all."

"You... you don't have to kill me. Why do you have to? I'm no threat to you."

"You're the only one who can do what you do to people's minds, Deacon. Given the chance, I'm sure Skulduggery would think up a way to use your skills against me before I built up a defence."

Tears ran down Deacon's face, and he clasped his hands before him. "Please... I don't want to die..."

"It's OK," said Darquesse. "You won't feel a thing."

She waved her hand and he exploded into atoms.

Now was the tricky part. She still had control over those atoms and she spun some of them, manipulated them, changed them as much as she was able, as much as her limited knowledge allowed, and she took them and brought them together and a little yellow rubber duck appeared in mid-air and fell to the floor.

It bounced with a slight squeak.

Darquesse grinned, and left.

24

A FINE PAIR OF SPECIMENS

Clarabelle gave them the signal, and Scapegrace and Thrasher hurried into the Medical Wing.

They were but minutes away from uncovering the Sanctuary's dark little secret. If what Clarabelle said was true, if their old bodies were still here, then questions had to be answered. Questions like, why? What for? When? Where? Fair enough, the last two questions were probably immaterial and the first two meant the same thing, but Scapegrace was going to find answers to, essentially, that one question, and he was going to find answers today.

When they were sure that none of the busy doctors and medical personnel were looking, Scapegrace and Thrasher clambered on to a gurney and lay flat. Clarabelle immediately threw a white sheet over them. They lay very still as she wheeled them along.

This was the risky part. They were out in the open. If someone noticed Clarabelle acting strangely, it'd all be over. What would happen to them then? Would China Sorrows order their 'disappearance'? Would all three of them mysteriously vanish? How deep did this secret go? How far did this conspiracy spread?

As she wheeled them, Clarabelle hummed that song from *Frozen*. Thrasher started humming along with her and Scapegrace glared at him. Funny – now that he had a purpose once more, he found his capacity for becoming irritated with Thrasher was growing. He hadn't had the energy to tell him to shut up in weeks. He felt all that about to change.

Clarabelle stopped humming. So, thankfully, did Thrasher. Then it was the gurney that stopped.

"Clarabelle," said a woman's voice.

"Hello, Doctor Synecdoche," said Clarabelle.

Scapegrace held his breath. They were going to be discovered. Oh dear God, they were going to be discovered.

"What do you have there?" Synecdoche asked.

"Body parts," said Clarabelle.

"I'm sorry?"

"Body parts. Parts of a body. All gross and icky. I put the sheet over them because they're far too disgusting to look at."

Synecdoche was silent for a moment. "Where are you taking them?"

"Through there."

"I see. And where did you get them?"

Scapegrace looked at Thrasher out of the corner of his eye. Thrasher was sweating. He felt it, too. This was it. This was the end.

"Skulduggery Pleasant told me to put them somewhere safe," Clarabelle said. "He told me they're part of a very important case he's working on. These are the remains of Lewis Holmes."

Clarabelle said that name like it was supposed to mean something.

"Who?" Synecdoche asked.

"Lewis Holmes. You haven't heard of him?"

"I'm afraid not."

"Lewis Holmes died horribly while saving the world," said Clarabelle. "He went up against an evil Warlock and the Warlock tricked him, drugged him and dismembered him. That means he cut off his limbs."

"I know what dismembered means, Clarabelle."

"The evil Warlock left him for dead," Clarabelle continued, "but Lewis survived. According to Skulduggery, Lewis attached and tied four tourniquets, using only his teeth, and then he rose athletically to his buttocks and tracked down the Warlock with his keen sense of smell. Cornered, with no way out, the Warlock dived for his weapon, intending to use it to destroy the world. But Lewis bravely rolled into his path."

"Is any of this true?"

"Skulduggery said they fought for eight days and eight nights. The Warlock's blade separated Lewis from several body parts, including his favourite ear, but Lewis gave as good as he got."

"Clarabelle, I'm really quite busy."

"On and on they fought. The Warlock may have thought it would be an easy battle, but he didn't know that Lewis had been trained in more fighting arts than he'd ever heard of. And the more injuries Lewis got, the more dangerous he became. It would be accurate to say that after his dismemberment, Lewis Holmes became a true master of unarmed combat."

"Oh dear God, Clarabelle."

"The Warlock fell backwards, impaling himself upon his own weapon, and Lewis Holmes lay there, panting, gazing up at the night sky. Triumphant."

Scapegrace waited. It seemed unlikely that anyone would believe such a story, especially someone as intelligent as a doctor, but Clarabelle had told it quite convincingly. He'd almost been convinced himself.

"And how did Lewis end up here?" Synecdoche asked.

Hell.

"Hmm?" Clarabelle said.

"If he survived eight days of fighting and blood loss without any arms or legs, what killed him in the end?"

"Oh," Clarabelle said. "Oh, yes. Well, he was lying there, being all triumphant and out of breath, and, like, a pack of wolves found him and ate him."

"Wolves."

"Yes."

"And where did all this happen?"

"A land far, far away. Britain."

"Clarabelle... you made that story up, didn't you?"

Scapegrace waited for Clarabelle's cunning reply.

"*Nnnnno*," she said slowly.

"There is no Lewis Holmes, is there?"

"There is," Clarabelle insisted. "His remains are under this sheet. I can show them to you if you want, but they're so disgusting you'll probably explode your brain in horror."

"Lewis Holmes doesn't exist, does he?"

The sheet covering Scapegrace bunched suddenly as Clarabelle gripped it. "He does. He's right here. I'll show you if you don't believe me."

Oh dear lord, she was going to pull the sheet off. She believed her own story. She was going to pull the sheet off and then it would all be over.

"Clarabelle, wait," Synecdoche said. "You don't have to. It's OK. You've been working really hard to fit in and... I believe you. I do. Go on now, you'd better put those remains somewhere safe."

"I will," said Clarabelle.

Scapegrace heard Synecdoche walk away, and suddenly the gurney was moving again.

"She believed me!" Clarabelle whispered.

Scapegrace was too relieved to answer.

The subdued bustle of the Medical Wing quietened, and the light beyond the sheet changed. They were in a new room. The gurney's wheels squeaked. Clarabelle turned them into another room, and the light changed again.

"OK," Clarabelle said, pulling the sheet away, "we're here."

Scapegrace and Thrasher sat up. It was a large room filled with electronic equipment that beeped and chattered. The centre of the room was taken up by a water tank in which floated Scapegrace's old body. Beside it was Thrasher's corpse.

Scapegrace got off the gurney and approached the tank. It was surreal, seeing his old self like this. The body was rotten and burnt, though not as rotten and burnt as he'd remembered. In fact, it wasn't looking half bad, all things considered. His eyes refocused on his reflection in the glass. Within the tank, Scapegrace was dead and decrepit and decomposing. Outside the tank, he was tall and strong and beautiful. But as he looked from his new face to his old one, he realised that the old one was home, and it always would be.

"So these are Lewis Holmes, are they?"

They turned. Doctor Synecdoche came forward, sighing. "Clarabelle, for the last time, this is a restricted area. That means unauthorised people cannot just wander in. We have a lot of sensitive projects being researched and we have to be strict about this. I've told you before about this kind of thing."

"But these are my friends," said Clarabelle, blushing. "They miss their old bodies."

"That's not the point, it's just..." Synecdoche shook her head. "Oh, Clarabelle, what am I going to do with you?"

Clarabelle hung her head.

Scapegrace stepped up, his eyes narrowing. "Don't blame her. We found out about this and forced her to take us here. It's time you answered a few of our questions, Doctor. What are you doing with our bodies? Nye told us that once our brains were taken out of them, they'd be destroyed. Burned."

Synecdoche nodded. "That was the plan, but then one of the other doctors requested that they be kept intact to study the effects certain procedures have on necrotic tissue."

Scapegrace jabbed his finger at her. "So *that's* your dark little secret!"

"I'm sorry?"

"The secret you've been keeping! The conspiracy!"

She looked genuinely puzzled. "Uh, there is no conspiracy, and it's not a dark little secret. You should probably have been informed that your old bodies were still intact, but apart from that administrative oversight, everything that has occurred here has been above board."

"Oh."

Thrasher peered more closely at the glass. "They don't seem as rotten as they were."

"They're not," said Synecdoche, turning away from Scapegrace. "We've actually been able to reverse a lot of the damage done by simple day-to-day wear and tear. It's been hugely beneficial to work on such a fine pair of zombie specimens as these. Usually this sort of research is conducted on slabs of meat. The work we're doing here could have far-reaching benefits across a whole array of medical and scientific areas."

Thrasher raised his eyebrows. "Really?"

"Oh, yes," said Synecdoche. "You two should be proud of yourselves. You're going to make a real difference in the world."

Thrasher looked back at Scapegrace. "Do you hear that, Master? We're going to make a difference."

Was this it? Was this what Scapegrace had been searching for? The chance to do something important, the chance to make a difference... Sure, it wasn't what he'd had in mind. In truth, it had nothing to do with him. It was his old body that was doing all the work. But still... it was something. *He* was something. He *mattered*. Maybe this could be it. Maybe this could be his pathway to contentment. He wasn't going to save the world, but by contributing to the world of science, well... That was something to be proud of. Finally.

An odd thing happened to his face. His facial muscles contracted and pulled and his mouth twisted.

"Master!" Thrasher exclaimed. "You're smiling! And it's beautiful!"

25

GOING TO AMERICA

exter Vex was talking with Saracen Rue when she walked in, and they both turned and Vex smiled and came over, arms out for a hug. "Welcome back," he said, and Darquesse hugged him. He smelled of pine needles and fresh air. She could have tightened her grip and crushed his spine, and all of those tightly-bound muscles underneath his shirt would have been for nothing. But she didn't. She behaved.

Saracen Rue, though. She was curious about how he would react to her. *Saracen Rue knows things*, that was what people said, after all. She wondered if he'd be able to see through her act. But he just came over, wrapped her up in another big hug, said nice things and gave her a lovely, happy grin.

So she didn't crush his spine, either.

She got hugs off Gracious O'Callahan, clad in a Captain America T-shirt, and Donegan Bane, clad in extraordinarily tight jeans, and she got a friendly nod from Dai Maybury. Poor Dai. So cool, so aloof, and so recently an only child. She wondered how he'd react if she told him what she'd just done to his brother. Probably not well, she figured.

Skulduggery walked in, followed by Stephanie and Fletcher.

"Six renegade sorcerers are hiding out in the New York Sanctuary," Skulduggery said, adjusting his cufflinks. Little black skulls that Valkyrie had bought him as a Christmas present. "If these renegades are being monitored, if they're secure, we leave them alone. If they're roaming free, however, they present a clear and present danger to the sorcerers around them and the public at large, and we *will* take them down. Questions?"

"What do we do about Zafira?" asked Vex.

"If Grand Mage Kerias is harbouring these renegades because she doesn't think they'll be treated fairly by us – that's fine. If she has some other agenda, we'll take that into account. Kerias was one of Ravel's staunchest supporters, remember. We do not turn our backs on her for a moment."

Nods all round. Even Darquesse nodded.

"Everyone link up," Skulduggery said. "Fletcher, teleport us straight into the lobby area, if you please."

Darquesse held Vex's hand and Donegan's, and she had time to blink once before they were in New York.

Sorcerers jumped back in surprise and two Cleavers started forward. Skulduggery turned his head to them and they stopped, and resumed their positions by the door.

"What the hell do you want?"

They turned to the young woman with the scowl on her face.

"Adrasdos," Vex said. "It's been a while."

Adrasdos. A Necromancer. Darquesse looked her up and down. There was a sword hilt in a sheath on her hip, and to Darquesse it pulsed with cold power. That was her object, clearly, the same way that Valkyrie's had been a ring, and Solomon Wreath's was a cane. That little hilt contained all her power. Delightful.

Adrasdos was looking at Vex with a confusing mix of emotions on her face. Anger at their presence, but a secret delight at seeing him in particular, it seemed. Did they once have a thing? They probably once had a thing.

"Dexter," Adrasdos said. "It's... good to see you. It's nice. But you can't just teleport into the lobby like this."

"We were going to call ahead," Skulduggery said, "but we thought Grand Mage Kerias would appreciate a surprise visit. Is she in? We need to speak with her. I'm here to extend an invitation to a celebration."

"I'll make sure she gets it."

"Apologies," Skulduggery said. "Grand Mage Sorrows insisted we deliver it in person."

Adrasdos chewed this over. "Sure," she said. "Follow me."

They went deeper into the building. Darquesse brought up the rear, taking her time. She smiled at everyone she passed. She didn't care about appearing friendly, she just needed to practise smiling without menace.

"Valkyrie!"

She turned. A dark-haired girl ran up, excitement bouncing in her eyes. Darquesse had only seen her once before, when Valkyrie had gone up against her in London.

"Hello, Ivy," she said.

Ivy's eyes widened. "You know my name? *Seriously?*"

"Of course," said Darquesse. "It's not every day someone beats me in a fair fight."

Ivy giggled. "Aw, I didn't beat you! You're the one who knocked me out, remember?"

"Only because you talked too much."

Ivy giggled again. "That sounds like me, all right! Hey, heard you were Darquesse all along. What was that like? I bet it was amazing. Like, scary and deeply, y'know, unsettling, obviously, but I bet it was just... wow. Was it wow?"

"It was wow."

"I knew it! I knew it! But I was delighted you came back. I mean, I heard that last night and I was, like, oh, cool! I know I've said this before, but, literally, I am your biggest fan! So what're you doing here? You here for long? Can I introduce you to some of my friends?"

"Flying visit," said Darquesse, resisting the urge to punch her neck.

"Aw, that's a shame. Hey, d'you think, y'know, maybe some day when you're not busy—"

"I'm busy a lot."

"Right, yeah, OK, gotcha. You probably have to go off now, yeah? Could you do me one favour? Just one, I swear, and then I'll go away!"

"What kind of favour?"

Ivy dug around in her pocket, pulled out a thick black marker. "Could I have your autograph?"

"Uh... sure."

"Oh, you are the best!" said Ivy. "And could you sign my face? Just across it. From one side to the other. Thank you *so* much!"

Darquesse hesitated. "Sure," she said. Ivy did her best to stay still, and Darquesse wrote Valkyrie Cain from the left cheek to the right. Navigating over the nose was tricky, but she managed it, and handed the marker back.

"Oh my God, that is so cool," Ivy breathed, crossing her eyes in an attempt to look down at her own face.

Stephanie appeared at the corner. "Hey," she said, "we're waiting for you."

Ivy's eyes almost bugged out. "Two of you? There are two of you?"

"It's a long story," Stephanie said.

"We could be triplets! Oh my God, this is the coolest thing ever!"

Darquesse nodded. "We need to go away now."

"Thanks, Valkyrie!" Ivy squealed. "Thanks, Other Valkyrie! Love you both!"

"Sure," Darquesse said, and joined Stephanie as she walked quickly away.

They continued in silence, and caught up to the others as they were entering the Hall of the Elders. Adrasdos glared at them, but Stephanie ignored her and Darquesse didn't take it personally. Adrasdos was glaring at practically all of them, apart from Vex.

Grand Mage Zafira Kerias sat alone in the middle of the three chairs, the light illuminating her from above. It was all very impressive.

"This is a rare honour indeed," Zafira said, smiling benevolently. "It's enough to make one wonder what I could have done to deserve such esteemed attention. Surely it can't be for a mere invitation to a party, as Adrasdos tells me you've claimed?"

"I'm afraid we misled her to gain an audience with you," said Skulduggery.

"Such chicanery, Detective Pleasant."

"Indeed. And of course we apologise. Our real reason for being here is these renegade sorcerers we've been looking for. Six of them. You've been sent the list of their names, I trust?"

Zafira nodded. "I received the list, yes. I can't remember who was on it, but I'm sure I'd have—"

"We know they're here," Stephanie said, and Zafira's eyes narrowed at the interruption. "We know you've been hiding them. Just tell us the truth and we can go."

"And which one are you, I wonder?" Zafira said, looking from Darquesse to Stephanie and then back again. "Are you the reflection or the real thing? It's all very confusing. I must admit, I'm stumped. Flummoxed, even. Detective Pleasant, please help me out."

"That's Stephanie," said Skulduggery. He turned. "And that's Valkyrie."

Darquesse smiled to herself.

"The reports were right," Zafira said. "It could almost pass for human, couldn't it? If I hadn't known that one of them was a fake, it might even have fooled me. Nevertheless, please remind the reflection of its manners. It is not polite to interrupt when real people are—"

"Stephanie is polite enough," Skulduggery said. "She just has very little patience for the games people play."

Zafira observed them without speaking for a few moments. "The sorcerers on your list did come here, seeking refuge," she said. "They were in fear for their lives after Grand Mage Sorrows sent her death squads after them."

Donegan put up his hand. "I am not a death squad."

"And neither am I," said Gracious.

"Those sorcerers are not refugees," Skulduggery said. "Their powers are unstable. They need to be isolated and closely monitored until the effects of the Accelerator wear off."

"So you claim you've not been sent here to kill them? How can I believe that you're telling the truth?"

"I sincerely don't care what you believe," Skulduggery said. "If they've turned themselves in to you, if you're taking responsibility for them, then our work here is done. Deal with them as you see fit."

He turned to go, and Zafira sat forward. "I could turn them over to you."

Skulduggery looked round. "Why would you do that?"

"I heard some of them killed sorcerers as well as Warlocks, when they were out of control. Maybe you have some criminal charges against them? If you can guarantee their safety, we will of course hand them over. Providing you reciprocate."

"And what is it you want?"

"You have Erskine Ravel in a cell, do you not? Erskine and I have a... history. I would greatly appreciate it if he were transferred to one of our prisons here, where we can monitor his condition."

"His condition?" said Vex. "His condition is twenty-three hours of untold agony a day, followed by one hour of respite, where he gets to eat, drink, and look forward to the next twenty-three hours."

Zafira nodded. "And what have you done to alleviate his suffering?"

"Ravel's pain is a result of a direct link to Darquesse," said Rue. "It can't be alleviated."

"But really," Zafira responded, "how hard have you tried? He killed your friends, after all. You can't be feeling overly concerned about his well-being, now can you? Have you run any more tests since Darquesse was captured? Have you found out why the link is still active, now that she's trapped in a Soul Catcher? It shouldn't be active, should it? My experts tell me so. The moment Darquesse was pulled into that Soul Catcher, the link should have been severed and Erskine's pain should have ceased. There's a mystery to be unravelled there. Let us solve it for you."

Skulduggery's head tilted. "How close were you? In the run-up to the war, I mean. Were you by his side when he hatched his plans? Were you there when he decided to betray and kill his friends and overthrow mortal rule on earth?"

"Of course not," said Zafira. "I knew nothing of—"

"Don't insult our intelligence and we won't insult yours. The only reason you're not in chains right now is because Grand Mage Sorrows thought it prudent not to issue arrest orders for *everyone* at the same time. We know what you did, but as long as you do what we tell you, we'll pretend that we don't. Do I make myself clear?"

Zafira reddened. "You cannot speak to me like that. I am the Grand Mage of—"

"Do I make myself clear?" Skulduggery said, louder this time.

Zafira glared.

"I'll take that as a yes," he said.

"I had hoped this conversation would be a little friendlier," Zafira responded, "but fair enough. We both know where we stand now. That's something, at least."

"I'm glad you think so. We'll be leaving now."

Zafira waved a hand dismissively. "Give my love to China, won't you? You know, when I think of how far we've come, I can't help but feel proud of our forgiving attitude to people who've wronged us. Why, now we have one of Mevolent's most fanatical followers running the Irish Sanctuary, and bullying every other Sanctuary into doing her bidding. It truly is a great time to be—"

The door burst open and a sorcerer Darquesse had met once ran in. What was her name? Vinette, or something? "Grand Mage," Vinette said, her face flushed with alarm. "We have a situation."

26

WEIRD FEELINGS

Chaos reigned, and Darquesse was enjoying every minute of it.

Alarms went off. Sirens screeched. Teams of sorcerers were sent into different parts of the New York Sanctuary. More teams were coming back, bloodied and carrying injured comrades. The renegades were going nuts and it was seemingly impossible to figure out where they all were. Darquesse sat with Skulduggery and the others in the lobby, and they made themselves comfortable. It was only when Zafira Kerias stalked up to them that this changed.

"Detective Pleasant," Zafira said, panic biting at her words, "we seem to have an emergency."

Skulduggery looked around, then nodded. "Yep."

Zafira grimaced. "I would appreciate any... assistance you could give us. Most of my operatives are at least twenty minutes away."

"You're officially requesting our assistance?"

"Yes, yes, whatever. Will you help?"

Skulduggery stood up. "We'd be delighted. Where would you like us?"

"Lower levels," said Zafira. "We sent two teams down there and we've yet to hear anything back."

"Then that is just the place we want to be," Skulduggery said. "We'll let you know when we've found them."

Darquesse set off with everyone else, grinning to herself. This was *fun*.

They took this weird elevator-type thing down to the lower levels. Down here, the wail of the sirens was reduced to a distant scream.

"Stay together," Skulduggery said, his gun in his hand as he led the way down the corridor. "We don't know what these particular renegades can do and we don't know if their powers are ebbing or surging. In any given minute, they could either kill us all with a look or fall down at a harsh word. They are not to be underestimated."

He didn't have to say this to Vex or Rue, and the Monster Hunters didn't need to hear it. These words were for Stephanie and Fletcher and Darquesse. To protect them. Little gestures like that made Darquesse smile.

There were bodies up ahead.

Two dead. One unconscious. She recognised the injured girl. Tia. Blood ran from the gash above her eye. They moved on silently. Darquesse could sense the power ahead of them, lying in wait, but she didn't say anything. She'd seen the list of renegades. She knew which one this was. Star, her name was. A pretty name. She was English, and her power was jumping and jiving along with her nerves.

Star burst from hiding when they got close. She took them all by surprise – all except Darquesse, who watched Dai go flying and Fletcher go reeling. Star hit Gracious and he flew back off his feet. Oh, this glorious power was making her strong! Darquesse nearly laughed to look at it. Skulduggery grabbed Star and she grabbed him and they went down. Stephanie and Saracen lunged, tried to pull her back. Vex and Donegan ran in, and between them they managed to haul Star off Skulduggery. Star twisted free, her hands lighting up. Before Darquesse knew what she was doing, she stepped forward, used her magic to send a column of air slamming into Star's face. Star spun like she'd been hit with a hammer.

Odd, this new urge to lend a hand.

Darquesse watched Star charge through the others, come straight for her, swinging a punch. Darquesse could have increased her body's density in an instant, watched Star shatter her fist upon impact. But she didn't. She let the punch land, let it launch her backwards. She hit the ground and rolled and before she'd even finished sprawling, Skulduggery and the others were there, protecting her. She watched them fight, watched Star cover up under the onslaught. Star broke left, launched herself at Saracen. They went down, Saracen scrambling beneath her as they turned over, and Star let out a roar as her arm was snapped. She managed to get up, but Skulduggery kicked her knee sideways and Darquesse heard it go *pop*. Another roar from Star as she staggered, her magic boiling within her.

Darquesse could have killed her from where she lay on the ground. She could have burst her like a balloon, or taken her head off with a stream of energy. She could have got up and grabbed her and torn her heart from her chest. She didn't do any of that. What she did do was to reach out with her magic and smother Star's, keeping it from boiling over. She saw the confusion in the renegade girl's face, as something that should have happened didn't happen. Gracious finished the fight with a right hook that wiped the confusion away, replacing it with a look of serene relaxation as Star slumped to the floor. Donegan shackled her wrists.

Stephanie stood over Darquesse. One hand held the Sceptre. The other was reaching out to her.

Darquesse hesitated a moment, then clasped Stephanie's hand, and allowed herself to be pulled to her feet.

"You OK?" Stephanie asked.

"Yeah," said Darquesse. "Suppose I'm a little out of practice."

Stephanie shrugged. "It'll come back to you."

That was it. That was all she was getting. Stephanie wandered away, slipping the Sceptre into her backpack. Darquesse watched her go. She frowned. What was this she was feeling? This odd sensation?

Was it... warmth?

She shook her head, trying to dispel it. It felt both weirdly comfortable and uncomfortably weird, all at the same time.

She realised they were fussing over Fletcher. He was sitting against the wall, holding his head.

"I'm fine," he muttered.

Saracen crouched in front of him, his hand splayed. "How many fingers am I holding up?"

Fletcher counted, frowned, then counted again. Finally satisfied, he nodded and said, "Six."

"Oh, God," Stephanie muttered. "He's brain-damaged."

Saracen helped Fletcher to his feet. "He's fine, he just needs a doctor."

"Be right back," Fletcher said, and stood there. He blinked at Saracen. "Hello, Doctor."

"You haven't teleported," Stephanie said.

"Oh."

"He'll need someone to walk him back," said Skulduggery. "Valkyrie, can you do it?"

Stephanie frowned. "Her?"

"Valkyrie can protect him if they meet one of Star's friends and, to be honest, we need you and the Sceptre to stay with us."

"Right," Stephanie said, unconvinced. Darquesse wished she'd put up more of an argument. She didn't want to miss out on the fun.

As the others went on, Fletcher walked over to her on shaky legs. He looked pale. "You might have to carry me."

"I'm not carrying you."

"What if I fall over?"

"I'll drag you."

"That sounds painful."

They started walking back the way they'd come. He walked so *slowly*.

"Can you teleport yet?" she asked.

"I'll try," he said, and took a moment. "Have I teleported?"

"No."

"What about now?"

"No."

"I don't think I can teleport," he admitted. "I need a clear head. My head isn't clear. It's ouchy."

"Maybe I *will* carry you."

"Really? That'd be cool. I don't like walking. It's boring and it takes forever."

He talked on, but Darquesse wasn't listening. There was someone up ahead. Someone with bubbling, boiling power. Male. Big. Strong. Darian Vector, maybe. Darquesse allowed herself a smile. Looked like she wouldn't be missing out on the fun, after all.

They got to the weird elevator thing. "Up you go," said Darquesse.

Fletcher looked confused. "Weren't you supposed to take me to a doctor?"

"No. I was to take you as far as here, and go on by myself. Up you go now. We're going to need you to teleport us home when all this is over."

"I think Skulduggery meant you to stay with me."

Darquesse took Fletcher's arm, led him into the elevator, and stepped out. "There," she said. "Get well soon."

The doors closed before he could respond.

Darquesse continued down the corridor. It was dark here. Quiet. Empty. Perfect.

A slight sound behind her, and she turned.

Darian Vector loomed over her. Handsome. Unshaven. A gleam in his eyes that was bordering on insane.

"Look who we have here," he said. "You're either the reflection or the real thing. Doesn't much matter which. Only thing that matters is that you're not *her*."

"Darquesse," said Darquesse.

"What's it like," said Vector, "to go from being that powerful to being... you? What's it like to go from killing everyone in sight to quivering in fear?"

"I'll let you know when I start to quiver."

"Still talking tough, eh? Let's see how tough you talk when I pull your arms and legs off. You killed some friends of mine."

"Do I look scared? Do I look the slightest bit intimidated? Even someone like you, Vector, even someone as obviously stupid and intellectually stunted as you has to be wondering why that is. Am I bluffing? Am I expecting back-up to arrive in the nick of time? Am I as stupid as you are?"

"Stop calling me stupid."

"Or," Darquesse continued, "am I really as confident as I appear? If so... why? Why am I this confident? What secret am I holding? What do I know that you don't? Or, to be more precise, what *else*?"

Vector's lip curled. "Did you just call me stupid again?"

"You're missing the point. You're letting your pride get in the way of your thoughts. I'm standing here insulting you, openly mocking you, and yet I'm not threatened by the horrible death you're promising. So I ask you again – why do you think that is?"

Vector's eyes narrowed. "You're trying to make me believe you're still her."

"Yes."

"But you're not."

"Can you be sure?"

"The Skeleton Detective wouldn't hang around with you if you were still her."

"You don't think I can fool Skulduggery? Really? Especially when he secretly wants to be fooled?"

She saw it all. She saw his shoulders slump a little. Saw his fists open slightly. Saw him swallow, and his eyes widen. She saw the blood drain from his face.

He stepped back. "Please..."

"You were saying something about pulling my arms and legs off?"

"Please don't kill me."

"You were saying something about making me quiver in fear?"

"I surrender. Please, I surrender."

"And you seemed insulted when I implied you were stupid. Almost like you were going to argue. Tell me, Vector... are you going to argue?"

"N-no."

"So you are stupid?"

"Yes. Are you going to kill me?"

Darquesse hesitated. "I should. I mean... I want to. I think. You're annoying, so..." She raised her hand, and Vector flinched. But she hesitated again. "Something's wrong," she said.

Vector saw what he thought was his chance, and his fist came round and shattered against Darquesse's jaw. He howled, and reeled away.

"Y'know what it is?" Darquesse asked. "It's humanity. That's what it is. Humanity is contagious. I'm around people who do good for five minutes and already I'm thinking of doing something good, too. Isn't that ridiculous? It's like there's something inside me that wants to be part of a group, or it wants them to like me or... or something like that. Bizarrely ridiculous. And pointless. No matter how much I might want to seem like one of them at this particular moment, it's only a matter of time before I go back to being me."

"You should try being good for a little longer," Vector said, clutching his broken hand.

"Ah, you're just saying that because you think I'm going to kill you in a minute."

"Are... are you?"

Darquesse shrugged. She hated spoilers. "I shouldn't be spending this much time with them," she said. "I should go back to Tanith and Sanguine and the Remnants. None of them have a conscience, and none of them want to do nice things for anybody. Skulduggery and the others are infecting me with, like..."

"Decency?" said Vector.

She snapped her fingers. "Yes. That. Exactly. You're not so stupid, after all, are you?"

"Please."

"Stop begging. Unless I have a personal interest in seeing you beg, it's boring."

"I – I can help you."

"How could you possibly help me?"

"There's a... thing. A creature. Found in the Caves of the Void."

It took Darquesse a moment to access that memory. The Caves of the Void were what people called the caves beneath Gordon's house.

"It's resistant to magic," Vector continued. "A group of scientists managed to capture it when it was young, and they transported it over here to study. They call it a Gnarl. It's waiting for your friends."

"It's free?"

"I think so. I mean, that was the plan. I only caught a bit of it, and I wasn't supposed to even hear that. But I picked up a lot of other things. I eavesdropped on the deal Kerias tried to make with you. She was going to betray us. She promised us refuge and then she offered to hand us over. You can't trust that woman. You didn't go for her deal so she's sent you down here, where the Gnarl is waiting. She's going to say it was an unfortunate accident, but really it's to teach China Sorrows a lesson."

"Zafira thinks one creature will be enough to kill everyone I came in with?"

Vector swallowed. "From what I heard? Yes."

Darquesse grunted. "Must be an impressive creature." She chewed her lip. "Wonder what it's like."

27

THE GNARL

She took the stairs down. The concrete walls became rock. The electric lighting gave way to the occasional lamp hanging overhead. She reached the bottom of the steps and walked till she came to a cavern. A viewing window had been cut out of the rock wall. Behind it, a narrow tunnel, barely wide enough to squeeze through. There was an intermittent breeze, but it wasn't coming from the tunnel. And it was hot. It was hot like breath.

Darquesse ventured forward. She could hear the creature breathing, but she still couldn't see it, even when she shifted through the visual spectrum only available to her. Every living thing had its own energy signature. She could see sorcerers through walls by focusing on their magic, but she couldn't see this Gnarl thing. That was... unsettling.

Something shifted in the dark and her eyes returned to normal in time to glimpse a huge head brushing the top of the archway. She moved back quickly, getting behind cover. She peered out again. The creature, a quadruped ten times her height, stepped into the cavernous room. It had legs like stone pillars, scaled armour around its body and head, and two sharply curving tusks. There was no trace of magic coming from it at all. What a curious beast.

Darquesse walked out into the middle of the floor. It tracked her movements, growling deep within its throat. It had no obvious weak points, but she had yet to encounter an opponent who could withstand her power, so she let her magic pour from her eyes in twin streams. The blast hit the Gnarl on the shoulder, should have melted right through it. Instead, the wound sizzled a little, like a blister.

The Gnarl charged.

Darquesse rose to meet it. She flew straight for its head, hit the armoured plates and bounced off, went tumbling through the air. Its tail, it had a *tail*, whipped round, caught her across the waist, in between the armoured clothes. Bones broke. She smacked into the ground and sprawled.

She lay there for a moment, blinking in surprise.

Her bones healed, her internal organs righted themselves and she got up. The Gnarl turned, the ground juddering with every step.

She didn't understand how creatures of the Void were immune to magical attack. Nobody did. People had theories. They had their tests. But then, nobody understood magic, either. Not really. They did their best to confine it to disciplines and restrict it with rules, but nobody knew what magic was or where it came from or how it worked. Not really.

Someone who understood magic, though... Someone who genuinely understood magic could reshape the universe.

And her next step was the *Hessian Grimoire*.

But first, she had to survive this encounter.

Darquesse raised her hand, wondering if she could take the creature apart atom by atom, but it was all wrong. She couldn't see it the way she saw everything else. She couldn't figure it out. She couldn't see how it *could* be figured out. She tried to burn it in black flames, but she could find nothing for those black flames to burn; it was like the Gnarl wasn't even there.

"Those clothes must be astonishing."

She turned. Grand Mage Zafira Kerias stood at the viewing window.

"I don't know how you survived that, Miss Cain," she said, "but you're not going to be so lucky twice."

Keeping one eye on the Gnarl, Darquesse edged over. She was three steps away when an energy shield spread within the window, sealing Zafira safely inside.

"You think you've won," Zafira said. "You think that's it for Ravel's plans. Well, it's not. There are still people like me, people who recognise what he was trying to do. And we will not stop, do you hear me? I don't care if I have to have every one of you killed. We will seize control of this world and every mortal will—"

Darquesse pressed her hand against the energy shield and quickly found its frequency. The shield retracted and Zafira's eyes widened.

"What? How did you—?"

Darquesse took hold of her, yanked her through the window. She held her up for a moment, dangling like a doll.

"Oh my God," said Zafira, eyes bulging with terror. "You're not Valkyrie Cain. You're—"

"Yep," said Darquesse.

Then she tossed Zafira high into the air.

The Gnarl snatched her into its mouth. Zafira's screams ended abruptly when its molars popped her head like a freshly-laid egg.

Watching the creature eat was fascinating. Not a pretty sight, but a mesmerising one. It chewed with its mouth open. Zafira proved both crunchy and squelchy, but an insubstantial treat. She was gone in mere seconds, and the Gnarl turned its beady eyes back to Darquesse.

It lowered its head and charged. She moved at the last moment, barely saving herself from being gored. Even so, the impact lifted her, tossed her into the air, and the Gnarl caught her in its jaws. She barely had time to register that she was actually in this creature's mouth before its teeth closed on her, pierced her left arm and leg, cutting through the armoured clothes like they were nothing.

She blocked the pain, and took in many things simultaneously. The first thing was the smell, which was disgusting. The second was that not even a trace of Zafira remained. The third was the Gnarl's flat tongue, which nudged against her, wet and sticky. It was dark in here, but she saw the teeth begin to part as the Gnarl prepared to chew.

The thought came to her that maybe being eaten alive wasn't a great lifestyle choice, so she extended her free hand and energy burst from her fingertips. It seared the roof of the Gnarl's mouth. She'd been hoping it'd go straight up into the brain, but it appeared that the inside of this creature was just as durable as its armoured hide.

Her arm and leg were suddenly free and she pulled them back, healing them, but before she could fly for the gaps between the teeth, the tongue moved beneath her and she cursed as she slid down the convulsing throat. She plunged into darkness and cold, and everything she grabbed for was wet and slimy and moving. The walls of its gullet constricted, but she stopped herself before they trapped her, spun in place and then flew upwards. Ricocheting around in its throat, she flew back towards the light, and a moment later she burst from its mouth. She kept flying till she was at the other end of the room, then turned.

Darquesse was annoyed, frustrated, and dripping with mucous. Saliva matted her hair. Her clothes had two bloody holes torn through them. She wanted to go somewhere, grab a shower and dip her head into a bucket of potpourri in an attempt to rid herself of the smell.

But if she left, this Gnarl would go hunting and it'd eventually find Skulduggery and the others.

"So what?" she muttered.

There it was again – that infection of decency. Let the Gnarl kill them. What the hell did she care? They had been trying to kill her, after all. The only reason they were nice to her now was because they thought she was Valkyrie. If they knew the truth, the last thing she'd see would be Stephanie pointing the Sceptre at her.

Nope, the smart thing to do was to fly down to that little tunnel and follow it all the way out.

But when she looked at the Gnarl, she knew she couldn't leave. She couldn't let this thing beat her.

She flew at it, twisting to avoid the tusks. She landed on its back, punched downwards, not making the slightest dent on its hide. The tail swished at her, but she was already flying out of range. She didn't understand this. The Gnarl was impervious to magic, sure. But shrugging off energy blasts was one thing – Darquesse could get her head round that, even if she didn't understand how it worked yet. Shrugging off magic-augmented strength, though? Ignoring pure, physical strength, just because it was magical?

She flew to the rock wall, punched it, grabbed a rock the size of her head before it fell. She threw it at the Gnarl. It hit between its scales like a bullet. The Gnarl screeched in anger and pain.

Darquesse hovered over it. It *could* be hurt, then, just not by anything magical.

The Gnarl reared up on its hind legs and almost snagged her foot with its teeth. She flew up, burrowing through the cavern ceiling. She changed direction, carving a large circle through the rock. She kept going, the circles getting gradually smaller and smaller as she picked up speed, and then there was a rumble and a roar and the ceiling fell in, knocking the Gnarl to the ground and smashing its skull as it was buried in rubble.

It was almost disappointing.

Darquesse glared at the dead creature as she landed, then turned and squeezed through the tunnel. It widened and she could walk quicker. There were lights now. And steps. She followed them to a platform that took her upwards. When she stopped, a door slid open, and she stepped into Zafira Kerias's private quarters.

She took a shower, washed herself and her clothes. While she dried, she held up her jacket, examined how the reinforced fabric needed to knit back together. It wasn't easy. Ghastly's clothes were phenomenally complicated as far as armoured clothes went, but she had put people back together atom by atom. She could handle a jacket and a pair of trousers.

When she was done, she dressed, made sure she was presentable, and left Zafira's quarters through the window. She re-entered the Sanctuary and managed to blend in with a crowd that included Skulduggery and the others, hauling two shackled prisoners after them.

"How's Fletcher?" Stephanie asked in among the confusion.

"He's going to be fine," Darquesse told her. She thought for a moment, and offered a reassuring smile. Stephanie seemed to accept it.

They met another group of sorcerers, American this time. Adrasdos in the lead. They had Darian Vector in shackles. Vector looked up, saw Darquesse. She stared at him, but didn't react. He looked away quickly, and she gave another smile, but this one was for herself and herself only.

While they waited for Fletcher to be cleared by the doctors, Darquesse went for a stroll. She noted the growing alarm when the sorcerers around her failed to locate their Grand Mage. She could have told them what had happened, could have come right out and said it... but she didn't, and that interested her.

Obviously, she wanted Argeddion's location and, if possible, a chance to peek at the *Hessian Grimoire*, but there were easier ways to achieve both those things. She could kill everyone who tried to stop her and just take the book. She could promise to end Ravel's suffering in exchange for Argeddion's new name. There. Simple. But here she was, pretending to be Valkyrie Cain, working alongside Skulduggery and the others like she was part of the group. Like she belonged.

She stopped walking.

Did she want to belong? Was there some part of her that wanted Valkyrie's old life? Did she want people to like her?

There were many things Darquesse could do to make people like her – even now, with the limited knowledge she possessed. She could purify the air and clean the oceans. She could reinforce the ozone layer. With a little research, she could spread a virus around the world that would eradicate cancer. She could disarm nations, end wars, stop conflicts before they even started. She could do more than save the world – she could make the world a better place. Then maybe that warm feeling deep inside her would stay. Maybe it would never leave.

All she had to do was make a decision. It wasn't too late. She could continue with the act until she felt it was safe to tell the truth, and then she could prove herself by helping people and saving lives. Because maybe she was wrong. Maybe people *were* more than energy. Maybe their personalities *did* matter.

Darquesse turned, walked back the way she'd come, her smile growing wider. She was on the cusp of a brand-new day.

Fletcher was up and ready to teleport by the time she rejoined the others. They were already in place, with a space for Darquesse between Skulduggery and Vex. They'd waited for her. She had that warm feeling again. She held their hands, everyone else linked up, and Skulduggery nodded to Fletcher. Right before they teleported, Vex moved slightly, inching away, and Darquesse noticed Stephanie looking at her.

They teleported to a dark room and Skulduggery and Vex whipped their hands away and China was standing right in front of her with something black and metal on her arm and she reached out and touched Darquesse and

28

there was a crack and Stephanie watched Darquesse slump to the floor of an empty room in the Irish Sanctuary even as she yanked the Sceptre from her backpack.

China stepped away, deactivating the Deathtouch Gauntlet as Finbar rushed in from the shadows.

"Her brain is dead!" he cried. "Her consciousness has left the body!"

There was an inhuman screech and Stephanie ducked as something flew past her. Finbar stepped back, waving his hand like he was swatting a fly. Fletcher hopped away, hands over his head, cursing, and then Stephanie felt it nipping at her and she recoiled, swinging a fist at thin air.

"Keep it away!" China commanded, pulling the Soul Catcher from her robes. She hurled it to the floor and it exploded into a thousand pieces, unleashing the swirling light within, unleashing Valkyrie. The light sank into Darquesse's dead body and Skulduggery knelt by it.

There was another screech, but this one was drawn out and anguished, and it faded as Finbar's gaze flickered up to the ceiling.

"She's gone," he said, his voice suddenly quiet.

China tossed a seven-pointed star to Skulduggery. It was made of thick metal and inscribed with dozens of delicate symbols. Stephanie had seen one before in the Medical Wing – a Sunburst, it was called. Skulduggery pressed the star against Darquesse's chest, held it there while the symbols began to light up.

No one said anything. No one moved.

When all the symbols were lit, they flashed red and instantly faded. Skulduggery felt for a pulse. Didn't find one.

He tapped the Sunburst again. Once more, the symbols began to light up.

Stephanie's hand was hurting. She looked down, realised she was gripping the Sceptre so tightly her knuckles were going white. She returned it to her backpack as quietly as she could.

The symbols flashed red. Still no pulse.

She'd been right. They all knew it. It hadn't been Valkyrie communicating through Finbar. It was Darquesse all along – though once Valkyrie had been dragged out and trapped in the Soul Catcher, Darquesse had gone on to fool everyone, Stephanie included. Only Skulduggery noticed anything wrong. Only he noticed the tiny differences, picked up on the tiny clues. Only he knew to make the call to China, to get Fletcher to fake an injury and teleport home in preparation. And now here they were, with Darquesse dragged, kicking and screaming, from Valkyrie's body and Valkyrie put back in. But no pulse. No brain function. The Deathtouch Gauntlet had been more effective than they'd anticipated.

Skulduggery held his hand above Valkyrie's mouth, searching for the slightest breath. He tapped the Sunburst yet again. "It's not working. It's not *working*."

Nobody else moved until China stepped forward. "Skulduggery," she said gently, putting a hand on his shoulder. "You have to let her go."

He ignored her, and threw the Sunburst to Gracious. "Fix it."

Gracious could only stand there as Skulduggery interlaced his fingers and started pushing down on Valkyrie's chest with his palms. A nudge from Donegan, and Gracious peered at the star, turned it over in his hands. He was something of an inventor, but Stephanie could tell by his face that he was no expert on Sunbursts.

Skulduggery continued giving CPR to Valkyrie's dead body. Fletcher disappeared, arriving back a few seconds later with Synecdoche. The doctor went immediately to Valkyrie's side.

"We need a Sunburst," she said, checking for vital signs.

"We tried," China told her. "It didn't work."

Synecdoche looked up, the colour draining from her face. She stopped checking for vital signs.

Stephanie felt sick.

"Finbar," Vex said, "can you detect Darquesse's presence?"

"She hasn't come back," Finbar said numbly.

"How long can she survive in her current state? Finbar? Finbar, I need you to focus."

Finbar looked at him. "But Valkyrie..."

"We can mourn for Valkyrie later," Vex said. "We need to make sure Darquesse won't return."

"Right," said Finbar. "Yeah. Darquesse is... she's what people call an untethered entity right now. She won't survive long outside the... outside Val's... um, outside the body."

"Could she take over any *other* body?"

Finbar frowned. "Maybe a Sensitive, if they were willing or, I don't know, taken by surprise. But if she did, she'd burn out that body within hours."

"No ordinary sorcerer could withstand Darquesse's level of power," Synecdoche said. She stood up, reluctantly leaving Skulduggery on his knees alone. "Valkyrie is... was... a descendant of the Ancients – that made her special."

"My family," Stephanie said, her eyes widening. "They share the same bloodline. Darquesse will be going after them!"

China looked at her. "Your family is safe. I have my best Cleavers protecting them, each one armed with a new and improved Soul Catcher. If Darquesse even goes near them, she'll be trapped. We're not going to let her gain even the tiniest of footholds. Valkyrie will not have died in vain."

"She's not dead yet," Skulduggery snarled without raising his head from the CPR, but of course she was. They all knew it.

The fact remained that Stephanie had *warned* them not to trust the miracle of Valkyrie's communications, and they hadn't listened. Maybe if they had, they'd have been able to plan a little better, maybe prepare a little more, and maybe Valkyrie would still be alive, Stephanie would not be crying these hot tears, these awful tears, maybe they would not have had to rely on some magical defibrillator, on the Sunburst thing that Gracious O'Callahan was still fiddling with, to bring her back to life.

Gracious closed the back of the Sunburst, screwed it shut with his penknife, and tossed it over to Skulduggery. "Try it now."

Skulduggery pressed it into Valkyrie's chest. It lit up. The symbols flashed red.

The Sunburst beeped.

And Valkyrie sucked in a deep breath and opened her eyes.

29

THOSE WHO LIVE IN DARKNESS

Four days after Gant and Jeremiah Wallow had visited Danny's store, Etta Faulkner comes in to convince him to protest against the plans for the proposed Starbucks. He listens and nods and murmurs where appropriate, but makes sure not to commit to anything. He knows how easy it is to get sucked into someone else's struggle, and he's determined to sit this one out. When she has exhausted herself of her righteous fury, Etta collects a few essentials into a basket and brings them up to the till to pay.

"Terrible thing, what happened in Giant's Pass," she says as Danny rings up her purchases.

Giant's Pass is a small town about six hours north. It's just like all those other towns that are just like Meek Ridge, except it's even further from civilisation. Danny has never been there. "What happened?" he asks as he packs Etta's things into a bag.

"You didn't hear?" Etta says, her eyes glittering. "Killings. Murders. Whole family is what I heard."

"Seriously?"

"Found this morning, they were. Parents and children, though the children were in their twenties, or close enough to them. It's all over the news."

"That's awful," says Danny. "They catch whoever did it?"

Etta shakes her head. "He's on the loose, that's what the reporters told me."

"You talked to reporters?"

"Uh-huh. Down the street, not ten minutes ago. Asking me my opinion on it. I said it was shocking, that something like this could happen in such a quiet town like Giant's Pass, where everyone knows everyone else. They liked that, I think. They'll probably use it in their report. They said they'll send a camera crew to talk to me. I might be on the news. They said it was something to do with anti-Irish racism or something."

Danny closes the bag over, and freezes. "Anti-Irish?"

"First I've heard about something like that, but they seemed pretty sure."

"Why would it be anti-Irish?"

"The family that was killed were the Fitzgeralds or the Fitzgibbons or something. They seemed really sure that the family was targeted because of their nationality. Doesn't make a whole lot of sense to me, but I guess I'm not in full possession of the facts."

"What were they like, the reporters?"

"Don't know which paper they're from," says Etta, "but one was tall, about my age, and the other was shorter, with a beard and long hair. Fat."

In that instant, Danny knows what has happened. Gant and Jeremiah aren't Feds or US Marshals or paparazzi, they are killers. They went to Giant's Pass, asked around for anyone Irish. They found the Fitzgeralds or the Fitzgibbons or whoever they were, paid them a visit, expecting to find Stephanie. When they realised their mistake, they had to silence the witnesses, or maybe they were so annoyed at getting it wrong that they killed the whole family out of spite. Either way a family is dead, and suddenly the pressure is on to find their actual target before the police find them.

Danny hurries to the backroom, grabs his coat and pulls it on as he rejoins Etta in the store. "Did they ask if there were any Irish people in Meek Ridge?"

"Yes," she says, sounding a little surprised that Danny has guessed correctly. "I said half of the families here could probably be traced back to Ireland, but there are no *Irish* Irish, apart from that Edgley girl."

"You told them where she lives?"

"Yes. Told them how vulnerable she was, living up there all on her own."

Danny's car keys are in his hand and he's running out the door before Etta can ask what's wrong. He slips in the snow, but manages to reach his car without falling. The engine starts first try.

He drives to Stephanie's place. The gate is open. He parks, carries on on foot. He feels stupid, moving like a soldier under fire, flitting from tree to tree like he's being watched, but at the same time he feels this is an entirely fitting response to the situation.

The Cadillac is parked in the driveway beside Stephanie's pickup truck. With the angle, with the cold glare of the sun and all that packed snow on the rear window, it is impossible to see if there's anyone in it. Danny stays crouched down for another minute. No movement, no sound. The house is quiet, too.

He creeps forward, leaving deep footprints. If he suddenly has to run, there'll be nowhere he can go where they couldn't easily find him. He ignores the voice in his head telling him this is a bad idea. Of course it's a bad idea. He doesn't need a little voice to tell him that.

One more step and he's close enough to peer through the rear window. It's dark in the Cadillac, much darker than it has any right to be. He can't see anyone in the gloom, but he can't be sure, so he creeps up along the side, careful not to touch the car itself. It isn't that he's afraid an alarm might sound, alerting Gant and Jeremiah to his presence. It's just that he doesn't want to touch the car. He has the absurd notion that touching it will make him sick.

The back seat is empty. Lots of space in there. The front is empty, too. Tidy. Neat. No coffee cups or scrunched-up gas receipts. It is showroom clean. That Mr Gant sure knows how to take care of his automobile.

For the first time, Danny becomes aware of the footprints in the snow leading from the Cadillac to the house. Gant's footprints are narrow and long and, judging by the depth, he's a deceptively light man. Danny follows them up round the hood, where they're joined by Jeremiah's heavy footprints clumping alongside, drag marks between each one. Both sets of footprints lead up to the porch, and on the porch there's freshly-shod snow all the way up to the front door.

He should kick the car. That's what he should do. Kick the car, set off the alarm, get Gant and Jeremiah running out here, away from Stephanie. By the time they got outside, Danny would already be backing away. They might be able to track him easily, but they wouldn't be able to catch him. One is fat and one is old. He'd get away. He'd probably get away. Unless Jeremiah has a gun, and he's a good shot.

Kicking the car is Plan B, Danny decides.

He moves up to the side of the house. Peers through the kitchen window. He sees Gant pouring some orange juice into a glass. He drinks. It's a tall glass and he drinks the whole thing. His Adam's apple bobs up and down unpleasantly.

Jeremiah comes into the kitchen, says something to Gant that Danny can't hear. They haven't found Stephanie, though, and that's all that matters. Gant folds his arms, taps a long finger against his chin, and before Danny can duck down, Gant's head swivels and they lock eyes.

Coldness sweeps through Danny's veins and freezes his heart.

Then Jeremiah goes one way and Gant goes the other and Danny falls away from the window, starts scrambling. He's been afraid before in his life, but not like this. Never like this. This is real fear, and real fear jolts so much energy through his system that for a moment he forgets to stand, and he just crawls on his hands and knees through the snow. He's breathing fast. Too fast. Hyperventilating. It occurs to him that running would be better than crawling and he rises like a sprinter from the blocks but awkwardly, his legs shaky. The jolt of energy passes and now he's tired, he's sluggish, doesn't know what the hell is happening because all he wants to do is sit down and curl up, but of course he can't, he has to get back to his car, he has to get away.

Jeremiah Wallow walks round the corner of the house.

"It's Danny!" Jeremiah says. He holds a tyre iron in his hand. "Look, Mr Gant, it's Danny!"

Danny backs away, turns and stumbles, sees Gant walking round the far corner. Danny slips on ice and falls, gets up, throws himself into a run. He ploughs deep furrows into the snow covering the garden. Already his legs are tired, but he can't rest. He has to make it to the trees. He's faster than they are. They can't catch him. He glances back at Jeremiah, sees him plodding in slow pursuit, then glances over at Gant and Gant runs across the snow, barely making a dent, running like an athlete fifty years his junior, and he slams into Danny and Danny goes spinning through the air, goes rolling through the snow towards Jeremiah.

The tyre iron crashes into his shoulder and Danny cries out, twisting on to his back, and Jeremiah swings again and it hits Danny's leg and this time Danny screams.

"Jeremiah, Jeremiah," says Gant, like he was scolding him. Jeremiah straightens up, his face a little red from the exertion. Gant stands over Danny and smiles kindly. "Hello, Danny. I'm quite impressed with you, I am forced to admit. You had us fooled. Did he not have us fooled, Jeremiah?"

Jeremiah nods. "Had me fooled."

"Hear that, Danny my boy? You had Jeremiah fooled, and Jeremiah is no fool, are you, Jeremiah?"

"No flies on me," says Jeremiah.

Gant laughs. "Yes! Exactly! No flies on you, Jeremiah! And yet, you had us fooled, Danny my boy. That first day, we followed you right past this place, did we not? You must have seen us and, being the good guy that you are, the straight shooter, you didn't want to lead us straight to the home of our quarry, so instead you led us to the house of some old-timer we wouldn't be bothered with. That was some quick thinking, Danny. That was thinking on your feet. Aren't you impressed, Jeremiah?"

"I'm impressed," says Jeremiah.

"But only grudgingly," Gant says with a chuckle. When the chuckle dies, Gant says, "Yet actions have consequences. They have repercussions. It is a sad fact of life. Jeremiah, I want you to take Danny into the house and tie him up. Then I want you to take the car to the old-timer's place, and I want you to beat him to death with the iron bar in your hands."

"No," says Danny, still hissing in pain. "He didn't have anything to do with it!"

"Sometimes the repercussions of our actions are not felt by us directly. Sometimes they're inflicted upon the innocent and the ignorant. Bystanders, if you will."

Danny tries to fight, tries to struggle, but Jeremiah Wallow is surprisingly strong for someone so flabby. He handcuffs Danny, and drags him into the house. When Danny tries to shove him back, he kicks Danny's injured leg and Danny screams and falls back on to Stephanie's sofa. Jeremiah gets two pieces of rope. One piece he ties round Danny's neck, wraps the other end round a door handle behind him. That one keeps him upright. The other piece he ties round Danny's ankles, then loops it round the chain of the handcuffs. That one keeps him sitting. Then he goes away to beat Eddie Sullivan to death, and leaves Danny in here with Gant.

Gant stands by the bookcase, fingernail scraping lightly from book to book, spine to spine. He slides an old paperback from the shelf, a book by an Irish horror writer Danny had once liked. Same last name as Stephanie. A small part of him wonders if they're related. There couldn't be too many Edgleys in Ireland. There couldn't be too many Edgleys *anywhere*.

"How much do you know?" Gant asks, flicking through the pages.

Danny's shoulder is most likely broken. That's how it feels anyway. Every time he moves, he has to bite back a shriek. The rope around his neck is tight, but not tight enough to choke him, and it's rough against his skin. The handcuffs are decorated with ornate symbols that Danny doesn't understand, and even if he could get his feet free, he doubts his injured leg would carry his weight for more than a few steps. All this he thinks about while Gant waits for an answer, and then one more thought comes into his head. If he somehow manages to rid himself of the ropes and the cuffs, if he somehow manages to stand and put up a fight, he has Gant himself to deal with, and the old guy is tougher than he looks.

"I don't know where she is," Danny says.

Gant puts the book back on the shelf and turns to him. "Her boots are just inside the door," he says. "I dare say she would not have left this house in simple shoes – not if she were merely going for a walk. Tell me, Danny, what kind of dog does she have? I saw a bowl, and some dog food. Is it a big one? It is, isn't it?"

"Big enough to rip your throat out," Danny says.

Gant laughs. "Quite! Yes, indeed! Big enough to rip my throat out! Provided I don't kill it first. She didn't take the dog for a walk. She didn't even lock the house. Granted, she lives apart from the populace, undoubtedly assumes that those gates of hers would keep out any undesirables... but with the amount of security in place, it leads me to believe that she always locks up after herself, no matter what. Better to be safe than sorry, that's her motto. But if she did leave quickly, then where are the tracks? Where are the footprints in the snow? Did you call her, Danny my boy? Did you warn her?"

"I don't have her number."

"I find that difficult to believe."

"She has my number. I don't have hers."

"Ohh... and what does that tell you? That she doesn't like you, or merely that she doesn't trust you?"

"It tells me that she values her privacy."

Gant smiles. "Indeed it does. But when I asked the question *how much do you know?* I was not asking whether or not you knew where Stephanie Edgley had got to. I was simply asking how much do you know?"

"About what?"

"About the world, and the world beneath it. The world alongside it. The people in the shadows, in the darkness. Magic, Danny. I'm talking about magic."

Danny waits for him to break out into another one of his chuckles, but Gant stays distressingly straight-faced. Oh, hell. Danny isn't just at the mercy of a killer – he's at the mercy of a madman.

Gant raises an eyebrow. "Judging by your silence, you don't have the first clue as to what I may be talking about. Very well. Try not to let it concern you overly. Forget I ever said anything. Pretend we're just two people in a house, making conversation and passing the time."

"What are you going to do with me?" asks Danny.

"Probably kill you."

The admission hits Danny harder than any iron bar. His throat tightens. His stomach lurches. "Why?"

"Because you've been an obstruction," says Gant. "You've been an annoyance. And you've seen my face, Danny my boy. You can identify me, describe me to the authorities and make my life very awkward."

"I don't even know your full name."

"Cadaverous," the old man says. "Cadaverous Gant. Pleased to make your acquaintance."

"I won't tell anyone," says Danny.

"We both know you're lying. You shouldn't lie, Danny. Lying is bad."

"So why... why am I here? Why aren't I dead yet?"

"You may yet prove useful. I have heard many things about the person you know as Stephanie Edgley – many contradictory things. Some say she is noble; others say she is evil incarnate. If she is noble, I can use you to lure her into the open. If she's evil incarnate... well, a drastic rethink would be in order. I am, of course, hoping that she'll be noble. Noble people are easier to predict, easier to provoke, and easier to kill."

"What has she ever done to you?"

"To me?" asks Gant. "Nothing."

"Then why do you want to kill her?"

"Because of what she is, and what I am."

"And what are you?"

Cadaverous Gant just smiles.

30

FORGIVEN

alkyrie Cain looked at herself in the mirror. She slowly tapped a finger against the glass, touching her own reflection.

Her again. It was her again. No more looking through Darquesse's eyes. No more fighting to hang on inside her mind. The person she saw in that mirror was the person she was. It was an odd feeling, but a welcome one.

Reverie Synecdoche walked in. "You're dressed," she said.

Valkyrie picked up her jacket, slipped it on. "I am. I need to go home. I haven't been home for... a while. You can let me go, can't you?"

Synecdoche hesitated. "Well... yes. If the Sensitives cleared you—"

"They did," said Valkyrie. "They poked around my head all afternoon, making sure there was no trace of Darquesse left inside. Or that I wasn't pulling a double bluff. They concluded that I'm me again."

Synecdoche smiled. "Good. Your tests have come back, and you'll be happy to learn that you are in unnaturally perfect health with no obvious side effects."

"Darquesse liked to keep me running in tip-top condition," Valkyrie said. "It's all downhill from here, I suppose."

Synecdoche smiled again, but it was a professional smile, the smile that quietly conveyed how busy she was and, really, if you had nothing further to ask, she should be getting back to patients who needed her help.

"I'll see myself out," said Valkyrie.

Synecdoche nodded, spun on the heel of her sensible shoe, and then she was gone.

Valkyrie left the Medical Wing. The doctor had been right – she was feeling great. Strong and energetic and well rested. Her body was a temple. Her mind, however, was a ramshackle old cabin in the middle of a forest. It leaked. There were draughts. The doors wouldn't shut properly, there were noises from the attic and something had died under the porch.

Her mind needed help.

She found the others in the library in the North Tower. There were four libraries in the Sanctuary, but this was the smallest and the least used. Vex sat with his feet on the table opposite Saracen. Gracious and Donegan searched the shelves and, judging by their dismay, they were searching in vain for copies of books they had written. Stephanie and Fletcher sat together in the corner, talking quietly. No sign of Skulduggery or Dai Maybury.

Saracen was the first to see her. Everyone else looked round.

"Hi," she said.

"Come on in," said Vex. "Pull up a chair."

Valkyrie took a few steps, but didn't sit. "I want to thank you," she said. "You saved me from... myself, and you stopped me from doing things that I'd never, ever be able to come back from. You risked your lives and I'm just so... grateful."

"We look after our own," said Vex.

"Once a Dead Man, always a Dead Man," said Saracen.

Stephanie stood. "You should apologise to Dai," she said. Fletcher got to his feet, reached for her, but she pulled away.

"No. She has to apologise. Dai has no brothers left thanks to her."

"Go easy," Fletcher said softly.

"It's OK," Valkyrie said. "She's right. Of course I have to apologise to Dai. I have to apologise to everyone. Including all of you. I've been trying to figure out a way to explain it, but... I don't know. There was a movie I saw once. Dad made me watch it. It was a Western, and I don't like Westerns."

"What was it called?" Gracious asked.

"I don't remember."

"Who starred in it?" asked Donegan.

"That guy, you know. He's tall and he looks at people like he's going to shoot them all the time. He was the cop in that other movie, called that guy a punk and made him think about how many times he'd fired his gun because he'd lost track."

"Clint Eastwood," said Gracious.

"Yeah," said Valkyrie. "Anyway, there's a scene in it, in this Western he was in, and this other cowboy, dressed all in black, was told to go for a gun."

"Lee Van Cleef," said Gracious. "At the end of *For a Few Dollars More*."

"Whatever," Valkyrie said. "So he's told to go for his gun and there's this big long pause, because the guy who told him to go for it, the sheriff, is armed and he's ready to fire."

"Wait," said Donegan. "It can't be *For a Few Dollars More*. El Indio wasn't the sheriff."

"I'm pretty sure he was the sheriff," Valkyrie said. "The other cowboy was in a jail cell. The sheriff was that guy from *Superman*, and the cowboy was from *Harry Potter*."

Fletcher frowned. "Harry Potter was in a Western?"

"Oh my God," said Stephanie. "It was *Unforgiven*, OK? Will you please let her get to whatever point she's trying to make?"

Valkyrie continued. "So the sheriff makes this other guy, a third guy, I think he was in that film with Elvis and Tony Soprano and

Brad Pitt lying on a couch, and he's very nervous, but anyway the sheriff makes him give the cowboy a gun, and he tells the cowboy to pull the trigger, to shoot him and escape. So the cowboy reaches out for it, but he doesn't know if it's loaded or not, and the guy from *Superman* is standing there just waiting for him to grab it. But the *Harry Potter* guy can't, so he sits back down. Then the sheriff, the *Superman* guy, he takes the gun and he opens it up and all these bullets fall out and the other guy's like, 'Aw, I could have shot him.'"

"My mistake," said Stephanie. "There was no point."

"It was that fear," said Valkyrie. "The fear that if you make a move, the other person's going to shoot you. Like they're just waiting for you to do it, like they set the whole thing up to get you to make this mistake, and when you grab the gun, it's going to be empty, and they're going to open fire.

"That's what I thought was going to happen. Darquesse pushed me to one side so... so completely that I was... I was nothing. I was tiny and insignificant and powerless, and it felt like I was barely hanging on, like if I stopped concentrating I'd stop existing. And it was as if she was watching me and giving me all these chances to peep my head out just so she could chop it off."

"You should have been stronger," said Stephanie.

"I should have been," Valkyrie said. "But I wasn't. I gave up. It was a huge, unimaginably huge, mistake, but I gave up. It was just too hard to deal with everything that was happening. I should have kept fighting. The moment I gave up, I was just shoved to one side, and all I could do was watch. Well, watch and... When Darquesse did those things, killed those people, it was me, even though it wasn't. It's... kind of hard to explain."

"We understand," said Gracious. "It's Jean Grey and the Phoenix Force. We all understand."

"I have no idea what that means," said Vex, "but we get it, Valkyrie. We do. We've all seen what Darquesse was capable of. To have her living inside your head, as a part of you, that must have been... difficult."

Stephanie barked out a laugh. "I'm sorry, is that it? Are we letting her off the hook now? She killed people."

"You killed my cousin," Valkyrie said.

"And no one is letting me forget it," Stephanie responded. "But everyone here's acting like they're never going to bring up your little slide to the Dark Side ever again."

"We've all made mistakes," Skulduggery said from behind Valkyrie. She turned, saw him standing there with Dai Maybury.

"Some more than others," Skulduggery continued. "Long life means more time to work for redemption. We all have a second chance now. Valkyrie is back with us, and Darquesse is a few angry thoughts on the horizon. No Darquesse means no apocalypse. The future we needed to avert has been averted. We won."

Valkyrie looked at Dai. "I am so sorry for what I did."

"Wasn't you," said Dai. "Deacon wasn't much of a brother, but I'm still going to miss him. And when I do, I'll lay the blame squarely at the feet of the person who killed him – Darquesse. Not you."

Valkyrie gave a single nod, tears in her eyes.

Skulduggery clapped his hands once. "OK, speeches are over. Darquesse's ghost, because I refuse to call it an untethered entity, is still out there. It's up to Valkyrie and myself to track it until it dissipates. Fletcher, you take Stephanie home – she's earned a rest from all this craziness. Then get back here. The search for the Remnants continues. If anyone finds themselves with a spare moment, as unlikely as that sounds, you can lend a hand in the hunt for Doctor Nye. It was broken out of prison early this morning by a person or persons unknown. Nye is not an immediate threat, though, so keep your priorities straight. Let's get to it."

Chairs were pushed back and people stood up, and Skulduggery put his hand on Valkyrie's back and they were the first ones to leave.

She walked with him to the car. Moments later, the Bentley emerged from the brightly-lit car park into the darkness of Roarhaven's streets.

"Before we go wherever we're going," she said, "could we stop by Haggard? I haven't seen my family in, y'know, ages, and I just want to check in on them and... I just didn't think I'd ever see them again."

"Haggard *is* where we're going," said Skulduggery. "I would have asked Fletcher to take you, but I wanted to talk to you without anyone else around. How are you?"

Valkyrie put her head back, closing her eyes. "I'm good," she said. "I'm... good. I probably shouldn't be. I should be traumatised. When I was Darquesse, I did all these horrible things. I killed people. Murdered them. I can't blame her for that. It was me." She turned to look at him. "But now that she's gone, now that I'm back in control, all those doubts and fears and bad thoughts have just... evaporated. Everything that led me down that path towards giving in, letting her take over... it's gone. All of it. Isn't that brilliant?"

"Yes," Skulduggery said. "It's brilliant."

"Then why are you saying it like it so clearly isn't?"

"Why do you think?"

"I don't know, I'm not you, am I?" She watched the streets they drove past. "I suppose it might be because you think this is all some kind of repression. I'm not ready to face up to everything I've done so I'm pushing all the bad stuff away. Is that it?"

"And if it is?"

"Then I suppose I can only repress it for so long before it all comes crashing down on me."

"Are you ready for that?"

"Probably not," she admitted. "Were you ready for it when you took off Lord Vile's armour?"

Skulduggery was silent for a moment. "No," he said. "And I'm still making up for the things I did."

"But you had five years of death and destruction. I've only had a few weeks."

"You think the length of time makes any difference? People

still died. You're going to feel exactly how I felt. But you're stronger than me. You might be able to deal with it better."

"You know," Valkyrie said, "for a skeleton, you can be really morose. We used to have great conversations where we'd insult each other the whole time. Can we go back to those, please?"

"Of course," Skulduggery said. "The moment you tell me what else is wrong."

Valkyrie's smile threatened to vanish, but she managed to keep it up. "Trade," she said. "You tell me how you knew it wasn't really me, and I'll tell you what's wrong."

Skulduggery shrugged. "Little things. Little movements. Little facial expressions. One big thing."

"Oh?"

"Darquesse never asked to go home."

Valkyrie thought about this. "Huh."

"Now your turn," Skulduggery said. "What's wrong?"

She took her time. She chewed her lip. Her stomach flipped and churned. She didn't want to say it. She didn't want to say it out loud. To say it out loud would be to admit the awful, awful truth.

"When Darquesse was kicked out," she said, "she took all my bad feelings and my horrible thoughts with her and... and she took something else."

"What?"

"My magic," Valkyrie said, looking at him. "She took my magic."

31

CREEPY KID

Being a Monster Hunter sucked.

The main problem was that they spent most of their time searching for monsters to hunt. The Remnants did not want to be found, and Fletcher had lost count of how many small towns they'd checked. They all had divining rods now and, apart from Gracious and Donegan, they all felt astonishingly stupid.

But that still didn't stop the others from prying into Fletcher's personal life.

"What's wrong with you?" Gracious asked as they walked through the darkness. "I thought you'd be delighted to have Valkyrie back."

"I am," said Fletcher, doing his best to concentrate on the ridiculous twig in his hands. "Of course I am. We all are."

"Then why the sour face?"

Donegan glanced back. "That there is the expression of a man torn between two lovers."

Saracen seemed amused. "Is that true, Fletcher?"

"No," Fletcher scowled. "I'm going out with Stephanie. That's all there is to it. I was with Val, but she dumped me for a vampire, of all things, and now I'm with Steph. End of story."

Gracious passed. "No regrets about that?"

"None," said Fletcher. "And when did this become a group discussion anyway?"

"We're Monster Hunters," said Dai. "We share things."

"Do you think maybe you hooked up with Stephanie because you couldn't have Valkyrie?" Saracen asked.

"What? No. God, no."

"Because it'd make sense."

"That's not why I did it."

"It's only natural."

"Saracen, I'm telling you, Steph isn't a consolation prize, OK?"

Saracen smiled, satisfied. "Good. Good man."

Vex rejoined them. "What are we talking about?"

"Fletcher is experiencing conflicting emotions over Valkyrie's return and what it means for his relationship with Stephanie," Donegan informed him.

"Gotcha," said Vex.

"It must be weird, though," said Gracious. "Going out with Stephanie when we all thought Val was gone... that's one thing. But going out with her now that Val is back... well. That's weird, isn't it? Isn't that weird? It's going to be weird for Valkyrie."

Dai nodded. "Going to be very weird for Valkyrie."

"It doesn't have to be," said Fletcher. "It'd just be like if I were going out with her identical twin sister, if she had one."

"But even that's weird," said Donegan.

"That is weird," said Gracious.

"You're looking at this all wrong," Fletcher said. "Val is fine with this. Or she will be."

Saracen raised an eyebrow. "She doesn't know?"

"About me and Steph? Not in so many... no."

"Are you going to tell her?" Gracious asked. "Or will Stephanie?"

"Can I tell her?" Saracen asked. "I'd love to see her face."

"I'll tell her," Fletcher said, glaring. "I just haven't had the chance, that's all. A lot's been going on, and now we're back hunting for Remnants and... I just have to wait for the right moment."

217

"When you tell her," said Donegan, "do you think she'll hit you?"

"No," Fletcher snapped. "At least I hope not."

"Buy her something to soften the blow," Gracious advised. "Here, what should Fletcher buy Valkyrie to soften the blow?"

"Something she can't throw at him," said Vex. "Like a kitten. I used to have a kitten, her name was Sabrina, and she used to dig her claws into me whenever she sat on my lap. I wanted to throw her across the room every single time, but I didn't. Because she was a kitten, and she was cute. So buy her a kitten. Or an ostrich."

Saracen stopped walking. "OK," he said. "Something's wrong here."

Donegan looked up hopefully. "Is your divining rod buzzing?"

"No, my bloody divining rod isn't buzzing," Saracen said, throwing down his twig. "Follow me. And be careful."

They followed him out to the street. A small child sat in the middle of the empty road, head raised to the night sky. He was singing to himself, his soft voice carrying on the breeze.

"*Twinkle, twinkle, little star, how I wonder what you are...*"

"Right," said Gracious. "Because that's not creepy at all."

Wary of an ambush, they walked out till they were standing in a line. Eventually the boy stopped singing, and looked at them. Black veins riddled his smiling face like an insane jigsaw.

"You should run," the boy said.

"First, you leave that body," Vex replied. "The body of a child is going to do you no good."

The boy got to his feet. "Actually, this is probably the best body to have right now. You're not attacking me, are you? No one wants to hurt a kid."

"I hate kids," said Dai.

The boy laughed. "I won't be in this one for long, don't worry. I'm just here to deliver this message: you should run."

"Remnants aren't usually in the habit of warning people," said Saracen.

"Things have changed," said the boy. "My brethren have gone on – most of them anyway. I'll join them later, once you understand that we're not the threat you think we are."

"You're Remnants," said Saracen. "You are *exactly* the threat we think you are."

"Then why haven't we taken over this town? Why aren't we killing everyone?"

"Because Darquesse told you to lie low."

The boy shook his head. "Darquesse doesn't give us orders any more. She only thinks she does. We're not going to disobey her, of course – we're not stupid – but we're not going to help her, either. We have our own plans now."

"Where are the others?" Vex asked.

"I'm not going to tell you that."

"Things will go better for you if you do."

"Better for me? Oh, no, no, no. I've given you the warnings. It's your time that's up, not mine. If you had just turned round and gone home, you could have remained yourselves for the next few days. That would have been something, at least. But now you're ours."

"I don't think so," said Vex.

The boy smiled. "Oh, it's already begun."

Dai cracked his elbow into Vex's jaw and Vex went down. Saracen spun and Dai slammed a headbutt into his face that sent him staggering against Donegan. Fletcher glimpsed a Remnant darting from the shadows. It latched on to Vex and prised open his mouth.

Gracious knocked Dai off his feet as more Remnants flitted towards them. He grabbed Fletcher's hand and Fletcher linked up with the others, and in the space of a heartbeat they were back in the Sanctuary. Safe. Secure.

And down two men.

32

THE JOB OFFER

Vincent Foe liked mortal bars.

There was something refreshingly anonymous about them. He could drink here and not worry about running into someone he'd wronged in the past. And he had wronged a lot of people, it had to be said. Such were the casualties of the war he was waging, a war to take out as many people as possible when he died. It was an unusual war, he freely admitted. In fact, during all his time on this earth, he had met only four other people who shared his dream, and three of those were now in what was commonly referred to as his 'gang'.

Among the nicer names that people called them, nihilists was one. He didn't mind that label, though his was a brand of nihilism that neither Kierkegaard nor Nietzsche would ever have truly recognised. He saw himself as a fundamentalist existentialist, harbouring deep-seated psychopathic and genocidal tendencies. All he wanted to do was be responsible for the destruction of the world and everyone in it – himself included.

But until that opportunity presented itself, he was content to sit in mortal bars and ponder the pointlessness of life.

"Vincent Foe."

He turned his head slightly. The woman who had spoken was small, with wild brown hair.

"I know you?"

"We've met." The woman smiled.

"Sorry. I don't recognise you."

"You wouldn't," said the woman. "This body is new. Well, new to me. A rental, shall we say? I was recently evicted from the body I'd been using. I found this one and, while it's not perfect, beggars can't be choosers."

The mortals in the bar drank and chatted and paid not one whit of attention to Foe and the woman.

Foe studied her face. She looked sick. She was sweating badly and her eyes were bloodshot.

"And what do you want with me?" he asked carefully.

"If you could possibly tear yourself away from working for China Sorrows, I have a job for you which will probably result in the imminent destruction of the human race."

Foe narrowed his eyes. "What did you say your name was?"

"I'm the one they're all scared of," said the woman. "I am Darquesse. Are you interested?"

Foe didn't want to appear too eager, so he took his time before shrugging and saying, "Yeah. Maybe. What've you got in mind?"

33

MISADVENTURES IN BABYSITTING

Losing Dexter Vex and Dai Maybury to the Remnants was a serious blow. Part of Valkyrie wanted to stay in the Bentley when the call came through, to return to Roarhaven with Skulduggery while all of this was going on, but another part, a stronger part, wanted to be home. She was glad she'd listened to it. The moment she walked through that front door, she felt lighter, better. Happier. And now here she was, raising her eyebrows at her father.

"I have babysitting advice for you," he told her while he put on his coat. "I made this mistake once and your mother has never let me forget it. This is invaluable, and I learned it the hard way. You ready?"

Valkyrie stood with her back to the roaring fire, and grinned. "I'm ready."

"Do *not* lose the baby," her dad said. "Do *not*. Understand? Also, the term *babysitter* is misleading, because neither can you *sit* on the baby. I sat on you once when you were really small, but thankfully your head just popped back to its original shape once I noticed. You were under there for a few minutes, actually. I was surprised you were even alive."

"I won't sit on Alice."

"Well, you say that, but it's a surprisingly easy thing to do. She's soft, like a cushion."

Valkyrie's mother walked in. "Did you sit on our child?"

Her dad shook his head. "No. I did not. Not recently. You ready to go?"

"I am," said her mum. "Steph, sorry for dumping you with Alice on your first night back, but that's what you get for staying at Gordon's place all week. Alice is wonderful, she is a wonderful, wonderful child, but we *really* need a break. If I'd remembered how tiring it was to raise a kid, I'd have probably got someone else to do it."

Her dad nodded. "Outsourcing. Clever."

"She's ready for sleep, so just give her a bottle, tuck her in, and then go to bed yourself. You look tired."

Valkyrie smiled. "That sounds nice."

She walked them to the door.

"Don't open the door to strangers," said her dad. "Unless they're selling something. Then open the door and see if I'd like it. If I'd like it, buy it for me. But nothing cheap. I have standards. Nothing too expensive, either. My standards aren't that high."

"Have a good time," Valkyrie said, closing the door behind them.

She went back into the living room, put the guard in front of the fire, and scooped Alice into her arms. She climbed the stairs, put her sister in the cot with her bottle and tucked her in. Alice looked up at her until her eyelids began to close, then Valkyrie sneaked out. She crossed the landing to her bedroom.

Stephanie was sitting on the bed, her backpack beside her. "Enjoying being back?"

Valkyrie's smile faded a little. "I am, actually, yes. It's good to come home."

"I know what you're trying to do."

"And what is that, exactly?"

"You're trying to replace me."

"I'm trying to replace *you*? You are *my* substitute."

223

"*Was!*" Stephanie said, springing to her feet. "I *was* your substitute! And now you're threatened because you've realised that I'm a better daughter to them than you ever were."

Valkyrie's lip curled. "You're insane. But then we all knew that when you murdered Carol. You really think I'd be comfortable with you living with them full time? How do I know you won't slip up and have to kill someone else? How do *you* know you won't do it?"

"Because I've changed. I've evolved."

"You can't be trusted."

Stephanie laughed. "And you can? We both saw a future where you killed our parents, where you killed our sister. I've evolved *from* a killer. You've been evolving *into* one. Tell me again which one of us can't be trusted, and then tell me which one of us is trusted. It's not you. I've been working very closely with Skulduggery these last few weeks. Seems like I can replace you in every aspect of your life. I'm a better daughter, a better partner, a better girlfriend..."

Valkyrie frowned. "What?"

"You shouldn't have cheated on Fletcher. I'd never do that to him."

"You're... you're with Fletcher? You can't be. You're a copy of *me*."

"That's what I used to think. Now I realise that I'm an improvement."

Valkyrie stared at her. "Stephanie, this isn't going to work out. I thought it could, but it can't. You're going to have to leave."

"I'm sorry?"

"What are you, deaf?" asked Valkyrie. "Leave. Leave the country."

"And where do you suggest I go?"

"Anywhere. I don't care. Go to America, get a dog, find a life."

Stephanie took a step towards her. "You think *I'm* the one who's going to run away? Seriously? You've already run away once. You ran away and let Darquesse take over. We both know

224

you're the weaker one. So here's my counter-proposal, Valkyrie. You take off. What use are you to anyone now? You don't have any relevance. You've failed everyone. You don't even have any magic any more, do you? Don't look so surprised. I can see it in your eyes. At least I have *this*."

She reached for the backpack, pulled out the Sceptre, and Valkyrie stepped back involuntarily.

Stephanie's eyes narrowed. "Wow."

Valkyrie felt the heat rise to her face. "I wasn't—"

"Wow," Stephanie said again. "You thought I was going to kill you, didn't you? You actually thought I was going to do it."

"In my defence—"

"In your defence *what*? I've already killed Carol – why not you, too? I'm not that person any more. I told you that. I told everyone that. They all know I've changed. Even Skulduggery knows. You're the only one who's still treating me like a *thing*."

"Hey," said Valkyrie, "if you want to have this conversation, let's have this conversation. But let's do it when you're *not* holding the Sceptre, OK?"

Stephanie pointed it straight at her. "This? You're scared of this? You're scared of what I'll do with this?"

"Don't joke around," Valkyrie said, her pulse thundering in her ears. "Your thoughts activate—"

"I know!" Stephanie said, almost shouting. She lowered her voice immediately, but the anger remained. "I know how to use this, and it's not going to go off accidentally. I've been thinking about it since I got home, actually, thinking of all the people it can kill and the destruction it can cause, and you know what? I don't want it any more. You're back. You can go off and have adventures. That's what you're good for. But me? I'm done with all that. I quit. I never want to use another weapon. I never want to hold this thing again."

Valkyrie watched her grab the backpack and stuff the Sceptre into it. She zipped it up and the zip got stuck and Stephanie cursed and muttered and Valkyrie reached out. "Here, let me—"

Stephanie yanked it back. "No. This has nothing to do with you. Amazing, isn't it? Something that has nothing to do with you. This is about me. This is about my decision." She stormed past Valkyrie, slamming the door.

The room was quiet without her. Valkyrie waited a few moments to see if she'd storm back in. When she didn't, Valkyrie hung up her jacket and pulled her boots off.

Stephanie walked in. She wasn't carrying the Sceptre any more.

"There," she said. "I've put it away. Happy now?"

"Where is it?" asked Valkyrie.

"You don't have to worry about where it is. You just have to worry about what you're going to do with your life. Because this life is mine."

"I'm not going to argue with you about this," said Valkyrie. She sat on the bed and took off her socks.

Stephanie's eyes widened. "What do you think you're doing?"

"Getting ready for bed, what does it look like?"

Stephanie put her hands on her hips. "And who says you're getting the bed?"

Valkyrie laughed. "Seriously? Who says?" She stood up. "I say, because it's my bed."

"You haven't been sleeping there for quite a while," Stephanie responded. "It's mine now."

"Listen, *Stephanie*, here's the way it is. My bed. My room. My family. My rules."

"You gave up your family, *Valkyrie*. What is it the lawyers say? You've relinquished your rights. You gave in. You let Darquesse beat you."

"And now I'm back."

"But that's got nothing to do with you. We brought you back. You did nothing."

The anger rose. Valkyrie's eyes narrowed. "Screw you," she said, bumping Stephanie's shoulder as she strode out.

She was halfway down the stairs when she realised Stephanie was following her.

"You didn't overcome Darquesse with the force of your will," Stephanie said. "Your true and noble self didn't triumph over her evil. If we hadn't risked our lives to get you back, you'd still be a tiny, insignificant voice in the back of her mind."

Valkyrie walked into the living room and Stephanie followed, right on her heels.

"You don't deserve this new freedom. Do you understand that?"

Valkyrie whirled. They stood toe to toe.

"You think you and Skulduggery share a lot, don't you?" said Stephanie, a sneer on her lips. "He became Lord Vile, you became Darquesse. You both did terrible things. But here's the difference. Skulduggery reasserted himself. He was strong enough, he fought hard enough, to push Vile down, and re-emerge as the Skulduggery we all know and love. But you? You weren't strong enough."

"Shut up."

"You didn't fight at all," said Stephanie. "You needed us to pull you out. You say that bed is yours? No. You gave up your claim to all of this when you let Darquesse take over, and you haven't earned any of it back."

Valkyrie jabbed a finger into Stephanie's chest. "You are not taking my family."

"They're not your..." Stephanie faltered, and then frowned. "Did you leave the patio door open?"

Valkyrie turned, just as Tanith Low stepped into the room.

Stephanie lunged at her and Valkyrie grabbed the poker. Tanith kicked out, sending Stephanie hurtling over the couch. Her sword flashed and she spun, and Valkyrie blocked the blade with the poker, the impact jarring it from her hands. She grabbed Tanith, drove her back against the wall, got a knee in the belly for her trouble. The wind rushed out of her.

Her reinforced jacket was upstairs.

Tanith's face was riddled with black veins, and her hand curled round Valkyrie's throat. "Where is Darquesse?"

"Please," Valkyrie gasped, "you don't have to do this..."

Stephanie got back to her feet and Tanith's eyes flickered, and Valkyrie saw her chance. She grabbed what she could of Tanith's body, jammed her hip against Tanith's and wrenched her body round, flipping Tanith into the armchair. The armchair fell and Tanith tumbled out of it, but came up immediately, still with the sword in her hand.

Valkyrie went left. Stephanie went right.

Tanith darted forward and Valkyrie stumbled, narrowly missing the sword. Stephanie went for the poker, but Tanith spun into her, sweeping her legs. Stephanie crashed to the ground and Tanith swung the sword and Valkyrie rammed into her from behind, wrapping her in the tightest bear hug she could manage and pulling her back over her outstretched leg. Tanith flung her sword away before she landed on it. She hit the ground and Valkyrie tried keeping her down there. But Tanith was a squirmy one, and she was stronger than Valkyrie even without the Remnant inside her.

She grabbed Valkyrie's head with both hands, started to twist. Valkyrie felt the cartilage in her neck about to pop and she panicked, tried getting the hell out of there. Stephanie's shoe came in, connecting solidly with Tanith's jaw. There was a mad scramble for the sword, but Tanith got there first, swung round and the blade pressed against Valkyrie's throat.

They all froze.

"Bring Darquesse back," Tanith said.

"We can't," said Valkyrie.

"How did you do it? How did you regain control?"

"I didn't. She's not with me any more. She was thrown out. She's gone."

"Gone?"

"Cassandra called her an untethered entity."

Tanith looked at them both. "A ghost?"

228

"Kind of."

"Oh," Tanith said. There was a long pause. Then Tanith sighed, and took the blade from Valkyrie's throat. She went and sat on the couch.

Valkyrie and Stephanie looked at each other.

The black veins faded, and Tanith's lips returned to normal. "Sorry," she said.

Stephanie frowned. "I don't get it. Are you going to kill us or not?"

Tanith hesitated.

"Please say not," said Valkyrie.

"I don't know," Tanith said. "I mean... I should kill you. Killing you would make sense. You took away Darquesse, and I want Darquesse to destroy everyone. Or... I did."

Valkyrie made a decision. She righted the armchair and sat in it. "You changed your mind?"

"I don't know," said Tanith. "The more I think about it... yeah, maybe. The Remnant part of me is, like, whoop, let's kill everything. But the human part of me is all, why? Killing everything would make the world so boring. And to be honest, I think the Remnant part of me is also starting to think along those lines, even though it'd never admit it."

Stephanie sat down slowly, rubbing her jaw. "So you're not going to kill us?"

"Probably not. I mean, don't let your guard down or anything. I don't want to make a promise I can't keep, but as of right this second, no, I have no intention of killing either of you. But I may change my mind."

"Well, that's progress," Valkyrie said. "That's something, isn't it?"

Tanith nodded. "I think so. I mean, it feels like I've just taken a big step. That's how it feels. It feels important."

"Admitting you have a problem is the first step towards recovery," Stephanie said.

"That's what they say, isn't it? And I do have a problem. I

sometimes want to kill everything. I don't have a conscience and occasionally I do things that could be labelled as, you know..."

"Evil," said Stephanie.

"Right. Yes. Evil. Occasionally I do evil things. I don't mean to be evil. I'm not evil just to be evil. But evil things happen and I'm responsible."

"Are you going to take Moribund's advice?" Valkyrie asked.

Tanith looked surprised. "You know about that?"

"I overheard you talking to Sanguine about it. Or Darquesse did."

"Who's Moribund?" Stephanie asked.

"This guy who has a Remnant bonded to him," Valkyrie told her. "But he decided not to be evil. He decided to be good. He said all Tanith has to do is pretend to be a good guy for long enough, and then she'll be a real one."

"Will that work?"

"I don't know," Tanith said. "I haven't really tried it yet. But now that Darquesse is gone... Is she gone? Really gone?"

"Uh," said Valkyrie, "I really don't want to make you decide to kill us again, but... she's *mostly* gone. Finbar said that untethered entities like her can only last for so long in that state before they just... evaporate. She's being driven by the need to survive, but that'll only sustain her for so long."

"And is there a way she *could* survive?"

"She could possess someone, someone open to possession. But that wouldn't last long. An ordinary body wouldn't be able to withstand her level of power without burning out. All the Sensitives are sleeping in protective circles tonight in case she tries to sneak in."

"But she's still alive? In a way? Hmm." Tanith stood up.

Valkyrie and Stephanie got to their feet quickly.

"Are you going to try and kill us again?" Valkyrie asked.

Tanith sheathed her sword. "Naw. I don't know what I'm going to do. The apocalypse seemed like a really good idea a few years ago. Now... I don't know. Maybe I'm just not that into it any more. You should remember to lock your doors, by the way. I just walked in here."

"Yeah," said Valkyrie. "Thanks."

Tanith gave them a smile. "I think I'll leave through the front."

When Tanith was gone, they tidied the living room and locked the patio door. Then they went back upstairs, and looked in on Alice, who had slept through the whole thing.

Stephanie went to the bathroom while Valkyrie went into her room. She stood there for a while before walking out. The door to the bathroom was open, and Stephanie was examining herself in the mirror.

"You OK?" Valkyrie asked.

Stephanie probed her cheek with her finger, and winced. "Ow. Look at that. That's going to swell up something fierce by the morning."

Valkyrie went back to her room, took a clot of dirt from a bundle of tinfoil, and ran it under the cold tap.

"Let's see," she said. Stephanie turned to her, and Valkyrie rubbed the mud into her skin. "That feel better?"

"It's starting to," Stephanie said.

"Did you think Tanith was going to kill us?" Valkyrie asked.

"For a moment. Well, a long moment. What about you?"

"At first, yeah. Hey, thanks, by the way. You probably saved my life."

Stephanie shrugged. "Ah, you probably saved mine, too. That was a nice little flip you caught her with."

"Saw that, eh? Yeah, it wasn't bad. I'm really starting to miss my magic, though."

Stephanie grinned. "I started to seriously regret not having the Sceptre with me."

Valkyrie laughed. "I bet. The moment you put it down, *bam* – here's Tanith!"

"Typical," Stephanie said, drying her face with a towel. "There.

231

Black eye averted, I reckon. Hopefully, that's the last time I'll ever have to do that."

"Are you really going to quit?" Valkyrie asked as they walked back to the bedroom.

"Of course," said Stephanie. "You sound surprised."

"Well, yeah. I don't know how you could leave it all behind. I mean, you're me, essentially."

Stephanie glanced at her as she got ready for bed. "What are you talking about? I'm not you. I just pretended to be you. The moment I became aware, really aware, was the moment I stopped being you and I started being me. I've got no interest in risking my life to save people I've never met. I would kill and die for my family and the people I love, but everyone else can take care of themselves, as far as I'm concerned."

"So you won't miss being Skulduggery's partner?"

"Not one bit," said Stephanie. "But that's mainly because he was never that comfortable around me. There were times when he was fine, when he was like how he is with you. And then it was as if a switch were flicked, and he remembered who I really was. I'm not going to miss that at all."

"And you're not going to miss the adventure, or the excitement...?"

"Maybe a little," said Stephanie. "At first, anyway. But I'm looking forward to being normal again. It sounds dumb, but being normal is what I find exciting."

"Yeah," said Valkyrie. "That does sound dumb."

They laughed.

"I want to say goodbye tomorrow, though," said Stephanie. "You know, to Skulduggery and China and, like..."

"Fletcher?"

"Well... I don't know if I'd have to say goodbye to..."

"What exactly is, uh, going on between you two?"

"I don't know," said Stephanie. "I don't know how he feels about, like, the whole thing, or what he'll do when I tell him I'm quitting..."

"But you like him?"

"Well... yeah."

"And he likes you?"

"I think so."

"And you're going to want to continue... seeing him?"

"Maybe," said Stephanie. "Yes. If he wants to, I mean. I don't know how he'll react to me being normal."

"And how are *we* going to do this?" Valkyrie asked. "You and me and my... you and me and *our* family?"

"Well," Stephanie said, thinking it over, "I suppose we could... we could choose not to treat it any differently. I mean, if you're cool with it, I'd spend most of my time here, and a couple of times a week I could stay in Gordon's house while you take my place. It won't be as easy as getting the memories straight into our heads, but we could just, y'know, tell each other what's been happening before we switch places."

"Tell each other," Valkyrie echoed. "How revolutionary."

"I know, right?"

"You realise we're going to be arguing a lot, yeah?"

Stephanie shrugged. "I'm OK with that if you are."

"Well, at least it'd be intelligent conversation."

Stephanie rolled her eyes. "That's such a Skulduggery thing to say."

"Shut up," Valkyrie said, laughing. "Well, I suppose if tomorrow is your last day risking your life, you should probably be the one to get the bed."

"Maybe," said Stephanie. "Or, y'know... it's a pretty big bed, for a single. We could share it."

Valkyrie smiled. "Cool."

"But I get the good pillow."

34

SAYING GOODBYE

Watching Valkyrie and Skulduggery together, Stephanie was actually jealous of all the things she'd been denied. She envied that relationship, the confidence that Valkyrie exuded around Skulduggery, where she knew she would have his support and understanding no matter what. Stephanie didn't have that kind of relationship with anyone. She was still treading with a light foot, even around Fletcher. She couldn't afford to screw up. Not yet.

It'd get better, though. She knew it would. It was already better now than it had been at the start. The more she was around people, the more she changed their attitudes towards her. To Skulduggery, to China and Saracen and the Monster Hunters, she wasn't just the faulty reflection any more. She was Stephanie. A person. An individual.

It was just typical that just as she was about to reap the rewards of all the work she'd put in here, all the things she'd done, she'd reached the point where it was time to leave it all behind.

But she was glad to go. Mostly. She wasn't wired the same way that Valkyrie was. She wasn't dissatisfied with life in Haggard, with life as a normal person. She wasn't drawn to danger, or adventure, or darkness. Her original purpose as a reflection was to carry on with Valkyrie's normal routine – was it really so hard to believe that she'd grown to love that routine? Her parents, her sister, her friends, her town, her future... these were all things that interested her. These were all things she needed. She certainly wasn't going to miss hitting people. She certainly wasn't going to miss being hit.

But even so... she was envious.

"Mortal female, forty-six years old," Skulduggery was saying as he and Valkyrie walked through the Sanctuary. Stephanie trailed after them. "We'd been keeping an eye on her as she'd displayed some psychic tendencies in the past. Nothing too earth-shattering, but enough to register as an untrained Sensitive. Her body was found early this morning. Little more than a dried-out husk."

"Darquesse?" Valkyrie asked.

Skulduggery nodded. "Looks like it. From what we can gather, Darquesse couldn't have possessed her for more than three hours before she burned up."

"Where was the body found?"

"In a field near Ashbourne. Her car was nearby."

"So Darquesse possessed this woman and that's as far as she could get?" asked Valkyrie. "What's in Ashbourne?"

"Our operative on the scene noticed some fresh tyre tracks nearby. A motorbike."

"Tanith?"

"Maybe."

"I don't know," Valkyrie said, and glanced back at Stephanie. "What do you think? Tanith was talking last night like she was ready to call it quits."

"She could have changed her mind," said Stephanie. "Darquesse could have called her after she left us, when she was still in this woman's body, and convinced her to come back."

"I don't want to assume it's Tanith until we've at least verified that the tyre tracks match her bike," said Skulduggery. "Maybe it's not her. Maybe it's someone else entirely who's got nothing to do with any of this."

They met two sorcerers coming the other way, escorting a man in a nice suit with a harried look on his face. Skulduggery held up a hand, and all three slowed to a stop.

"Keir Tanner," Skulduggery said. "Do you know who I am?"

The harried gentleman, Tanner, nodded distractedly. "Of course. Not too many living skeletons around, even in Roarhaven."

"Indeed there aren't," Skulduggery said. "Valkyrie, Stephanie, Mr Tanner here is Chief Warden of Ironpoint Gaol, scene of the audacious midday escape by our old friend Doctor Nye. Any idea how this escape occurred, Warden Tanner?"

Tanner sighed. "Someone got in, bypassed the security protocol, sneaked Nye to the surface where, we think, it stowed away on a truck."

"Forgive me, Warden," said Skulduggery, "but you make that sound astonishingly easy."

Tanner flushed. "We're a low-security prison, Detective Pleasant. The Sanctuary knew that when they shipped Nye to us, but we were the only place with a cell big enough to accommodate it. And Nye wasn't even a security risk, at least not according to the file I was sent."

"That doesn't mean we expected someone to be able to walk the prisoner out the front door," Valkyrie said.

Tanner ground his teeth. Stephanie could almost hear it. "I assure you, we are conducting a thorough investigation into how this happened. Now, if you'll excuse me, I came here to help with organising a search, not to be berated by a mass murderer."

Stephanie's eyebrows shot up and Skulduggery slammed Tanner against the wall. The other two sorcerers tried to pull him back, and Valkyrie just stood there, stunned.

"Let go of me!" Tanner commanded, his face flushed bright red. "Release me this instant!"

Ignoring the attempts to separate them, Skulduggery leaned in close, and whispered something into Tanner's ear. Whatever he said, it was enough to turn that flushed face deathly pale.

Skulduggery stepped away. The sorcerers grabbed Tanner, hurried him onwards. They passed Stephanie and Tanner looked terrified.

"Where were we?" Skulduggery asked when Tanner was gone.

"Is that how people see me?" Valkyrie asked in a quiet voice.

Skulduggery didn't have an immediate response to that.

"Some of them," said Stephanie. "Especially here. They look at you – they look at *me* – and all they see is the face of the person who killed all their loved ones. They hate Darquesse. They hate us. You're just going to have to get used to it."

Valkyrie looked at her. "You've had to endure this since that day?"

"You'll learn to ignore it. Or almost ignore it."

Valkyrie chewed her lip for a few seconds, then said, "So much for the moral high ground."

Stephanie laughed. "Yeah, you can't stay up there any longer."

"I loved that place," Valkyrie muttered.

"The moral high ground is overrated," Skulduggery said, "and the view's much better from down here. Come along, troublemakers."

"Actually," Stephanie said, "I just want to say goodbye to the Engineer, if that's OK?"

"By all means," said Skulduggery.

"I'll come get you when we're ready to go," Valkyrie said. Stephanie nodded, and headed off by herself.

Within minutes, she'd left the new Sanctuary behind, and was back in the cold and dark remains of the old. She got to the Accelerator Room, and the Engineer looked up.

"Hello, Stephanie," it said.

She grinned. "And how do you know I'm not the recently-returned Valkyrie Cain? Is it because I'm not wearing black?"

"Not at all," said the Engineer. "You walk differently. You are lighter on the balls of your feet, whereas she walks like she has a weight upon her shoulders."

Stephanie's grin faded. "That's... kind of sad, actually. I would've thought she'd be the cheerier one."

"I suppose it cannot be easy, being the architect of the world's demise."

"You're depressing me."

"Oh!" said the Engineer. "Well, I certainly did not intend to do that. I should point out that visions of the apocalypse and prophecies of doom rarely turn out to be accurate. So far anyway."

"I'm going to miss these chats of ours."

"You are leaving?"

"Retiring," Stephanie said. "I'm going to leave the fighting to Valkyrie. She can save the world. I just want to live in it."

"In that case, I wish you a happy retirement," said the Engineer. "Would you like to know how long before the Accelerator overloads, for old time's sake?"

Stephanie opened her mouth – then paused. "No," she smiled. "That's not my problem any more."

"Very well. Have a nice life, Stephanie."

"You too, Engineer," she said, and walked out. And that was it. That was all she'd needed. A simple choice like that, and it all changed. Her future opened up before her. Blossomed like a flower. Every opportunity, every avenue, came into sudden, vivid clarity. She would be a good daughter, a great sister, a wonderful girlfriend, a decent person. She would finish that Stephen King book. She would go to college. She would live and love. She would be vibrant and happy and thoughtful and strong. She had long outgrown her limitations as a reflection, and now she would outgrow her limitations once more.

Stephanie laughed.

The fist caught her in the side of the head and the corridor tilted and threw her to the unsteady ground. She rolled, not sure which way was up. She got her feet under her and straightened her legs, staggered against the wall. The whole world spun and the wall wasn't there any more and she was falling through an open door.

A man appeared in the doorway, a giant of a man, muscled arms bursting from his sleeveless denim jacket, long black hair in tangles. She knew him. She knew his face, ugly as it was. Obloquy. He was one of Vincent Foe's little band of nihilists. She backed up unsteadily, expecting Foe to make his presence known. But it seemed that Obloquy was here alone. Obloquy the giant, the thug. The Sensitive.

But of course it wasn't Obloquy. Not really. He was sweating, and his movements were clumsy. He was a vehicle that someone was taking for a test drive, and not planning to return.

"Darquesse," Stephanie said.

Darquesse twisted her male face into a leering grin, and swung a punch. Stephanie saw it coming. She ducked under it and lunged, going for Darquesse's eyes, but Darquesse was already raising a knee.

It was an awkward move, but it caught Stephanie right in the belly. Her jacket was open, unzipped, and the knee took the breath out of her. She stumbled away, her muscles in spasm.

"Did I hear right?" Darquesse asked, following. "You're retiring? You're saying your goodbyes? Did you honestly think that was going to happen? Really? You think you're the one, out of everyone, who gets a happy ending?"

Stephanie straightened, sucking in air. She tried to zip up her jacket but the zipper was stuck.

Darquesse brushed her matted hair out of her eyes. "I mean, I understand it. That desire. A happy ending sounds nice, doesn't it? I had a happy ending in mind, too. I was going to do what you were trying to do. I was going to fit in. I was going to belong. But they weren't content with that. They wanted Valkyrie back. Wouldn't settle for anything less."

"You don't look well, Darquesse," Stephanie said. Her voice was weak. Her lungs couldn't draw in enough breath to shout for help.

"I *don't* look well, do I?" Darquesse agreed. "I can feel my organs boiling inside me, and there's nothing I can do to stop it."

"Must suck."

"I might not be able to use my powers, but this body will do the job. It's enough to kill you."

"I'm not going to die," said Stephanie. "I've got too much to live for."

Darquesse closed in. "Life and death are just two ways in which energy moves. Two possible paths out of a billion. Look. I'll show you."

She moved in and Stephanie dodged under her swipe, slammed a boot heel to the side of her knee and watched her shift her weight drastically. Her instinct was to go for the head – always go for the head – but Darquesse had picked this guy for his size. Stephanie would need to work her way up.

Darquesse lunged, grabbed Stephanie's right arm and threw a punch that would have taken her head off if she hadn't stepped in to smack her forehead into Darquesse's mouth. Darquesse howled, blood spraying from burst lips. Maybe the blow had broken a tooth or two. Stephanie hoped it had, because the headbutt had hurt her, too, sent bright flashes of light exploding behind her vision. Darquesse stepped back, both hands at her face, and Stephanie crouched, threw an uppercut right into Darquesse's groin. Darquesse made a sound like a stone door being opened, all grinding and hollow, and she doubled over, eyes bulging for a moment before screwing shut in slow-delivered pain. Stephanie danced back a step and kicked, her toe catching Darquesse just under the chin. That should have put her down. Instead, her big man's legs shook a little, and after a moment she straightened up again.

Stephanie feinted one way, went the other, foot swinging for that knee. What was it Patrick Swayze said in that movie Tanith had made her watch? Take the biggest guy in the world, shatter his knee and he'll drop like a stone. Damn right. Look at Darquesse now, lurching, hobbling, her bloody face contorted in pain, her breath coming in ragged wheezes. All Stephanie had to do was keep dictating the distance between them until she could break off and run.

Darquesse dropped back, glaring at her.

"You're not much without magic, are you?" Stephanie said. Her breathing was back under control. Her voice was strong again. She kept circling, getting closer to the door.

"New body," Darquesse responded, blood dribbling from her mouth. "Takes a while to get the hang of things. Also, male. There's some vulnerable spots I'm not used to."

"You've got more muscles to make up for it."

"Suppose I do," Darquesse said. "But I can't be relying on stuff like that, can I? I have to remember who I am. Have to remember my training. Which, now that I think of it, is exactly the same training as yours. This is going to be interesting, isn't it?"

Darquesse smiled, and took a limping step forward. Stephanie took one back. Darquesse wiped the blood from her mouth, looked at it, then flicked her hand out. Drops of blood splattered across Stephanie's face and she flinched, and in that split second Darquesse forgot about her limp and dived across the space between them. A huge hand grabbed Stephanie's shoulder and the other ripped the jacket off her. A punch cracked her ribs, then an elbow came in with the force of a wrecking ball, shattering her jaw.

Pain screamed through her body and she fell into the corridor. They went down, Darquesse a crushing weight on top. Stephanie tasted blood, swallowed broken teeth. She squirmed frantically, shifting her hips. She went for the eyes, but Darquesse kept her head out of range, so Stephanie grabbed the hand that gripped her shoulder, swung her legs up, tried to force Darquesse into an arm bar, but Darquesse got her feet beneath her and she stood, taking Stephanie up, lifting her off the ground, and then she let herself fall and Stephanie hit the floor and Darquesse landed on her and Stephanie's arms and legs splayed wide open with the impact.

She felt thick fingers at her throat, but her body was too stunned to react.

Then she heard voices. Valkyrie. Fletcher.

She tried to shout, but her jaw sent fresh waves of pain crashing through her. Darquesse abandoned the choke, went searching through her jacket for something. Stephanie's body was starting to respond again. Darquesse took a wooden sphere from her pocket, twisted the hemispheres in opposite directions, and a bubble rippled out, enveloping them both just as Valkyrie and Fletcher came round the corner.

"You don't think it's weird, do you?" Fletcher asked in a low voice, oblivious to Stephanie and Darquesse only a few paces away. Stephanie wanted to call out, for all the good it would do with the cloaking sphere preventing sound from escaping the bubble, but Darquesse's fingers were squeezing her throat and she could barely breathe, let alone shout.

"Actually, yeah," Valkyrie said, "I think it's very weird, to be honest. You're doing things with her and she's me, essentially, so even though we've broken up, you're still getting to do stuff with... OK, listen, it's just unsettling."

"Amazingly, this isn't all about you," said Fletcher.

"Oh, really?" Valkyrie said, not bothering to hide her scepticism.

Stephanie tried a closed-mouth roar as they passed right beside her, but they didn't even glance down.

She felt Darquesse tighten the choke and she tried to squirm backwards and Darquesse shifted her weight forward and Stephanie caught her in a beautifully-timed scissor sweep, flipping

Darquesse on to her back with Stephanie on top. She scrambled to get up, dropping hammerfists on to Darquesse's nose when she tried to hold on to her. Stephanie fell sideways and Darquesse turned over, and they got to their feet.

"Hi," she heard Valkyrie say from the Accelerator Room, "have you seen Stephanie?"

"I did indeed," the Engineer responded. "She was here two minutes and forty-nine seconds ago."

Stephanie called out. It came out as a gurgle from her broken mouth.

Darquesse grinned.

Stephanie rushed forward, her hands sliding over her own head, those elbows smashing whatever was in front of her.

"Typical," Valkyrie said as they walked out into the corridor. "You know, she does this just to show me that she's her own person."

"Don't be mean about Steph," Fletcher said. They stood there, looking at each other. "I like her and she likes me. You remember what that was like, don't you? Back when I was irresistible to you?"

Valkyrie laughed. "You were never irresistible."

Stephanie hooked her left hand round the back of Darquesse's neck, started driving more elbows into her face, desperate to get the space she needed to just lunge out of the sphere's bubble.

"Of course I was," Fletcher said, grinning. "You were totally into me. Before the vampire came along, of course. You and your bad boy phase."

"It didn't last long."

Fletcher shrugged. "Didn't have to."

Darquesse flipped her over her hip and Stephanie slammed to the ground. Darquesse twisted the arm she still held and even through her broken jaw Stephanie screamed as her bone snapped.

"I really never meant to hurt you," Valkyrie said. "You were my first real boyfriend. I didn't know what the hell I was doing."

"You think I did? You were my first girlfriend."

Valkyrie frowned. "I thought you said I was your fourth."

Fletcher laughed. "Yeah... may have exaggerated about that part."

Valkyrie's eyes widened. "Oh my God."

He laughed again. "Yeah," he said, and went quiet for a moment.

Darquesse let go of her arm and Stephanie turned over, tears in her eyes, started dragging herself towards the edge of the bubble.

She didn't look back, but she felt Darquesse standing there, watching her as she neared the edge.

"I really like Stephanie," Fletcher said softly.

"I know," said Valkyrie. "And if that's what it is, then I have no problem with it. But she deserves your honesty. So are you sure you like her because of her, or do you like her because of me?"

Stephanie reached out, her hand passing through the bubble, her fingers curling, digging into the floor, dragging herself after them. All they had to do was look round. All they had to do was see her hand.

Fletcher took a deep breath. "No," he said. "I'm not sure."

Strong fingers closed round her ankle and Darquesse hauled Stephanie away from the edge of the bubble. She sobbed in pain and desperation as she was flipped on to her back, and Darquesse knelt over her, those hands round her throat, squeezing. The face she wore, Obloquy's, grinned down at her with a bloody mouth.

Stephanie scraped at those hands, dug her fingernails in, tried to claw at that face, tried to bend one of those fingers back, tried to do something, anything, to stay alive, to keep going, to see her family again, her mum and her dad and her baby sister, please Christ, she didn't want to die, she'd worked so hard, she'd done so much and come so far and she was a person now and she loved Fletcher and she loved her family and she loved this world that was getting darker and dimmer and the sound was muting and she couldn't hear any more or feel or touch and then it was gone and it was all black clouds of cold and then even they were gone and she

35

THE LOSS

Footsteps echoing in the empty corridors, they continued their lazy search for Stephanie until finally Valkyrie took out her phone.

Fletcher was being adorable today – he had a way of doing that, of dropping the grin and swaggering demeanour and allowing glimpses of the young man underneath to shine through. She liked him when he was honest, and it was in those moments that she was reminded of why she'd fallen for him in the first place. Those feelings had long since faded, of course, but what remained was a connection that would never be forgotten. They had been each other's firsts. That meant something. No matter what else happened, that meant something.

And as long as he didn't break Stephanie's heart, or as long as she didn't break his, it always would.

Stephanie's phone rang and rang, and just when Valkyrie was about to hang up, it was answered.

"Valkyrie."

Valkyrie frowned. "Hey. What are you doing answering Stephanie's phone?"

"Come down to the Accelerator Room," Skulduggery said. "Is Fletcher with you?"

"Yes."

"Bring him."

He hung up.

Fletcher waited for an explanation. Instead, Valkyrie took hold of his arm. "The Accelerator Room," she said.

He shrugged. When his shoulders lifted, they were in the middle of another brightly-lit corridor in the new Sanctuary. When they fell, they were standing beside the Accelerator.

The Engineer stood in the doorway, looking out. It turned. "Terribly sad," it said.

Valkyrie's frown deepened. She hurried past the robot. There was a group of people in the corridor outside, huddled round someone who'd collapsed. With Fletcher behind her, they approached, just as Reverie Synecdoche crouched down over the still body.

Valkyrie froze. Fletcher bumped into her. He was about to apologise when he saw what she was looking at – when he saw the burnished red trousers, the dark hair. The blood on the face. The grave expression worn by Synecdoche.

"Stephanie?" he said.

Skulduggery looked up, saw them. "Out," he said to the other people crowding around. "Everyone I didn't personally ask for, leave immediately."

There was a hesitation, and then the crowd dispersed, saving their murmurings for when they were upstairs. Valkyrie and Fletcher stayed where they were, staring.

On the ground behind Synecdoche was another body – a big man who looked like he'd also sustained a lot of damage. Obloquy.

Fletcher walked forward. He looked unsteady. "Is she OK?" he asked, like he hadn't any breath left in his body.

"I'm sorry," said Synecdoche. "There's nothing we could do."

Fletcher stayed very still, then suddenly fell sideways, hit the wall with his shoulder, slid to the floor. He never took his eyes off his girlfriend. "We were here," he whispered. "We were just here. Talking."

"He must have attacked her immediately after you left," Synecdoche said.

Stephanie's face had a look of terror etched on to it that was making Valkyrie feel sick. She'd put up a fight. A hell of a fight. It hadn't been enough.

"Obloquy," Valkyrie said. Speaking felt oddly clumsy. Her face felt numb. "He's a Sensitive."

Skulduggery nodded. "Darquesse possessed him. He's dead, too. His body is burnt out, just like the mortal woman this morning."

Synecdoche's hand began to glow, and she passed it over Stephanie's body. "Strangulation," she muttered, almost to herself. "Broken arm. Broken jaw. But asphyxiation is the probable cause of death." She moved Stephanie's body, ever so slightly, and a cloaking sphere rolled out from underneath.

It came to a stop against the wall. It *nokked* slightly.

"Oh, God," said Fletcher when he saw it. "She was here. She was being killed and we couldn't see her." He stood up, looked at Valkyrie. "You think she heard? You think she heard what we were saying?"

"I... I don't know," said Valkyrie.

Fletcher covered his face with his hands. Valkyrie went to comfort him, but he jerked away, and when she stepped towards him he vanished.

She looked back at Stephanie's body, tears spilling on to her cheeks. Skulduggery walked over, and he pulled her gently into him and hugged her, and she let herself cry.

36

JOINING THE STREAM

Skulduggery was barking orders and issuing commands and people were doing things with determination, with urgency, and all Valkyrie could do was stand there and be numb. Eventually she walked away, went wandering through the Sanctuary, found herself in the Dining Hall. She hadn't eaten in hours. She got a plate of food, sat at a table by herself, and realised she wasn't hungry. She pushed the plate to one side and rested her head on her arms.

The numb feeling didn't go away.

"I heard about your reflection."

Valkyrie raised her head and wiped her eyes. Solomon Wreath sat opposite her, laying his cane before him on the table and folding his hands over it. Wearing black, as usual. Being handsome, as usual. Looking concerned. Which was new.

"She was more than just a reflection," Valkyrie said.

He nodded. "So I heard. You have my condolences."

Valkyrie sniffed. "You're a Necromancer. Should you really be consoling me when someone dies? Isn't that against your rules?"

"Consoling someone has nothing to do with the person who has passed on, and everything to do with the people left behind."

"Remind me again what happens when we die?"

Wreath smiled. "In my religion? We re-enter the Great Stream of life and death. Stephanie will be unique, though. You and I, we would just flow back to where we came from. But from what I've heard, your reflection became whole, attained actual life, and as such she would probably be the only person to actually *add* to the stream, instead of merely replenishing it."

"Well, that's Stephanie," Valkyrie muttered. "Always has to be the awkward one."

"Has there been any sign as to where Darquesse is now?"

She shook her head. "Scuttled back into the shadows. Anyone with any psychic talents is being watched. If we keep denying her vessels, maybe we'll starve her out of it. God, I don't know. I'm too tired to think about all this. What are you doing here anyway?"

"I decided to pay you a visit when I heard you'd fallen prey to your darker nature."

"That was weeks ago."

"I was a little tied up. But I get back, finally, and you have it sorted without me. Almost."

"Yeah, almost."

"I notice you're not wearing your ring," he said. "Is that it, then? When your Surge comes, you've decided on Elemental magic?"

Valkyrie hesitated. "It's... more complicated than that. I lost my ring. Right now all my Necromancer powers are in a dinky little amulet... not that I can access them."

"The amulet has been taken from you?"

"My magic has been taken from me."

He frowned. "I'm sorry?"

"Darquesse *is* my magic," she said in a quiet voice. "When we separated, she took it all, left me with nothing."

Wreath sat back, staring at her. "I've... never heard of anything like that ever happening."

Valkyrie offered up a half-smile. "Yep. I'm unique."

"No magic *at all*?"

"Not a peep."

"How distressing."

"I'm pretty distressed, all right."

"So what are you going to do?"

"I don't know," she said. "I thought my life was going to be magic and monsters and fighting and... whatever. But if I don't have magic, then..."

"Does that mean a mortal life?" Wreath asked. She could have sworn he had paled slightly.

"It might." Over his shoulder, she saw Skulduggery walk in. "Oh, hell," she muttered.

Wreath's smile reappeared. "It's Skulduggery, isn't it?"

"Please don't annoy him."

"Me? When have I *ever* annoyed the great Skulduggery Pleasant?"

Skulduggery arrived at their table. Wreath smiled up at him. "Hello."

"I will shoot you in the eye," Skulduggery said.

Wreath glanced at Valkyrie. "I think I've annoyed him."

"What are you doing here, Wreath? How the hell did you get in the front door?"

"The Cleavers love me," Wreath said. "I told a few jokes, we had a few laughs, they invited me in. Also, I shadow-walked past them. I'm sure they won't mind, though."

Skulduggery motioned to someone behind Valkyrie. "And I'm sure you won't mind if I assign one of them to stick by your side while you're here."

"Not at all," said Wreath. "I love making new friends."

A Cleaver came over and Skulduggery nodded to Wreath and said, "Don't let him leave your sight. Valkyrie, if I may?"

She got up, followed him to a quiet corner. "We were just talking," she said.

"Wreath doesn't bother me," he responded. "I need you to go home. In all the confusion, we've let something very important slip our minds. You need to go home and claim the Sceptre."

"Me?" she asked, frowning. "No, you should be the one to control it. I don't even have any magic any more."

"That won't stop the Sceptre from binding itself to you."

"No, I mean, I don't have any magic, so what use am I to you, long term?"

He tilted his head. "Meaning what? You're thinking of walking away?"

"I don't... I don't know. I don't want to. I want to... I want to do this for the rest of my life. But without magic, I'll just be a hindrance."

Skulduggery folded his arms, and tapped one gloved finger against his chin. "Hmm."

"You see?"

"I think so."

Tears came to her eyes again. "So... you agree? I mean, you think I should... stop? With Stephanie gone, I could just go home and be normal and... You think I should do that?"

He sighed. "If you think it's best."

She went cold inside. "Really?"

He reached out, and flicked a finger against her forehead. "Don't be such an idiot."

"*Ow.*"

"Go home, claim the Sceptre. I'll call you in the morning."

"That *hurt.*"

"Good."

He turned.

"I just hope I can find it," she muttered.

He turned back, and looked at her for a long moment. "I'm sorry?"

"Stephanie hid it. We were arguing and... anyway, she hid it. It's not down a well, or anything. I mean, she didn't bury it. It's still in the house, somewhere. She was so set on giving it all up and having a normal... a normal..."

"Life," said Skulduggery.

"Yes." Valkyrie's throat felt very tight all of a sudden.

"Well," said Skulduggery, "you'd better look for it, hadn't you?"

Valkyrie nodded, but hesitated before walking away. "If you hear anything about where Darquesse has gone..."

He nodded to her. "I'll call you immediately. Now for God's sake, go home."

When she was done with everywhere else, she searched Alice's room. She ransacked every millimetre of the wardrobe, she checked under the changing table, she rooted through the big box of toys in the corner. She was about to leave when she glanced at the cot.

Stephanie wouldn't have put it anywhere near the cot. The risk of Alice accidentally touching the black crystal would be far too great. Never in a million years would Stephanie have put her – *their* – little sister in danger like that. But...

But Alice wouldn't have been in danger. Alice was an Edgley, the same as Valkyrie. She would be able to survive direct contact with the crystal. And the cot... who would think to search a baby's cot for the most powerful weapon in existence?

Valkyrie lifted the cot, checked underneath, then stood and lifted the blankets. The mattress bulged slightly. She took it up. The backpack containing the Sceptre was jammed down between the gaps. It was half open.

She yanked the bag free, pulled the Sceptre out, held it tightly. The ownership of the Sceptre should have passed to her upon contact. But she had a cold feeling in her belly. She looked around for something to disintegrate. Finally, she opened the window, pointed the Sceptre into the clouds and tried to fire.

Nothing happened.

It hadn't bonded to her. Meaning it had already bonded to someone else.

Valkyrie sank down on to her haunches and closed her eyes. "Oh, Alice..."

37

BROOKING NO ARGUMENT

he nightmare was vivid. Valkyrie woke with her heart thumping, her hands gripping the sheets. She lay very still, until she was sure it was just a dream. After a moment, tears came to her eyes, and she started crying.

Then her phone rang, and she cleared her throat and answered.

"Stephanie's body is gone."

Valkyrie sat up, her eyes wide and her bad dream forgotten. "*What?*"

"Doctor Synecdoche was found unconscious an hour ago," Skulduggery said. It sounded like he was walking. "She identified Vincent Foe as one of the people who assaulted her when she was checking the body into the morgue. That was at three o'clock this morning."

Valkyrie checked the time on her bedside clock. "The body's been gone for *six hours?*"

"Synecdoche is OK, no one else was injured, but there's no sign of the body and no sign of Foe."

Valkyrie threw the covers off and got out of bed, started gathering up her clothes. "Do we know why they did it? Obloquy was part of Foe's gang – is this revenge against Darquesse? Somehow?"

"I don't think so," said Skulduggery. "Very possibly, it's the opposite. I think they're working together."

She almost fell over putting her trousers on. "So Obloquy allowed himself to be possessed?"

"Maybe. Remember, Foe and his friends are their own peculiar brand of nihilists. They want the world to perish, themselves along with it. When they turned up last night, they were allowed in to view Obloquy's body, then they were forgotten about. They hung around until Stephanie's body was wheeled in, and they grabbed it and disappeared. We're trying to track them, but I don't like our chances, not with a six-hour head start on us."

Socks. Socks. Where the hell were her socks? "So if they're bringing Stephanie's body to Darquesse, what is she going to do with it? Can she inhabit it?"

"Unlikely," said Skulduggery. "Leaving aside the fact that she'd be trying to possess a corpse, Stephanie wasn't magical. She didn't share your genes – she wasn't descended from the Ancients. Even if, somehow, Darquesse managed to possess a dead body, Synecdoche estimates she'd burn it out within seconds. I don't know what her plan is, but we'll figure it out. There is one piece of good news, though. Creyfon Signate has found Mevolent's dimension. If we hide Ravel over there, we can lure Darquesse in any time we want."

"Well, that's just wonderful," Valkyrie said, finding her socks. "Especially seeing as how we don't have the Sceptre to use any more."

"Positive attitude, Valkyrie."

"Yeah, whatever. I'll drive over now and help you with..."

She paused, one sock on.

"Valkyrie?"

"I'll be in Roarhaven as soon as I can," she said, continuing to dress. "I just remembered something, and I want to check on it first."

"OK. Is the Sceptre stored away?"

She sat on the bed, jammed the phone between her jaw and shoulder, and pulled on her boots. "Yeah. Sorry about that. The most powerful weapon in the world and the only one who can use it is my twenty-month-old sister."

"Don't worry about it," Skulduggery said. "At least it hasn't fallen into enemy hands. That's the main thing. OK, I have to go. Don't do anything stupid."

He hung up before Valkyrie could summon any indignation, and she finished dressing and hurried downstairs. She hopped in her car while munching an apple. Not the most satisfying breakfast ever, but it'd have to do. She drove to Gordon's house.

When she walked into the study, the Echo Stone lit up in its cradle on the table, and Gordon Edgley appeared before her. Sort of. The image was faded.

Gordon frowned. "This is odd," he said.

Valkyrie tapped the stone, shifted it in its cradle, and the image became clearer.

"Looks like I need a service," Gordon said. "Hello, Stephanie. I hope you're here to bring me news of my niece."

Valkyrie frowned. "What do you...?" Her eyes widened. "Oh, Gordon! I am so sorry! I didn't come to see you! I didn't explain!"

"About what?"

"It's me. It's Valkyrie."

Gordon's frown deepened. "But... but Valkyrie became Darquesse..."

"I'm me again! I'm so sorry, I didn't get a chance to come and tell you."

A smile broke out across Gordon's features. "My favourite niece has returned to me! Tuesdays were always my favourite days!"

"It's Thursday."

"Closely followed by Thursdays! Valkyrie, it's so good to have you back! I bet there's a tale needs telling..."

"There is," she said, "but we're kind of pressed for time. Gordon, a lot has happened. Obviously. I'm back, Skulduggery's fine, the

Sceptre is at my house and it's bonded to Alice, but that's another story entirely, and Darquesse is... she's an untethered entity."

"Things *have* been happening."

"And Stephanie is... dead."

"Oh," said Gordon. "Oh, that's inconvenient."

"It's a little more than *inconvenient*, Gordon. She... she was a person. And she's dead."

"I'm sorry," said Gordon. "I didn't mean to be insensitive. But keep in mind that she did try to kill you."

"I remember."

"And she *did* kill poor Carol."

"I remember that, too. But all she wanted was a family. All she wanted was to be normal. And now she's dead and I... don't really know how to feel."

"Did you like her?"

"Yes, actually. She was... I liked her. She had a thing with Fletcher – as weird as that sounds. She liked him, he liked her..."

"That must have been very confusing for him," said Gordon.

"I'd say so. She was building up her own life. She had a boyfriend, for God's sake. Yes, it was my ex, but it still counts."

"How did she die?"

"Darquesse."

"Oh."

"And now the body's gone. We think Darquesse has it."

"Well, that won't last..." Gordon's voice faded and his image flickered.

Valkyrie tapped the stone again. "Hey. Gordon, hey, I can't hear you."

The image steadied. Gordon blinked. "Can you hear me now?"

"Yes."

"Oh, good. Now what was I saying? Oh, of course. The body won't last long. An entity of Darquesse's power can only survive in her original form – in this case, you. She'll burn out any temporary vessel within—"

"I know all that," said Valkyrie. "I don't think she's taken possession of Stephanie yet, though. She had someone else steal the body."

"Huh," said Gordon. "Do you know why?"

Valkyrie hesitated. "I'm wondering if, before she hops into Stephanie, she's going to try to do something to make sure she can possess her without burning her out."

"Do you have any idea what that might be?"

"When I was Darquesse, I spent a lot of time collecting information on how magic works. I can't remember most of it, and the stuff I do remember I don't understand any more. But I remember some things. Like a story about a pool in the caves below us, where ordinary weapons were turned into God-Killers."

Gordon nodded. "Yes, the Source Fountain, as it's called. Anathem Mire mentioned it in the journals he kept when he went exploring."

"Did he find this fountain?"

"He did indeed. Fascinating properties, that water, turning ordinary objects into magical items. Simply fascinating."

Valkyrie looked at him. It took him a moment. Then his eyes widened.

"Oh, my! You think Darquesse is going to put Stephanie's body in the fountain!"

"Why wouldn't she? Why wouldn't that work? It'd be like marinating the body in magical juices, right? And when it's done marinating, she takes it out and this non-magical body is suddenly capable of absorbing whatever magic is poured into it. That's how the fountain works, yeah? How long would it take? To marinate?"

"I don't know," said Gordon. "Hours, certainly."

"Darquesse has already had it for hours."

Gordon flickered, but his voice remained strong. "Then we have no time to waste. Whoever took the body will still have had to get it down there, past all those horribly nasty creatures. If we're lucky, that's delayed them. If we're really lucky, it's killed them. I suppose we'll soon find out."

"We?"

"Oh, yes," said Gordon, putting his hands on his hips. "You really think I'm letting you go down there without me? I've read Anathem Mire's journals from cover to cover. I know his maps, I know his notes, I know every short cut and every dead end off by heart. You're taking me down there, young lady, and I will brook no argument."

Valkyrie raised her eyebrows. "Fair enough."

"Excellent. So what do we do now?"

"I'm going to call Skulduggery."

"Splendid. I shall continue to stand here with my hands on my hips. Hurry along now. We have heroics to undertake."

38

ENEMY TERRITORY

There is a soft click, and the wall across the room opens up, and Stephanie peeks out.

A door. A hidden door. A panic room. She's had a panic room installed.

Xena pokes her head out, sniffs the air and growls, and Stephanie hurries forward, her finger to her lips. Xena pads after her, tail wagging with suppressed ferocity, hackles raised. Stephanie crouches at Danny's feet, fingers digging into the knotted rope. As she works, Danny can hear Gant and Jeremiah talking. Gant is telling Jeremiah to wash the blood off the tyre iron.

Stephanie hisses a curse. She can't get the knot untied. Instead, she rises, pulls at the rope around Danny's throat. It loosens instantly, and Stephanie hauls him to his feet, spins him in place. He falls backwards into her arms, and she starts pulling him towards the panic room, his heels dragging along the floorboards. They are halfway there when they hear the footsteps coming back.

Danny glances over his shoulder at the room. Too far. They'll never make it. Before he can whisper at Stephanie to drop him, she drops him. He falls heavily, jarring his injured arm, hears Stephanie whisper an order to Xena. The dog runs into the panic room, spins and waits for Stephanie to join her. Instead, Stephanie ducks behind the sofa, aims a fob at the panic room and the hidden door swings closed just as Cadaverous Gant walks in.

Danny stops squirming. Gant looks down at him, frowning slightly.

"Danny my boy," says Gant, "how am I ever supposed to trust you if, the moment I leave the room, you try to effect an escape, however ill-judged and badly executed it may be? What does that say about you, Danny? Does that say you cannot be trusted? I fear it might." Gant picked him up off the floor with easy strength. "Now please, return to your seat."

There is nothing Danny can say or do, and so he hops back to the sofa on his good leg, and sits. He has no way of telling if Stephanie is still hiding behind it.

Jeremiah enters, laying the tyre iron on a side table, and finishes drying his hands on a dishcloth. "Do you think she knows we're here yet?"

Gant goes to the window, looks out. "She knows. She's watching us right now. I can feel it."

"Then we should string Danny up outside," Jeremiah says. "Cut him a little. Let him bleed out. She'll have to come save him, won't she?"

"Will she?" Gant says. "What do we know of this girl, Jeremiah my old friend? The bare minimum, that's what. We have been unable to undertake our usual copious amounts of research and, as a result, we are at a distinct disadvantage. She might be walking away right this very moment, leaving the poor unfortunate Danny in the hands of two highly irritable killers."

"Should we go?" Jeremiah asks. "How about we kill Danny and leave him here for her to find? She'll think we've given up, killed him in frustration, and she'll come back and we'll grab her and kill her."

"A sound plan," Gant says, nodding, "and in normal circumstances, it might stand a chance of working. But something tells me Stephanie Edgley is not a girl to be taken in so easily. What were we told about her?"

"She's resourceful," Jeremiah says, almost grudgingly. "She is not to be underestimated."

"Indeed," says Gant. "We've done very well so far, Jeremiah. She was impossible to find and yet we found her. We are standing in her house. We have forced her to hide. These are things we should be proud of. But we cannot afford to be overconfident. Overconfidence is a killer. If she knows we are here, she may very well be gone already. If she intends to save Danny, however, she is unlikely to be caught out by any of our usual ruses."

"So what do we do?" Jeremiah asks.

Gant is silent for a moment. "We currently stand in enemy territory, Jeremiah. This is her house and, as we both know, one's house is one's domain. She knows it well. We don't know it at all. There may be two of us, but here *she* has the advantage. We need to take that away from her. Put Danny in the car."

"Where are we going?"

Gant turns to him. "Home, Jeremiah. If she wants to save him, she'll have to follow us."

"And if she doesn't?"

"We kill him, and start looking for her all over again. Put Danny in the car, there's a good lad."

Gant walks out, and Jeremiah kneels down to untie Danny's feet. When he's done, he attaches the piece of rope to Danny's bound wrists and uses it to pull him off the sofa. Then he walks out, tugging Danny along behind him.

Danny glances back and sees Stephanie, still crouched behind the sofa. Her face is tight, tense but expressionless. He catches her eye, but she doesn't move as Jeremiah yanks on the rope, tugging him from the room. Danny stumbles on his injured leg and Jeremiah walks on, not giving a damn if Danny falls and has to be dragged out. He manages to stay on his feet, however, and a moment later he's limping out into cold air and snow.

Jeremiah goes to the back of the Cadillac, opens the trunk. Danny gets his good leg under him and charges, aiming to ram him with his shoulder and hobble on, but Jeremiah steps out of the way and Danny slips and falls, coughs out a gurgle as the taut rope cuts off his air.

"Don't misbehave," says Jeremiah, looping the rope round his hand. "You really don't have much of a chance of emerging from all this alive, not if I'm being honest, but you'll live longer if you're good. Now hop in."

Jeremiah pulls on the rope and Danny is jerked to his feet. Standing, the pressure on his windpipe is lessened. He looks into the trunk.

"I don't have to get in there," he says. "I'll behave. I'll be good."

"In," says Jeremiah.

"I'll freeze."

"It's more comfortable than it looks. In."

"Jeremiah, please, you can let me go. I won't tell anyone, I swear."

"Me and Mr Gant are driving away," says Jeremiah. "You can either climb in the trunk right now without any more complaints, or I'll tie this rope to the tow bar and we'll drag you behind us the whole way home. It's a long way, Danny. You're gonna be a red smear on the road before we get fifty miles. Up to you."

Danny climbs in.

39

FINDING THE
FOUNTAIN

alkyrie led the way down the stone stairs, her torchlight pushing back the gloom with every step, Skulduggery behind her and Gordon drifting through solid objects with barely concealed delight. Cold down here. The ground flattened as much as it was able and they walked quietly through a tunnel carved into the rock, till the walls around them vanished and the ceiling disappeared and they emerged into the first of many caverns. Slivers of captured sunlight criss-crossed its length and breadth and Valkyrie put away her torch so that she could grip the tranquilliser gun with both hands. She liked the tranq gun. Skulduggery held its long-barrelled twin. He liked to keep them as a set.

Unspeaking, they took the tunnel to their right, walked on through patches of darkness and light. Around them, the skittering of tiny legs, of sharp claws on stone. The tunnel got narrower. The first hints of claustrophobia crowded at the edges of Valkyrie's mind. The first time she'd come down into these caves, they had been searching for the Sceptre of the Ancients. The second time, she'd been held captive by what was left of Anathem Mire. Her last trip down here had not been any happier. The memory of being dragged into a tightening hole, too narrow to even move her arms, slipped by her defences and she took a shallow breath. Then she caught herself, made her heart turn to steel, and she pushed the fear away from her. If Skulduggery noticed the slight hesitation in her step, he didn't say anything.

Something brushed by her foot and she jumped back, clenching her jaw to stifle the scream. There was more skittering now, these little creatures drawn to the magic that held Skulduggery together. Valkyrie forced herself onwards, swinging her feet to kick them out of her way. Her boot connected solidly with some living thing of bloated but yielding mass, then another that was made of sturdier stuff, and the others seemed to get the message – stay out of the way of the girl in black.

They went over a bridge that crossed a chasm, out of which belched steam and cold winds that tossed Valkyrie's hair and threatened to snatch her off the edge. Then they took a tunnel as wide and tall as a chapel but as long as a racetrack. The ground got slippery. Somewhere, the sound of running water, all gurgles and rush.

They got to another bridge, a narrower one, and Skulduggery stopped, his hand out, reading the air.

"Just once," he said, "I'd have liked things to have gone without a hitch."

On the other side, a creature emerged from the shadows.

The size of a small tiger, its grey and black fur was short and fine, and grew up around the protrusions of bones at its joints and around its skull.

"Mire had a name for these things," Gordon whispered. "He called them Phalanx Tigers. They were responsible for the death of more than one expedition member."

"Well, maybe this one's friendly," Skulduggery muttered.

The tiger padded slowly across the bridge, and Skulduggery went to meet it.

"Easy, girl," Valkyrie heard him say as he raised his gun. "Just stay very still..."

The tranq gun whispered just as the tiger growled, and the dart bounced off its rows of teeth. Its *multiple* rows of teeth.

Its jaws opened in two directions. Its mouth was vast. The teeth looked sharp, and they were everywhere. It leaped at Skulduggery and he dodged, barely. The tiger landed and spun without pause, and Skulduggery took off, lifted into the air. But the tiger jumped, collided with him and they went down. Those jaws closed over his forearm and Skulduggery yelled in pain. He used the air to roll himself sideways, took the tiger with him, and they rolled off the edge of the bridge and fell.

They dropped into the chasm. On the way down, the tiger released Skulduggery's arm.

The tiger continued to fall, as Skulduggery swooped up and landed beside Valkyrie.

She glared at him. "You let it fall."

He held up his torn sleeve. "It bit me."

"It was a tiger. You don't let tigers fall. They're endangered."

"Up there, yes," he said. "Down here, no. You also seem to be forgetting the fact that it bit me."

"Still," she said, scowling, "cruelty to animals."

"What about cruelty to me?" he asked, loading another dart into the gun.

"Um," said Gordon, "if I may? Mire called those things Phalanx Tigers for a reason. From the Latin, meaning battle line. They never hunt alone."

They looked back over the bridge, where a dozen Phalanx Tigers were grouping.

Skulduggery wrapped his arm round Valkyrie's waist. "We're getting out of here."

"Wait," said Gordon. "If you lead them away, your magic will make them follow you. They'll ignore Valkyrie."

Valkyrie frowned. "I don't want to be left behind."

"You don't have to be. Skulduggery, lead them east. You'll get to a narrow tunnel. Go through it, turn right. There'll be a gap they can't cross but you can. Take the only tunnel you see, and it will lead you straight to the other side of this bridge, where we will be waiting."

The tigers were crossing the bridge.

"Good plan," Skulduggery said. He handed her his gun. "Valkyrie, get behind that rock. I'll meet you over the other side."

Gordon disappeared into the Echo Stone and Valkyrie couldn't think of a good enough reason why she shouldn't do as suggested. She hurried away, got behind cover, and peeked out at Skulduggery, waving hands that were full of flames.

The tigers broke into a run, and the flames went out and Skulduggery started sprinting. They caught up to him easily so he started flying. He led them away.

Valkyrie peeked out. No stragglers. She emerged, and jogged to the bridge. She looked straight ahead as she crossed it. The bridge was the width of a country lane and she could walk a country lane without stepping on to the grass verge on either side. She should be able to do this without a problem. But there was no grass verge here. There was only a drop and darkness. She could feel her heartbeat.

She got to the other side, kept walking without looking back. Finally, she stopped, tucked one of the guns into her waistband and took out the Echo Stone. Gordon flickered into existence.

He looked around. "Did my plan work?"

"He led them away," Valkyrie said. "How long will it take him to get back to us?"

"A few minutes," Gordon said. "We could play I spy while we wait. I spy, with my little eye, something beginning with c."

"Caves," said Valkyrie.

"You're really good at this."

"We should probably conserve the stone's power."

"Ah, yes, I suppose you're right. Let me know when Skulduggery gets back."

He faded again, and she waited.

Gordon reappeared. He looked around. "Where's Skulduggery?"

"He hasn't got back yet," Valkyrie said. "It's been half an hour."

Gordon's smile dropped. "Oh. That's... that's unexpected."

"Are you sure your directions were accurate?"

"Absolutely," said Gordon. "There is no doubt in my mind. I suppose... I suppose there may have been a cave-in over the years, something that could have cut off the tunnel, but..."

"Do you think he's in trouble?"

Gordon was quiet for a moment. Then he brightened. "I know what's happened. If there was a cave-in, and there may very well have been, he probably went further on. The next tunnel he found would lead him on a more complicated route, but so long as he kept going in roughly the same direction, he'll rejoin us shortly. Not here, though – further on. Do you think it's wise for us to go on alone?"

Valkyrie glanced back at the bridge. "I don't know, but I don't like the idea of being here if those tigers decide to come back."

"A wise precaution," said Gordon. "Very well, then, straight on we go. Oh, I do love adventures. I like this one especially, because I don't have to walk anywhere."

Valkyrie grunted, and started walking.

She followed Gordon's directions, even when she was sure he was making it up as he went along. But every time he said they were about to encounter a particular feature, that feature duly appeared, so she stopped doubting him. He led her through the light and into the dark, and it was while she was in the shadows that her foot kicked something that clattered across the rock floor.

She flicked on the torch and crouched. The light glinted off empty shell casings.

"Hmm," said Gordon. "A lot of bullets were used here."

"Automatic weapons," Valkyrie said, scattering the casings

with her fingers. "High-powered rifles. Explosives, too, judging by the craters on the wall over there – looks like rocket-propelled grenades. All recent."

Gordon sounded impressed. "You're turning out to be quite the detective."

"For my fifteenth birthday, Skulduggery gave me a three-month course in ballistics. Some of it stuck." She stood up. "Whatever attacked them was driven away. Doesn't look like Foe or any of his friends were hurt."

"At least we're getting closer," said Gordon. "Let's keep going."

Valkyrie put her torch away and walked on for another ten minutes, and then Gordon said, "There's something up ahead."

She advanced cautiously, tranq gun in hand, but what at first appeared to be a person lying down turned out to be a bundle of old clothes. She nudged the bundle and it rattled.

"Bones?" Gordon asked.

"This looks like the suit Anathem Mire was wearing," Valkyrie said. She looked around. "This is familiar. Are we heading to that messed-up house of his?"

"We're heading to the fountain," said Gordon.

"Maybe he built his house near it."

Gordon nodded. "That would make sense. According to his journals, the fountain is in a cavern that the creatures here stay away from. If he were going to build a house of magic, that would be the only place to do it. But then what is his body doing all the way out here?"

"He promised he'd find me," Valkyrie said. "He was convinced I was to be his wife, or his queen or whatever, and I'd stay forever in that house that moved and changed and melted and... Anyway, I escaped, and when I was running off he was screaming at me, *I'll find you, I'll find you,* blah blah blah. I think he tried to do exactly that. I think he tried to follow."

"So his spirit returned to his body," said Gordon, "and he gave chase. But he was vulnerable from the moment he left that cavern, and the creatures here got him. Picked his bones clean."

Valkyrie grimaced. "Couldn't have happened to a nicer chap. Think his spirit is still around?"

"Without a form to inhabit, it would have dissipated long ago," Gordon said. "Pity. I would have liked him to sign his journals. They were surprisingly well written. Come along now, the fountain can't be far from here."

It wasn't. Five minutes later, Valkyrie stepped into a vast cavern. The last time she'd been here, there had been a replica of Gordon's house in the exact centre. Now there was nothing. The ground was flat and the cavern, as far as she could see, was empty.

"Can't see a fountain or a pool or even a puddle," she whispered.

Gordon pointed. "That way. We can't see it from here, but there should be an opening in the cavern wall that leads to the chamber with the fountain."

Valkyrie chewed her lip. "Darquesse could be in there. With Foe and Mercy and Samuel."

Gordon nodded. "We should wait for Skulduggery. Good idea. Better safe than sorry, after all."

She looked back, willing Skulduggery to appear. "No. We have to do something. If they're in there, maybe I can, I don't know, delay them."

"You have no magic."

"I have the tranq guns. And I have my shock stick. It's fully charged. If I'm lucky, I can take out three or four of them."

"I do not like this plan," said Gordon.

"It's barely a plan."

"That doesn't make it better. Please. Wait here. For all we know, Foe and his friends took a wrong turn somewhere and there's no one even in there."

Valkyrie stood. "Then there won't be any harm in taking a look."

She crept out and, when nothing bad happened immediately, she started jogging. Gordon was swept along with her.

"There," he whispered.

She saw it. A crack in the cavern wall. No more than a fissure. She reached it, breathing slightly more heavily, and listened. No sounds from within. No light in the dark.

She squeezed into the fissure.

Once she was past the opening, the tunnel widened slightly, enough for her to walk normally. The gloom lifted. There was light ahead. She slowed.

The tunnel opened into a cave the size of her back garden. Shafts of sunlight, squinting through the gaps in the ceiling, reflected off the Source Fountain, which was no wider than a paddling pool. Vincent Foe sat with his back against a rock. Samuel, the vampire who dressed like an accountant, lay asleep, head resting on a folded jacket of burnished red. Stephanie's jacket. Mercy was playing a game on her phone. The quiet little beeps were the only sound in the cave apart from the occasional gurgle of water.

Samuel turned his head and opened his eyes. "The girl is here."

Valkyrie bit back a curse, then decided *what the hell*, and stepped into plain view, tranq gun in hand. But instead of charging at her, Foe merely nodded, and Mercy didn't even look up from her game.

This was not what Valkyrie had expected.

"You took Stephanie's body," she said, after another few seconds of relative silence.

"Yeah," said Foe.

That was it. Nothing more.

Valkyrie inched forward, till she could see into the fountain. Stephanie's corpse lay in the water, still clad in her black T-shirt and burnished red trousers, weighed down with rocks.

Valkyrie stepped back again. "You're preparing the body for Darquesse."

271

Foe nodded. Then he got up, slowly, and stretched, like he'd been sitting there for hours. "What's the matter, Valkyrie? Not sure what to do without the Skeleton Detective around to issue orders?"

She narrowed her eyes. "How do you know he's not around?"

Mercy laughed, and finally put her phone away. "Because that was the plan, silly girl."

Valkyrie didn't like that. Oh, she didn't like that one little bit. She backed up further. "What plan? You were expecting us?"

Foe glanced at Mercy, who shrugged, and then he looked back at Valkyrie. "Expecting? Kind of. We knew there was a strong chance you'd come down here, but it wouldn't have been a total loss if you hadn't."

"Where is she? Where's Darquesse?"

Foe looked at Mercy. "Want to tell her?"

Mercy smiled. "Love to. Valkyrie, you've actually saved us quite a hazardous trip, so thank you. Were it not for you, we would have had to go back up ourselves to bring her down here. So, from the bottom of our hearts, thank you for saving us the trouble."

Valkyrie frowned. "But I didn't. I didn't bring anyone down with me."

"Well," Gordon said from behind her, "that's not *strictly* true."

40

FAMOUS LAST WORDS

Valkyrie felt herself go ashen-white with shock. "Gordon?"

Gordon's image flickered as he walked by her, to the edge of the pool. "I'm afraid not," he said, peering in. "You have to understand, the Echo Stone had all the properties I needed for a place to rest. I figured if it could store a personality then it could store a – what was it? Untethered entity? – even if it is just temporarily. Sort of like a summer home, you know? Mr Foe, you can take my body out now."

Foe and Mercy waded into the pool while Gordon turned back to Valkyrie. "So I moved some furniture around," Darquesse continued, "knocked down a few walls, redesigned the interior..."

"What did you do to Gordon?"

A wince. "Ah. Yes. Unfortunately, the previous tenant proved... uncooperative. So I had to evict him."

"What do you—?"

"I mean he's gone, Valkyrie. I wiped his consciousness before I moved in."

Valkyrie's insides went cold and plummeted. "You murdered him!"

"Gordon died six years ago. It's taken him this long to shut up about it, that's all."

Foe and Mercy laid Stephanie's body on the ground, then Foe took a Sunburst star from his jacket and placed it on her chest. It started to light up.

"Isn't that cool?" Gordon's image said. "Skulduggery used one on you. It kick-starts the brain as well as the heart, and the entire central nervous system along with it. Higher chance of a successful revival than a regular defibrillator, and this one has been tinkered with to increase its power. Just what I need."

The sigil on the device pulsed red.

"Wish me luck," came Gordon's voice, and then his image disappeared and the Echo Stone flashed with a bright light. All at once, Valkyrie's head was filled with a torturous shrieking and she ducked back, stumbling, as Foe and the others did the same.

Then the shrieking went away and Stephanie's body gasped and sat bolt upright.

"Wow," said Darquesse.

Foe took her hand, helped her to her feet. Darquesse wobbled unsteadily.

"Do not let go," she said. "Until my blood starts flowing properly I won't be the most agile person in the world. Oh, this feels good. This feels right." Samuel helped her into her jacket. "Valkyrie, how do I look? What do you think of this colour on me? I like it."

Valkyrie glared. "I'm going to kill you."

Darquesse smiled. Her wet hair hung down over a face that was already starting to get some colour back into it. "With a tranquilliser dart? No you're not. Even while I'm waiting for this body to adapt to the power levels I need it at, I'm still stronger and better than you. You really want to see which one of us would win in a fight? Really? Then let's go. I can't access most of my power yet, I can't even move properly, but I bet I can still rip your head off."

"There can be only one," Foe said, grinning.

Darquesse frowned at him. "I'm sure that's referencing something I'm too young to get, but either way, shut up. This is between me and—"

Valkyrie whirled, made to break for the tunnel, but only managed a few stumbling steps. Tanith stood before her, her lips black and her face riddled with black veins. Her sword was in her hand and her eyes were fixed on Valkyrie.

"You're not going anywhere," Darquesse said. "I know how much you hate being the hostage, so let's just call you the Emergency Negotiation Device and leave it as that. I'm sure Skulduggery, if he's even still alive, has a last-resort plan to take me down... but if I keep you with me, I think I'll do OK. Mercy, would you put some shackles on our guest and find her somewhere to sit?"

"My absolute pleasure," Mercy said, grinning. She came over, smacked the gun out of Valkyrie grip, and Tanith's sword came up, almost lazily, and cut Mercy's hand from her wrist.

Mercy stared at the stump and the blood and, before anyone could even react, Tanith took her head off.

Then she grabbed Valkyrie and pushed her into the tunnel.

"*Run.*"

Valkyrie ran. She ran from Vincent Foe's screams of rage and Samuel's echoing snarl, then she turned sideways, squeezed out through the fissure. She stuffed the Echo Stone into her jacket as she stumbled out into the cavern. Tanith wasn't following her.

She sprinted on.

She left the cavern and retraced her steps as well as she could, alternating between jogging and sprinting whenever her lungs and legs would allow it. But she got lost. It was inevitable, really. Only a matter of time.

She had to stop. She sank down, sat with her back to a tunnel wall. It had all gone wrong. They were supposed to have *won*, for God's sake. Darquesse had been reduced to an untethered entity.

She was a ghost. She should have been nothing more than an annoyance. A nuisance. How the hell had this happened?

Valkyrie took the stone from her jacket. "Oh, Gordon," she whispered.

The stone lit up weakly, and Gordon appeared before her.

She jumped to her feet. "Gordon! You're OK!"

Gordon's image flickered, and he frowned. "Hello? I can't... I can't see anyone. Who is that? Who's talking?"

She waved her hands in front of his face. "It's me, it's Valkyrie."

Relief washed over him, but he still wasn't looking at her. "Oh, thank God. Darquesse, she was here. She took over—"

"I know," said Valkyrie. "But she's gone now. Are you OK?"

"I'm fine," said Gordon. "Not a bother on me. The stone, on the other hand..."

"What? What's wrong with it?"

His eyes widened, and focused on her. "I can see! I can see you! I don't mind admitting, that was getting a little worrying. I could hear you, but couldn't see a single..." He looked around. "I know this. See that rock formation? See how it looks like an old man's face? Mire mentioned this tunnel. If you keep going straight, you'll come to a chasm. I don't know how you'd cross it, but the stairs to my house are on the other side. Maybe if you fashioned a rope bridge out of hair and spiderwebs..."

"What's wrong with the stone, Gordon?"

He hesitated. "It's in the process of being wiped clean. Darquesse thought she'd got rid of me, but I was just pushed into a little corner and I've been huddling here ever since. I thought that once she left things would get back to normal, but I seem to have misjudged her."

"But if the stone is wiped clean—"

"Then my personality will be wiped away. I fear I may only have moments left."

"No," said Valkyrie. "No, please, there must be something we can do."

"Darquesse altered the stone so dramatically that there's no way to stop the——"

He talked on in silence.

"I can't hear you!" Valkyrie shouted. "I can't hear you any more!"

Gordon frowned again. He pointed at the stone, mimed shaking it. Valkyrie grabbed it, did as she was told. She smacked it into her open palm a few times, and all at once the sound came back, just as Gordon was launching into the chorus of 'My Lovely Horse' from *Father Ted*.

"OK," she said, "I can hear you. Stop singing."

Gordon chuckled softly. "So how are you, my favourite niece? Finding yourself in trouble again, are we?"

"Gordon, I've already lost you once. Please don't make me go through that again."

"I am sorry, Valkyrie. It's not up to me. It's not up to you, either." He started to fade. "But look on the bright side," he said. "I get to have a second death scene."

Stupidly, she reached for him, and her hand passed through his shoulder. "Wait, just... let's think about this. What if we shut down the stone until I find someone to fix it? Can we do that?"

"Valkyrie," Gordon said, his voice distant, "there are some inevitabilities you can fight against. There are some you can't. This is one of the latter."

Tears ran down her face. "Please."

"Hush now," he said. His image was still fading. "All those stories I told when I babysat you, do you remember them? They all had one thing in common. Do you know what it was?"

She shook her head.

Gordon smiled. She could see the rock wall through his smile. "The brave princess, the brave mermaid, the brave rider on her brave horse, whatever you wanted the story to be about... the brave little girl always won in the end. That's what separates real life from the majority of the books I wrote – sometimes, the good guys do actually win."

"Please don't die."

"The mentor figure dying is all part of the hero's journey, my dear. Look at Obi-Wan Kenobi in *Star Wars*, or Gandalf the Grey in *Lord of the Rings*. How are you supposed to reach your full potential if you're coddled every step of the way?"

"I've been coddled?" asked Valkyrie. "When? Why wasn't I told this was the coddling part?"

His smiled widened. "You'll be fine without me."

"I really wanted Alice to meet you."

"And I wanted to meet her, too... And I wanted to talk to my brothers again, and Melissa... though not Beryl."

"She's not that bad any more."

"Please, let me have my pettiness."

Valkyrie wiped her eyes. "Sure."

Gordon was quiet for a moment. "It's funny," he said. "I always imagined my death would include a lot more coughing, and long... gaps... between... words... and maybe even a cheek to brush my finger against. Something dramatic like that. Maybe even enough to prompt the shedding of a few tears upon the telling. But would I be able to go through with it without even *attempting* to subvert the norm and skewer expectations?"

Valkyrie smiled despite her tears. "You have been known to skewer."

"That I have, my niece. That I have."

"If it makes you feel any better, you have me crying."

"It does make me feel better, actually." A look of alarm crossed his face. "Famous last words! I need to say my famous last words! They must be at least on a par with those uttered by James French or Dominique Bouhours, and maybe even as memorable as those uttered by Oscar Wilde on his deathbed. You must promise me that when you get out of here, you'll have these inscribed on my headstone, OK?"

"I promise."

"Good, thank you. I actually came up with these years ago. They've gone through a lot of rewrites, but that's what you get for being a writer, really. Always tinkering. Never satisfied. But finally, they're perfect, and I get to use them." He cleared his throat, puffed out his chest, opened his mouth, and then frowned. "No, wait—"

And then he disappeared.

Valkyrie stared at the space where he had just been standing. She shook the stone, smacked it into her palm again. But Gordon didn't reappear. The stone was wiped. Her uncle was gone.

41

HERE BE DRAGONS

Valkyrie emerged from the tunnel. She recognised this place, this chasm. On the opposite side, she had run from a dog-faced monster, had leaped off the edge, grabbed the vines that had turned out not to be vines at all but tentacles, and had been pulled upwards towards the gaping mouth of a monstrous, gelatinous *thing*. Now Skulduggery hung there, those tentacles wrapped round his arms and upper body, suspending him over the bottomless pit like he was on some invisible crucifix. His jacket was torn and his hat was missing. His head was down. Apart from the swaying, he did not move.

"Skulduggery," she called, her voice guarded. He didn't look up.

She stepped right to the edge, keeping her eyes fixed ahead of her, not allowing them to peer down into the darkness. Every few moments, the tentacles, all of them, would tremble slightly. There was a rhythm at work here, a gentle heartbeat, and suddenly Valkyrie understood why Skulduggery wasn't being carried upwards. The thing that had once dragged her towards its long and many teeth had decided it would be better nourished by the magic it could drain from Skulduggery than by whatever nutrients it could scavenge by munching his bones. Valkyrie didn't know how much magic could be sucked out before he fell apart, but she assumed that her bad luck would hold and that time was running out. She backed up, away from the edge, took a breath, then broke into a sprint, got a toe to the edge and leaped.

She crashed into Skulduggery, arms wrapping round his waist as they swung back from the impact. She felt the emptiness beneath his clothes but held on, trusting in the quality of Ghastly Bespoke's work to save her life once again. They swung now the other way, back over the chasm, a pendulum of two. It was all Valkyrie could do to stay clinging on. She closed her eyes and gripped her own wrist, and eventually the swinging slowed and lost its momentum. When they were more or less hanging there, Valkyrie looked up for the first time, and wondered what the hell she was supposed to do now.

"Hey," she said. "Hey, wake up. Hey!"

He had no eyes to open, so it was impossible to tell if he were awake or not. She shook him again, then hung on as they swayed.

"What're you doing?" he muttered.

"Skulduggery! Thank God! Are you OK? Skulduggery? Hey, pay attention!"

His head moved, ever so slightly. "Right, yes. Sorry. What?"

"We're hanging over a bottomless pit of death. You're going to have to fly us to safety. Can you do that?"

"Sure," he murmured. He turned his head, looked at the tentacle wrapped round his upper arm. "That's new."

"I think it's feeding on your magic."

He nodded. "Get me free. Then I'll fly."

"You're sure? You won't need time to recover or anything?"

"No. Just... just get me free."

"OK. Listen, you don't happen to have a knife on you, do you? No? Hello? OK, I'm going to... I'm going to have to climb up, all right? I can get you free from up there, but you have to stay awake. Otherwise you'll just fall. OK? Skulduggery?"

"Yes," he murmured.

"Stay awake," said Valkyrie, and wrapped her right arm round his shoulder. She pulled herself up, clambering over him. He didn't notice. Her hand closed round one of the tentacles. The first time she'd found herself here the tentacles had been cold and slippery. Now they were warm and dry. The nourishment was doing them good.

Valkyrie twisted her hand round the tentacle and held on. Then she reached up with her other hand, grabbed another tentacle. Twisted, and held. Like this, she climbed, grabbing and twisting and holding. Her arms were already tired from hanging on to Skulduggery, but she kept going. It was slow. It got painful. She clamped her legs round the tentacles, the same way she'd seen in movies. It stopped her swaying too much.

She got halfway up and stopped to rest. Her fingers were burning from gripping so tight. Her arms and legs were on fire. Sweat dripped along her spine. She glanced down, then immediately closed her eyes as fear seized her heart and fright burst through her veins. No. Looking down was bad.

She opened her eyes again, but looked up, into the gloom overhead. "Hey!" she shouted. "You awake down there?"

Her voice echoed, but Skulduggery didn't answer.

Gritting her teeth, Valkyrie kept climbing.

Above her, the tentacles disappeared over a ledge. The last time she was up here, she'd been dragged over. She'd tried to pull away, but those tentacles had sought her out, latched on to her. They only loosened when she'd stopped struggling. She prepared herself for what was to come, and reached up, got her forearm over the ledge.

She hauled herself over.

The thing, whatever it was, was right where she'd left it. A grey, sickly mass – like a giant jellyfish with a huge, gaping maw. The only solid parts of it were those teeth. It was different now, though. It looked... healthier, somehow. The magic it was draining from Skulduggery was good for its complexion.

Valkyrie stood up. Her legs trembled. Her arms felt weak. She could barely close her hands. But the thing wasn't paying her any attention. Whether it was too preoccupied with Skulduggery, or whether it just didn't have any interest in non-magical prey, she didn't know. She didn't particularly care. Six years ago, she had cut through those tentacles with a heavy, sharp rock. She found that rock again, held it in her hand.

Four tentacles held Skulduggery. Only four. She moved back towards the ledge, crouching, careful not to look over the side. She did her best to group the tentacles together. She managed to push them a little closer. The blob behind her didn't seem to mind.

It soon would.

She flexed her fingers to get some feeling back. Then she held the sharpened edge of the rock over the thickest and juiciest tentacle. She wet her lips as she raised her hand. Then she smashed it down.

Thick green fluid burst from the wound, and Valkyrie started to saw the rock side to side as the tentacles convulsed. She kept hold of the remaining three, started cutting through, glancing behind her. More tentacles were springing from the blob's centre, searching blindly for whatever was causing it pain. Valkyrie cut faster, feeling the variation in resistance, the different textures, from rubbery to wet to sticky and back to rubbery again, and then she was through, and she looked over the edge and saw Skulduggery dropping.

Not flying. Dropping.

She looked back. The tentacles thrashed in their search. Dozens of them. Too many to dodge, to cut through, to hope they'd miss her. She dropped the rock, turned to the ledge, put her hands over her face and jumped.

Valkyrie fell.

She started screaming.

She fell past the point where Skulduggery had been hanging and plummeted into the chasm.

She twisted. The wind whipped at her hair. Her body turned. Still she screamed.

The chasm widened. She could no longer see the walls on either side. She fell through mist and darkness.

She looked down. Saw something. She blurred past it.

"Skulduggery!" she screamed, twisting again to look upwards. The thing was a dot now, rapidly retreating into the distance. No. It was getting closer. It was falling. No. Flying.

Skulduggery streaked after her.

She reached up, but he didn't take her hand. He stopped flying and started falling alongside her. He had his arms out, his hands moving.

The air began to buffet them both.

Their fall slowed. When he wasn't going to snap her in two just by laying a finger on her, Skulduggery pulled her close to him and they came to a gradual stop.

They hovered there, and she clung to him. Buried her head in his chest.

"Are you OK?" he asked softly.

She nodded. Suddenly realised how cold it was down here. Cold and dark.

"Darquesse?" he asked.

"Free," Valkyrie said, her voice trembling. "In Stephanie's body. We brought her down with us."

He nodded. "She was Gordon. I figured as much, when his directions led me to a dead end."

"He's gone," she said. "The Echo Stone is empty."

"Oh, Valkyrie. I'm so sorry."

She nodded. "Is there a reason we're floating?"

"Just have to get my strength back," he said. "Shouldn't be too long. Another few moments."

She looked down. All she could see was darkness below, so it wasn't vertigo that struck her. It was the open, yearning emptiness. It was the quiet. The awful, empty quiet. If he hadn't caught her, she'd still be falling even now. She doubted she'd have ever stopped.

Valkyrie frowned. "Huh."

"What is it?" Skulduggery asked.

"My eyes are playing tricks on me," she said. "It looks like... light down there."

They shifted slightly so that he could look down, too. Below them, in the deep and distant dark, a red light burned weakly.

"I see it," said Skulduggery.

"Wasn't there a second ago. Hey. Is it... is it getting brighter?"

Skulduggery tilted his head. "It's definitely getting bigger."

Her eyes widened. "It's getting closer."

"I have my strength back now," he said, and they started to rise.

"You might want to go a tiny bit faster," Valkyrie said, and suddenly there was a huge shape below them, unimaginably vast, filling the chasm with its darkness. She saw eyes, glittering and yellow, and that red light was flame that burned in a throat and reflected off teeth, and there was the sound of great wings beating. A rush of air boosted their ascent and Skulduggery rode that wave and they shot upwards as a screech, a terrible screech of inhuman power, blasted Valkyrie's eardrums and made her bones rattle.

They flew up, out of the chasm, and through the tunnel. Their feet touched down at a run and they kept running up the stairs, and into the cellar, and the floor closed up behind them and Valkyrie led the way up into Gordon's house. She ran into the living room, spun, her hair wild and her eyes wilder.

"Did you see that? Did you see that?" She couldn't help it – an excited laugh burst from her lips. "That was a dragon! A dragon!"

Skulduggery shook his head. "A dragon."

"There be dragons!" Valkyrie yelled, spinning in a circle before collapsing on to the couch. Immediately, she was up again, bounding to her feet like she was on a spring. "This is amazing! That is fantastic! It was huge! It was massive! What if it gets free? Do you think it'll get free? Do you think I could ride it?"

Skulduggery fixed his tie and buttoned his jacket. "I'm sorry?"

"Ride it. Put a saddle on it and ride it. Wouldn't that be cool? Wouldn't that be the best thing to ever happen ever in the world?"

"Probably not, all things considered."

"Don't you want me to ride a dragon?"

"It would eat you," said Skulduggery.

"Not necessarily. I could make friends with it. It could be my pet. Or I could be its pet, or whatever. Did you know there were dragons? Did you know there were dragons and you kept it from me?"

"I didn't know. I thought... I didn't think they even existed. They're in stories, in legends, and we have Dragon Eye jewels and dragon thread and dragon this and that, but no one ever seriously thought these things came from actual dragons. That would have been... ridiculous."

Valkyrie stopped her twirling, and the smile faded. "I wish Gordon were around. He'd have loved this."

The house was quiet.

She pulled the tranq gun from her waistband. "Here."

"Ah," he said, "thank you. And the other?"

"I kind of lost it."

"You lost it?"

"Kind of," said Valkyrie.

"They're a set of two."

"Now it's a set of one."

"That's not really a set, though."

"I'm really sorry."

"That's OK," he said tenderly. "You've been through a lot."

She nodded. Moments passed. Her head felt heavy. So did her heart. Then she thought about the dragon and her heart

286

lifted. She spun. "Do you think it'll try to escape or will it go back down into the pit?"

"I don't know," Skulduggery said. "I know absolutely nothing about dragons. I suppose there's no reason to think it's going to find a way out now, if it hasn't before. We woke it from its slumber. Hopefully, it'll go back to sleep."

Valkyrie grinned. "Dragons."

42

BRAINSTORM

China's voice filled the car. "Where is Darquesse now?"

Skulduggery overtook a slow-moving tractor and guided the Bentley round a hairpin bend. "We don't know," he said. "There are dozens of hidden entrances to those caves. She could be anywhere."

There was an edge to China's words that had not been there before. "How long before she's at full strength?"

"Days, if we're lucky. China, we need to get Ravel ready to shunt. We're out of time."

"Agreed," said China. "Get back here now."

The call disconnected, and Skulduggery looked at Valkyrie.

She kept staring out of the window. She was fully aware of how hyper she'd been, and now how quiet she'd become. But the mood had settled over her like she was in the shade of some great monolith, and there had been nothing she could do to stop it.

She'd returned the Echo Stone to its cradle. She had hoped a simple recharge would bring Gordon back. It hadn't. The stone was empty. There was no coming back from that.

Her eyes were tired. They stung, and wanted to close. She longed to go to bed, to curl up under the covers and never come out.

"She's going to win," she muttered.

"Nonsense," Skulduggery said.

"We can't stop her. You know we can't."

"She said it herself, it's going to take some time for her new body to acclimatise to her power. She's in a weakened state. What's the first thing I taught you about getting into a fight?"

"Never fight on their terms."

"And this is exactly what I meant. In a few days, she'll be back to full strength and ready for us. So we don't give her those few days. We fight her when she's not ready. Are you with me?"

"I suppose."

"That doesn't sound very enthusiastic."

"I'm really not in the mood."

He jammed his foot on the brake.

"Jesus!" Valkyrie said, bracing herself as the Bentley screeched to a halt. She stared at him. "What the hell did you do that for?"

He tilted his head. "I lost my hat," he said. "You haven't once asked what happened to it. I'll tell you what happened to it. I lost it. As we speak, it's probably making its way down the digestive tract of a particularly fashion-conscious Phalanx Tiger. I await your condolences."

"Uh... I'm sorry about your hat."

He leaned closer. "Why? It's only a hat. It's a garment, made specifically for the head. True, my dear friend Ghastly Bespoke made it just for me, but it's still only a hat, and I have many more that he made for me."

Valkyrie frowned. "Right. What's your point?"

"Why do I need a point? I mentioned it simply because it's something that happened. But things happen all the time. Some of them are good things. Exciting things. Things like seeing a dragon. Things like Tanith covering your escape. Other things are bad things. Distressing things. Things like losing a hat your friend made for you. Or losing the last echoes of your uncle.

Things happen, Valkyrie, but life carries on regardless of how we feel."

"Are you trying to cheer me up? Somehow?"

"You don't need to be cheered up. You just have a decision to make. Allow yourself to wallow in misfortune..."

"Or?"

He shrugged. "Or don't."

They started driving again.

"That was your pep talk?" she asked.

"Sort of. I also wanted to talk about my hat. But mostly it was a pep talk. Did it work? Are you pepped? I could give you another one, if you like. About a torn jacket."

She sighed. "The first one was fine, thank you. What's that song you're always whistling? 'Accentuate the Positive'?"

"I have literally whistled that *once* since you've known me."

"Whatever. So let's do that." She clapped her hands, sat up straighter, forced herself out of her black mood. "OK then, so in this new spirit of positivity, let's brainstorm. Let's kick around some ideas. How will we defeat Darquesse?"

"The God-Killer weapons."

"OK, yes, good. Anything else?"

"I've been thinking about this," Skulduggery said, "and I've come to the conclusion that we should bring Melancholia out of her coma."

"That's it!" said Valkyrie, clapping her hands again. "See, *that's* the kind of brainstorming we need! Now do you have any ideas that are actually useful? Because obviously waking up Melancholia is a truly dreadful one."

Skulduggery said nothing.

"Oh, come on," said Valkyrie. "We can't wake her up. She's the Death Bringer. Sure, when you get to know her, she's not that bad, but she's unhinged and she tried to kill us. Really? Waking her up is your best idea? Something tells me she's not a morning person."

"We're going to need her as reinforcements."

"So who's going to convince her to help us?"

"Well... you're probably the closest thing she has to a friend."

"That's the saddest thing I ever heard."

"I know," said Skulduggery. "I know."

43

SHUNTING RAVEL

Erskine Ravel screamed.

The doctors were giving him foul-smelling liquids to drink with his meals, to make sure he didn't rupture his vocal cords. He did a lot of screaming. He did a lot of screaming and sweating and crying and begging. Twenty-three hours of agony a day. This was what it looked like.

Valkyrie felt no pity.

She watched the Cleavers drag him into the room. Dressed in prison orange with his hands shackled before him, he writhed and kicked, but they had no trouble holding on. He needed a shave and a haircut.

Creyfon Signate walked over. Unlike Ravel, he no longer wore his jumpsuit. He was now a free man, dressed in a free man's clothes. More than that, he was a free man with a purpose. "I've already shunted over a few times," he told them. "It should be fine. The Sanctuary in the other dimension is a ruin, but this room is intact with an easy climb to the surface. No one around – that I could see anyway."

Skulduggery nodded. "The Cleavers will protect you if anyone turns up with bad intentions. Return here every four hours and we'll brief you on the situation. We're sending a doctor with you to monitor his condition, but the moment you shunt, Ravel's pain should disappear. This means you cannot let your guard down. Understand?"

"I can handle it."

"Ravel was a Dead Man," Skulduggery said. "He's one of the most dangerous individuals I've ever known. Do not take your eyes off him."

Signate nodded, suitably chastised. "Yes, sir."

"Avoid contact with the natives. The world you're shunting into is run by Mevolent. The mortals are his slaves. The Resistance is crumbling. It is not a place you want to find yourself for any length of time."

"Yes, sir."

"China is working on something that will hide Ravel from Darquesse's view once he's back. When you return, you'll shunt him directly to this room. If she senses his presence before we're ready, Darquesse will come straight for him."

"You can count on me."

"Good luck, Mr Signate."

Signate gave them a small bow, and rejoined his group – eight Cleavers, two sorcerers, one doctor, Signate himself and Erskine Ravel.

"I quite like the fact that he's in pain," Valkyrie said.

"Me too," said Skulduggery.

"You're sure the pain will end once they shunt?"

"It should."

"Damn."

"Damn indeed."

Signate closed his eyes. The group began to flicker.

A moment later, they were gone.

Valkyrie sighed, and followed Skulduggery out. "Any word on when Melancholia will be awake?"

"Tomorrow afternoon," he answered. "So you get to spend the night at home, and I get to change into another suit. One with a hat."

"All your suits have hats."

"Not this one," he said quietly. "Not any more."

She glanced at him. "What do you think Darquesse will do to Tanith? I mean... will it be bad?"

"I don't know. Sincerely. Darquesse has proven herself to be most unpredictable. As has Tanith, for that matter. We can only hope."

"I don't like hoping," Valkyrie said. "I prefer knowing."

They crossed into warmer, busier corridors, and walked up to Saracen Rue talking with Gracious O'Callahan and Donegan Bane.

Saracen saw them coming. His usual smile was absent. "China told us," he said. "Just when we think we're in the lead..."

"How is the search for the Remnants going?" Skulduggery asked.

"Badly," said Gracious. "Dexter and Dai know our strategies. We still have a few tricks up our sleeves – you don't get to be Monster Hunters without being incredibly sneaky – but they've vanished into the woodwork again."

"And we're not as mobile as we'd like," Saracen added. "Any sign of Fletcher?"

Valkyrie shook her head. "We don't know where he is. He's not answering."

"We messed up." Saracen rubbed a knuckle against his forehead like he was fighting off a headache. "We went in unprepared and we paid for it. We went looking for the usual signs of violence and unrest. We expected the Remnants to have taken hosts. But they haven't. There have only been a few. A handful. I've never seen them exhibit this kind of behaviour before."

Donegan nodded. "It's almost... disciplined."

"Darquesse may have something special in mind for them," Skulduggery said. "But as for right now, if they're not causing havoc, let's take the opportunity to regroup and restrategise. We have other things that need our attention."

Valkyrie watched Saracen. His jaw was tight.

"Has Ravel gone?" he asked.

Skulduggery looked at him. "Yes. If we're right about that psychic link, Darquesse should be aware that he's fallen off the grid. She'll come looking for him, but not yet. She has to build up her strength first. Our task is to build up our strength faster. We need the city's shield ready to activate. We need the fortifications secure. We need people in place. Once that's done, we'll bring Ravel back. Darquesse should sense him again, and hopefully she'll be compelled to re-establish that pain link. But she'll have to do that in person."

"You're expecting her to just walk into Roarhaven before she's at full strength?" said Saracen.

"Yes."

"You expect her to do this because of her hatred for Ravel."

"Among other things, yes."

"OK then. But can you do me a favour? Can we spring the trap *after* she re-establishes that pain link?"

"We'll take what we can get," Skulduggery said, his voice grim.

Saracen nodded, walked away.

Valkyrie looked at Gracious and Donegan. "We saw a dragon," she said excitedly.

They took a moment to stare at her.

"What?" said Donegan.

"A dragon," she said. "A real one. It lives in the caves. We saw it, didn't we, Skulduggery?"

"We saw it," Skulduggery said, almost reluctantly.

Gracious's eyes nearly bugged out of his head. "Seriously? You seriously saw a dragon? A proper dragon?"

"It was huge," Valkyrie said, grinning. "Bigger than anything. It had wings, and I think it breathed fire."

"A fire-breathing dragon!" Gracious said, clinging to Donegan's arm. "We must see it! Where is it?"

"Down this bottomless pit."

"Damn it! I hate bottomless pits! I was trapped down a bottomless pit for *days* once."

"That wasn't bottomless," Donegan said.

"It felt bottomless."

"You were at the bottom."

"Well, it was a long way down."

"This pit really was bottomless," Valkyrie said. "I think it was anyway."

"A fire-breathing dragon living in a bottomless pit," Gracious said happily. "We should give it a name. All great dragons have names. Smaug. Drogon. Fin Fang Foom. Puff. They all have names."

"Gordon," said Valkyrie.

"Gordon the dragon?"

"He would have loved that."

Gracious nodded. "Yeah. That's nice. But how about Destructorface?"

"Gordon it is," said Donegan, leading Gracious away.

"Spreading joy is a special gift in dark times," Skulduggery said, his hand on Valkyrie's shoulder. "And you have made those two the happiest Monster Hunters in the world."

"I do what I can."

"Come on," he said. "Let everyone else worry and work for the next few hours. You deserve a night off."

44

A BETTER PERSON

Smell, someone had once told Valkyrie, was the single most powerful trigger of memories. Somewhat ironically, she didn't remember who'd told her that, or why, or where she was when she was told, though she had no reason to doubt the truth of it. But when she woke from her bad dream and walked down the stairs of the house she'd grown up in and the smell of roast chicken was waiting for her, she wasn't transported back to one particular time or one particular occasion. Instead, memory piled upon memory to form an indistinct sense of warmth and belonging and love and home, and a smile grew up from within her so that when she reached the kitchen she was beaming.

Her mother was at the table, eyes fixed on the laptop while her dad hovered over her shoulder, pointing at the screen.

"Click that," he said. "That looks important. We should click it and see what it does."

Her mum batted his hand away. "Go on, shoo. You're not allowed near this."

"But it's mine."

"Hiya," Valkyrie said, crossing straight to the oven.

"Good morning, sleepyhead," her mum said. "Lunch will be another half an hour or so."

Valkyrie opened the oven, inhaled the steam that billowed out, and closed it again, her mouth watering. "Oh, I'm starving," she said. "What are you doing?"

"Your father has a mission," her mum said, sighing.

Her dad stood straighter. "That USB thing. It's a video. We're downloading something that'll let us play it. Well, we think we are. We might not be. To be honest, we haven't a clue what we're doing."

"I know what I'm doing," her mum said, a little annoyed.

"Ah, a USB," Valkyrie said. "How quaint. Half an hour, you say? I'll be right back."

"Leaving us so soon?" her mum asked.

"Just going to pop over to Fergus and Beryl's and say hi."

Her parents stared at her.

"Why?" they both said at the same time.

Valkyrie laughed. "You're funny."

As she left the house, she heard her dad say, "No, seriously, why?"

She took the short cut across the beach. The tide was out and the sky was grey. A few joggers on the sand. Some people walking their dogs. She didn't know why she wanted to see her aunt and uncle. Some part of her just wanted to talk to them, to connect with them in some way. It was probably because of Gordon. She'd lost her favourite uncle for the second time and she was, what? She was grieving?

Valkyrie stopped walking. She was grieving.

Tears came to her eyes, but she wiped them away angrily. No. No crying. She'd cried enough. She'd deal with her loss later, when she had the luxury of time. She'd deal with it the same way she was going to deal with the guilt she felt over the things she'd done as Darquesse. She'd deal with it alone, without anyone around to see it. She walked on.

When she got to Fergus and Beryl's house, the car was gone. She thought about just turning round and going home, but knocked on the door anyway, and Carol's reflection answered.

"Hello, Stephanie."

Valkyrie looked at it. "Hi. Are Fergus or Beryl home?"

"I'm afraid not."

"Crystal?"

"She's out. With her boyfriend. She has a boyfriend now. He doesn't treat her very well."

"I know what you are."

Carol's reflection looked at her without expression. "What do you mean?"

"You're not her. You're not Carol. You're her reflection. The real Carol is dead."

"And you're Darquesse."

"No. I'm not."

"Stephanie came over and told me what happened. Valkyrie allowed you to take over and now you're free. Valkyrie's gone and Stephanie has assumed her rightful place as daughter and sister."

Despite herself, Valkyrie smiled. "Is that what she said? Her rightful place? Yeah, that sounds like her. What was the last thing Stephanie told you?"

"She came over about two weeks ago," Carol's reflection said. "She told me she's been helping Skulduggery Pleasant track you down. She couldn't wait for it to be over. Are you going to kill us now?"

"No. God, no. I'm not going to kill anyone. I'm not Darquesse. I'm me again, I'm Valkyrie. But Stephanie... she died."

The reflection's expression didn't change. "Oh. I'm very sorry for your loss."

"Yeah, you look it."

"Since you know I'm not really Carol, I'm not bothering to appear convincing. If you'd rather I respond with appropriate emotions—"

"No," Valkyrie said quickly. "No acting. This is fine."

"OK. Then if you're not here to kill me, why are you here?"

"I'm not really sure," Valkyrie said. "I wanted to see Fergus. Don't really know what I'd have said to him, but... and I suppose I wanted to check up on you, now that Stephanie isn't able to any more. I wanted to see what you're like. How do you feel?"

"I don't feel. All my emotions are simulated."

"And what do you think of your family?"

"Are you asking what Carol thinks of her family or what this *representation* of Carol thinks of her family? Because I hold no opinion."

It sounded so familiar. It sounded just like Valkyrie's own reflection had, way back at the start. "So you don't see yourself as an improvement on the real Carol?"

"The only advantage I have over Carol is that she is dead and I am not."

"So what are your plans?"

"Stephanie told me what my role is," the reflection said. "I'm to take over as Carol until my family is dead. I will age with them, I will follow the course of Carol's life as it unfolds before me. I will get a job, probably get married and start a family of my own, and hopefully make my parents proud."

"*Can* you start a family?"

"I am flesh and blood. There's no reason why not."

"And what about Crystal?"

"Stephanie told me to avoid Crystal for the time being. As Carol's twin, she's more likely to spot the flaws in my performance. When enough time has passed, I will work to establish a sisterly bond. She'll notice some changes, but I'm confident these will be overlooked."

"And what about this boyfriend of hers?"

"Stephanie advised me on that also. She told me I'm my sister's protector. If Crystal's boyfriend damages her, emotionally or physically, I am to damage him physically in an appropriate, measured response."

"Huh," Valkyrie said. "Seems like you've got everything sorted."

"I know my role."

"How is Crystal doing?"

"At home, she's withdrawn. Sullen. The gap between us is affecting her, which is unfortunate but necessary. Apart from her boyfriend, she's making good friends, and spending more time out of the house. She's becoming quite sociable."

"Good," said Valkyrie. "That's... that's actually good. And Beryl and Fergus?"

"Mum is sad," Carol's reflection said. "But she's always been sad. She just disguised it with a sharp tongue. She thought money would make things better, but it hasn't. Dad is worried about her. I think he's worried about a lot of things. Stephanie told me that one of my jobs is to make their lives better by pretending they've been good parents. That is what I plan to do."

"OK," said Valkyrie. "Well, I'll... I'll head off, then."

"Very well," said the reflection, and went to close the door.

"Wait," said Valkyrie. "Listen. My reflection malfunctioned. She did some terrible things. But in the end... in the end, she'd changed. She had become a good person. I'd like you to become a good person."

"Very well."

Valkyrie stepped back. "OK," she said. "See you around."

The reflection gave a convincing smile, and closed the door. Valkyrie got to the top of the road and a car passed her. Fergus and Beryl, returning home. She waved, and kept going.

She hadn't walked through Haggard in months. It felt nice. It felt normal. It was cold, and it looked like rain, but her childhood had been spent here, on these streets, on that beach, running and playing and chatting and laughing. It had been a normal life. It hadn't been boring, as she had once thought. It hadn't been drab. It had just been normal. Haggard was her own personal sanctuary, the place she could go now and be the person she used to be. Here, nobody knew her secret. Here, she could be Stephanie Edgley again.

She got back to her house and walked into the kitchen. Her parents were sitting at the table, staring at the laptop.

She grinned. "You get it working?"

At the sound of her voice, they both looked up, startled. Afraid. Her eyes flickered to the screen. The video playing was of a war zone. Screams and shouts and a shaking camera. And there, in full view and perfect focus, was Stephanie Edgley, firing black lightning from the Sceptre of the Ancients.

45

A BRUTAL ACT OF KINDNESS

Darquesse stood over Tanith. "So, young lady," she said. "Do you have anything you want to say to me?"

Tanith looked straight up at her. Not confrontational, exactly. Just... confident. Assured. From where she was sitting, with her hands shackled to the radiator, that was quite a feat. "What did you have in mind?"

"Oh, I don't know," said Darquesse. "Perhaps an apology? You let Valkyrie escape and you cut off Mercy's head. The second one was funny. The first was not."

"What do you care?" Tanith asked. "You're getting your power back, aren't you? Let Valkyrie be free. Let her enjoy her last few days."

Darquesse hunkered down. "What is this? Why did you betray me?"

Tanith took a moment, like she was trying to figure it out in her own head. Then she said, "Valkyrie's my friend."

"But you're a Remnant. You have no friends."

"Then I also have no loyalty, so my betrayal shouldn't come as a shock to you."

Darquesse sighed, and stood up. "I'm not shocked. Not really.

303

I'm disappointed, though. I thought, out of everyone, you'd be by my side till the very end."

"I had every intention of doing that. But then I realised I had a choice. I could either be a bad guy, or a good guy. So I'm a good guy."

"And look where this choice has landed you. You don't even know the trouble you're in, do you? You think I'm going to chain you up, but eventually I'll let you out because, hey, I'm a fun girl. But that's not going to happen. Because of what you've done. Before today, I'd have found another way to do this."

"Do what?"

"You're right, of course," Darquesse said. "My power's coming back. I can feel it growing. It's a nice feeling. But you know what I can't feel? Ravel. He's not there any more. Tanith, he deserves the pain I've been giving him, you know he does. But right now, Ghastly's murderer is out there somewhere feeling fine. Feeling good. Feeling smug. He thinks he's beaten me. He thinks he's got away with it. But he hasn't. I'm going to find him and I'm going to do far, far worse things to him than he could ever imagine."

"Maybe he's dead," said Tanith. "Maybe he couldn't take any more and his body gave up."

"No," said Darquesse. "I'd have felt that. He isn't dead. He just isn't here any more. He's gone. They've taken him to the only place beyond my reach. They've shunted him."

"And what does this have to do with me?"

"I need to find Argeddion," she said. "I need to find him and absorb his knowledge. Then I'll be able to shunt after them and bring Ravel back. Now, there are two ways to track down Argeddion. The first is to read the *Hessian Grimoire*. Unfortunately, that is locked away in the Sanctuary, so that's not really an option any more."

"And the second way?"

"I'm going to need the kind of knowledge that only Kenspeckle Grouse had."

"So you want to ask my Remnant side some questions," said Tanith. "Well, I'm all for Ravel's eternal agony, so go right ahead. A lot of Kenspeckle's memories are closed off to me, but I'll answer what I can."

"I'm afraid that won't be enough, Tanith. I'm going to need Kenspeckle's knowledge for myself."

Tanith frowned. "I... don't understand."

"I'm going to have to take your Remnant."

Immediately, Tanith's eyes widened and her black veins rose. "You can't. You can't do that, it's impossible. The Remnant is bonded to me. It's a part of me."

Darquesse hunkered down again, closer this time, and said gently, "And like every part of you, it can be removed from the rest."

Tanith flinched away from Darquesse's hand. "No. Stop. It's not like you can just find the Remnant bits and put it back together."

"Actually, that's exactly what I'm going to do." Darquesse gave her a kind smile. "You forget, a Remnant once tried to take control of me, but I consumed it. I know the taste."

"Darquesse, wait, please don't do this. I'll be split into two again. I won't be me any more. I'll be Tanith and I'll be the Remnant. You'll kill me."

Darquesse's fingers closed round Tanith's chin, holding her head in place. "Look at me. Look how sad my face is. Don't think for a moment that this won't upset me. But I need to do it. I need the information that is resting somewhere below your thoughts."

"Help me find it, then," Tanith said desperately. "Help me unlock the memories and I'll tell you what you need to—"

"Tanith," Darquesse said softly, "I've made my decision."

Pulling a plaster off is best done quickly, so that's what Darquesse did. She wrenched open Tanith's mouth and jammed her hand in, breaking teeth. Tanith's eyes bulged, her lips burst and her skin tore as Darquesse shoved her hand down the throat, ignoring the sounds of breaking bones and the gurgle-spit of screams. Deep inside, her fingers puncturing organs and rupturing meat, Darquesse called the Remnant to her. She poured her magic through her arm, into her hand, and this magic dragged the Remnant from Tanith's being, corralling it, forcing it to take form. Piece latched on to piece and bit by bit the Remnant was put back together. Darquesse kept her eyes closed the whole time, seeing it in her mind, focusing on what she needed to happen. She was only dimly aware that Tanith had stopped struggling. She was only dimly aware of the massive damage she was doing, or the mere seconds Tanith had left to live.

And then the Remnant was whole again, and her fingers closed round it, and she pulled her hand out.

It writhed and squirmed in her grip, and she almost lost it for a moment, but then she opened wide and forced it into her own mouth. She swallowed, felt it tearing at her throat. Then it was inside her, and she took it apart once more. The memories of all its previous hosts washed over her. Tanith's were the most vivid.

Tanith lay at her feet. She was ruined. There was blood everywhere. Darquesse could sense her life about to leave her. Poor Tanith. She hadn't wanted to hurt her. Not really. She knelt, placed her hand on Tanith's cheek. She wasn't at full power yet – not even close – but even so she knit those broken bones and repaired those failing organs and healed that flesh and that skin, and when she was done she stood up and almost blacked out.

She chuckled as she steadied herself against the wall. That could possibly be her last-ever act of kindness, and she would never be thanked for it. Typical.

46

THE CONVERSATION

"I don't get it."

There was a paused image on the screen, showing Valkyrie in the middle of a battle she didn't remember. No, it wasn't Valkyrie, it was Stephanie, and it was the Battle of Roarhaven. Around her, sorcerers fought Warlocks and Wretchlings in a frozen blur of violence and death.

"I don't get it," her dad said again. "What is it?"

Ice water flooded Valkyrie's body. She was suddenly cold and sick and her head spun. No. No, no.

"When did you do this?" her mum said. "It looks real. It doesn't even look like special effects. When did you do this? Who did this?"

The USB. Someone had given this to them. Valkyrie tried to speak. She couldn't.

"Stephanie," her dad said, "the stuff on this video... I'm sorry, I don't understand what it is." He gave a shaky laugh. "I mean, it looks real, for God's sake. And the guy, the guy talking over it, he said you died. That you died saving us, saving the whole world."

Valkyrie knew what she had to do. She had to grin, make a joke out of it, demand to see the footage, squeal in delight at how realistic the effects looked. She had to give herself time to come up with an excuse. But she couldn't. She couldn't say anything.

"He talked about Skulduggery Pleasant," her dad continued. "Skulduggery Pleasant is that friend of Gordon's. He was at the reading of the will."

"You don't forget a name like that," her mum said.

Her dad shook his head. "No you don't. What's been going on, Steph? What have you been hiding from us? Gordon was mixed up with some shady characters, but I told him, I begged him, to keep all that craziness away from us. Away from you. For God's sake, Steph, tell us what the hell is going on."

"Dad," she said, "I..."

Alice came in, saw Valkyrie and cheered and ran over. Instinctively, Valkyrie scooped her up, hugged her, her eyes wide, her blood still cold. Alice babbled and yapped excitedly, and eventually Valkyrie put her down.

"I have to make a phone call," she said numbly.

Her mum shook her head. "Not until you—"

"I have to make a phone call," she repeated, and left the room. She made two calls, actually, standing in the hall, her voice low and even. When she was done, she walked back into the kitchen, stood against the cupboard while her parents watched the video again. Every few seconds their eyes would drift up to look at her, and then return to the screen.

She heard a voice she knew from somewhere, asking a question. Kenny Dunne. The journalist. She heard her own voice saying things she'd never said. "You don't know anything about me."

Kenny spoke again. "I know plenty. These people call you Valkyrie, but I know you as Stephanie Edgley, eighteen years old, from Haggard, in north County Dublin. Recently left school and is considering college. According to your old teachers, you're a bright girl who—"

There was a knock on the door, and her mum paused the

video. Valkyrie left the room, coming back a few seconds later with Fergus. When they saw who it was, her parents relaxed.

"Now really isn't a good time," Valkyrie's dad said.

"I know," said Fergus. "I warned her. What did I say to you, Stephanie? I said it was a sickness. This whole thing was a sickness."

"Wait," her mum said, frowning, "what's a sickness? Steph, you called him? Why? What does Fergus have to do with what's on this video?"

"All that stuff Gordon wrote about," said Fergus. "Sorcerers and monsters and magic. It's real, as insane as it sounds."

Both of her parents straightened up.

"Des," he continued, "remember the old stories Granddad used to tell us? About the Last of the Ancients and all that? About how we were magic? Turns out he was telling the truth."

Valkyrie's dad took a long time to answer his brother.

"*Magic?*" he said. "This is all about magic being real? Monsters being real? Granddad was nuts, Fergus. You've said it yourself a million times. He went nuts. The only person who bothered listening to his rants was Gordon – and you called *him* nuts, too."

Fergus nodded. "I was protecting you."

"You were, were you? Protecting me from what?"

"From the sickness," said Fergus. "Granddad had it, Gordon had it, and Pop made me promise to shield you from it if I could. You were the youngest and the smartest of us. I said I'd try, and I've been trying ever since."

Valkyrie wasn't used to seeing her dad angry. She was seeing him angry now. "I'm not sure when I'm supposed to laugh," he said. "I'm just waiting for the punchline."

Fergus raised his hand and clicked his fingers, and a flame leaped up from his palm. "This is all I can do," he said. "I can summon one little flame, and that's all. I can't throw fire or fly or turn invisible. But even this you think is a trick, don't you? A party trick." He closed his hand and the flame went out. "But it's not. It's real magic. Actual magic. But I can't convince you that we're telling the truth, not with my little party trick."

"So what are we doing here?" Valkyrie's mum asked.

"Waiting," Valkyrie said.

Twenty minutes of silence passed, punctuated occasionally by questions that went unanswered.

During this uncomfortable silence, her parents watched and rewatched the video.

Finally, there was another knock on the door. Valkyrie went to answer it.

She had briefly thought about calling Geoffrey Scrutinous. About having him rearrange her parents' memories, convince them that nothing on that laptop screen was real.

But they were her *parents*.

So she hadn't called Geoffrey.

She came back into the kitchen with a tall man in a black three-piece suit, white shirt, and black tie. His shoes were polished to a gleam. His gloves were leather. His hat was in his hand. The expression he wore on the face he wore was calm. Confident.

"Mum, Dad, Fergus... this is Skulduggery Pleasant."

Her dad stood up immediately. "What the hell have you been doing with our daughter?"

"Desmond," Skulduggery said, "please sit down. This will go a lot smoother if we remain calm. Before we begin, can I make tea for anyone? Desmond? Melissa? What about you, Fergus? Would you like a cup of tea?"

"Uh," said Fergus, "yes. Please."

"I'll make tea for everyone," Skulduggery said.

Valkyrie helped him. Nobody spoke while the kettle boiled. Nobody spoke while tea bags were dipped and milk added and spoons stirred. When everyone had a seat and a cup in front of them, Skulduggery sat. There was nothing special about where he sat, yet he made it seem like he was at the head of the table.

"You're not having one yourself?" Fergus asked hesitantly.

Skulduggery smiled. "No. I don't drink tea."

His hat was on the table at his elbow. He adjusted its position slightly. When he was ready, he looked up. "So you know about magic."

"Tell us what's going on," Valkyrie's mum said.

"That's why I'm here. I'm here to offer you proof that what your daughter is saying is true. But before you see that proof, I have to warn you. I'm dead."

Valkyrie's parents waited for an explanation. When one wasn't forthcoming, her mum said, "Figuratively?"

"Literally. I was killed three hundred years ago or thereabouts, when I was somewhere over a hundred and thirty years old. Tortured to death and then burned, had my remains thrown in a sack and then dumped in a river. For reasons too complicated to go into right now, I was able to put myself back together. This face you see is a mask. These clothes are, for want of a better word, enchanted, giving the illusion that my body has greater mass than it actually possesses."

"Uh," said Valkyrie's dad, "so what is it you think you are? A ghost? A zombie?"

"Neither. I am... unique. Even though I'm dead, it would not be inaccurate to call me a *living* skeleton."

"You're a skeleton?"

"Beneath my disguise, yes."

"But... we're all skeletons, aren't we?" responded Valkyrie's mum. "Beneath our skin?"

"What a wonderfully enlightened view you have," Skulduggery said, smiling. "Unfortunately, I'm not talking in riddles. I'm going to take off my glove now. I want you to prepare yourselves."

Valkyrie's folks glanced at each other.

"Sure," her mum said.

Skulduggery pinched the tip of his right thumb, pulling the glove loose. He went up the fingers, pinching and pulling at each one, and then, with unhurried elegance, he gently pulled the glove off, and laid it on the table. For a few seconds, it kept its shape, like there was a hand still in there, but then it deflated, and flattened. Not that Valkyrie's parents were looking at the glove. Their eyes, and Fergus's, were transfixed by the skeletal hand that clenched and unclenched for them to see.

"How are you doing that?" her mum asked, her voice breathless.

"Magic," Skulduggery answered.

"But how do they move? There's no muscles or..."

"If you would allow me to remove my mask?"

They nodded, and the tips of his phalanges tapped the sigils at his collarbones, and his face flowed away, revealing the skull beneath.

Her parents leaped up, their chairs sliding backwards. But once they were on their feet, they froze.

"Good God," Fergus whispered.

Valkyrie's parents stood there, staring. Their eyes were wide, their faces pale, but they weren't panicking. That was good. That was a good sign.

Her mum screamed.

"Sorry," she said immediately after. "I don't know where that came from."

"Quite all right," Skulduggery said. "You're handling this whole thing remarkably well, all things considered."

"You're a skeleton," Valkyrie's dad said.

"I am."

"But how do you stay together?"

"Magic."

"How do you talk?" her mum asked.

"Magic."

"Do you have a brain?" asked her dad.

"No," said Valkyrie. "But he has a consciousness."

"That's amazing," said her mum. "Just... astonishing. Is there a God?"

"That depends on which one you mean," Skulduggery said. "Most of the gods we've encountered have been insane."

"You've met gods?"

"Oh, yes."

"I've punched one," said Valkyrie.

"But if you're asking if there's such a thing as the Judeo-Christian God, the one spoken of in the Holy Bible, I'm afraid I have no answer for you. To me, death was darkness and stillness with no sign of an afterlife."

"My wife and I go to mass every Sunday," said Fergus, visibly angry. "Don't you sit there and tell me there's no God."

"I would never presume to do any such thing," Skulduggery said calmly. "I believe in logic and reason, but I've seen wonders that defy explanation. I have had the pillars of my own belief shaken again and again as new truths come to light. Just the other day, your daughter and I saw a dragon. I had *no idea* those existed."

"A dragon?" repeated Valkyrie's dad.

"A big one. I could never tell you that what you believe is wrong, any more than I could tell you that what you believe is right. It seems to me that the universe holds far too many secrets to trade in absolutes, and anyone who tries runs the risk of being found out a fool. I am many things, but I like to think that a fool is not one of them. As I said, the circumstances surrounding my death were unusual, so my experience should not be held up as an example of what happens to us after we die. Desmond, Melissa, would you like to rejoin us at the table?"

Valkyrie's parents looked down, as if they'd only just realised they were standing. They pulled their chairs back to the table, and sat.

"So it's real," said her dad. "But then that video... What we saw on that was real. What that man said about Stephanie was real..."

"But we saw her die," her mum said, her voice shaking.

"May I?" Skulduggery asked, holding up his skeletal hand. The laptop spun and slid across the table to him.

"Wow!" her dad said, then caught himself. "I mean... cool."

Valkyrie leaned in to Skulduggery as he moved the video forward. Scenes of battle were intercut with interviews. She glimpsed footage – grainy and out of focus – of the Haggard pier in darkness, recognised it as the night Caelan had died, and then Skulduggery let the video play as normal. The battle raged in Roarhaven and Kenny Dunne spoke over it.

"...abandoned my plans to make this footage public. What would the world do if they knew about people like this? But I couldn't ignore the sacrifice made by your daughter."

The terrifying figure of Charivari fired a stream of energy at Saracen Rue, catching him full in the chest.

"Stephanie was a hero. She didn't ask for thanks, she didn't ask for recognition. But as her parents, you need to know what she lived for, what she fought for..."

Dexter Vex dodged a stream meant for him, and there was Stephanie, searching through the rubble, looking up just as Charivari fired at her. There was a bright flash and she was gone.

"...and what she died for."

Skulduggery dragged the video back a few seconds, and paused it. "Yes," he said. "This isn't footage of her death." He turned the laptop and it slid back to the other side of the table. "Look in the background, on the left. What do you see?"

Valkyrie's mum peered at it. "People fighting."

"Look!" her dad said, pointing. "That's Fletcher! I'd know that head anywhere!"

"Press play," said Skulduggery, "and watch what happens right before the massively scary gentleman fires at Valkyrie."

Her mum glanced up. "Her name is Stephanie."

"Of course," Skulduggery said. "My apologies."

Her parents clicked play and Fergus crowded in.

"He disappeared!" Fergus cried.

"Fletcher is a Teleporter," Skulduggery said. "He saw what was about to happen and he teleported your daughter to safety."

Valkyrie's mum looked confused. "Fletcher's one of them? I mean, one of you? He's... magic? Really?"

"That would explain the hair," her father mused.

"But he seemed like such a nice boy."

"He is a nice boy," Valkyrie said. "He's also a sorcerer."

Her mother closed the laptop, and looked at her. "How did you do all this? When did you find the time? Steph, you never leave the house."

Now was not the time to tell them about the reflection. There would never be a time to tell them about the reflection. "I sneaked out," she said. "I skipped some school. Not a lot, but some."

"You almost got killed."

"Mum—"

"No, Steph. You almost died. Does... I don't know, does this happen often? When did all this start? How long has it been going on?"

"A few years."

"Years? And how many times has your life been in danger in those few years? And you, Mr Pleasant—"

"Call me Skulduggery."

"I don't think I will. How can you justify bringing a child into all this?"

"Mum—" Valkyrie started, feeling the heat rise in her face.

"Stephanie, quiet," her mother said sharply. "You're eighteen now. You can argue that you're an adult. But a few years ago you were very much a child. I want to know what the hell is going on. Well, Mr Pleasant? You dragged a child into harm's way again and again from what I understand. What's your excuse?"

Skulduggery tilted his head. "Excuse?" he said. "I don't have one. I don't need one."

"I think you'll find you bloody well do."

"Valkyrie is my partner."

"Her name is Stephanie."

"Her name is also Valkyrie, and she's my partner. She came into this willingly, after I saved her life at her uncle's house. She proved utterly capable and, as it turned out, invaluable. Over the last few years I've been berated by friends and colleagues over this partnership, and I have been advised to dissolve it. They all thought Valkyrie should be leading a normal life. But she's meant for greater things than a normal life. She's meant for amazing things. She has saved lives. She has saved me. She has saved the world.

"I understand your urge to protect her, to shield her from danger and threat. I once felt that urge, too, for my own child. Long ago. But if you think I'm going to apologise for, as you say, dragging her into harm's way, you're going to be sorely disappointed. There's nothing I would change about the last few years. Valkyrie has proven herself to be an astonishing individual and one I would gladly lay down my life for, such as it is. How many people leading normal lives would you be able to say that about?"

"Until the end," Valkyrie said softly.

Skulduggery looked at her, his head tilting gently.

"No," her mum said. "I don't care what you say, or how eloquently you're saying it. It ends here."

"Mum, no," said Valkyrie.

Her dad spoke up. "Steph, you can't continue with this... madness. You'll get yourself killed. Do you want Alice to grow up without a sister?"

"Doing what I do is just like being a cop or a soldier."

"And we wouldn't want you to do those things, either."

"Wait, wait," her mum said. "It's taking a while for some of this to sink in, so forgive me for being a bit slow. But Steph, are you... are you *like* these people? Are you magic?"

Valkyrie hesitated. "I... don't know. I was. But something happened and... I don't know if I am any more."

Her mum looked at Skulduggery. "Well, that decides it, doesn't it? If she's not magic, then she can't continue being your student."

"Partner," Valkyrie and Skulduggery said at the same time.

"Student, partner, whatever. No magic, no job. That makes sense, doesn't it?"

"We'll have to see," Skulduggery said. "If, by the end of our current assignment, her magic has not returned to her..."

"I'll make the decision," Valkyrie finished. "But until then, I'm not stopping."

"We haven't agreed that," said her mum. "We'll need to think about this. Your dad and I will have to talk about it ourselves, and once we—"

"Mum," Valkyrie said, "no. You don't get to make this decision. I love you, but this has nothing to do with you. I'm the only one who gets to decide."

"Steph, no, you're still our daughter—"

"Yes I am." Valkyrie stood. "And as your daughter, it's my job to keep you safe. So that's what I'm going to do."

She walked out, leaving the smell of a roast dinner behind her.

47
THE DEATH BRINGER WAKES

She left her car at home and they drove to Roarhaven in the Bentley. She ran over the conversation a hundred times, trying to see how she could have handled it better. She came up short every time.

"You're angry, aren't you?" she said. They left Dublin, started hitting the narrower roads.

Skulduggery shook his head. "This isn't about me."

"But you had all those reasons for not telling my parents. Second Lifetime Syndrome and all that. People I love growing old while I stay young. You warned me."

"What happened was not your fault," he said. "This was Kenny Dunne's act of honourable intent, misguided as it may have been."

"So you're not mad?"

He inclined his head towards her a fraction. "Your parents knowing the truth is a complication you could do without. It may lead to greater complications further down the road. If there is a road."

Valkyrie dropped her face into her hands. "All I want to do is protect them. They're going to try to stop me from doing that."

Skulduggery was silent for a moment. "Your mother echoed a valid point you yourself have made."

"I know," Valkyrie muttered.

"Without magic..."

"I'm useless."

"Not useless. Far from useless. But without magic, your future opens up. You can now walk away without losing anything. You don't have to give up magic if you no longer have it."

"I'd be losing this," she said. "The job. Helping people. I'd be... I'd be losing you."

He looked at her. "You'll never lose me."

Tears pricked at her eyes. She looked away. "When this is over, I'll think about... everything. Until then, I'm in this all the way."

"Very well." They were on a lonely road now, a road that led to nowhere but Roarhaven. "In that case, we should probably have the conversation."

She looked back at him. "Which one would that be? The birds and the bees? I've already had it."

"The conversation?"

"The birds and the bees."

"Right, yes, well... I'm talking about the other conversation. The less fun one. The fact is, Valkyrie, going up against Darquesse... we might not make it this time."

"What? What about everything you were saying earlier about accentuating the positive?"

"Again, you brought up that particular song."

"Of course we're going to make it," Valkyrie said. "Making it is what we do. Darquesse is just another bad guy we have to defeat."

"She's more than that. The threat she poses is more valid than any you and I have faced before."

"You saying she's going to win?"

Skulduggery paused. "No. I think she'll be defeated. I think you will be instrumental in bringing about her downfall. But it won't be without its costs."

She shifted in her seat. "I don't like this conversation."

"I didn't think you would. But it's something we need to acknowledge."

"Why? It's a thought we're both having, and now we know we're both having it, so fine, it's there, it's out, we're discussing it, let's never discuss it again."

"One or both of us may not survive the next few days."

She whacked his arm. "What the *hell*, Skulduggery? I told you we didn't need to discuss it further! I know this! Don't you think I know this? But I don't want to talk about it! It upsets me! It makes me angry and sad and makes me want to cry! I don't want to think about living in a world where you're not in it, all right?"

"All right," he said. "All right."

Valkyrie looked away, tears in her eyes once more.

"Although I was kind of assuming you'd be the one who didn't make it," he muttered.

She whirled. "What? Why am I the one who dies?"

He shrugged. "It seems like the kind of thing you'd do. I'd find a way to cheat death at the last second, but you... you're just not that bright."

"I... I can't believe you just said that."

"I didn't mean it in a bad way."

She folded her arms. "I'm not talking to you any more. I don't know why I *ever* talk to you."

"Maybe you tried talking to yourself, but you were starved of intelligent conversation."

Valkyrie glared. "I find it incredibly worrying that the only way you know to take my mind off my troubles is to insult me."

"I find it really funny."

"I know you do."

They got to Roarhaven, parked and walked to the Medical Wing. Valkyrie was immediately whisked away, brought to a secure room with a half-dozen Cleavers standing outside.

Melancholia St Clair lay in bed, hooked up to IVs and beeping monitors. Her hair, previously so lustrous and healthy, was lank and spread out over her pillow like a dull blonde halo. Her eyes were closed. Her pale skin was marred by a curious network of pink, raised scars, sigils that Vandameer Craven had carved into her entire body in order to capture her Surge.

For any other sorcerer, the Surge was a painful, but relatively brief, burst of pure power that solidified their magical discipline. Thus sorcerers who were stronger in Elemental magic would forever more be Elementals, while those stronger in the Adept disciplines would be confirmed as Adepts. Melancholia's Surge, however, had been captured and redirected into a never-ending loop of increasing magic, transforming her into the Death Bringer the Necromancers had been waiting for.

And now here she was, waking up after so long with her legs strapped down and her wrists in shackles.

"She's in a light sleep," Synecdoche said from behind Valkyrie. "She woke earlier, but was too disorientated to ask questions. She should be more lucid now."

Valkyrie frowned. "Should I... Should I wake her?"

"She's slept long enough," Synecdoche said, leaving the room. "I'm sure she'd appreciate it."

There was an empty chair by the bed and Valkyrie sat in it. Then she reached forward, nudged Melancholia's leg.

"Hey," she said softly. Then, louder, "Hey."

Melancholia opened her eyes. It took her a few seconds to focus. She blinked, and looked around. "Where am I?"

She sounded like she needed a glass of water.

"In the Sanctuary," Valkyrie said. "How are you feeling?"

"What happened?" she said. "Where's Vile? How did I get here?"

"Calm down," Valkyrie said. "You're safe."

She tried to sit up. "I'm in shackles."

"Of course you're in shackles. The last time you weren't in

shackles you tried to kill almost half the population of the planet."

"I planned it," Melancholia said. "I didn't try it. There's a difference." Quickly, very quickly, she was becoming her old self again. "So where's Vile?"

Valkyrie glanced at the door to make sure no one could overhear. "What's the last thing you remember?"

"You and me, running through those caves. I remember Skulduggery Pleasant turning into Lord Vile and coming after us. Did you know they were the same person? That's insane."

"Yeah. You can't tell anyone about that, by the way. That's our little secret. He's not Lord Vile any more. He's all better."

"Oh, that's reassuring," Melancholia said, rolling her eyes.

"What else do you remember?"

"Hold on, hold on, let me think." Melancholia frowned. "I remember getting outside, and it was night, and he was still coming and I was so tired, I was too tired to even... and you punched me."

"I did."

"That wasn't very nice."

"I needed you to try to kill me."

"Why?"

"Darquesse. You've heard of her, right?"

Melancholia frowned. "That's the sorcerer all the Sensitives are worried about."

"Yes it is. And she's me."

"I'm sorry?"

"She's me. Darquesse is my true name. Back then, she only came out when my life was in danger. I needed her to come out to stop Lord Vile, so I had to make you try to kill me. This particular story has a happy ending, though, because after a really messy fight, Darquesse went away and Vile went away, and everyone lived happily ever after. Except you, who went into an induced coma."

"A coma? They put me in a coma? Why?"

"You're the Death Bringer, one of the two most powerful Necromancers who have ever lived. And you were unstable, both magically and... mentally."

Melancholia blinked at her. "Harsh."

"But true."

"But still harsh. So I've been in a coma for... how long?"

"A year and a half."

Her eyes widened. "What? A year and a half? What the *hell*?"

"They had to do it."

"*A year and a half?*"

"Please calm down. If you don't calm down, they'll come in here and sedate you."

Melancholia stared at her, then did her best to relax. "Wow. Eighteen months. That's... So I'm twenty-two. I am twenty-two years old. Right. That's a bit of a shock."

"I'd say so."

"So what did I, you know, what did I miss? Anything good?"

"Over the last year and a half?" Valkyrie said. "Well, the Necromancers kind of retreated into their temples. There was this guy called Argeddion and he wanted to make all the mortals magic. We stopped him, don't worry. You missed a war between our Sanctuary and virtually the whole world. Erskine Ravel betrayed us, killed Ghastly Bespoke and Anton Shudder. Now China Sorrows is in charge and everyone is doing pretty much what we tell them. Oh, also, there are aliens now."

"*Really?*"

"No."

"I hate you so much."

"But everything else is true. And Darquesse – and this has just happened over the last few weeks – Darquesse kind of took me over and killed a load of people, but now she's out and she's inhabiting my reflection's body and we think she's going to destroy the world."

"So now there's another you out there—"

"Not me."

"So now there's someone out there who looks like you and sounds like you and is, in fact, you, except she's evil, and you need to stop her, and that's why I've been woken up. Right?"

"Basically."

In spite of everything, Melancholia smiled. "So you have an evil twin."

"She's not my twin," said Valkyrie, "she's just... I mean, OK, evil, sure, you can call her evil, but she's not, I wouldn't call her... Why are you laughing?"

"I'm sorry, but that's just really funny. So why do you need me? Can't your skeleton friend just turn into Vile and go after her?"

"First of all," said Valkyrie, "I told you to shut up about that. Second, Vile is hard to control. Third, even if Skulduggery could control Vile, Darquesse is just too powerful. We need all the heavy hitters we can find."

"And what happens to me when it's over? Providing I survive, of course? I'm put back in my cosy little coma?"

"No. You'll be set free, but..."

"But what?"

Valkyrie hesitated. "But we'll need to cut you off from magic."

Melancholia was already pale enough, but now she went paler. "Permanently?"

Valkyrie nodded. "I'm sorry. I wish there were another way, but everyone I speak to says the same thing. Craven's experiments on you resulted in a level of power that is just too unpredictable. Once Darquesse is taken care of, China's people will try to contain as much of your magic as they can, and Sensitives will put up walls in your mind. Your memory will be altered and your personality will be slightly... rewritten. They've been doing that a lot lately and—"

"You're talking about killing me."

"No, we're—"

"Yes, Valkyrie. Changing my memories and my personality until I'm no longer the same person. That's killing me."

Valkyrie sat forward, her hand on Melancholia's. "The alternative is worse. The alternative is putting you back in that coma, or you walking around with your fluctuating power. You'd be a danger to everyone – yourself included. At least this way you'll be able to live a normal life."

"A *mortal* life," Melancholia said. "What do I know about living as a mortal? They pass you in the street, these dull-eyed cattle, going about their grey little lives, rushing home to watch their favourite television shows, inane people doing mundane things... and you want me to be one of them? You want me to give up the magic that makes life worth living? Tell me this, Valkyrie – if this is such a wonderful opportunity, would you do it? Would you give up magic?"

"I didn't have to."

"But if you were in my situation and had my—"

"It was taken from me."

Melancholia frowned. "What?"

"When they pulled Darquesse from my mind, she took all the magic with her."

"You're... mortal?"

"It's not so bad."

Melancholia looked at her. "You're lying."

"I'll get used to it. So will you."

"I... I don't think I'll be able to."

"I'll be there to help when you need it."

"But I hate you."

Valkyrie smiled. "No you don't."

"No, I do. I want to kill you and stuff."

"We actually became friends in those caves."

"That's not what happened," said Melancholia.

"We're pals. We're buddies."

"If my wrists weren't in shackles, my hands would be round your throat."

"You want to hug my throat because we're friends."

"I really hate you."

Valkyrie squeezed her hand. "I'm going to leave you alone for a bit, let you think about it. It's a huge decision to make. But at least you get to make the decision."

Melancholia had tears in her eyes she was trying to fight against. "Your face is stupid."

Valkyrie squeezed her hand again, and left.

48

A NEW ROARHAVEN

Tanith woke.

There was the taste of blood in her mouth, and she had the king of all sore throats. She felt sick, like someone had stomped on her insides. Apart from that, though, she seemed to be fine. Unhurt.

She took a look around. She was sitting on the floor in a small room, shackled to a radiator. She didn't remember how she'd got here. The last thing she remembered was...

She shook her head. Unimportant. What was important was getting out. The shackles were tight, and the radiator solid. There were scrapes where her chain was looped. Someone had been in this exact same situation, and recently, too. She wondered if they'd managed to escape.

Footsteps. She pressed her back against the wall. Billy-Ray Sanguine walked in.

"Should have known you'd be involved," Tanith said. Her voice was rough. It surprised her. "What the hell is going on? Where are the others?"

"Others?" Sanguine said, closing the door behind him. His shirt sleeves were rolled up. His tie was loose. He looked comfortable, like this was home to him.

"Yes," she said. "Others. As in the people who are going to tear your head off when they come to get me. Skulduggery. Valkyrie. Ghastly. The *others*."

She didn't get a smirk in response. She'd been expecting one. Instead, he nudged his sunglasses further up the bridge of his nose. He almost seemed shy. "What's... what's the last thing you remember?"

Tanith hadn't been expecting that, either. She was going to dismiss the question, ignore it and bombard him with questions of her own, but the fact was...

"Fighting," she said. "Fighting alongside Valkyrie and Skulduggery against... against everyone."

"The Remnants," Sanguine said.

It came back to her. Christmas. The Remnants taking over. She sat forward. "Is that what you are? Did they get you, too?"

"No, Tanith," Sanguine said. "I ain't a Remnant. But all that... all that happened a little over two years ago."

"*What?*"

"The Remnants, most of them at least, were trapped in that Receptacle thing. Everyone woke up with sore heads and no memory of what had happened. Everyone except..."

He trailed off.

Her frown deepened. "You're lying."

"No I'm not."

"You're lying," she said. "You really expect me to believe that I've had a Remnant inside me for two years? Then answer me this – how the hell did I get rid of it?"

"Wasn't your choice," Sanguine said. "Darquesse re-formed it inside you and dragged it out."

She sneered. "Oh, so now Darquesse is loose."

"Yeah. And she's Valkyrie." Sanguine frowned. "Well, she was. Now she's the reflection... Listen, it's complicated as hell. I'd love to explain everything, I really would, but we don't have time. You killed someone, a nasty piece of work called Mercy.

One of Vincent Foe's people? You cut her head off, and Vincent is none too happy about it. I have a feeling he might be waiting till Darquesse is looking the other way and then he's gonna come in here, wanting your head in compensation. You've gotta get outta here." He reached for her.

"Touch me and you'll never use that hand again."

Sanguine froze, and pulled his hand back. "Tanith, a lot of stuff has happened since you been gone. Darquesse is here. There was a war between the Sanctuaries. The Remnants are out – again. They've taken over this little town called Thurles, or something like that. Things have happened and you gotta be ready for—"

"Why are you talking to me like we're friends?"

"Because we're..." He faltered. "Because I thought we were friends," he said at last. "We've been through a lot together recently. We were partners, more or less."

Tanith laughed. "Now I know you're lying. I'd never partner up with someone like you."

Colour rose in his cheeks. "Yeah, well, I guess your standards slipped. Listen, you can either let me get you outta those shackles, give you back your sword and let you hightail it outta here, or you can give me attitude and bad manners and wait for your head to be chopped off. Up to you, princess."

"Why would you help me?"

He stared at her. "Like I said, we were friends."

She didn't trust Sanguine, but he'd been true to his word. She was free, with her sword on her back and her head on her shoulders. She didn't understand it, though. Didn't understand any of it. She leaped across rooftops until she came to the neighbourhood she was looking for. Across the street, a man took his dog for a midnight walk. Nothing suspicious about him. Nothing suspicious about his dog, either. It all looked very normal. Very civilian. Very mortal.

But this street was full of sorcerers – or it had been, the last time Tanith was here. Every one of these houses was more than it appeared and, as such, she had to be careful. If she had, in fact, spent the last two years as a Remnant, then who knew what kind of enemies she'd made?

When the man was gone and there was no one else around, Tanith dropped to street level. One hand on the hilt of the sword hidden beneath her coat, she hurried to the door of Bespoke Tailors, and slammed her fist against it.

The shop was dark. She knocked again, harder this time. No lights flicked on inside. No one home.

Back when telephones had been stationary things with rotary dials, Tanith could recite the numbers of dozens of people without even thinking about it. But things were different now. She doubted she'd ever tapped out Ghastly's actual number in order to call him, or Valkyrie's or Skulduggery's, for that matter. So here she was, alone in Dublin City, with no idea how to contact her friends.

She didn't even know where the Sanctuary was. The last thing she'd heard, there were plans to use Roarhaven as their new base of operations. She didn't like that idea. It was a small grey town full of narrow-minded, spiteful people. The Torment had lived in Roarhaven, and probably a few other Children of the Spider. Anyone who didn't like mortals could find a sympathetic ear in that horrible little place. Unfortunately, it was her best chance at getting in touch with her friends.

She didn't have any cash to pay for a taxi, so she jumped from rooftop to rooftop until she found a motorbike she could steal. She didn't even have a pen and paper to leave an apologetic note.

She hot-wired the engine, pulled out on to the road, and gunned it.

She got lost twice. She'd only been to Roarhaven once, years ago, and the turn was hard to spot, but as she followed the winding road she started to think that maybe some of this was familiar.

When the road straightened, Tanith knew she'd come the right way.

She saw tail lights ahead of her. A car parked at the side of the road. An elderly man waved to her as she slowed.

"Afraid the road's closed, miss," he said.

"The Sanctuary's up here, is it?" Tanith asked.

The smile remained on his face. "The what? I'm sorry, I'm not familiar with the—"

"My name is Tanith Low. If the Sanctuary is in Roarhaven, I'd like to come in. I've been possessed by a Remnant for the past two years. I'll wait, while you call it in."

The elderly man lost the smile. He nodded to her and backed away. Tanith stayed on the bike, but turned off the engine. She heard him speak into a radio, but couldn't make out the words. Thirty seconds later, he came back – but kept his distance.

"Miss Low," he said, "some Cleavers are on their way now to escort you in. I have been asked to try to shackle you. Would you be agreeable to that?"

"That depends," said Tanith. "Who's Grand Mage?"

"China Sorrows."

Tanith frowned. "How the hell did she manage that?"

"I couldn't possibly comment," said the old man. "So... the shackles?"

Tanith sighed and held out her hands. By this stage, the headlights of a truck were approaching.

This was a different Roarhaven to the one she had visited. It wasn't a town any more – it was a city. As she was driven through it, Tanith glimpsed the old drabness still present in places, but this only made the newer buildings appear all the more glorious.

When she was here last, the Sanctuary had been a low, charmless, circular building. Now it was a palace. It had towers and steeples, a brightly-lit beacon to keep the darkness back. The inside was just as glorious, even though she was escorted through it with a ring of Cleavers around her.

Once the doctors had determined that there was no Remnant present, her shackles were removed and Tanith was taken to a quiet room for debriefing. She was brought a coffee. She drank it while her stomach rumbled. She waited for whomever they would send.

The door handle rattled and Valkyrie burst in.

"Oh, thank God," Tanith said, actually laughing. "I was getting worried for a—"

She didn't get a chance to finish. She didn't even get a chance to stand up. Valkyrie wrapped her in a hug so tight it was hard to move.

"You're alive," Valkyrie whispered.

"You sound surprised."

Valkyrie hugged her tighter. "I saw you yesterday. You were covering my escape."

"I helped you?" Tanith said. "Even when I had a Remnant inside me?"

Valkyrie released her and stepped back, smiling. "Even then," she said.

Valkyrie had changed. She was taller, for a start. Stronger. Tanith had felt it in the hug, and now she saw it in the shoulders.

"You look great," she said.

"It is so good to have you back." Valkyrie ignored the chair and sat on the corner of the table.

"I'm going to take your word for that," said Tanith. "To me, I only saw you a few hours ago. Val, Sanguine said some strange things. I know a lot has happened since I've been gone, but some of what he said was pure nuts. He said you were Darquesse."

Valkyrie took a breath. "He wasn't lying."

"But... but then what—?"

Valkyrie half smiled. "Funny. I've just had this conversation with Melancholia."

"Melancholia... The blonde Necromancer? Annoying?"

"Who later became the Death Bringer," Valkyrie said. "Darquesse was my true name, but I couldn't handle the power. It took on a life of its own, a personality of its own. Now it has a body of its own – my reflection."

"You're... You're the one all the Sensitives had the nightmares about?"

"I was. Now she is."

"And Sanguine said I worked for her? For Darquesse?"

"I'm afraid so," said Valkyrie. "The Remnant in you glimpsed the apocalypse that Darquesse would bring about. You've been helping her."

"And Sanguine was my partner?"

"Is that what he said?"

"He said we even had our own gang at one stage."

"Yes you did – though partners may be stretching it a bit. He did what you told him."

"Well, that's something," Tanith said. "At least I didn't let my standards slip too much."

Valkyrie adjusted her position. "And he didn't say anything else?"

"Sanguine? No. Were you hoping for something in particular?"

"No," said Valkyrie. "Never mind. It's really good to have you back. I've missed you."

"And I've missed a lot. Care to fill me in over some food? I'm starving."

"Yeah," said Valkyrie. "Yeah, of course. Come on."

They walked. Valkyrie was hiding something, but Tanith didn't press it. It was bad news. Whatever it was, it was bad news.

Before they got to the food, Valkyrie's phone rang. She listened for a moment, her eyes widening. Then she hung up. "Come on," she said, and took off at a run. Tanith ran alongside her.

They got to a large room filled with thin, mirrored pillars. The perfect place to find someone like China Sorrows. Tanith hung back by the door while Valkyrie ran in, joining China and Skulduggery and a thin, dishevelled man.

"What happened?" Valkyrie asked. "Where's Ravel? Where's everyone else?"

"Mr Signate was about to tell us," China said, turning her gaze on the dishevelled man. "Please continue. You were saying that our plan worked...?"

Signate nodded. "It did. It worked. I mean, first things first. Shunting Ravel to another dimension did break the link to Darquesse, like you thought it would. The pain went away instantly. The look of relief on his face was just... anyway. So, we arrived. It was quiet. The room we'd shunted into was unsuitable for spending any length of time in, so we set up camp on the surface. Ravel was in shackles. We established a perimeter and I'd turned in for the night."

Tanith didn't know what the hell he was talking about, but from the look of panic on Valkyrie's face she knew this was bad.

"Then I woke up," said Signate. "There were people fighting. There were those Cleavers, like you said, the Redhoods, and there were so many of them and there were people in robes and..."

Skulduggery tilted his head. "What happened, Mr Signate?"

"I'm... I'm not a fighter. I'm not a soldier. There was nothing I could do. I ran to an injured Cleaver, one of ours, the only one I could get to, and I shunted us both back here."

"The Cleaver's being tended to in the Medical Wing," said China. "I think we can assume the rest have been killed."

"What about Ravel?" Valkyrie asked, like it was the only question that mattered.

"I saw him," said Signate. "Only for a moment, but I saw him. He was running. He may have got away in all the confusion. I'm sorry, I just don't know."

China looked at Skulduggery. "Well?"

"We need him back," Skulduggery said. "The one constant when it comes to Darquesse has been her insistence that Ravel be punished."

Tanith frowned. *Punished?*

"Shunting him out of her clutches has undoubtedly got her attention, but if we want to draw her in, we need him here."

"More than that," China said, "Darquesse has a tendency to develop new abilities at a frightening rate. If she learns how to shunt and she goes after Ravel, if she finds him before we do, we've lost our only chance to predict where she'll be."

"We need to go," Skulduggery said. "Now."

"I agree," said China. "But you have to realise that Mevolent is now aware of our incursion, and he may very well be expecting another visit. If I order—"

"You don't have to order it," Skulduggery said. "I volunteer."

"Me too," said Valkyrie. Then she hesitated. "Well, if..."

Skulduggery looked at her. "If what?"

"If you want me. There's probably not a whole lot I'd be able to do."

He looked back at China. "Then we both volunteer. But us two – no more. A larger group would be easier to detect."

China nodded. "Agreed. Mr Signate, you will shunt my detectives over and you will facilitate their return trip. Skulduggery, Valkyrie, I would like to tell you to take an hour to prepare, but time is of the essence. If Ravel is on foot, you need to start tracking him down immediately. If Mevolent's forces have taken him... you'll need to get him back."

Skulduggery nodded. "We leave in five minutes."

Valkyrie hurried over to Tanith.

"What the hell is going on?" Tanith asked when they were out in the corridor again. "Mevolent? He's dead."

"Our Mevolent is dead," said Valkyrie, "but about a year ago we shunted into an alternate reality where he's very much alive and pretty much ruling the world."

"And you're going back there? And what's this about Ravel? Why does Darquesse want to punish him?"

Valkyrie hesitated.

"What is it?" Tanith asked. "You're holding something back, something bad, but we don't have time for that any more. We have minutes before you leave. So just tell me what this terrible thing is that's happened and get it over with."

Whatever it was, Tanith's anger wasn't going to bring it to the surface any quicker.

Valkyrie licked her lips. "They told me you tried Ghastly's place before you came here."

"I did. He wasn't in."

"No," Valkyrie said quietly. "He wasn't."

49

STOPPING FOR GAS

Amazingly, Danny falls asleep.

It isn't easy. The Cadillac's trunk is smaller than it looks, and it's cold and uncomfortable and every bump in the road jars his injured shoulder. But after an hour or so he closes his eyes, and only opens them again when the car slows to a crawl. He checks his watch in the red glow of the tail lights. He's been asleep for nearly two hours.

The car stops, and he can hear muffled voices, and then car doors opening and closing. He stays very quiet, tracking one set of footsteps as they lumber away, and another as they get closer. There's a loud rattle, and for a moment he doesn't know what it is, then metal bangs lightly against metal and he knows even before the gurgle and splash sounds that they're at the pumps of a gas station.

There's a knock on the lid of the trunk.

"You doing OK in there, Danny my boy?"

Danny frowns. He sincerely doesn't know how to answer that.

"Danny?" Gant says again. "You OK?"

"I'm fine," Danny calls. He realises how loud his voice sounds.

It takes a moment for the most obvious plan in the world to occur to him, and he starts shouting. "Help! Somebody help me! I'm trapped in here! Call 911!"

He hears Gant's chuckle. "That's the spirit. How are the legs? Pretty cramped, I would imagine. And the bladder? I don't know about you, Danny, but long journeys tend to put a squeeze on things, if you know what I mean. If you want to use the restroom, just let me know."

"I want to," Danny says at once.

"You sure? You wouldn't be saying that in a bold attempt to be let out of the trunk and make your escape, now would you?"

"I need to go," says Danny. This isn't a lie. He's suddenly become aware of the pressure that has built up.

The gurgling stops, and the trunk clicks and lifts. It's night, and the gas station's lights fill Danny's eyes and he gropes blindly about as he sits up. He feels Gant's long, strong fingers at the ropes that bind him, then they loosen and fall away. Gant helps him clamber awkwardly out of the trunk. Once out, he stays bent over, rubbing his legs to get some feeling back into them. Gant goes back to filling the car.

The road is unlit but the gas station is of a more than modest size. There's another car at the pumps, a station wagon, and two more in the parking slots. That means people. That means a way out. Danny straightens up.

"Go use the restroom and then come back," Gant says. "No dilly-dallying."

Danny nods, and limps stiffly across the forecourt. His left shoulder isn't as badly injured as he had feared. It hurts like hell and he can barely move it, but the pain has lessened considerably. His leg, though, has improved a lot. He keeps his limp, keeps up the act, but by the time he pushes open the door and enters the gas station, he's fairly confident he could break into a run if he has to. First place he looks is the counter. Jeremiah Wallow stands there, stuffing a Twinkie into his mouth as he waits for the attendant to come out of the backroom. Jeremiah catches Danny's eye, puts a finger to his cream-covered lips.

Danny goes to the men's room. There are two urinals and one stall, and the stall is empty. The window is too high to get to and too small to squeeze through. Danny relieves himself, then goes back to the door, peeks out, and steps into the ladies' room across the way. It too is empty. Where the hell is everybody?

He goes to the door. How long will Jeremiah wait until he comes looking? Will he come alone, or will he call for Gant? He'll probably come alone. He'll wander down, thump his fist against the door of the men's room, tell Danny to hurry up, and then Danny can spring at him, knock him out with... what, exactly? Danny doesn't have a weapon. He's seen a heap of old TV shows where people were knocked out by a swift chop to the back of the head, but he doubts he'll be able to do that. What then? Will he charge, tackle Jeremiah, bring him to the ground? But what if Jeremiah gets on top? He outweighs Danny by maybe eighty pounds, and Danny has never been much of a wrestler.

No. The more he thinks about it, the less and less it seems like a good idea to choose this place as a battleground. Taking a breath, Danny limps out of the restroom as calmly as he is able.

"You took your time," Jeremiah says from the counter.

"I'm hungry," says Danny.

Jeremiah shrugs. "Grab yourself something to eat, then. But I'm not paying for it."

Danny scans the shelves of quarts of oil and wiper fluid. Nothing sharp, nothing heavy, nothing that can be used as a weapon. He follows the aisle to the sandwiches, and picks two, carries them to the counter.

Jeremiah is licking cream from his moustache. "How's that trunk working out for you?" he asks, grinning.

"It's cold," Danny says. "Where are we going?"

"Mr Gant's house."

"Is it far?"

"Far enough."

"How long will I have to stay in that trunk?"

Jeremiah shrugs. "We might be there by morning. We might not. From here on out we travel by back roads. Things are gonna get a sight bumpier for you."

Danny puts the sandwiches on the counter beside the till. "Jeremiah, can I ask you a question? Who are you? Why are you doing this? Why are you so interested in Stephanie?"

"That was three questions," Jeremiah says. "Four, if you count the asking of the first question as a question. I'll answer one of them. Which one you want answered most?"

Danny hesitates. "Why are you so interested in Stephanie?"

"Because she's special. She's not like you regular people. She's special like I'm special, and Mr Gant is special. Special people are littered through this world and some of them are nice and some of them are nasty. Mr Gant and I, we are unashamedly nasty, and it's our job to find the nice special people, like Stephanie, and pluck them from this earth like you'd pluck a flower from a garden."

"What makes you special?"

Jeremiah's tongue finds that last dollop of sugared cream on his whiskers, and he sucks it in between his soft pink lips. "Everything," he says.

Danny looks at him, and the stillness of their surroundings suddenly veer from strange to unnatural. "Where is everyone?"

Jeremiah looks back at him innocently. "Everyone?"

"The people who work here," says Danny. "The people who own those cars outside."

Jeremiah's head twitches towards the backroom. "They're all in there," he says. Says it like it's nothing. Says it like it isn't even something worth saying.

Moving slowly, Danny steps round Jeremiah, and limps behind

the counter. Jeremiah doesn't try to stop him. His mouth dry, Danny puts one foot into the backroom, glimpses the bodies stacked in the corner, and immediately steps back.

"She's following us," Jeremiah says, eating one of the sandwiches Danny has left on the counter. "Mr Gant has seen that pickup of hers, way back in the distance. Mr Gant talks about fishing sometimes. He says this is like reeling in a fish once it's hooked. You bring it closer and closer until it's out of the water and flapping around on the deck of your boat. Course, in this case she doesn't even know she's got a great big hook in her mouth. That just makes it funnier."

There's a loud honk from outside. Gant getting impatient. Jeremiah takes his gun from his pocket, points it at Danny's belly. "Time to go. Want to take your other sandwich?"

"I'm not hungry any more," Danny says, his voice quiet.

Jeremiah gives another little shrug. "Suit yourself. Back in the trunk for you."

50

THE CARD TRICK

Darquesse stood in the rain until she was nice and wet. Levitt was watching her. She liked Levitt. He was a quiet man even when he had a Remnant inside him. She appreciated the fact that he never spoke. The ability to shut up was something she respected in a man.

When she was wet enough, she walked up and knocked on the door. Knocking on the door was nice. She could have smashed through it. She could have made it disappear. She could have turned it into a million bubbles. But she knocked, and she waited, and it was nice.

Movement. Sounds. A latch being lifted. The door opened and a man in his early thirties stood there, a pleasant expression on his face. Argeddion.

"Hi," said Darquesse. "I'm so very sorry for disturbing you, but my car broke down and I don't have my phone with me. Could I possibly use your phone to call home?"

"Of course," Argeddion said, stepping to one side. "Come on in. The phone's on the table there."

Darquesse gave him a grateful smile and hurried over to the phone. She started dialling a non-existent number as he left her alone in the hall.

"Hi, Mum," she said. "Car's broken down. Yes, I know you did, and you were right. Could you come and pick me up? I'm at a house opposite the park entrance – you know the one with the big iron gate? No, it's fine. His name is..." She took a step sideways, peering into the kitchen. "Excuse me, could I have your name?"

Argeddion came back, smiled as he handed her a towel. "I'm Michael Tolan."

She took the towel, started drying her hair one-handed. "His name's Michael Tolan. No, Mum. He's normal. He's not scary."

Argeddion chuckled. "I'm a teacher, not a serial killer."

"Hear that, Mum? A teacher. Yep. I'm fine. OK. OK, thank you. Love you. Bye. Bye bye bye bye bye." She put the phone down. "Thank you so much. She'll be here in ten minutes."

"You can wait in here if you want."

"Oh, no. I couldn't. I'll wait in my car."

"It's lashing out," he said, "and I've put the kettle on."

"Well," said Darquesse, "a cup of tea does sound nice."

He smiled, and she followed him into the kitchen. "Excuse the mess," he said while he poured the boiling water into a mug. "I've just moved into the area, and I'm not used to visitors."

She sat at the table. "How long have you been a teacher?"

He laughed. "Too long, but I just started at St James's last September."

"And how do you find it?"

"It's a great school. Did you go there?"

"Naw, but a lot of my friends did." He handed her a mug of tea. "Thank you, Mr Tolan."

"Outside the classroom, people call me Michael."

She smiled. "Thank you, Michael. You don't look like a teacher."

"No?" he said, leaning against the cooker. "What do I look like?"

"I don't know. A doctor. Or a scientist."

"I must look intelligent."

"Or a magician, maybe."

"Wow. Well, that's new. I look like a magician?"

Darquesse shrugged, and sipped her tea. "Magicians come in all shapes and sizes."

"I suppose you're right."

"Ever tried doing magic?"

He shook his head, amused. "Not that I can recall."

"You're missing out."

"Oh, really? You sound like you know what you're talking about. Can you do tricks?"

"Illusions, Michael. I can do some. Do you have a deck of cards handy?"

"I should have," said Argeddion, looking around. "I remember unpacking them here, putting them..."

She watched him search through a few drawers. Finally, he uttered a small cry of triumph, and came back to her with a box of playing cards, still in its clear plastic wrapping.

"Perfect," she said, taking it from him. He sat down as Darquesse peeled off the plastic, her favourite part, and opened the box, sliding the cards into her hand. She shuffled them thoroughly and fanned them out. "Pick a card," she said. "Any card."

Argeddion drew one from the pack, glanced at it, and kept it close to his chest. Darquesse shuffled the pack again, then laid them face down on the table and splayed them with one gentle sweep of her hand.

"That was a brand-new pack?" she asked.

"It was," he said.

"You bought it? You put it in that drawer?"

"Yes."

"There is no possible way for me to have interfered with that pack?"

"None whatsoever."

"Please hold up your card."

Argeddion did so.

"The seven of clubs," she said. "So, if every single one of the cards on this table turns out to be the seven of clubs, you'd have to be pretty impressed, wouldn't you?"

He laughed. "I suppose I would."

Grinning, she swept the splayed cards right-side up.

"Um," said Argeddion, "I don't think it worked."

Darquesse looked at the perfectly ordinary pack of cards before her. "Oh, that's right," she said. "I hate card tricks. Here's something else."

She clicked her fingers and every one of Argeddion's fingers on his right hand snapped backwards. The seven of clubs fluttered to the floor as he fell out of his chair, screaming.

She went to the window, waved, and a moment later the front door was kicked open, and Levitt walked in. Darquesse didn't bother with words. She took hold of the back of Argeddion's shirt and grabbed a handful of his hair. She turned him towards Levitt and pulled his head back. He tried struggling, but he was no match for her.

Levitt's throat bulged as the Remnant climbed out. Levitt himself collapsed, and the Remnant flitted across the space between them and latched on to Argeddion's face. Within seconds, it was forcing its way down his throat. She released him and he fell to his knees, the screams replaced by gagging. Another moment and even the gagging was forgotten.

She returned Levitt to his essence while she waited, just for something to do.

Argeddion rose, black veins running across his face. "Interesting," he said.

"How much can you remember?" Darquesse asked.

He frowned. "I remember everything as Michael Tolan. These false memories they implanted, false experiences... they're really very good."

"What about your memories as Argeddion?"

"They're... hidden. Obstructed. But I can... I can get through them if I..."

His eyes widened suddenly, and he smiled. "There," he breathed. "There..."

Darquesse gave it as long as she possibly could, and then she grabbed him, rammed her hand into his mouth and forced it down his throat.

Argeddion struggled. He wasn't strong yet, but she could feel his power returning to him. It wouldn't be long now.

She drew the Remnant into her hand, closed her fingers round it, and yanked it out.

It squirmed and squealed in her grip and Argeddion collapsed, his throat in ruins and his jaw smashed. Darquesse opened wide, forced the Remnant into her own mouth. She swallowed, feeling its little claws ripping her insides to shreds. She smiled, healing everything instantly. The Remnant struggled inside her, tried to escape, but she kept it where it was. After a few moments, its natural processes took over, and she felt it try to slink into her mind. Instead, she pulled it in, isolated it, extracted its memories. Once she was done, she burned it, fed on its power.

So many memories. It would take time to sort through them. Luckily Darquesse had plenty of experience with this. In some ways, it was a lot like Valkyrie absorbing the reflection's experiences, back in the old days.

She was brought back to the present by Argeddion getting to his feet. His power was returning. She could see it. Within moments, he would remember how to heal himself.

She poured her magic out through her eyes. A beam of energy, no thicker than a pencil, burrowed through Argeddion's heart. He stepped back, then fell. She watched his life leave him, watched his essence rejoin the Great Stream, as the Necromancers called it – a stream that would soon be bursting its banks.

51

THE TEMPLE OF THE SPIDER

reyfon Signate flickered and disappeared, leaving Valkyrie and Skulduggery alone to creep through the darkness.

Redhoods stood guard, surrounding the remains of this dimension's Sanctuary. Their scythes looked every bit as nasty as the Cleavers back home, but somehow their red uniforms were even more unsettling than the grey. Grey was the colour of neutrality. Red was the colour of violent, passionate intent.

"Can't see any survivors," Valkyrie whispered. "I count seven dead Cleavers, three dead sorcerers. No sign of Ravel."

"If they caught him, he's either dead or already on his way to Mevolent," said Skulduggery. "Come on."

Staying low, they moved away, seeking refuge in the night's darkness.

"What do you think Mevolent will do to him?" Valkyrie asked.

"Torture," Skulduggery said. "But after what Ravel's been through, mere torture would be a blessing. He'll be interrogated. He'll eventually tell Mevolent everything he wants to know about our reality. And if Mevolent has a Shunter on staff, and there's no reason to think he doesn't, that could spell trouble for us."

"You think Mevolent would invade?"

"Possibly. The last time he received a visitor from our dimension, it was Darquesse, and she proved to be quite a threat. Mevolent's not the type to sit around and wait for trouble to strike."

"And what if they didn't catch Ravel?" Valkyrie asked. "How do we find him, then?"

"He knows about this place. He's read the reports. He knows the layout of the city, and how to get in."

"You think that's where he's going?"

"He fought against Mevolent his whole life, but take the worship of the Faceless Ones out of the equation, and what do you have? What ties Mevolent and Ravel together?"

"They both want sorcerers to rule over the mortals."

Skulduggery nodded. "The city's the place for him – certainly somewhere to find like-minded individuals, if nothing else. Besides, he knows we'll be coming after him. The city's the best place to hide. If he went there of his own free will, we grab him, slap him around and drag him back. If he was brought there as a prisoner, we rescue him. Then slap him around and drag him back."

"OK," said Valkyrie, and wrapped her arm round him.

He looked at her. "Uh..."

She blinked. "What? We're flying there, aren't we?"

"Not with the Redhoods and the Sense-Wardens on high alert. We'll be walking. It's safer."

"Oh," she said, and took her arm back.

"If you want to hug me, you just have to ask," he said.

"Shut up."

"It's sweet, actually."

"Shut up."

They started walking. When Valkyrie got too tired, Skulduggery carried her and she slept with her head against his chest. He was an unsurprisingly smooth walker. She only woke on the few occasions he had to hurry behind cover as a Barge passed overhead, or dodge behind a tree to avoid someone on the road.

The sun came up and he let her down and they walked together. Sometimes they talked. Other times they didn't. The silence that would accompany them was comfortable and easy.

They got to Dublin-Within-The-Wall a little before midday. The wall that surrounded the city was gigantic, even by Roarhaven standards. They watched mortals in ragged brown clothes bring carts of goods in and out through the massive gates.

"If he came here himself," said Valkyrie, "that's how he got in."

"He did come here himself," Skulduggery said. "We crossed his tracks a few times on our way here."

"You're sure it was him?"

Skulduggery nodded. "His shoes are standard-issue prison wear. They leave a mark like no other."

"He was right in front of us? So, if we'd just been faster, we would have caught up to him?"

"Maybe," said Skulduggery. "Or maybe we'd have overshot and alerted him to our presence, and lost our chance forever. We did the right thing. We took our time and we made sure. He's ahead of us, and I think you're right – I think he's already in the city."

"So how do we get in?"

Skulduggery didn't answer. He just led her away from the gates. When they were out of sight of even the sharpest of eyes, they approached the wall itself.

"OK," Skulduggery said, "you can hug me now."

She scowled at him. "We're going to fly over the top?"

"Not quite. Come. Hug."

Valkyrie sighed, and they hugged, and they leaned against the wall...

And the wall cracked and crumbled and they moved into it, into the cold and the dark and the dirt and the stone and the pebbles, and they were turning, revolving, the whole world rumbling, and then light burst through the darkness and they were out the other side, Valkyrie coughing and staggering and gasping. "Since when can you do *that?*"

"What do you mean?" Skulduggery asked, using the air to brush the dust from his suit. "We've done that before, when we were going to get the *Hessian Grimoire* from – oh."

"That wasn't me," said Valkyrie. "That was Stephanie."

"Yes. It would appear so."

"Awkward."

"Indeed it is. Let's skip by it, what do you say? So, yes, I can walk through walls now. I can't do it as well as Sanguine, and there are some materials I just can't pass through at all. But it's a neat little trick when you're in a tight spot."

"You are full of surprises, aren't you?"

He shrugged. To some people, that may have been a modest gesture. But to Valkyrie, it was a shrug that said, "Yes. Yes I am."

She had to smile. "So where to now? If Ravel's in here, where would he go?"

"The first thing he'd do is look up old friends," Skulduggery said. "The last time we were here we passed a peculiar church. Do you remember it?"

"Everything here is peculiar. A Faceless Ones church?"

"No, which makes it peculiar. Come on. We'll have to stick to the back streets, but I think I know the way."

He'd only been here once before, and already he was talking about short cuts. But Valkyrie didn't argue. If Skulduggery thought he knew something, he generally did.

They walked for almost two hours. Skulduggery's façade was used only when absolutely necessary, but even so it was close to failing when they got to where they were going. The church was nothing compared to Mevolent's Palace, or the Faceless Ones' churches, or even the Sanctuary in Roarhaven, but it was bigger and more impressive than any place of worship Valkyrie had ever seen back home. She frowned at the iconography built into the structure.

"The Children of the Spider?" she said. "They have their own church?"

"Apparently so," Skulduggery responded. "And if Ravel has gone anywhere for refuge, it's here. He planned the takeover of Roarhaven with them. It makes sense he'd seek them out in this reality."

He checked the street, made sure there were no City Mage patrols, and they hurried through the open doors.

Immediately upon entering, they saw a cage suspended by chains. Within that cage, an old man with a long grey beard and long grey hair was forced to crouch, an old man Valkyrie knew as the Torment.

Skulduggery's façade failed in that instant, and it flowed back off his skull.

The Torment peered at him through narrowed eyes. "Skeleton," he said. "I'd heard your bones had turned to dust decades ago and you were carried away on a stiff breeze. Unless you're another unfortunate who has had his flesh stripped from his body."

"No," Skulduggery said. "Same unfortunate, I'm afraid."

The Torment shifted his attention to Valkyrie, his frown deepening and his lip curling beneath all that hair.

"And what exactly are *you*?"

She sighed. "Save your disgust, OK? I've heard it before. You don't like me because I have the blood of the Ancients in my veins, and I don't like you because you're old and nasty and creepy and you stole Gandalf's beard."

"I don't know who this Gandalf is, but that is not why you disgust me, you insolent little—"

Valkyrie jabbed her finger at him. "No insults. You hear me? I'm not in the mood and we don't have the time. By the looks of it, you've been in that cage for a while now, and people in

351

cages probably don't get many opportunities to chat to people who aren't in cages, so embrace this chance while you can, you miserable old goat."

"What my friend is trying to ask," Skulduggery said, diverting the attention back to him, "is why *are* you in a cage? This is a Temple of the Spider. Surely this is your home?"

The Torment sat cross-legged, and didn't answer.

"Maybe this is a self-punishment thing," Valkyrie said. "But instead of, like, whipping himself or wearing one of those shirts made of hair, whatever they're called—"

"Hair shirts," Skulduggery said.

"—maybe instead of doing that, he locks himself in a cage so that more people can see how he's suffering. He probably thinks he's being really dramatic and noble."

"I don't think that's it. But this cage isn't even bound. It wouldn't stop magic from being used."

The Torment sneered. "My magic, as you put it, is to grow into a beautiful spider that would dwarf the likes of you. This cage stops me from growing. It does its job."

"I'm sure it does." Skulduggery took a step closer. "We're looking for a friend of ours who might have come through here a few hours ago."

"The man Ravel," said the Torment. "Yes, he was here. He seemed surprised when the others found him. I do not think it was what he was expecting."

"Where is he?"

"They took him away. They're deciding what to do with him now. They'll argue and debate, but eventually they'll do what they always do – bring him to Mevolent like the spineless, gutless whelps they are."

Skulduggery tilted his head. "That's why you're in here," he said. "You wouldn't bend the knee."

"Mevolent worships the Faceless Ones," the Torment said. "In order to ensure their own survival, the Children of the Spider have taken to worshipping them as well. I stood against it, as did Madame Mist and a handful of others. But our own brothers and sisters betrayed us. I was the only one left alive after the purge, such as it was, and now here I sit, another of Mevolent's trophies."

Valkyrie remembered the lifeless body of Mr Bliss floating in that tank in Mevolent's Palace. He did seem to have a thing about displaying his enemies for all to see.

"We need to get Ravel back," Skulduggery said. "Where's he being held?"

The Torment uttered a sound that may have been a cough or a laugh. "Why would I help you, skeleton? You're a dead thing who should have given up any claim to life a long time ago. And the girl... Even she doesn't know what an abomination she really is."

"In your reality and ours," Valkyrie said, "you're still a gigantic asshat."

"If you help us," Skulduggery said, "you'll be hurting Mevolent. You'll be hurting all those people who betrayed you. That's worth something, isn't it, to that withered little heart of yours? Even here, trapped in a cage, you can still manage to slip the knife in and give it a fun little *twist*."

"Or I could ignore you," said the Torment, "and by ignoring you, hurt you. At least then I'll be able to see the frustration on the face of the abomination."

"Please call her Valkyrie. I'll never hear the end of it if you keep calling her... the other thing. And you're absolutely right – by not helping us, you'll be able to see with your own eyes the frustration that results. But we haven't hurt you, have we? We may offend your delicate sensibilities, but we have never, and I can say this with absolute certainty, we have *never* acted against you. But Mevolent? Those Children of the Spider? They are directly responsible for your imprisonment. They are directly responsible for the death of Madame Mist. And this is your chance, finally and at long last, to strike back, in whatever small and meagre fashion it may be. You can't tell me that wouldn't be far more satisfying than causing us this trifling little moment of annoyance."

"You talk a lot."

Skulduggery nodded. "That has been said."

The Torment settled back. Just when Valkyrie thought he wasn't going to utter another word, he spoke. "He was here, your friend. He saw me caged, talked to me like he knew me. Before he said too much, he was taken away. The Terror likes to make regular offerings to his lord and master Mevolent – I expect your friend will be one such offering before long."

"So he hasn't been handed over yet?"

"As far as I am aware, he is still being held in the Confessional, in the uppermost tower. If you are considering a rescue attempt, I wholeheartedly endorse such an idea, as it will surely get you both killed."

"Do you have a better idea?"

"No, and nor do I feel the need to supply one. Time, however, is not on your side. The hour is almost upon us when Baron Vengeous pays the temple a visit."

Valkyrie frowned. "Vengeous is dead. The last time I was here, I saw Anton Shudder kill him."

The Torment curled his lip behind his beard. "Death means little to Mevolent's generals, though I admit Vengeous is not the man he once was. That pool of Mevolent's, the one he bathes in daily, has properties as strange as they are unnatural. Baron Vengeous is a man transformed, and when he arrives, your friend will undoubtedly be passed into his custody."

"Well then," Skulduggery said, "we'll have to endeavour not to be here when he shows up. Top of the stairs, you say?"

Skulduggery didn't wait around for an answer. Valkyrie shot another glare at the Torment, then followed Skulduggery through the archway. They passed three Children of the Spider. Valkyrie tensed, ready to fight, but Skulduggery just walked by, acting like he owned the place. It was one of his favourite tricks, and it usually worked. Nobody likes to bother someone who looks busy. Not even a walking skeleton.

They got to a vast hall housing the stairs, the sight of which made Valkyrie start. The base of the staircase was ridiculously wide, but then it split into narrower tributaries at the second floor, tributaries that curled and spiralled and split again and again and got narrower and narrower as they rose, criss-crossing, into the gloom overhead. Supporting pillars of varying thicknesses stood like impossibly tall trees, so tall their tops could not be seen from where Valkyrie stood. Skulduggery slipped through the forest of pillars like this was something he saw every day. Valkyrie trailed after him, seemingly unable to close her mouth, and the only thought in her head was a fervent wish that the Children of the Spider had been wise enough to install elevators.

Skulduggery stopped walking and looked straight up. From this position, they had an unobstructed view of the ceiling high above. Valkyrie stepped close and his arm encircled her waist.

They lifted off the ground, flew upwards, eliciting a few startled cries from people who blurred by too quickly to see. They reached the top and landed behind a man with unusually large hair. Probably a new craze sweeping Dublin-Within-The-Wall. He turned and Skulduggery hit him, and he bounced off the ground and lay still.

They hurried down a corridor that narrowed the further they got. Another guard was stationed ahead of them. They walked right up to him and just as he was about to deny them entry, Skulduggery punched him. This one didn't go down as easily, so Skulduggery smashed his head against the wall. They moved on to a junction, heard a cry of pain, and a moment later Erskine Ravel ran round the corner.

He saw them and his eyes widened. He raised his hand, but Skulduggery was already splaying his. Ravel flew backwards, tumbled and got up, staring straight into Skulduggery's gun.

He froze.

Valkyrie checked round the corner. Three people lay unconscious. Beyond them was an open door and another unconscious person. A pair of shackles lay on the floor nearby.

"Why?" Ravel asked. "Why did you come? Why bother? You could leave me. Why don't you? You can just walk away. And it's not like I'll have a happy life here. I'm probably going to be caught again, taken to Mevolent, tortured until I die. That's the thing about Darquesse's punishment – the agony was exceptional, but I was never going to die from it. Mevolent's way seems a lot fairer."

"You think we'd let you off that easily? After what you've done?" asked Skulduggery.

"You deserve a lifetime of agony," Valkyrie said, rejoining them.

"I thought I did," Ravel said. "But what Darquesse did to me... that's what we'd label cruel and unusual. I can't go back to that. I just can't. You have no idea what it was like. You've no idea what something like that does to you. I'm exhausted. I need to recover. I need to get strong again."

"You need to put those shackles back on and come with us," Skulduggery said.

"No!" Ravel said, almost shouting, before visibly calming himself. "No. You're not taking me back. Darquesse will find me and it'll start all over again."

Skulduggery thumbed back the hammer of his gun. "This is not a negotiation."

Ravel offered a wan smile. "You won't shoot me. You need me alive."

"I'll settle for wounded."

"Go ahead. Wound me. Hope the wound slows me down but doesn't bleed me dry. Hope it makes me more co-operative and not more stubborn."

Skulduggery didn't respond for a moment, and then he gave

a shrug. "Very well," he said, passing his hat and his gun to Valkyrie. "Hold these."

Ravel chuckled softly as Skulduggery stepped towards him, and flexed his fingers, readying his magic. Before he could raise his hands, however, the door opened beside him and four unsuspecting Children of the Spider walked out.

Alarm swept over their faces, and Ravel lunged at one and Skulduggery dived at another. Ravel was still recovering from Darquesse's punishment, so the dismantling of his opponents wasn't as precise or as polished as Skulduggery's, but it was impressive nonetheless. Valkyrie had seen Skulduggery fight like this before, alongside Ghastly or any of the other Dead Men, giving battle with the absolute assurance that the person by his side was doing his job. The Children of the Spider didn't have time to even cry for help. Fist collided with chin and elbow smashed into jaw and forehead met nose, and in moments Skulduggery and Ravel were standing over four unconscious, broken bodies.

"You're going to need my help getting out of the city," Ravel said. "I came here looking for assistance. It's obvious I'm not going to get it, so I need to escape, too."

"And when we're out of here," Skulduggery said, "you'll surrender?"

"Not a chance. But we can have that argument once we're clear."

From somewhere close, running footsteps. A whole lot of running footsteps.

"Come on," Skulduggery said, turning to the window. He flicked his hands and the glass exploded outwards, and then all three ran forward and jumped.

Air rushed.

It brought Valkyrie to Skulduggery's side. She hung on. The street hurtled towards them. No Redhoods gathered below. Not yet.

They slowed, following Ravel's trajectory, and landed at the same time.

"Get to the back streets," Skulduggery instructed. "Get under cover as fast as—"

He stopped talking. Valkyrie glanced at Skulduggery, then at Ravel, noticed how pale he'd become. Then she saw what they were looking at. Three men, walking up the street towards them.

Baron Vengeous.

Lord Vile.

And Mevolent.

52

THE DEVIL COMES
TO PLAY

The world got very quiet all of a sudden.

Baron Vengeous wore his grey hair short and his grey beard tight. His uniform was spotless and his boots were polished, his sabre still in its scabbard at his belt. All of this Valkyrie expected. She did not expect his skin to be so pale as to be almost blue. His face, usually so stern, so filled with anger, was slack. Lifeless. Anton Shudder had, it seemed, killed him – but Mevolent had not let him rest.

Lord Vile's black armour twisted lazily around him, savouring the calm before the storm.

Between his two generals, and taller than either of them, Mevolent wore his battlesuit of grey chain mail and black leather. His tattered cloak, covered as it was with sigils, caught the breeze as he walked. The hood was down. His face, that gaunt, nicotine-yellow face, was hidden behind his metal helmet's screaming visage.

Shadows curled round Vile and he disappeared into them. At that same instant, he stepped out of the swirling shadows right in front of Skulduggery.

They stood there, looking at each other.

"You'd think we'd have a lot to talk about, you and I," said

Skulduggery. Vile didn't answer, so Skulduggery continued. "You'd think we'd have questions that needed answering. But I don't. All I need to know is that you're still here. You didn't fight it, like you should have. You weren't strong enough to control it."

Vile's armour grew spikes.

"I've done terrible things," Skulduggery said. "Things I will never make right. But there's one thing I know. There's one thing of which I'm certain. I'm a better man than you."

Shadows crashed into Skulduggery and sent him flying.

Ravel snapped his palms against the air, but Vile was already moving. In a blur of shadow, he batted down Ravel's arms and took his legs from under him. Before Ravel could recover, the shadows grabbed him and threw him.

Ravel rolled to his feet, but now Vengeous was behind him. That slack face didn't change its expression as he wrapped his arm round Ravel's throat. Ravel was lifted off the ground. The choke came on instantly. A few seconds later, he collapsed.

Valkyrie stood motionless. Her shock stick was still on her back. Vile was watching her, waiting for her to make a move. For all he knew, she was Darquesse, here to tear the city down. One slight twitch on her part would probably lead to him lashing out, killing her in an instant.

She left the stick where it was.

And then, from the street to the west, a siren.

Vile and Vengeous looked round. With that particular slow confidence that characterises the most powerful player on any field, Darquesse came walking.

Vile looked at Valkyrie, quickly deciding she was not the threat he thought she was. He rejoined Mevolent and Vengeous, and the siren cut off.

Darquesse gave them all a smile, and pointed at Ravel, who was doing his best to get to his feet. "I just want him," she said loudly. "I learned how to shunt and came all this way simply to make sure he didn't run off. Hand him over. You can do what you want with the others."

Vile and Vengeous remained silent. Only Mevolent spoke. "I've been waiting for you."

Darquesse laughed. "I bet you've thought about nothing else. But I'm not here for a rematch. You don't interest me. None of you do. Only him. Only Ravel."

Mevolent turned to observe Ravel for a moment. "He doesn't appear to be that special."

"Oh, but he has sentimental value," said Darquesse. "I won't bore you with the details. I don't have much sentiment left, to be honest. But he has earned a special place in my heart. Give him to me, and I'll let you live."

As if by a silent command, Redhoods melted from doorways and alleys, surrounding Darquesse. She shook her head as she rose into the air. "You do not want to test me, Mevolent. I have punishments to deliver."

Valkyrie became aware of Skulduggery standing at her elbow. They watched as Alexander Remit teleported in, passed Mevolent a brown metal gun, and vanished again.

It was the size of a shotgun, but thicker, like a rocket launcher. Glowing sigils ran around its circumference. Mevolent's right hand curled round the grip; the mouth of the barrel was open and jagged, like the thing had teeth.

Darquesse surrounded herself with a bubble of energy as she hovered there. "You're not going to hurt me with toys," she said.

A single beam of green light burst from the gun, sliced straight through the energy shield and hit Darquesse square in the chest.

The bubble vanished and Darquesse dropped. She landed on her feet, staggered a little, then straightened up and laughed. "That's it? That barely tingled."

Then a Cleaver hit her from behind and she went stumbling to the ground.

Valkyrie's eyes widened.

A kick came in that snapped Darquesse's head back. She sprawled, got up, the confusion vanishing from her face as anger swarmed in. She grabbed the nearest Redhood and tore him apart. A scythe came for her and she caught its blade in her hand and snapped it, then took out its wielder with an eye blast.

Mevolent fired again, the beam hitting Darquesse in the side just as she waved her hand.

A scythe flashed and took her fingers.

Darquesse screamed, clutching her hand, too shocked by the sight of her spurting blood to do anything about it. The Redhood whirled, taking her legs out from under her. She hit the ground and tried to scramble away. Her jacket bunched up, exposing her back, and the Redhood impaled his blade in her flesh.

Her scream was cut off. Her mouth was open but no sound came out. Pain danced in her wide eyes.

And then, as if the pain had only been an act, her eyes narrowed and the terror washed away. Black flames consumed the Redhood and burned him from existence. She stood, pulled out the scythe and dropped it with one hand even as her fingers grew back on the other.

The other Redhoods closed in. She swept her arms wide and they exploded into nothing. Then she fixed her glare on Mevolent.

She dived into the air and flew at him, but he caught her again with that dazzling green light and she fell into the street.

Lord Vile shadow-walked to her side. She sprang up, waved her hand, but nothing happened. Tendrils of darkness lashed at her face, drawing blood and cries of pain. She ran, slipping and sliding away from the shadows. She didn't even see Baron Vengeous waiting for her. He ran her through with his cutlass, finding the space between her jacket and waistband, and Darquesse gasped, gagged, fell sideways, sliding off the blade.

Her strength returned and she swung wildly, but Vengeous was already calmly stepping away.

She got up, healing her injuries. But instead of attacking, she stayed where she was, looking from Vengeous to Vile to Mevolent. Her face was tight with anger, but tempered with something else – the realisation that she was not going to win this.

She started to flicker, slowly at first and then faster. The gun in Mevolent's hands was getting ready to fire again, but before he could aim she straightened up, looked over at Valkyrie and gave her a shrug, and then she shunted.

Mevolent lowered the weapon.

Hands seized Valkyrie from behind. Skulduggery tried to fight, but there were too many Redhoods. She glimpsed Ravel being thrown to the ground and shackled, and then someone hit her and the world spun. Her knees gave out, but she wasn't allowed to fall.

Baron Vengeous came into view. From this close, he looked like a corpse. "Take the skeleton and the Elemental to the Racks," he told someone. "I want them screaming before the hour is up."

"And the girl?"

Vengeous barely glanced at her. "Take her to Professor Nye. Tell it, it can do whatever it likes to her."

53

THE END IS NYE

Strapped to another damn table.

This one was elevated so that Valkyrie was almost vertical. She couldn't see the mechanism that raised it to this position. She couldn't tell if it was magical or mechanical. It was silent, though, and smooth, the result of thought and effort and ingenuity. This was the work of someone who liked to get straight down to business.

Professor Nye stooped low to get through the door of its laboratory, and once it was through it unfurled to its full gangly height. The surgical scrubs it wore were a deep red, and the leather apron was old and black. Like its counterpart in Valkyrie's dimension, it wore a surgical mask and cap, so that only its small yellow eyes were visible.

"Professor," its assistant said, hurrying to its side, "we have a new patient. Female, approximately eighteen years old. In good health." The assistant's name was Civet. He had assisted Kenspeckle Grouse back in the reality Valkyrie knew, before the Grotesquery had killed him one lazy afternoon. He'd been a goofy guy. Here, he assisted a murderous sadist.

"I can see all that," said Nye in that curious, high-pitched voice, pulling the clipboard from Civet's hand. "The only thing I *can't* see is why she's here."

"Baron Vengeous sent her to us," Civet said. "She was with the living skeleton and another man. The Baron wants to know more about her."

Nye leaned in, its long fingers tracing lightly down Valkyrie's arm. "This jacket is armoured," it said, almost in wonderment. "I haven't seen quality like this in... I don't think I've *ever* seen quality like this." It moved to the cabinets, taking out trays of instruments. "Remove her clothes," it said. "I want every centimetre of this material examined."

Civet nodded, stepped forward, and Valkyrie glared. "Touch me and die."

Despite the manacles and the straps holding her down, Civet faltered.

Nye looked round, saw the distance between its lackey and Valkyrie, and pulled down its surgical mask in annoyance. Its skin was as pallid as the Nye that Valkyrie had known, but this one had not had its mouth sewn shut or its nose cut off, and so its ugliness was marginally less horrifying. "She intimidates you? She's powerless, you cretin. She's tied down. What exactly is she threatening you with?"

"She, ah, appears easily agitated."

"And yet harsh words are the only things she can throw at you. Are you afraid of harsh words? No? Then remove her clothes before I remove your skin."

Nye turned back to its trays of sharp-bladed tools, and Civet took one more hesitant step closer to Valkyrie. He reached out to unzip her jacket and she bared her teeth. He thought better of putting his hands anywhere near her mouth, and dropped them to waist-level, where he hesitated again. He glanced up, saw her glare, and looked away quickly. After another moment's hesitation, he knelt, one hand on her ankle.

"If I take the manacle from around your foot so I can get at your boot," he said, "are you going to kick me?"

"Without a doubt," said Valkyrie.

"That's what I thought," Civet said miserably.

Nye came back, shoving Civet out of its way. "Leave me, you buffoon. You can strip the clothes from her corpse, as that's all you're good for."

"Yes, Professor," Civet said, bowing as he took his leave. "Sorry, Professor."

"What are you going to do to me?" Valkyrie asked.

"Poke you," said Nye. "Prod you. Do unpleasant things."

"Why?"

"Because I can," it said, reading the information on the clipboard, "and it amuses me, and you're a curious creature. You are clearly mortal, with no aptitude for magic, and yet..."

"And yet what?"

Nye examined a nearby monitor. "And yet there is something..."

The last time Valkyrie had been strapped to a table like this, she'd had an autopsy performed on her while she was still conscious. She doubted this Nye would be any gentler. She couldn't escape. She had no magic and her shock stick was on a table across the room. The only thing she could do was delay the inevitable, offer up distractions.

"I'll save you some time," Valkyrie said. "I found out my true name. My true name then took on a life of its own, and was recently separated from me."

Nye swivelled its head towards her. "You offer this information freely?"

"I want to know what I am even more than you do. You said there was something. What is it? Is it magic?"

Nye blinked a few times. "I... I do not know, I... ah..."

Valkyrie sighed. "I get it, OK? You're not used to the people you experiment on asking questions, but I need this to happen, so buck up, bucko. I don't have a true name any more. My magic has left me. Can I get it back?"

"I've never heard of anyone being separated from their true name before," Nye said. "It will take some time for me to come up with a hypothesis, and there – there are so many tests to run and I... I don't, I don't think I can do this."

"Do what?"

It didn't answer.

"Do the tests?"

"I can't work with you when you're like this!" it blurted. "To every one of my specimens, I am the last thing they see! Terror is what I am used to – terror is what I like! I prefer my subjects to scream and beg, not ask to see results!"

"I'll scream my questions, if that helps."

"It won't," it said sadly. "I'll know you're only trying to make me feel better."

"Well then, it looks like you're in for an uncomfortable few hours, Professor. Unless of course you'd like to tell Mevolent you were unsuccessful."

Nye's small eyes narrowed.

"Run your tests," said Valkyrie. "When you're done and you have an answer for me, I'll behave."

Elsewhere in Dublin-Within-The-Wall, Skulduggery Pleasant and Erskine Ravel were being tortured. She knew this. She didn't give a damn about Ravel's discomfort, but she was worried about Skulduggery. She just didn't think it was fair. He'd been tortured so much in the course of his lifetime, after all. That's how he'd died. Nefarian Serpine had tortured him for three days, using that red right hand of his, employing all manner of barbaric techniques and cruel instruments. Skulduggery had died screaming, looking into the face of the man who had killed his wife and child. And now he was back on the torture table while Mevolent or Vengeous or even Vile took turns.

"Curious," Nye muttered.

Valkyrie looked up. "What is?"

"You said you'd pretend to be unconscious."

"Well, now I'm pretending to wake up. What's curious? What?"

Nye sighed. "It's merely a theory, based upon the most rudimentary of tests already run, and I do not know how to explain it, exactly."

"Please," said Valkyrie, "use small words."

"Your magic is, indeed, gone. When your true name was taken from you, all your magic went with it. But my tests did pick up something. And that something led to a thought, and the thought to an idea, to a theory, and lastly to a hypothesis. Our true names act as our link to the source of all magic, this we know, and every sentient being has such a name. In theory."

"Only in theory?"

"Magic is too vast a subject to be mastered. We view magic one way, from one perspective. Who are we to say that ours is the only perspective? Warlocks and witches are virtually extinct thanks to Mevolent's purges a hundred years ago, but they didn't follow our rules and yet they had access to the source, and their access was arguably purer than our own. There could be a thousand different aspects to magic that we don't know about, that are invisible to us, that we will *never* know about."

"And what does this have to do with me?"

"You do not have a true name, and yet there is, as I have said, something. Or rather, the complete *lack* of something. Which is, in itself, rather something."

"I know you're trying to dumb it down for me, but I think you've gone a smidge too far."

"My tests show nothing," Nye said impatiently. "Absolutely no trace of magic within you. Zero. Even in the most mundane mortal, there's a sliver of a trace. Not enough to ever activate or ever affect anything or be affected, but a sliver nonetheless. But within you, there is nothing."

"So Darquesse took everything with her."

"Yes. But that's not important. The complete lack of magic may not necessarily indicate that there's no magic within you. It may instead indicate that there's something *blocking* you from magic."

"But since I don't have a true name—"

"Then you're an empty vessel," said Nye. Almost excitedly. "You are something unique. Something I've never seen before. And, like any empty vessel, you're just waiting to be filled."

"So how do I get... filled?"

"I do not know. As I said, all this is conjecture. I will know more after the autopsy."

"I'm sorry," said Valkyrie. "The what?"

"I've done all I can with your living body," said Nye. "Once I've dissected you, I'll know more."

"I won't be much use to you dead."

"That's what every living person says. They're always wrong."

"But there have to be more tests you—"

"This is why I do not like conversing with specimens on my table," said Nye, interrupting her. "Arguments. Discussions. Appeals to my humanity. I am a Crengarrion. I am not human. I will now cut you up into little pieces that I will weigh and catalogue. You only interest me from this point on as a collection of body parts."

"What about the soul?" Valkyrie asked. "The Nye in my reality was always looking for the soul. Don't you want to do that?"

Nye leaned over her. "The soul? I found where the soul resides four years ago. Rest assured, I'll be dissecting that also."

Civet came back in. He walked stiffly. He looked terrified. "Professor..."

Nye turned to him. "Yes? What is it? What do you—?"

Civet was shoved sideways into the wall, and a silenced pistol gripped by a red hand was aimed straight into Nye's startled face.

Nye raised its hands. "Wh-what is this?"

"What does it look like, you ridiculous creature?" Nefarian Serpine asked. "It's a damn rescue."

54

THE DEAL

In Valkyrie's reality, Emmett Peregrine was a Teleporter who had been dead for years, killed by the Diablerie. In this reality, he was alive and well and waiting for them in the corridor outside Nye's laboratory. With her stick in one hand, Valkyrie grabbed his arm and Serpine took hold of the other, and suddenly they were outside.

Valkyrie stepped away from them both. They were in a small village. People hurried by. She could hear the sea. She could smell fish on the evening air.

Peregrine disappeared, and Serpine turned to Valkyrie and smiled. "Hello, Valkyrie."

"What do you want?"

"That's all the thanks I get?" he said. "I just saved your life. A little gratitude would be nice."

"What do you want?"

Serpine didn't seem overly wary of the stick in her hand at all. "Valkyrie, this may come as a shock to you, considering the history you've shared with both me and my counterpart from your dimension, but I'm not altogether a bad guy. I have my good moments. I have my redeeming features. In the time since you were last here, I've taken over as leader of the Resistance. Are you shocked?"

"I don't care enough to be shocked."

"Not caring is a sign of shock. After China Sorrows was so tragically killed during Mevolent's attack on Resistance territory, I put myself forward for—"

"You killed her."

"Eh?"

"You killed China. You broke her neck."

Serpine frowned. "You saw that?"

"Darquesse did," said Valkyrie. "Which means I did."

"Ah," said Serpine, "well, it was a chaotic day. Lots of people did lots of things. It was very confusing. Who knows who did what?"

"I know you killed China."

"Let's not get bogged down in specifics," he said, speaking quietly. "Yes, I killed China, but in a more general sense, China was killed and I was nearby. That's just a lot softer to say, isn't it? It isn't nearly as spiky as *I killed her*. So let's stick with China was killed, and I was nearby, and let's not tell anyone the rest. It'd just complicate matters – for you, as well as me. And now here I am, striking a blow against tyranny by releasing you, Valkyrie Cain. You're welcome, by the way."

"Why?"

"Because I am in need of you. Come. Walk with me."

"No," said Valkyrie.

He sighed. "You're stubborn. Some people might find that admirable. I find it annoying."

Valkyrie looked around. "Are all these people sorcerers?"

"Hmm? Oh, no." He chuckled. "Not at all. Look at them. What a sorry state we'd be in if they were."

"So this is a mortal village?"

"Yes. It's the perfect hiding spot. There's enough depressing mundanity here to frighten off even the most ardent of Sense-Wardens before they get too close."

"Isn't it dangerous?"

"We can handle it."

"Not for *you*," she said, glaring. "For them. The mortals. If Mevolent finds out your base is here, all these innocent people will be caught in the crossfire."

Serpine nodded. "So?"

"So these are the people you're supposed to be protecting."

"Who told you that? It's not our job to protect them. Our job is to fight Mevolent."

"And if you beat him?"

"*When* we beat him."

"What then? Are you going to rule over these people just like he did?"

"Of course," said Serpine. "What did you expect? You really think we'd let mortals run the world? Look at them. Watch them stumble and fumble. Gaze into their dull eyes. Can you see even the faintest glimmer of intelligence? Mortals are not fit to run their own lives, Valkyrie, let alone the world."

"If you give them a chance—"

"They don't want a chance. They need guidance. They need wisdom. The oldest mortal is still only a child compared to a sorcerer. Would you trust children to run your life?"

"They're not children."

"You haven't had your Surge yet, have you? So you're as young as you look, and as such you've probably still got sentimental attachments to a mortal family or friends... But you'll learn. You just need a few more years. Please, would you come with me?"

Valkyrie glowered, but she couldn't just stand in one place until she thought of something better to do. They walked up the road a little, to a tavern.

"You are not buying me a drink," she said.

Serpine smiled. "I can be quite charming when I put my mind to it, you know. You might even find yourself liking me."

She didn't even bother responding to that, and he laughed.

They walked into the tavern. Immediately, the atmosphere was different. The people in here held themselves straighter than those outside. They were stronger. More alert.

Sorcerers.

A girl drifted over to them, pale, with a scar curling from the corner of her mouth.

"Valkyrie," said Serpine, "you remember Harmony, don't you? Harmony is my... assistant."

"Valkyrie," Harmony said. "A pleasure to see you again."

"Harmony used to tell me what to do," Serpine continued. "She used to mock me. I think it's fair to say she didn't like me at all. Maybe she despised me as much as you do. Would that be fair, Harmony?"

Harmony glared at him.

Serpine smiled. "But that didn't stop her falling for my charms. Oh, it was an illicit affair. Torrid, even. She hated me, yet was drawn to me. Very passionate."

"I really don't need to hear this," Valkyrie said.

"And then the dearly departed China Sorrows ordered me to help you and your skeleton friend to sneak into the city, and Harmony feared she'd lost me. You feared that, didn't you, Harmony? You thought I'd be killed. But I returned. And it was China who died so, so tragically. The Resistance was in tatters. It took someone special to draw them all together. There was only one man for the job. But then he died too, also tragically, and I was the only soul brave enough to replace him. After that, Harmony began looking at me with a newfound respect – nay, admiration."

Harmony set her jaw.

"These people needed me, Valkyrie. They looked upon me as a saviour. It has been a lot of responsibility and I... I admit it, I've made mistakes. How many mistakes did I make, Harmony? Let's count them, shall we? There was Flaring, and Shakra, Ashione and Kallista, Luciana and Rosella and Rapture, and—"

"A lot of mistakes," growled Harmony.

"But finally I came to my senses," said Serpine, "and we found our way back to each other. Now Harmony is in charge of holding my coat." He shrugged out of it and held it out.

Harmony's lips tightened, but she took his coat and didn't drop it as she walked away.

Valkyrie had had enough. "Why did you get me out of there? What do you want with me?"

Serpine motioned to a table, and they sat down. "That magic-sucking gun Mevolent used on your evil doppelgänger," said Serpine. "He's been working on it since the last time you were here. That's what I want. You owe me that."

Valkyrie frowned. "I don't owe you anything."

Serpine leaned forward, his elbows on the table. "I had the Sceptre in my grasp – my only means of defeating Mevolent and his psychotic, shadowy lapdog. But Darquesse took it back with her into your reality. So now you owe me one unstoppable weapon."

"How am I meant to get it?"

"I have a plan."

She shook her head. "I don't have any magic any more."

"I'm sorry?"

"I'm not going into details, but my magic was taken from me. It's gone. I can't help you."

"Someone took your magic? With a weapon like Mevolent's, or—?"

"No. It was something else."

"That's... awful," Serpine said. "No wonder you were defending mortals. You *are* one. Oh, that must be soul-destroying. You poor, pathetic thing..."

"Whatever," snapped Valkyrie. "So I can't help you."

"It doesn't matter. You don't need any magic. You just have to do what I say and try to be convincing."

"Convincing as what?"

Serpine's smile reappeared. "As Darquesse, of course."

"What?"

"I want that gun. The only way Mevolent will bring it out in public is if Darquesse shows up again. From what I've heard, though, it looks like she's run off back to your dimension with her tail between her legs. But has anyone ever told you that you look a lot like her?"

"How do you expect that to work?" asked Valkyrie. "He'll know it's me when he attacks and I die horribly and don't get up again."

Serpine shrugged. "We'll just have to make sure you don't die, then."

"I'm very eager to hear how 'we'll' manage that."

"We have recently come into possession of an extremely rare artefact." He took a cloaking sphere from his pocket. "Do you know what this does? It envelops the wielder in a bubble of invisibility. Quite an ingenious—"

"I know what it is. You want me to take the sphere into battle against Mevolent?"

"You won't be using it," Serpine said. "My Teleporter will. This is far too rare an item to entrust to someone who who might take it back to her own dimension. Peregrine will be right beside you every step of the way – invisible. Mevolent will use the gun, we'll let it hit you, and then Peregrine will teleport you a few steps forward or back. To Mevolent, it will look like Darquesse has found a way to overcome the effects of the weapon. When he abandons his broken toy to take you on with his bare hands, and he will, Peregrine will scoop it up and teleport it, and you, back to us. Questions?"

"What about Skulduggery?"

"If you agree to do this, Pleasant and Ravel will be waiting for you when you return."

"You're going to break them out?" asked Valkyrie.

"Naturally."

"I don't believe you."

"I'm hurt. Unsurprised, but hurt. The fact is, I would have gladly lied to you about rescuing them, but I knew how you'd be, so I actually have a solid rescue plan ready to swing into action. Tomorrow morning, everyone will be distracted by your heroic confrontation with Mevolent, which will allow a team of my best people to break into the dungeons. I can show you the plan, you can meet the team, you can satisfy yourself that they, at least, are honourable people. So long as you say yes right now."

"If you try to cheat me—"

"I wouldn't dream of it," Serpine said, extending his hand. "Well? Do we have a deal?"

Valkyrie hesitated, but not for long. Every moment wasted was another moment of pain for Skulduggery.

She grasped Serpine's hand, and shook.

55

THE EXILED

hina came from a meeting with Melancholia St Clair and Solomon Wreath, and instructed her pretty little assistant to run a bath. Melancholia had been polite in the presence of authority, but Wreath had been his usual aggravating self. If she hadn't needed him to make Melancholia feel more at home in the Sanctuary, she would have arranged to have him escorted from the city gates days ago.

She undressed while she waited for her bath to be ready, and looked at herself in the bedroom mirror. Her head ached. Meetings, conflicts, anxieties, disruptions, expectations and responsibilities. These were the things that made up her life now. She had a troubled frown on her face. There was a small, invisible sigil by her left eye. Her fingertip grazed it lightly, and it glowed, and a feeling of slow warmth spread through her, cancelling out the ache and returning her forehead to its usual frown-free perfection.

Her pretty little assistant stood at the entrance to the bathroom. China removed a delicate bracelet and her necklace, placing them carefully on the dresser. There was a knock on the door, and the frown reappeared.

Her assistant rushed to fetch a bathrobe, but China strode across the room before she could find it and pulled the door open.

Tipstaff faltered midway into the first word of whatever he'd intended to say. Behind him, seven people stood calmly.

"Thank you, Tipstaff," China said, curtly. "That will be all."

Tipstaff bowed, his face flushed, and removed himself from her presence, leaving the seven visitors standing there. China addressed the black-haired man with the single scar marring his beauty.

"I don't like vampires, Mr Dusk."

He inclined his head ever so slightly. "I am aware of that."

"And yet you have still brought six of them to my private chambers. It's been a long day and it will be a long night. If Tipstaff brought you here, you have something of value to say, so out with it."

"We represent the Exiled," Dusk said, "vampires who have broken the most sacred of our codes."

"You've all killed other vampires."

Again, an almost imperceptible nod. "Because of this we've been cast out. It's not... easy, for a vampire to be alone. It's not safe – for us, or anyone else."

China graced them with a smile. "If you've all come here to be put down, I'm sure I can accommodate you."

"Put down like animals, you mean? I'm going to credit you with the intelligence I know you possess, Grand Mage, and choose to believe that you don't really think of us in those terms. You may not like our kind—"

"I despise your kind," China said. "So please, get to the point. I'm getting cold."

"We come to Roarhaven to request asylum."

"Request denied."

"You haven't heard us out."

"Mr Dusk, a burgeoning city like Roarhaven cannot have vampires within its walls."

"You have sorcerers here who've done far worse than any vampire has ever managed," Dusk said.

"And yet I would still prefer all of them to call round for afternoon tea instead of even one of you."

"Provided we have serum," said Dusk, "vampires can operate in a civilised society."

"The problem is nobody likes vampires, Mr Dusk. You unnerve people."

"Some people could do with a little unnerving."

Despite herself, China smiled again. "Indeed. But the answer remains no."

"But you still haven't heard us out."

She sighed. "Very well. Make your case. But be quick – my bath is calling for me."

"We want housing," said Dusk. "We want access to serum and we want the same rights as everyone else."

This made China pause. "In exchange for...?"

"Us."

"I'm sorry?"

"Vampires," he said. "Not only would Roarhaven be the first sorcerer city in the world, but it would also be the first magical community to count vampires among its citizens. It would show every Sanctuary on every continent that there's nothing Roarhaven is afraid of. There is no threat it cannot control. No beast it cannot tame."

"You're offering us your services? You'd be our tame vampires?"

He nodded. "We would be part of the city, and part of the Sanctuary. You would have your operatives, your sorcerers, your Cleavers... and your vampires."

China hesitated. "This has never been tried before."

"With good reason. But times are changing."

"And why exactly have you chosen now to make this offer?"

"Darquesse. A pack of vampires might not last that long against her on its own, but as part of a strategic plan..."

"So you think you're swooping in to aid us in our hour of need?"

"We need you. You may have a need for us. This is an opportune time for a deal to be made, I think. Would you agree?"

China had to admit, she liked the idea. The first magical community to have its own vampires. What a signal that would be. What a message that would send. Dusk was right – Roarhaven would instantly develop the kind of reputation she needed it to have. And as for what it would do for China's *own* reputation...

"Come in," she said. "Talk to me while I bathe."

56

TOE TO TOE

howtime.

The midday sun distant and indifferent over her head, Valkyrie walked the wide street, forcing herself to stroll with confidence towards the Palace, watching the people scatter and the street empty. Even the Redhoods stayed back. The white-robed Sense-Wardens watched her, but didn't try to peek into her mind. They had learned their lesson when they'd tried that against Darquesse.

She felt vulnerable. The only disguise she needed was a change of clothes, which meant she'd had to leave her black ones behind. The outfit she'd been given – red, like Darquesse's – wasn't even armoured. She didn't like this. Not one bit. She had to resist the urge to reach behind her to check if Peregrine was still there. She couldn't even hear his footsteps.

Her mouth was dry. She really wanted to lick her lips, but was afraid that would make her look nervous. She couldn't afford to drop the act, not even for a moment.

Valkyrie stopped walking, put her hands on her hips, and smiled.

They'd expected Mevolent to appear long before this. Maybe he wasn't coming. Maybe he didn't believe for a moment that she was Darquesse. Maybe someone was going to shoot her from a rooftop before Peregrine had a chance to teleport her to safety. One bullet, right between the eyes. How stupid would she feel then?

She was almost relieved when Mevolent drifted down from the sky. Almost.

He didn't have Vile or Vengeous with him. Were they too busy torturing Skulduggery and Ravel, or were they sneaking up behind her? She wanted to look round, but kept her eyes fixed straight ahead.

"Sorry about yesterday," she said loudly. "You caught me unawares. Shall we pick up where we left off?"

Her voice only trembled a little, right at the start. She didn't think he noticed, though. She hoped he didn't.

Mevolent brought the magic-sucking gun out from beneath his cloak. Valkyrie kept the smile, and wondered if this was going to hurt.

The beam hit her and it was hot against her skin, and hit with enough force to drive her back one step. But with no magic to drain out of her, once she'd got over the initial impact, all she felt was a mild tingle. Even so, she mimicked Darquesse's earlier reactions, and fell to her knees like she was exhausted.

Mevolent cut off the beam and strode forward. Before he had a chance to finish her, Valkyrie stood up, felt Peregrine's hand on her back, and suddenly she was on the opposite side of the street.

"Is that it?" she asked, forcing a grin on to her face. "Is that the only setting it's got?"

Mevolent raised the weapon and fired again. This time when the beam hit her, Valkyrie laughed.

Peregrine teleported her three strides to the left. "Your little toys only work on me for a short time," she said. "Then I learn. I adapt. We have a race of beings in my universe – we call them the Borg. They taught me everything they know about adapting to new weaponry. You cannot defeat me, Mevolent. Resistance is futile."

Mevolent fired again, and again. After each blast, Valkyrie forced her smile to grow wider.

He leaped at her and suddenly she was on the opposite side of the street, watching Mevolent land.

She tried to give a laugh, but all that emerged was a strangled bark that she really hoped nobody heard.

Mevolent turned to her. Valkyrie did her best to look arrogant. After all those years of *being* arrogant, it should have come to her a lot more naturally than it did. "I'm not here for you," she said. "I'm here for Skulduggery Pleasant and Erskine Ravel. Give them to me and I will leave this depressing little reality and never come back. You have my word."

Mevolent observed her from behind his helmet. Then he dropped the magic-sucking gun, and held out his hand. For a moment, he stood there like that, and then the God-Killer broadsword drifted down from the rooftops and settled into his grip.

Involuntarily, Valkyrie reached behind her, grabbing for Peregrine. Her fingers grasped at nothing but air, and her entire body went cold.

"Are you there?" she whispered, trying not to move her lips. "Hey!"

But there was no response, and no reassuring pat on the back. The moment Mevolent dropped the gun, Peregrine had moved. She was alone.

Mevolent walked forward slowly, the flat of the broadsword resting on his shoulder. The magic-sucker, on the ground behind him, disappeared, scooped up by the invisible Teleporter.

She couldn't run. Even if she had somewhere to run to, she was nowhere near fast enough to get there. She couldn't fight. She didn't even have her armoured clothes – not that they'd do any good against a God-Killer. That sword was going to slice her in two so cleanly she doubted it'd get any of her blood on its blade.

"Stop!" she screamed.

Mevolent stopped walking.

Fear turned to fury inside her, and bubbled from her belly to her throat. "You think you can kill me?" she roared, and found herself striding forward. "You think I'm going to be killed by the likes of *you*? I am Darquesse! I have lived inside nightmares since before I was even born! I was always here! I was always *meant* to be here! I'm going to kill every man, woman and child, every animal, plant and organism in my reality and I'm going to do it because I can! I am a *god*, you pathetic little man. I am the darkness at the end of the day. I am the cold that overcomes the heat. I am *inevitable*, you insignificant little *toad*. Who the hell are you to think you can threaten *me*?"

When she finished talking, she was standing right before him, glaring up through the eyeholes of his helmet and seriously regretting this course of action. She wanted to pee. Her left leg was shaking so much she thought she was going to collapse. Thankfully, Mevolent's sword was still resting on his shoulder. He seemed to believe that she was who she said she was, that she was capable of carrying out her threats to—

Mevolent's left hand rose, unhurried. Valkyrie forced herself to ignore it, to keep her glare fixed. His hand went to her face, cupping her chin. The slightest squeeze would crumple her jaw, she knew, but she was all out of ideas and staying very still and looking very angry seemed to be the best thing to do in her current situation.

She felt him observing her for the longest time, as if he were peering into her soul and weighing up what he found there. If he found her strong enough, he might just let her go. If he discovered her weakness, he'd kill her where she stood.

His hand left her face.

"You are not Darquesse," he said, and even as he was stepping back to swing the sword, Valkyrie felt hands on her from behind and then she was indoors.

She recognised this place, the darkness and the smell. It was the dungeon beneath Mevolent's Palace. The cloaking sphere retracted and Peregrine stuffed it in his coat. He held the energy-sucker in his other hand.

"You came back for me," Valkyrie said, her eyes wide.

"Of course," said Peregrine. "You think I'd leave you there? We're the good guys, Valkyrie."

"Indeed we are," said a voice behind her, and she turned as Serpine joined them, Skulduggery and Ravel following behind in shackles, escorted by a team of grim sorcerers. "See? Your colleagues, as promised. I am nothing if not a man who sometimes keeps his word. Peregrine, what is that wonderful object you're holding? Is it, perhaps, the weapon I've been waiting for?"

Peregrine handed it over and, while Serpine gave it a cursory examination, Valkyrie rushed over to Skulduggery. "Are you OK? I wanted to get you out sooner but—"

"You got me out when you could," Skulduggery said. "You have no need to apologise."

"Where's the key?" Valkyrie asked Serpine. "The key to the shackles, where is it?"

"I'm sure I don't know," Serpine mumbled, his attention still on the magic-sucker, "and I'm sure I don't care to." Satisfied, he looked up. "Your skeleton friend has a habit of hitting me, so he's going to remain in shackles until you go home, which hopefully will be very soon. Peregrine, I think it's time we all got out of—"

"Company!" one of Serpine's sorcerers snarled as Baron Vengeous stormed towards them.

"Oh, this should be fun," Serpine said, aiming the magic-sucker at him.

He pulled the trigger and nothing happened.

Serpine shook the weapon. "Work, damn you."

"Get us out of here," Skulduggery ordered, and everyone linked up, and before Valkyrie had formed her next thought they were back in the small fishing village on the other side of the country.

"Damn it, why won't it work?" Serpine yelled, stalking away from them. He tried firing at the sky, spun and aimed at Peregrine, but again nothing happened. *"Why won't it work?"*

"Maybe it doesn't work because you don't know how to work it," Valkyrie said. "Maybe it's not so simple as pulling the trigger. You're like a kid who gets a toy on Christmas morning and flings it away when it doesn't work first time."

"Why the hell would kids get toys at Christmas?" Serpine said. "And why are you still here? Don't you have a dimension to get back to?"

"We don't rendezvous with our Shunter for another twenty-six hours," Skulduggery said.

"Well, that's just annoying, isn't it? Do yourself a favour and stay out of everyone's way." He tossed the magic-sucker to one of his men. "And you. Get this working. I'll be in my chambers." He stalked away, shouted Harmony's name. She emerged from a doorway and hurried after him with a scowl on her face.

Peregrine passed a small key to Valkyrie. "For the shackles," he said. "I'm assuming you've arranged to meet up with your Shunter in Roarhaven? Whenever you need to go, come find me."

"We will," she said. "Thanks."

Peregrine and the other sorcerers dispersed. Valkyrie ignored Ravel and unlocked Skulduggery's shackles.

"You OK?" she asked.

"I'm fine," Skulduggery said, adjusting his cufflinks. "That is a *very* useful weapon they've just stolen."

"It is," said Valkyrie. "It's called a magic-sucker."

"That the technical term for it, is it?"

"Yep."

"You know... taking down Darquesse would be a lot easier with that weapon."

She nodded. "I was just thinking that. But Serpine's not going to let us simply take it. We already have a Sceptre from this reality. Taking the—"

"How can you stand to talk to him?" Ravel asked, his voice dripping with disgust.

Skulduggery turned to him slowly. "I'm sorry?"

"Serpine," said Ravel. "For hundreds of years, hunting down that man was what drove you. What drove us. We chased him across the world to make him pay for what he did. He killed our friends, Skulduggery. He killed your—"

Skulduggery moved, and all at once they were standing so close that Skulduggery's hat brim was touching Ravel's forehead.

"I know what Nefarian Serpine did," Skulduggery said in a low, quiet voice. "And the Nefarian Serpine who killed those people is dead."

"They're the same man."

"In a lot of ways. But the Serpine who just walked away from us is not the one who killed our friends. I carried around that anger for long enough. I let it change me. Do you really want me to pick it up again?"

Ravel hesitated. "He's the enemy."

Skulduggery didn't say anything to that. He didn't have to. Ravel took a step back, and looked away.

Skulduggery turned back to Valkyrie. "Serpine thinks he has twenty-six hours in which to get paranoid. But we can take the magic-sucker, steal some horses and get to Roarhaven in ten – just in time to make our actual rendezvous with Signate."

Valkyrie smiled. "You are sneaky."

"When I have to be."

They waited around for two hours for their chance. It was getting dark by then. Valkyrie, clad once again in her black clothes, kept watch. Ravel stood beside her. His hands were still shackled, and the shock stick was on her back and fully charged. If he tried anything, she was ready. Minutes passed.

Skulduggery emerged from the doorway, the magic-sucker wrapped in a blanket. Not a word was spoken. They moved through the village quickly. They got to the stables.

"Stop."

Valkyrie froze. Ever so slowly, she turned, saw Skulduggery and Ravel do the same, as Serpine walked up. Behind him, a squad of sorcerers armed with shotguns and automatic weapons.

"I knew I couldn't trust you," Serpine said. "I knew this would prove just too tempting. You come in here, cause trouble, then disappear with something that belongs to us. Well... not this time. This time you fail. Hand it over."

"Why?" Skulduggery asked. "It's not like you can get it to work."

"We will," said Serpine. "And if we don't, so be it. But you're not taking it with you."

"We just want to borrow it, really. We'll bring it right back."

"Drop it at your feet, or I'll give the order and all three of you will be blasted apart."

Skulduggery put the weapon on the ground slowly, then straightened up, hands in the air.

"If I ever see you again," said Serpine, "I'll assume you're here to try and steal something else, and you will be treated as an enemy. You can leave now."

Valkyrie and Skulduggery backed away from the magic-sucker, taking Ravel with them. At any moment, Valkyrie expected Serpine to give the order to shoot, but as soon as it became clear that he'd already lost interest, she relaxed. She watched him gesture to one of his sorcerers, instructing him to fetch the weapon. Instead, another sorcerer went to get it, a man in a tattered coat and hood. She glimpsed his face, frowned, and reversed her course.

"Valkyrie," said Skulduggery, but she ignored him, stepped closer, peering under that hood as the sorcerer bent to pick up the weapon. His face was unshaven, his lips stretched into a grin. In fact, his whole face was stretched, like it was a mask pulled too tight. The sorcerer raised his head, she saw blackness curling from his empty eyes, and she knew it was a mask – a face cut from another man's head.

"Lord Vile!" she cried, and Vile straightened, tendrils of shadow tearing his clothes to shreds as they lashed out at the startled sorcerers. Bullets raked his armour, either bouncing off or being absorbed into it, and Serpine cursed and dodged back, stumbling to avoid a shadow that would have taken his head off.

Skulduggery grabbed Valkyrie's arm and they ran, joining Ravel behind cover. Bullets whined and fire whooshed and energy sizzled, and screams mixed with shouts until the sound of people dying became the only thing they heard. Valkyrie raised herself up, took a peek. Bodies lay strewn about, and only Vile and Serpine remained standing.

Red energy coursed from Serpine's right hand and met the stream of darkness that flowed from Vile's fist. At first, they seemed evenly matched, but as Valkyrie watched she could see that the darkness was inching forward, bit by bit, and Serpine was showing the strain. He was pale, and sweating, and his arm was trembling.

The magic-sucker caught her eye. Vile had dropped it or someone had snatched it from him – either way it was on the ground once again. She remembered how it had looked in Mevolent's hands, how he had held it. Right before he pulled the trigger his left hand had tightened on the barrel. Maybe that was it. Maybe activating the sigils there was all that was needed to ready the trigger.

Serpine's legs gave out and he dropped, the red energy dissipating and the shadows glancing off his shoulder. He grunted, went sprawling, and Vile's shadows turned sharp.

Then Vile hesitated. To him, this Nefarian Serpine was the

man who had murdered his wife and child, the man who had been responsible for turning him from Skulduggery Pleasant into Lord Vile. Valkyrie reckoned that killing such a man was bound to make anyone relish the moment.

Valkyrie ran from cover, snatched the weapon up, but even as she aimed Vile was turning, sending a shadow shard out to meet her.

What happened next happened slowly. The magic-sucker buzzed slightly in her hand and she felt it activate, felt the beam ready to burst forth. The shadow shard came around like a whip, caught the weapon at its exact centre, a hair's breadth from Valkyrie's forefinger. The gun split as it tried to fire and light erupted from within and filled Valkyrie's vision.

She wasn't aware of being thrown back. She wasn't aware of Vile stumbling. She wasn't aware of her own screaming. All that she was aware of was the pain, and that was enough.

57

A WORLD OF PAIN

Valkyrie missed the long trek back to Roarhaven. That trek, as long as it was, was entirely replaced by never-ending pain.

Skulduggery would later tell her that following the explosion, Lord Vile had shadow-walked away, injured. Serpine had picked up the two halves of the magic-sucker, examined them, cursed, and had Peregrine teleport him away. Skulduggery had then bound Valkyrie's arms and legs so she would be easier to manage, and took her with him on his horse. Ravel went on ahead, his horse tethered to Skulduggery's. It was slow-going, and they missed their rendezvous, but they made the one after that, and Signate shunted them into the circle that China had devised in the Sanctuary in their own dimension. They'd left Ravel in that circle, hidden from Darquesse.

Valkyrie missed all that. All she saw were blurred faces and faraway voices. If she were lucky, unconsciousness would snatch her away from the pain for hours at a time.

She wasn't lucky very often.

58

VALKYRIE'S
AFFLICTION

isjointed. That's how Tanith felt. Like nothing
fitted right. Like she'd lost the rhythm of how
her life was lived. She couldn't shake the feeling
that she was stumbling. She couldn't shake the feeling that her
feet were suddenly leaden.

She was dealing with a life interrupted, and she was lost and
alone and she had no one to help guide her back. She hadn't
called her family. She wanted to leave that until she had a handle
on where things were going. Which would be a nice change.

Ghastly is dead.

Those three words haunted her. They waited at the end of
every thought. Sometimes they'd fade a little, allow her a
distraction, a moment of engagement. But they never left her
alone for long. They were persistent, those three little words.

She took to exploring Roarhaven. She'd tried to help with
preparing the city for Darquesse's wrath, but she only got in the
way. Saracen Rue was too busy to talk and while she'd read their
books, she'd never been introduced to Donegan Bane or Gracious
O'Callahan. Her Remnant-self knew them, apparently. It was
funny. Her Remnant-self had had a better grip on her life than
Tanith did.

Mostly, she just hung around the Sanctuary and waited for Valkyrie to get back. She was there when they shunted in. Thank God. She'd even visited Ravel in his little circle. She used to fancy him. He was so smooth, so charming, so good-looking. And those eyes – those beautiful golden eyes. But now she hated him.

Ghastly is dead.

She needed to get out. She needed to get on her bike and ride.

She left Roarhaven in a cloud of dust. She didn't know where she was going. She got on to the motorway, joined the traffic, found herself taking a familiar exit.

Oh. So *that's* where she was going.

She pulled up outside Valkyrie's house. Knocked on the door.

Melissa Edgley answered it. Desmond passed behind her, with little Alice scampering around after him.

Tanith smiled. "Hi," she said. "I'm—"

"I know you," Melissa said. She looked agitated. "You came to our house a few years ago after Christmas. You were Stephanie's substitute teacher."

"Ah," Tanith said. "Right. That actually wasn't me – not really. And I don't remember it, so I apologise for anything I may have said or done. I was possessed at the time by this horrible little thing that turned me evil for a few years. I just got rid of it, actually. Today is my first Saturday Remnant-free for over two years. My name is Tanith Low, and I suppose I *was* a teacher to your daughter, actually. I handled half of her fight training."

Melissa stared at her.

"Valkyrie told me you found out about the whole magic thing. I, uh, I didn't misunderstand or anything, did I?"

"Where is she?" Melissa asked. "She hasn't been answering our calls and we don't know where she is. Is she all right?"

"She's in the Medical Wing in the Sanctuary. Basically, she's in hospital. I thought you'd probably be worried about her, and it would never occur to Skulduggery to let you know these things."

394

Melissa went very pale. "Take us to her."

"That's not a good idea."

"She's our daughter and you'd better—"

"Melissa," Tanith said, talking over her, "it isn't a good idea to take you to see her because seeing her would distress you too much."

"What's wrong with her?"

"She's in pain," said Tanith. "A hideous amount of pain, if I'm honest. But it shouldn't be too long now before it passes."

"What happened?"

"It's a long story, and full of aspects that you'd find confusing, so I'm going to stick to the simplest explanation, if that's OK with you. Valkyrie and Skulduggery went away to do a job. While they were gone, she was caught in an explosion of sorts."

"An *explosion*?"

"Of sorts. Physically, she's fine, she's uninjured, but she is in an incredible amount of pain. Our doctors didn't know what to make of it at first, until they realised that it wasn't nearly as complicated as they'd feared. In fact, Valkyrie is going through something that everyone there is very familiar with."

"What?" Melissa asked. "For God's sake, what's wrong with her?"

"It's a magic thing."

"But she's not magic. She told us herself, she lost her magic."

"So she did," said Tanith. "But the facts are the facts, and the fact is the explosion kick-started her Surge. What she'll be when she emerges is anyone's guess."

59

THE CORPSE TRAIL

The Cadillac slows, the high whine of asphalt replaced by the crunch of roadside gravel, and then there's nothing. Apart from some residual ticking, even the engine is silent. Danny stops his teeth from chattering long enough to hear a few muffled words of conversation from up front. He doesn't get all of it – he's too cold and he has a pounding headache and he's nauseous and he desperately needs to pee again – but he catches the gist of what they're saying. They're afraid they've lost Stephanie – or rather, they're afraid that Stephanie has lost them.

Jeremiah suggests they loop round, to see if they can pick her up again, but Gant is against the idea. He doesn't want to make it obvious that they're luring her in. They talk about this for a few minutes, with Jeremiah coming up with suggestions like an eager employee trying to impress his boss. Gant, for his part, grows increasingly irate, and Jeremiah eventually gets the message and stops suggesting stupid things.

There's movement, and then a door opens – only one – and someone gets out. Gant. His footsteps move along the side of the car, and stop somewhere close to Danny's head.

"I need to pee," Danny calls.

There's the sharp bang of a fist on the trunk. "Shut up," says Gant, and a moment later Danny hears an approaching car. He catches a brief sweep of headlights through the cracks of the trunk, and then the car slows. It isn't Stephanie. Stephanie wouldn't pull up to where Gant was standing. He hears a voice, a man's voice, saying something, possibly offering to help in some way, and then he jumps as three gunshots ring out.

Gant's movements are unhurried as he gets back in the Cadillac. The engine fires up and they pull out on to the road and continue on.

Danny doesn't need to hear the conversation to know that that was a sign for Stephanie to follow.

A half-hour later, he can't hold it any longer. He unzips and pees into the carpet under the latch, the sense of relief momentarily overwhelming the bizarre sense of shame that threatens to engulf him. When he's finished, he zips up and shuffles back as far as he can, his jacket held up over his nose and mouth. He tests the air every few minutes until he can't smell anything rank, and begins to breathe normally again.

They haven't bothered tying him up after the gas station. They know he's beaten. He knows he's beaten. The acceptance is sudden and unexpected, but no less valid than the thought that follows after. He's beaten *now*, at this particular moment in time. But once they let him out of this trunk? Once he's got his strength back? Then he has a chance again.

The Cadillac slows again and he wakes. It's morning now. A thin line of warm sunlight falls across his face. He hears Gant say, "Excuse me," very clearly, like he's leaning out of an open window. Running footsteps approach. A woman's voice. An early morning jogger.

A thought surfaces in the murk of Danny's mind. The man in the car. The gunshots. A trail of carnage for Stephanie to follow.

"Run!" Danny screams. "Run! He's going to kill you!"

He hears the woman's voice. Not the words, but the tone – confused, suddenly wary – and Gant, trying to be soothing, trying to coax her closer. Then there's a scrape of rubber soles on the road, and the woman is running and Gant is cursing. Car doors open. A gun fires twice. More cursing.

"Go!" Gant shouts, and Danny hears Jeremiah take off in pursuit.

Gant gets back in the car and they leap forward, tyres spinning. The Cadillac swerves violently and Danny hits his head and jars his shoulder. The world rattles and bumps around him. They're off the road now, on some kind of dirt track. Branches scrape against metal. Water splashes. Another turn, and another, and for a moment they're going sideways and Danny is sure they're going to crash, but somehow Gant gets the big car back under control and they straighten out, picking up even more speed.

They take a long, wide turn, then brake, coming to a skidding, sliding stop, and the engine cuts out and the door opens and Danny hears the woman grunt. Something thuds heavily on to a crackling surface. Twigs. The ground is covered in twigs and old leaves and Gant and the woman are rolling around on it. The woman struggles fiercely. Gant curses. There's a burst of snapping branches and trampled undergrowth and another thud, and Jeremiah's heavy panting is added to the mix.

"Let go of me!" the woman shouts. "Let go! Let—"

There's a gunshot.

Danny lies in the darkness, listening to Jeremiah getting his breath back while Gant mutters to himself. After a minute, Jeremiah gets to his feet with great effort. He sighs a few more times, grunts, and Danny hears something being dragged, getting closer. It moves round the car to the trunk. A rattle of keys.

The trunk opens and Danny shields his eyes. He hears Jeremiah's cry of disgust as the smell hits him, and then Gant is saying something and Danny finally looks up.

"No!" says Danny, but Jeremiah drops the woman's body on top of him and slams the trunk shut.

Danny screams, shrinking back from the tangle of limbs and long hair, trying to push the body away, but his hands are suddenly wet with something warm and sticky. There's a new smell in the trunk now, the coppery smell of blood.

"That's what you get," says Gant from outside. "That's what you get."

Danny wants to scream and scream, but he locks it down, he keeps the screams clamped inside his chest, and he breathes fast and shallow. He can smell the woman's coconut shampoo.

Car doors close, and the engine starts, and the Cadillac reverses into a three-point turn and heads back the way it's come at a gentle pace.

When they get to the road, they stop, and Jeremiah comes round and opens the trunk again. His face is red from exertion. Dribbles of sweat run from his forehead. Glaring at Danny, he takes hold of the woman's torso and hauls her out. He lets the body fall at his feet, and looks in at Danny, his nose wrinkled in disgust.

Then he closes the trunk.

60

FREAKS

inally, the pain went away.

They ran a few more tests, then OK'd her release. She eased herself out of bed, her joints aching, and dressed slowly. She was zipping up her jacket when Skulduggery stopped by.

"Clarabelle tells me I've had the Surge," said Valkyrie.

"We've all gone through it," he responded. "It's not nice, but it's necessary. And at least you have magic again. How do you feel?"

"Tired. Sore. But most of all... different. I can feel the magic inside me, but it's not like it was. And I don't feel the air like I used to. I don't think I'm an Elemental any more." Valkyrie clicked her fingers. No sparks flew.

"They have a Nye over there," she said, carrying on clicking. "It's a professor. Still skulking around in the shadows. While you were being held by Mevolent, I was delivered into its delightful hands. After a few tests, it came up with a theory. When Darquesse was pulled out of me, I was left as an empty vessel. The Surge filled me back up but... with what?"

"Magic."

She stopped clicking. "But what kind? Nye said there could be all these different kinds of magic that even sorcerers don't know about."

"That's true," Skulduggery said. She joined him as he walked from the Medical Wing. "I've come across a few such examples. So have you, for that matter. The Jitter Girls. We have no explanation for them at all. We don't know how or why they exist. They just do. I don't know how you're going to turn out. You don't have a true name any more, Valkyrie. You're not bound by our rules. The magic that's within you right now has come directly from the so-called source, with no filtration."

"I could turn into a Jitter Girl?"

"Unlikely. From what we do know of the Jitter Girls, some very specific circumstances led to their present condition. You're probably closer to Warlocks and witches than you are to sorcerers right now. Put a smile on that face, Valkyrie. You're unique. Easily as unique as I am."

"Two freaks in a pod, eh?"

His head tilted, amused. "Wouldn't have it any other way." They walked on through the glorious corridors. This one had flowers and plants growing from the walls in bursts of vibrant colour. "Fletcher's back," he said.

"Is he OK?"

Skulduggery hesitated. "Yes. I think. He apologised, said he just had to get away. I don't think anyone holds it against him. How do you think he'll cope with Darquesse?"

"What do you mean?"

"His judgement. Will it be clouded?"

"By anger, you mean? I don't think so. Fletcher's not really a revenge type of guy. He'll do all he can to help, but he's not going to do anything stupid. No more stupid than usual anyway."

"Good. We'll be depending on him."

"He won't let us down," she said, and then smiled. "I'm really going to miss this, you know."

"Miss what?"

"This." Valkyrie waved at their surroundings. "Plans and

401

missions and briefings. You and me. If we all die, I'm really going to miss this."

"If we all die," Skulduggery said, "you're not really going to miss much of anything. But I appreciate the sentiment."

"And?"

"And what?"

"And is there anything in particular that *you're* going to miss?"

"Do you have anything particular in mind?"

"Well, I don't know," said Valkyrie, standing in his way to make him stop. "Maybe *someone* in particular? Maybe someone in particular who's standing very close to you at this very moment in time?"

"The plant?"

"No, not the plant. I said some*one*."

"And it's not the plant?"

"I know who you're going to miss most. It's OK to admit it."

He stepped round her, and continued on. "That's nice."

She caught up. "Seriously? After all this time, you're not going to give me this little piece of honesty? After all we've meant to each other?"

"You mean after all I've meant to you."

"I've meant just as much to you as you have to me."

"Debatable."

"Please just admit it," said Valkyrie. "You're going to miss me, aren't you?"

"Obviously," said Skulduggery.

"Thank you."

"Like a drowning man misses the land."

"Awww..."

"Like a hesitant man misses the chance."

"Yeah..."

"Like an oblivious man misses the point."

"I have a feeling you're mocking me somehow, but I can't put my finger on how."

They entered the Room of Prisms. China sat on her throne, sorting through a sheaf of papers. Saracen, Donegan and Gracious were talking with Fletcher and Tanith. To one side stood Solomon Wreath and Melancholia St Clair. To the other, Dusk.

"Woah," said Valkyrie.

Dusk looked at her, the scar she had given him reflected in a thousand tiny mirrors. "I bear you no ill will," he said.

She blinked. "Right. OK."

Skulduggery looked up at China. "Reading anything interesting?"

"Preliminary reports following our raid on the Church of the Faceless," China said, putting down the papers. "Finding a lot of names mentioned – possible worshippers we never knew about. Gettamein, Verdant, even your new friend Keir Tanner, the prison warden."

"He liked me," Skulduggery said. "I could tell."

China stood. "All right, then. Before we begin, I think we're all glad to see Valkyrie back on her feet, and we appreciate Fletcher being here after what happened. Tanith has also rejoined us."

Tanith smiled. "It's nice to be loved."

China ignored her. "First of all, what is our current situation as regards the Remnants?"

"We've lost them," Saracen said grimly. "Any chance we had of tracking them down vanished when they took Dexter."

"The moment they make trouble, though, we'll know about it," Donegan said. "So far, and this is both fortunate and worrying, there hasn't been a peep."

China nodded. "Focus your efforts here. Darquesse is our only concern from this moment on. How are we on that front?"

"Erskine Ravel is staying in the circle," said Skulduggery. "Darquesse hasn't smashed down the door, so I think we can assume it's doing an adequate job of hiding him from her senses."

"So we have our bait once again. How fares the trap?"

"That bit's trickier."

"I'm sure."

"Darquesse doesn't have an obvious weakness as far as we can see," Skulduggery said. "Like anything, if we hit her enough times, she'll eventually die, but the question then becomes what shall we hit her with?"

"Dear Liza," Gracious mumbled.

"The weapon Mevolent used," China said. "That had an effect on her, yes?"

"It drained her power for a few seconds at a time," said Valkyrie. "But we have no idea how it worked."

"Magical technology has been flourishing in that reality for the last two hundred years," Skulduggery added. "They're far more advanced than we are. We've no hope of replicating the magic-sucker."

China's lip curled. "That's what we're calling it?"

Valkyrie nodded. "That's the technical term."

"What about the Sensitives? Have they seen anything new?"

"I've just spoken with Cassandra," said Saracen. "They've been having the same dreams and visions. Details change all the time, but the result is always the same. Death and destruction."

China sat back down. "I want you all to understand something. I've been doing this job for a little over a month, and I like people doing what I tell them. It's fun. And I don't want the world ending just when I'm having fun.

"We use Erskine Ravel to lure Darquesse here. Once she's here, we engage her in combat. We throw everything we have at her – sorcerers, Cleavers... Dusk and his Exiled will be a part of our strategy, as, of course, will the God-Killer weapons. If they take care of the problem, wonderful. We can all go home early. But our main objective is to keep Darquesse busy. Keep her distracted. Valkyrie... this means you will more than likely encounter her on a one-to-one basis."

Valkyrie nodded.

China sighed. "Which means you'll probably need something to fight her with."

"I have magic again."

"But it hasn't manifested, has it? You feel it, but you don't know what it is. You might discover you possess the magical ability to talk to goldfish. Your magic might manifest as an offensive ability, or it may not. But you need *something*."

She nodded to someone out of sight and Tipstaff appeared from nowhere, holding out the Deathtouch Gauntlet for Valkyrie to take.

She glared. "I'm not wearing that."

"I'm afraid I'm going to have to insist," said China.

"What good is it going to do me?" Valkyrie said. "I'd need to get right up close to Darquesse to use it, and she'd kill me with a slap."

"I may have something to offer in that department," said Solomon Wreath.

China looked at him. "Go on."

"Twelve hundred years ago, the highest Clerics of the Necromancy Order got together and constructed a sigil which bestows upon its user incredible strength and complete and utter invulnerability. Are you aware of this sigil, Grand Mage?"

"Of course," said China. "The Meryyn Sigil – elegant and intricate, its beauty is marred only by the simple fact that it doesn't work."

"They were Necromancers," Wreath smiled. "You really think they'd let one of their secrets out without keeping something back? Physical activation is necessary in order for the sigil to start working. But the High Clerics, in their wisdom, decided that strength and invulnerability were gifts to be used only by those who had proved themselves worthy Necromancers – sorcerers who have mastered death. They thought the future would be full of such people."

"How many have there been?" Valkyrie asked.

"In the last twelve hundred years?" Wreath said. "None."

"And how does this help us?" asked Saracen.

"It doesn't help us," said Wreath. "It helps Valkyrie."

"Wait," she said. "When you say sigil... you mean a tattoo, don't you? No. I had one in the vision and I was wearing that gauntlet and there's no way I'm using either of them. No way."

"You might have to," said China.

All Valkyrie's old objections reared up, but one by one the arguments against them knocked them down before she had a chance to utter a word. Not wearing the gauntlet, not having the sigil... there was no guarantee that would be enough to save her family. In fact, without them, her family could even die that bit sooner.

"It doesn't even matter," Valkyrie said. "It's activated by someone who's mastered death, right? Well, that's not me."

"No," said Wreath, "but there's no rule that says the person who wears the sigil has to activate it. You can, for instance, send someone else to activate it. And if anyone here can be said to have mastered death, it's Detective Pleasant."

Skulduggery tilted his head. "What is involved in this activation?"

"I don't actually know," said Wreath. "There are three tests you'll have to pass. I'm sure they'll be no problem for you."

"Where do I take these tests?"

"Meryyn ta Uul. Also known as the Necropolis, the City of the Dead, the City Beneath... I can take you there, if you'd like. Valkyrie stays where it's safe, you pass the tests, activate the sigil, and suddenly she's invulnerable."

"For how long?" Valkyrie asked.

Wreath shrugged. "Long enough, I should think. If you truly intend to go up against Darquesse, though, you'll need every advantage you can get."

"Skulduggery," China said, "if you're OK undertaking the three tests in the Necropolis, I'll get the specifications for the sigil and apply it to Valkyrie personally."

Skulduggery nodded, looked to Wreath. "How long will you need?"

"A few hours," Wreath answered. "I've never been to the Necropolis myself, so I'll have to make enquiries. We may require advanced transport, though."

"Fletcher will accompany you," said China. "Valkyrie, I'll be ready in thirty minutes. Please come to my chambers. Everyone else, get back to work."

The group dispersed, and Skulduggery put his fingertips on the small of Valkyrie's back, and guided her out of the room.

"I'm not happy," she said.

"No? I thought you'd always wanted a tattoo."

"Not. Happy."

"Yes, well, I don't blame you. But seeing as how you're about to do everything possible to prepare yourself for the upcoming confronation, it is only good manners that I do likewise."

She frowned. "Where are we...? Oh."

They passed into the Old Sanctuary and walked in silence until they got to the Accelerator Room.

"Hello, Valkyrie," the Engineer said. "Hello, Detective Pleasant. Are you here to deactivate the Accelerator?"

"Not yet," said Skulduggery.

Valkyrie stayed by the door, making sure no one was going to walk in on them. She tried to keep her eyes from the spot where Stephanie had been killed, but her gaze kept dropping, kept picturing her there. Images surfaced of what her final few moments must have been like. To be that scared and that alone...

"You have three days, nineteen hours and one minute left," the Engineer said. "Plenty of time to decide who will give their soul."

"We're not here to shut off the Accelerator," Skulduggery said, "we're here to use it. Is that possible?"

"Of course."

"Would that affect the time we have left? From what I know of its processes, using it at this late stage could speed up the overload."

"You are quite correct," said the Engineer. "A full boost to your power would have a cumulative effect on the Accelerator's systems. If you wish to avoid that, I can reduce the level to which your abilities are enhanced. Instead of you reaching one hundred per cent of enhancement, you would reach sixty-three per cent. Still a significant boost, if I do say so."

Skulduggery looked back at Valkyrie. "Thoughts?"

"Many and magnificent," she said. "But you're the one who reckons we need all the help we can get."

"To start down this road, though," Skulduggery said. "It's dangerous."

"The roads we take usually are."

"You heard the lady," Skulduggery said to the Engineer. "But before we do this, can I count on your discretion?"

"I am a robot," said the Engineer. "I do not gossip. Please step into the Accelerator."

"Actually, I'm going to stay out here," Skulduggery said, and began unbuttoning his shirt. Tendrils of shadows seeped out from between his ribs. They collected in his outstretched hand, forming a spinning sphere of darkness that grew in mass the more the shadows flowed. Finally, the tendrils trailed off, and Lord Vile's power drifted from Skulduggery's hand to the Accelerator. It hovered over the dais, which began to tremble. A glow spread beneath the skin of the machine, and the sphere spun faster, expanding and contracting at an astonishing rate.

The glow in the Accelerator became a light that hurt Valkyrie's eyes. She looked up and down the corridor. No one coming. She examined her own shadow, stark against the wall. Then the shadow began to fade as the light behind her grew dim.

She looked back. The Accelerator had powered down, but the sphere was still spinning so fast it looked to be in constant danger of unravelling. She knew it was taking all of Skulduggery's self-control to keep it in one piece.

It darted to Skulduggery's hand. Now was the moment when it could all go horribly wrong. If the shadows morphed into armour and enveloped him, a supercharged Lord Vile would destroy this world just as readily as Darquesse.

Skulduggery's head twitched.

The sphere broke apart into a thousand tendrils and Valkyrie's heart lurched in dreadful and sudden fear – but the tendrils flowed up under Skulduggery's sleeve, up his arm, making his jacket bulge. They twisted at his shirt collar, curled out of his eye sockets, and then he arched his back and it was like he inhaled, and the shadows were sucked back inside his ribcage.

"See?" Valkyrie said. "Told you it'd be fine."

Skulduggery buttoned his shirt back up. "You told me no such thing."

"Yeah, but I thought it. How does it feel?"

He fixed his tie, and brushed lint from his lapel. "It feels..." he said, "angry."

"Yikes."

"It was necessary. Even if I don't have to draw on my Necromancer power for the three tests in Meryyn ta Uul, I dare say it'll be handy for when we go up against Darquesse. Engineer, thank you very much for your help. And your discretion."

The Engineer bowed, and they left.

Valkyrie looked at Skulduggery. "What are the chances of us just giving Ravel to Darquesse if she asks?"

"Slim. Ravel is the one thing we know she wants. Apart from that, we're blind. We have no idea where she's going to go or what she's going to do because we don't know what else is driving her."

"I should know what she wants," Valkyrie said. "I mean, shouldn't I? I'm her. OK, I'm not her now, but surely I was in her mind long enough to pick up a few things. Right?"

"In theory."

"So question me," Valkyrie said, turning to him. "Go on. Interrogate me. I have the answer. I must have the answer. I just can't recognise it. I don't know what's useful to you. Get it out of me."

"Interesting," Skulduggery said. "That might actually work. Very well, let's give it a go. What does Darquesse want?"

"I have no idea," said Valkyrie, then frowned. "That's a terrible start."

"It's less than auspicious, I'm forced to admit," Skulduggery said. "Valkyrie, Darquesse is you. She's your dark side. Your bad mood. She's still you, but she's growing. Evolving."

"Are you saying I'm not evolved?"

"She's evolving *beyond* you. Into what? What is she becoming?"

"What we've always feared," Valkyrie said, her voice so quiet it actually surprised her. "A god."

"And what do gods do, given the chance?"

"They punish people."

"Not all gods."

"All the ones I've heard about," she said. "The Faceless Ones were insane and ruthless and so mean and nasty that even though they can't exist here in physical form, they still want to get back in just to punish us for kicking them out in the first place."

"But Darquesse isn't like that."

"She *wasn't* like that," Valkyrie corrected. "She started off fine. She couldn't understand why people were having visions of her destroying the world. She didn't want to hurt anyone. But the more godlike she got, the less she cared about little things like people. She sees everything as forms of energy now. Life and death are the same thing."

"So she doesn't want to hurt us, exactly."

"Well, maybe not, but she doesn't view killing us *as* hurting us."

"Is that why she wants to expand her mind?"

410

"She wants to learn more about matter and atoms and energy. She knows a lot, but it's all... it's instinctive. She doesn't have the words to think it all the way through, and that's what she's after. When she has the words, when she has the framework to deal with all this, she'll be able to do what she wants to do."

"And what is that?"

"I don't know. She's growing, like you said. She's evolving. She goes up against something, she figures out how to beat it or control it, and then she moves on to the next thing."

"She's after a challenge," Skulduggery said.

"Yes," said Valkyrie. "That's when she's happiest."

"So what's her biggest challenge?"

"It's not us, I'll tell you that much."

"Then what is it?"

"I don't know, I—"

"Don't think about this, don't try to anticipate, just answer. What is Darquesse building towards? What is she evolving to meet?"

"I don't know," Valkyrie said, exasperated. "The Faceless Ones, maybe?"

Skulduggery tilted his head. "What?"

Valkyrie's eyes widened. "That's it. That's what she wants. She's evolving until she can beat the Faceless Ones, and then she'll find something else to fight. That's her goal. It has to be. Right?"

"It's definitely a challenge," Skulduggery said.

"Does this help? How can this possibly help?"

"In order to defeat your enemy," Skulduggery said, "first you must understand them. Up till now, we haven't been able to do that. Now we can – and we can adapt our plan to fit."

Valkyrie grinned. "I'm a genius."

61

THE PLAN

The God-Killer dagger was heavy in his belt. He could feel its entire weight, and had to resist the urge to constantly check to make sure it was staying in one place. One slip, after all, and that blade could nick him and then Sanguine would be no more.

It was a risk, carrying it. But it was even more of a risk to leave it behind.

Darquesse was fretting. No, fretting was maybe the wrong word. She was preoccupied. And puzzled. She couldn't keep still, pacing through the small living room, muttering to herself and occasionally looking up. She hadn't said much when she'd returned from that other dimension. All Sanguine knew was that she'd failed to bring Ravel back and that Mevolent had found some way to beat her. And that was not going down well.

"Like that," she said, snapping her fingers. "Like that, and I was helpless. Helpless. *Me.* I've never heard of anything like it. I'm pretty sure Kenspeckle hadn't, either. Argeddion, he might have been able to figure it out but... I didn't even know that was possible."

Sanguine watched her and didn't say anything. He was glad of this sudden preoccupation. So far, she hadn't said anything

412

about Tanith's escape, even though they all knew what he'd done. Vincent Foe and that creepy vampire sat across the room, and every so often Foe would glance at him. The vampire's gaze never wavered.

Someone knocked on the door. Darquesse barely noticed.

"I'll get it," said Sanguine. He did his best to walk the way he always did, but the dagger was making every movement stiff. He went to the wall beside the door, pressed his head against it. The wall crumbled and he poked his head out the other side, saw Dexter Vex standing there.

"She in?" Vex asked.

"She is," Sanguine answered.

He withdrew his head and opened the door, and Vex walked in like he owned the place. Sanguine followed him into the living room, and took up his usual spot by the window.

"You called?" Vex said to Darquesse.

She stopped pacing and looked up. There was a flicker of irritation on her face. "I did," she said. "Hours ago. You're late."

Vex gave a small bow. "Apologies. I found it hard to tear myself away from praising you to the others. But I am here now, and I, like my fellow Remnants, exist only to serve. What dost thou will, my mistress?"

Darquesse peered at him. "Are you being cheeky, Dexter?"

The corner of Vex's mouth twitched upwards in a smile. "Perhaps."

"Normally I don't mind cheeky," said Darquesse, "but today I'm in a bad mood. I'm cranky. I've been offered a glimpse of my own vulnerability, and I didn't like it. It's a reminder that no matter how powerful you get, there's always something out there that can topple you."

"Wise words," said Vex.

"When I return to full strength, I'll be back to my usual charming self, but right now, I want you to shut up and do what I tell you. The Sceptre is hidden in Valkyrie's house, probably

413

her bedroom. It's bonded to her baby sister so she won't be able to use it, but even so, if it's out there, it's a threat. It's something that can hurt me. Kill me. I cannot stand those things."

The irrational part of Sanguine's mind expected her to swing round and pounce on him, and he brought his hand closer to the dagger.

"I want it in my possession," Darquesse continued. "I'm thinking of hiding it on the moon, once I've mastered space travel."

"The Sceptre," Vex said, giving another nod. "We'll retrieve it for you, you have my word. Is there anything else I can help you with?"

Faced with Vex's calm demeanour, Darquesse paused, allowed herself to stop fretting. "Your brothers and sisters. Are they ready to strike?"

"They await your command."

"I haven't heard of any major Remnant disruption."

"You asked us to lie low," said Vex. "That's what we're doing."

"How have you kept them under control?"

Vex shrugged. "I like to think all they needed was the right kind of leadership. I'm their boss but I'm also their friend, you know?"

Darquesse took a moment. "You don't talk to me the way the others do."

"Because they're afraid of you," said Vex.

"And you're not?"

"Why should I be? You're going to destroy the world. You're my dream girl."

Darquesse grunted. "Next time I call, be here sooner."

Vex flashed her a dazzling smile. "Your wish, my lady."

He bowed again, and left.

Darquesse turned to Foe and Samuel. "Are you scared of me?"

Samuel didn't reply. Sanguine doubted anyone expected him to.

"I have a healthy respect for your power," said Foe. "In some circles, that may be seen as a type of fear."

"And you, Billy-Ray?" Darquesse asked. "Are you scared of me?"

He saw no point in lying. "Yes."

"And yet," Darquesse said, walking closer, "you released Tanith. You let her escape, and you stayed. You didn't even try to run. If you're so scared of me, why are you still here?"

"Because you'd probably be able to find me," Sanguine said. "I felt I had a better chance talking to you face to face than running from you. At the very least, I'd be able to see the killing blow coming."

"Interesting." She stopped just out of arm's reach. Did she know? Did she know he possessed one of the only weapons in the world that could kill her? He waited for her to take one more step. One more step, he decided, and he'd go for the dagger, no matter what.

"You miss her, don't you?"

He licked his lips. "Sorry?"

"Tanith. She's not here any more and that makes you sad. Hey, Billy-Ray, I remember being sad. Sad is not fun. So what are you going to do?"

"As regards...?"

"Me. Us. I think it's time to be honest with each other, don't you? You were only on my side because you were tagging along with Tanith, right? She's the only reason you were here."

"I guess."

"So what happens now? Are you going to leave me, too?"

She took another step forward. His hand remained where it was. The dagger remained where it was. He chose his next words with care. "Well, I mean... I figure this is the winning side, and I ain't never been on the winning side before, so I'll probably stick around. If you'll have me."

"You really mean that?" Darquesse said, clapping her hands in delight.

"Sure," he said, his heart sinking. "Why not?"

"What do you think, Vincent? What do you think, Samuel? Should we trust him?"

"Not one bit," said Foe.

"Oh, you are no fun!" Darquesse said, and turned her smile back to Sanguine. "This means so much to me. It truly does. You really want me to destroy the world? You really want me to end your life along with everyone else's?"

"Uh-huh..."

"Oh, that is good news."

"Though you might wanna kill me last. Because of the loyalty, and all."

"Loyalty," Darquesse said. "Of course."

She kept that delighted look on her face, but Sanguine wasn't fooled. "So what's the plan, boss?"

"The plan? Well... I've learned all I can as a physical form. I think my next state of being will be pure thought. Yes, I like that idea. But there are two things delaying me. The first is Erskine Ravel. He took Ghastly from us. I'm still angry about that, so I think, just for my own sense of closure, I need to find Ravel again and punish him. I need to drive him mad with pain, and then destroy him utterly. He doesn't deserve to live on as energy."

"And the second thing?"

Darquesse hesitated. "Valkyrie. It kills me to say this, it really does, but without her, I'm not all I could be. I'll never live up to my true potential until we're one being again. I'd like to see Mevolent using the magic-sucking thing on me *then*."

"Right. OK. So what are you gonna do?"

"End her life," Darquesse said simply. "Absorb her energy. Once I am whole, I'll be ready."

"Ready for what?"

She smiled. "For what happens next."

62

THE KNOCK ON THE DOOR

Fletcher teleported Valkyrie home. "Can I see?" he asked.

She put her fingers to her lips, went to her bedroom door and listened. Her parents were downstairs. She turned back to Fletcher, took off her jacket and showed him her arm.

"Wow," he said.

She pulled back the sleeve of her T-shirt, revealing the whole tattoo. Long swirls of solid black tumbled from her shoulder. They twisted round her bicep, linking with angular slashes that ran from the triceps to just above the elbow. Between these shapes were a dozen different markings that, by turn, bisected, separated and joined the two sections. It was a sigil comprised of smaller sigils, a tattoo that China had never tried before. She was, however, confident it would work.

"I was thinking of getting one," Fletcher said. "Not that, obviously. But a tattoo."

"Of what?" Valkyrie asked. "Your own face? I can see you with a tattoo of your own face. That'd be typical you."

Fletcher tried to smile. "Yeah," he said. "It would. But I was actually thinking of just getting *Stephanie* across my arm."

"Oh," said Valkyrie. "Right. Well, you know, that's... Listen, we haven't had a chance to talk since... since she died. I'm sorry about that, I really am."

"Don't be," said Fletcher. "I'm the one who ran. And when I got myself together enough to come back, you were going through your Surge. How was that, by the way?"

"Painful. You know when everyone tells you it's painful? You should really believe them."

"Oh, joy," he muttered. "I can't wait for mine."

"Fletch, are you OK?"

He smiled again, but this time it wasn't forced. It was sad. "I don't know, Val. On the outside, I feel normal things. I'm in mourning, I miss her, I think I may have loved her, maybe. I feel all that, and I think about that. But then, on the inside, I feel terrible. Like, guilty. Because of the things she probably heard, and what she thought before she died, and what she thought of me and... So I have these normal feelings of loss, but I also have these selfish feelings of *me, me, me*. And I don't know which is stronger. I'm not altogether sure I'm a nice person."

"You are, Fletch."

"But my sadness isn't all about Stephanie. A lot of it is about me."

"Of course. You've lost her. You've suffered a loss. You have to deal with that."

He shook his head. "Other people don't. Other people are capable of feeling sad for the person who died."

"How do you know? Can you look inside their minds? Maybe everyone feels this exact same way when they lose someone they care about. I mean, mourning *itself* is selfish, and there's nothing wrong with that."

There was a quiet beep from the triangular piece of metal on Fletcher's belt. "Time to go," he said. "We're going to have to follow a load of complicated directions to this Necropolis place. Sure, we'll be teleporting instead of walking, but we still have to travel slowly or else we'll miss clues or turns or whatever. Skulduggery reckons we'll be searching for at *least* a day."

"You'd better get going, then. Thanks for the lift home." On impulse, she hugged him. "You're going to be fine," she whispered.

He smiled, and vanished.

Valkyrie changed into jeans and pulled on a warm top. Then she took a few deep breaths, and went downstairs. Her parents were in the living room, playing with Alice. The mood was unusually sombre for playtime.

"Hi," Valkyrie said.

"Ste'nee!" Alice cried, and hurtled over.

"Didn't hear you come in," said her mum. She stayed on the floor, her feet tucked beneath her.

Valkyrie scooped up Alice. "Fletcher dropped me off. We teleported."

Her mum sighed. "Yes. Of course."

"Tanith said she'd been keeping in touch with you."

Valkyrie's dad nodded as he sat into his armchair. "She called over, then rang to tell us you were out of your Surge. Am I getting that right? Surge?"

"That's right."

"Oh, good. She said you were in huge amounts of pain."

"It wasn't that bad."

"She told us a lot about what sorcerers do," her mum said. "Told us stories. She told us about a man who can make people believe whatever he tells them."

"That's Geoffrey."

"You could have asked Geoffrey to brainwash us, couldn't you? Made us forget about this magic thing?"

"Yes," said Valkyrie. "I thought about it. But I didn't want to lie to you any more. It's just too hard. Too complicated. I think you have a right to know. No one else thinks that, by the way. If you have a mortal family, the generally accepted rule is that you keep them in the dark for as long as you can."

"And then what?"

"Then you leave. You come up with an elaborate story, or you disappear, or you fake your own death…"

"They wanted you to *fake your own death*?"

Valkyrie hesitated. "Sorcerers live longer than other people. They live for hundreds of years. Providing the world doesn't end in the next few days, and providing I survive, I'll probably stay looking eighteen until I'm at least forty or fifty."

Her mum had tears in her eyes as she stood. "You're never going to grow up?"

Valkyrie smiled. "I am grown up, Mum. I'm just going to age really slowly from here on out. I'll be the youngest looking forty-year-old you know."

"You'll be missing out on a normal life."

"What's so great about a normal life? I'm going to be strong and fit and healthy for centuries. I'm going to live an *extraordinary* life."

"If you can call that living. What about meeting someone? Falling in love? Raising a family?"

"I can still do all that."

"But we won't get to see it. We'll keep ageing. We'll die and you'll carry on and you'll have no one left. We won't get to see you start a family. I want grandchildren, Steph."

"Mum, you're not being fair."

"*You're* not being fair. This is about more than just you. When Alice is old enough, what's she going to think? Is she going to be like you?"

"Like me?"

"Magic," her mum said, making it sound like a dirty word.

"I don't know," Valkyrie answered, suddenly hurt. She put Alice down gently. "Maybe. Maybe not. But we don't have to tell her."

"And when she realises that her big sister isn't getting any older, or when she sees her big sister flying around on a broomstick or casting spells or whatever it is you do, she's not going to want to join in the fun?"

"Mum, I don't have all the answers."

"When you were born, I wanted you to be special. Of course I did. Every mother does. Every parent does. Please, God, let my child be the smartest and the prettiest and the best at everything. Let her have all the advantages in the world. But there's another thought, and it rests just underneath that one. That thought is please, please let my child be ordinary. Let her be just smart enough and just pretty enough and just special enough to get what she wants and be happy.

"Extraordinary people are outcasts, Steph. They're shunned. They're called names. They're hated and feared and misunderstood. I just wanted you to be happy."

"I am happy."

"Des, feel free to contribute. Don't you dare make me the bad guy in this."

Valkyrie's dad was silent a moment longer, and she knew he was sorting his thoughts into some kind of order in his head. When he was ready, he spoke. "I think it's wonderful."

Valkyrie looked up.

"You can't be serious," her mum said.

"I don't want our daughter risking her life any more than you do, Melissa. But that's what she does. She risks her life for others. It's amazing. It's... inspiring. When she was a kid, you never wanted to read her princess stories, do you remember that? You said she gets enough princess stories rammed down her throat from cartoons and toys and colouring books... You wanted her to colour in pictures of astronauts and footballers and you wanted to read her stories about adventurers and mad scientists. Remember, in spite of everything we did, she went through a pink stage anyway, where everything had to involve princesses? She got bored of that pretty quickly, didn't she?"

"Not conforming to society's view of what girls should be

is one thing, Des, and it's a good thing. But this? This is insane."

"It's what you wanted for her."

Valkyrie's mum looked shocked. "Are you saying this is my fault?"

"It's no one's fault, Melissa. No one is at fault. There's nothing wrong with what she's doing. She's a hero. Our job now is to support her."

"I can't support our daughter living a life like this. You can't expect me to. Jesus, Des, she's going to get herself killed!"

"She's fighting to save us all."

"Let someone else do it!" her mum shouted, and Alice started crying. "There are plenty of people with magic powers running around this place! Let them handle it!"

"It doesn't work that way, and you know it."

Valkyrie's mum picked up Alice. "If something happens to her, Des, if she gets hurt, if she... If our daughter dies, I will never forgive you."

Holding Alice tightly to her, she walked out. Valkyrie's dad watched her go.

"Do your best not to die, sweetie," he said quietly. "She's the only one who knows how to work the dishwasher." Then he followed after her.

Valkyrie went to bed early that night. She wanted to call Skulduggery to talk this through, but he was out trying to find the Necropolis. She would have called Tanith, but found herself hesitating. Even though the Remnant was gone, even though Tanith was back to her old self, ignoring the last two years was something Valkyrie couldn't do easily.

She realised, then, that the person she needed to speak to wasn't there any more, and she cried for Stephanie, and finally went to sleep.

*

The next morning started in silence. Valkyrie woke up early, nightmares driving her from slumber, but got up late, almost midday. She pulled on her dressing gown over a pair of light shorts and a T-shirt. She stood in her room and listened to her parents downstairs. She didn't even know what day it was. Was it the weekend? Was it a Sunday? She didn't want to go down. She didn't want to find out that her parents hadn't spoken to each other all night. Her folks never argued. There was never tension in the air.

She left her room. The door to Alice's room was open, and Alice lay napping in her cot. Valkyrie couldn't help it. She looked at her sister and smiled. Her baby sister always made her smile.

She went downstairs. Someone knocked on the door, and she went to answer it, tightening the sash round her waist as she did so. Her bare feet settled into the bristles of the welcome mat and her hand went to the latch, twisted it to the right. She pulled the door open, smiling politely in gentle anticipation. The smile didn't leave her face, even as she saw Dai Maybury standing there.

It left her face when he hit her, though. As she stumbled back, blood spouting from her nose, sudden tears in her eyes, her mouth was opening to, what? Curse? Cry out? Threaten? She'd never know, because he was already in the hall with her and he grabbed her and hurled her into the living-room door. It burst open under the impact and she sprawled over the armchair. She heard her mother's cry of alarm, and a rush of feet, and she raised her head in time to see Dai's hand collide with her mother's jaw. Her mum collapsed.

Valkyrie shoved the armchair out of her way and dived at Dai. He batted down her arms, keeping her fingers from his eyes, and she followed up with a headbutt that she realised, too late, he was expecting. His elbow cracked into her cheek and lights flashed behind her eyes, and he pivoted out of the way and let her own momentum take her into the wall. Her shoulder dislodged some family photographs. One of them, in a heavy frame, fell right on her foot. She didn't notice.

Her father came running in, charging straight at Dai, who watched him come and moved only at the last moment, hip-throwing Desmond Edgley to the carpet. Dai leaned over, hit him three times, and Valkyrie's dad stayed down.

The room spun and Valkyrie lurched upright. She went to run at Dai, but her knees bent without warning and she stumbled sideways, falling on to the coffee table. Dai walked by her. She watched him go, her eyes unfocused. He went upstairs.

She needed to get her head straight. She was stunned. Her equilibrium was shot. Blood ran from her nose. She was close to passing out. Concussion? Maybe. If she was concussed, then passing out would be the worst thing she could possibly do. She took a moment, breathed in through her mouth, working to sharpen her thoughts. Upstairs she heard movement. Dai was searching for something. What was he searching for?

The Sceptre.

Valkyrie stood. The sounds of the search upstairs had ceased. He'd found it. Her vision no longer swam. She was back in control.

She grabbed the poker from the fireplace as Dai came down the stairs. She ran into the hall, about to swing it at his head. Dai was calm. Why was he calm? She saw the backpack over his shoulder, the backpack containing the Sceptre. In his arms, he carried the sleeping beauty, little baby Alice.

Valkyrie froze, horrified beyond measure.

Dai drove a kick into her stomach so hard it launched her back off her feet. She hit the wall and bounced off, falling to her hands and knees and then curling into a ball. That dreadful panic seized her, the terror that comes with not being able to draw breath.

She forced open her eyes, manoeuvred her seized-up body around enough to see out of the front door, to where Dai was opening her mother's car. Moving with a calmness born of unnerving, unnatural confidence, Dai put Alice in the baby seat, and set about strapping her in.

Gritting her teeth, Valkyrie made her body straighten. Her muscles screamed at her, begging to contract, but she straightened her spine, arched her back, managed to suck in a sliver of air. Feeling sick, feeling weak, winded, terrified and desperate, she rolled over, pushed herself up, the poker still in her hand.

Satisfied that Alice was secure, Dai closed the door gently so as not to wake her, and put the bag containing the Sceptre on the passenger seat. He walked round the car, and when he was at the closest point to the house, Valkyrie ran at him. He saw her at the last moment, ducked the poker, but she kept coming, ramming her shoulder into his sternum. He fell back on to the bonnet and Valkyrie swung back towards his head. He rolled off the car, the poker striking the windscreen, cracking it, and he grabbed her wrist. Valkyrie let go of the weapon, jabbed her free hand at his eyes. Dai cursed, released her, stumbled away, trying to clear his vision.

She tore the sash from her dressing gown, looped it over his head from behind, and tightened. Dai gagged, fingers digging into his own neck as he tried to loosen the stranglehold. Valkyrie pulled him backwards, tightening the loop with vicious tugs. His heels kicked, pulverising the flower bed. Then he got his legs beneath him and he powered backwards, the back of his head crashing into Valkyrie's face.

They both went down, the sash lost amid the mad scramble. Her face stung with that numb feeling just before the pain kicks in. She felt his hands on her, pulling her up. She slipped out of her sleeves, leaving him holding her dressing gown. She spun, her hands latching on to the back of his neck, and she jumped, driving a knee into his solar plexus. She held on, kept throwing knees, just like Tanith had taught her, never letting up, never giving him a moment to counter.

She touched down with her right foot and her ankle gave, and in that moment Dai moved. His left arm snaked over her shoulder, his hand clutching her back, and his right shot down and under her legs, all the way under, his hand grabbing the back of her shorts. Suddenly Valkyrie was being lifted and turned, and she clutched at him, but there was nothing she could do to stop him from tipping forward.

They hit the driveway, Dai on top, and for the second time in less than a minute, her breath left her. She lay there, groaning, eyes open and blinking. Dai looked at her, the black veins running beneath his skin.

"Nice try," he said, and stood, brushed himself down. Valkyrie grabbed weakly at his ankle. He looked down at her hand, and slowly raised his foot. She lost her grip and her hand fell to the ground. He gave her a little smile, and stomped.

Valkyrie sat up, screaming, clutching her broken fingers to her chest, and Dai walked back to the car, got in behind the wheel, and reversed out of the driveway. Her screams had turned to sobs by the time he drove away.

63

THE CITY BELOW

The search for the Necropolis took them to Scotland. Fletcher's feet were sore. The night had been cold and he'd lagged behind Skulduggery and Wreath, finally giving up altogether and sitting down. He left the searching to the experts, and as long as he could keep them in sight, he could teleport to their side whenever they needed him.

Because of this he only heard snippets of the conversation. At first, silence had reigned. He knew the two men had never liked each other, and so he'd expected this. But gradually a conversation had sparked up, and he caught a few barbed comments every time he was close enough to listen in. They mentioned Wyoming once or twice, and the war – the old war, with Mevolent.

Fletcher left them to their argument. When he was hungry, he teleported off to grab something nice to eat. When he needed a warmer jacket, he teleported away to get it. When he needed to use the bathroom, he teleported to an annoying celebrity's house, and didn't bother flushing. But he spent most of his time not thinking about Stephanie.

When the sun came up all Fletcher wanted to do was sleep. He sat with his back against a tree and dozed until his phone rang.

"We've found it," Skulduggery said.

Fletcher stood. It was a cold day and the seat of his jeans was damp. He looked around, saw nothing but trees and rocks and sky.

"Turn south," said Skulduggery. Fletcher turned. "That's east. OK, that's north. There you go. See us?"

In the distance, Fletcher saw a burst of fire. He put away his phone and teleported over to Skulduggery's side. Wreath was standing at a doorway cut into a rock wall. Skulduggery still had his phone in his hand, and when he moved closer to the doorway, the screen blanked.

Skulduggery examined it. "A dead zone," he murmured. "Fletcher, stay close. We won't be able to use these."

Fletcher nodded.

The steps were black marble. Wreath led the way down, and Fletcher stayed beside Skulduggery. It was cold, and getting colder. Dark, and getting darker. Flames sputtered in the iron brackets that were hammered into the walls. The space was tight, and the ceiling sloped with them. Nobody spoke. Their feet echoed.

They kept going down. Once more, the cold got colder. Once more, the dark got darker.

And then the ceiling came to a sudden end and their surroundings opened to a vast city of concrete with a rock sky and a thousand glowing orbs of light. Fletcher stopped, frozen in an unexpected moment of awe. The buildings, featureless save for the narrow rectangular windows, formed a maze of right angles. The streets were narrow – made for people, not carriages. To set foot in this city was to be lost – Fletcher somehow knew this.

"We can go no further," said Wreath. "The living cannot cross into the Necropolis. Only the dead may go."

"Don't suppose you've got a map handy?" Skulduggery asked.

Wreath smiled. "Sadly, I do not. We'll be watching, though. There's a balcony in the rock wall that gives us a panoramic view of the place. We can shout out directions from there, if you'd like."

"Wonderful. So what can I expect?"

"In order to activate the sigil, you'll need to get to the square in the exact centre of the city. On your way you'll be faced with two challenges. I don't know what they are and I don't know how to beat them. Once you get past them, you'll face the Guardian in the final challenge. I'm assuming that one's a brawl, which should make you happy. I know how you like to hit things."

"One of my hobbies," Skulduggery murmured.

Skulduggery continued on, while Fletcher followed Wreath to a hidden staircase that led up to a long room with an open balcony. Fletcher hurried over, stood with his hands on the cold stone, looking down at the city. He saw Skulduggery almost immediately, a lone figure moving in the stillness. More than that, though, he *heard* him. He heard every footstep. Somehow the acoustics of this huge chamber fed the sounds from the city up into the balcony.

Wreath reached out, and Fletcher realised there was glass in front of him. At least, he thought it was glass. A few swipes of Wreath's hand and their view of Skulduggery was magnified.

"That's pretty cool," Fletcher said.

"Indeed it is," said Wreath.

They followed Skulduggery's progress for ten minutes. Shouted directions were not needed, as it turned out. Skulduggery was reading the air, somehow divining what path came to a dead end and what led on.

Then there was movement, and a shape emerged from the shadows.

"Who goes there?" the shape asked. The voice was male. Scottish. The viewing window showed a person in a black robe, wearing a porcelain mask.

Skulduggery stopped and observed the shape. "My name is Skulduggery Pleasant. I'm here to activate the Meryyn sigil. Do you mean to stop me?"

"No," said the shape, and Fletcher realised that it wasn't a mask he wore, but his actual face – porcelain and delicate and astonishingly creepy. "I am the Inquisitor. I mean only to test you. Whether or not I have to stop you will depend on the outcome."

"What's the test?"

"A simple one. A test of purity. You have no skin, I see. Nor blood nor organ."

"Correct."

"A curious creature. I know of some who would very much like to examine one such as you. Would you be willing to be examined?"

"Probably not."

"A pity," said the Inquisitor. "If you agreed to be examined, I could let you pass. I would deem that a worthy enough compromise."

"I'm not here to compromise," said Skulduggery. "I'm here to take the test and activate the sigil."

"But the route I offer you is easier. All it would require is your consent to be examined. I assure you, it would take no longer than the life of a day."

"I said no."

The Inquisitor was silent for a moment. "I know of some who know you, skeleton. They whisper in my ear even now. They know the things you have done. They know of the things done to you. They know of your wife and child."

Now it was Skulduggery's turn to pause. "What does any of this have to do with the test?"

"Your wife and child," said the Inquisitor, "murdered in front of you by a man whom you later turned to dust. They died screaming. They died begging you to save them. Your existence from that point on has been defined by that moment."

"If you're trying to provoke me, it won't work," Skulduggery said.

"These are not my words," said the Inquisitor. "These are the words being whispered into my ear."

"Who's doing the whispering?"

Now there was amusement in the Inquisitor's voice. "Ones who know you. Ones who are aware of you. Ones you would not wish to be aware of you."

"Any of them got such a thing as a name?"

"You and your kind rely so much on names," said the Inquisitor. "But there are those who do not."

"Fantastic," Skulduggery said. "Can we please get to the point before—"

"Your wife and child," said the Inquisitor.

Skulduggery stopped. "What?"

"They whisper to me also. They are here, in this city. Waiting for you."

"They're dead."

"And is this not the City of the Dead?"

"They've been dead hundreds of years," said Skulduggery. "They're gone. They're not here. No part of them is here. You're lying. Why?"

"If you believe that I am lying, you can pass on and I will not stop you."

"What about the test?"

"This is the test."

Skulduggery didn't move for a few seconds. Fletcher glanced at Wreath. The Necromancer had a slight frown on his face.

Skulduggery walked by the Inquisitor, and the Inquisitor stepped into the shadows and vanished.

"That was easy," said Fletcher.

"So it would seem," said Wreath.

Fletcher frowned. "It was too easy, wasn't it?"

Wreath nodded. "So it would seem."

64

CHASING ALICE

Valkyrie's mum helped her dress.

"Get Fletcher," her dad said, his eyes frantic. "He appears and disappears, doesn't he? He'll take us right to Alice."

"Fletch teleports to places, not to people," Valkyrie said while her mum guided her right foot into its boot. Her ankle was sore, but at least she could walk on it. The rest of her ached. Her ribs, her face, her jaw. Her left hand was already swelling up to twice its normal size. The pain would have been excruciating were it not for the leaves she chewed.

Her mother pulled the cuffs of Valkyrie's trousers down over her boots, and Valkyrie stood up from the bed. Hissing, she slipped her left arm through the sleeve of her jacket, and her mum helped her with the right, then zipped her up.

"We're coming with you," her mum said. She'd been quiet since Valkyrie had stumbled back into the house. Now Valkyrie knew why.

"No," Valkyrie said, limping out of the room. "This is dangerous. You have to stay here."

"Alice is our daughter and we're coming with you," her mum said.

Valkyrie got to the bathroom, grabbed a wet cloth and cleaned the blood from her face. Wiped her eyes, too. "Dai will kill you."

"I thought Dai was one of the good guys," said her dad.

"He is," said Valkyrie. "He's got a Remnant inside him. He isn't himself." She dropped the cloth, turned to them. "Dad, please say you understand why neither of you can come. I'm going after Alice. I know this world and I know these people and I'm used to things like this."

"We're wasting time," said her mum.

Valkyrie looked at her parents, realised there was no way she was going to win this argument, and her mother was right. Dai already had a five-minute head start on them.

"Fine," she said. "I'm driving."

"I'm driving," her dad corrected, already heading downstairs. "You're injured and your car is slow and you're not a very good driver."

Valkyrie limped quickly after him. "I'm a very good driver."

He grabbed his keys from the hall table and stood at the door impatiently. "Not at the speed we're going to be travelling at."

There were two roads out of Haggard – one going south, one going north. They took the one going south, and the old familiar countryside whipped by at a worrying rate. Going over the slight hills, the car actually left the road a few times, sending a wave of weightlessness churning through Valkyrie's belly. Melissa Edgley, in the passenger seat, held on tight, but didn't caution her husband to slow down.

Valkyrie's dad swerved round a tractor on a tight bend. Not even that elicited a complaint. Valkyrie realised her parents had become missiles, locked on to their target, unmindful of anything else.

For a curious moment she felt like she was a kid again, strapped into the back seat of the car while she took a drive with her folks. Maybe they were going to the cinema, or the zoo, or maybe to her uncle's house. Wherever they were going she was safe, because she was with her mum and dad, and nothing bad ever happened when she was with her mum and dad.

The pain from her hand brought her back to the present. Her fingers were now a deep, ugly purple that ran past her knuckles to the back of her hand. She could move her thumb, and her pinkie, but the others were useless. Every time the car took a turn, every time Valkyrie swayed in her seat, the pain stabbed at her despite the leaves that had left their usual bitter aftertaste in her mouth.

"Where do we go?" her dad asked, his voice tight.

Valkyrie looked up. Around the next few bends there was a straight stretch of road, and at the end of that was a junction. They could go right, towards Balbriggan, or straight, into Lusk, or left, towards Dublin.

"Left," she said.

"Where's he taking her?" her mum asked, keeping her eyes fixed on the road.

"Thurles," Valkyrie said. "That's where the other Remnants are. There's where Dexter Vex is." She didn't say why they wanted her baby sister. She didn't mention the Sceptre or the fact that in order for Vex to be able to use the Sceptre, he'd have to kill Alice. "She'll be fine," she said instead. "Dexter won't hurt her. He'll just use her to lure me in."

They got to the straight stretch of road. There was a line of slow-moving cars ahead of them, puttering lazily along. Valkyrie's dad beeped his horn and flashed his lights at oncoming traffic, warning them that he was about to do something stupid. Then he swerved into the middle of the road, overtaking everything in his path while other cars turned sharply to avoid a collision. He clipped a wing mirror and got a blast of a horn in response, but they'd already reached the junction. The car drifted a little as it made the turn.

Valkyrie's phone was in her left pocket. She reached across with her good hand, lifting her hips to allow her fingers access. She lost her grip, tried again, managed to pull it out slightly, like a turtle emerging from its shell. She lifted her hips again, got a firmer grip, pulled it out. Immediately, she dialled Skulduggery's number.

It went straight to voicemail. As she feared it would.

"Skulduggery's not answering," she said.

"You've got other friends," said Melissa. "Call them. Call the girl with the sword. Call all the magic people."

She couldn't. If it got out, that Alice was bonded to the Sceptre and the Sceptre was up for grabs, then her sister would never be safe again.

"Roarhaven's in lockdown," she said. "No calls in or out. But I don't need them. I can get Alice back myself."

"With our help," her dad said.

Valkyrie said nothing.

The day was pulling the brightness from the sky and by the time they reached Thurles it was beginning to get legitimately dark. The streets were quiet. Empty. No cars passed them. No one was out walking.

Valkyrie's dad slowed their car to a crawl. "I don't like this," he said. "It feels like a trap."

"How would you know what a trap feels like?" her mum said.

"I just know. Steph?"

Valkyrie nodded. "It feels like a trap. Pull over somewhere. I'll look around and come back."

"No chance," her mum said, turning in her seat. "We all go."

"And what will you do if there's trouble? These people will be trying to kill us."

"Then I'll fight," said her mum. "Anyone comes after me, I'll kick them between the legs."

Valkyrie sighed. "Mum..."

"I'm not staying behind, Steph. I've made my decision."

"Fine," Valkyrie said, biting back her frustration. She looked to the residential street ahead. After a few seconds, her scowl softened. "But don't kick them there."

"Why not? Isn't that the best place to kick them? Des, you don't likc being kicked there, do you?"

He frowned. "I don't like being kicked anywhere."

"First of all," Valkyrie said, "kicking anyone is a bad idea when you're in danger. You're panicking, you've got adrenaline shooting through you, you've got all these new instincts screaming at you. Your body wants to flee or fight – it needs to make itself lighter, so it wants to empty its bowels and its bladder. You're going to want to pee yourself. That's perfectly normal. But your legs are jelly. You're suddenly trembling so much your teeth are chattering. You really want to kick someone when you don't even know if your other leg will support you?"

"I suppose not," her mother said, frowning.

"And if you do kick, there's no guarantee you're going to hit what you're aiming for. And if you do hit what you're aiming for, the pain could take seconds to travel to his brain. He can do an awful lot of damage in those few seconds. Then there's also the risk that kicking him there will just make him mad."

"OK," her mum said, "fine, I won't kick them between the legs. But... is there anywhere I can hit them? I don't think I'd be able to punch very hard, and if they're all as strong as Dai Maybury was..."

"You can't build muscle on your throat," said Valkyrie. "The throat's vulnerable. And I don't care how many push-ups you can do, your eyelids aren't going to get any tougher. Everyone has eyes. Well, almost everyone."

"Throats and eyes," said her mum. "OK. That sounds straightforward enough."

Her dad pulled over. They got out. Valkyrie winced with every movement, but she limped to a small tree in someone's front garden and pulled three long twigs from it. She kept one for herself and gave the others to her parents.

"Hold these with your thumb pressed against it," she said. "Like this."

"Will this ward the Remnants off?" her mum asked.

Valkyrie shook her head. "We don't have anything to fight them with. Look, Remnants are little shadowy creatures that fly around and when they possess you, when they're inside, it's instantaneous. One moment you're you, the next you're not."

"How do they get inside?"

"They attach themselves to your face and force their way down your throat."

Her dad clamped his hand over his mouth.

"That won't do a whole lot of good, Dad. The point is, if we're spotted, a Remnant could possess one of us in a matter of seconds and the rest of us wouldn't know it. So, if you see one, you break the twig, OK? Just press your thumb down and the twig will snap. An unbroken twig means we're all who we say we are. A broken twig means one of us isn't."

Her mum suddenly hunkered down. "Oh, I don't feel well. My legs are weak. They're all wobbly."

"Then stay in the car," Valkyrie said.

"No, no. It's just nerves. It'll pass. Look." She forced herself to stand. She was so pale.

"Mum, I know you want to help, but if you're not ready for this you're going to be a hindrance."

"I won't be," her mum said. "My daughters need me. Lead on, Steph."

Reluctantly, Valkyrie started forward.

Their progress through the town was slow. They darted, as best they could, from cover to cover, but all too often they had to cross a lot of open ground without anything to hide behind. Thankfully, there was no one around to see them and raise the alarm, but the closer they got to the town centre, the warier

Valkyrie became. She stopped at a corner, the hairs on the back of her neck prickling. There. A woman holding a crowbar, standing with her back to Valkyrie. A sentry.

Valkyrie put her finger to her lips and motioned for her parents to crouch down, then she passed her twig to her dad and left them there. She moved silently. The woman tucked the crowbar under one arm and blew into her hands a few times to keep them warm, allowing Valkyrie to sneak up right behind her.

The shock stick was fully charged and ready to go, but she left it where it was. There was no telling when it might come in useful.

She waited until the woman had dropped her hands back down, then she wrapped her right arm round her throat. The sleeper hold came on at once and the woman jerked back, the crowbar falling, her fingers digging into Valkyrie's armoured sleeve. Valkyrie squeezed. Her broken hand sent white-hot daggers straight into her brain.

The woman powered backwards, slamming them both into the wall. Valkyrie banged her head, but didn't let go. The woman's Remnant-augmented strength was astonishing. She tried flipping Valkyrie over her shoulder, but Valkyrie wrapped her legs round her slim waist. They fell, the woman scrambling, panicking, but all she did was allow Valkyrie to adjust her position, to bend her knee round her foot. After a few more seconds, the woman went limp, and Valkyrie released her.

Her parents hurried up as Valkyrie got to her feet. Her dad handed her back her twig.

"That was so cool," he said.

"Yeah," she answered, trying not to cry with the pain. "I know."

They hurried on, passing another two sentries whom they left oblivious behind them. The streets became broader, more open. Valkyrie found herself wasting more and more time trying to figure out ways to progress undetected. They doubled back twice, tried a different route.

Frustration biting into her words, Valkyrie said, "Mum, stay here. Dad, head over to that corner and see if we can get across the street from there. I'm going to check further up."

She took off before either of her parents could object, the shock stick in her hand. Her leg was getting better the more she used it, but every step was causing her pain. She only had a few leaves left, though, so she withstood the discomfort. She reached the end of the alley, found herself at a wall she could easily have jumped over with the aid of her Elemental magic, but which now may as well have been a hundred metres high.

She cursed under her breath. Allowed herself a moment of pure anger and helplessness as she spun round, punching at nothing.

Then she got herself back under control, and retraced her steps. She saw her mother at the mouth of the alley, looking like she didn't have a care in the world.

Valkyrie slowed.

Her mother's anxiousness was gone. She was standing up straight, not looking scared any more.

A dread filled Valkyrie. Was she—

The twig. She needed to check the twig. Where was the twig? As she neared, she looked her mother up and down and—

There it was. Her mother still held the twig, and it was in one piece.

"Do I know you?" a man asked, just out of sight, and Valkyrie ducked back.

Valkyrie's mum shook her head. "Nope. Don't think so."

The man sauntered into view. He was middle-aged, wearing slacks and a heavy jumper. "You look nervous."

"Do I?" Valkyrie's mum said. "I'm not feeling very well. Something I ate, probably."

Valkyrie crept closer as the man nodded.

"Yeah," he said. "Listen, I don't mean to be rude or anything, but... but you *are* one of us, right?"

"One of...? Oh, you mean, am I... do I... Am I possessed?"

The man laughed. "Yeah, that's what I mean."

Valkyrie's mum laughed along with him. "I don't take any offence at that at all, don't worry. In fact, I take it as a compliment."

"Good!" the man chuckled.

"But the real question is, how do I know for sure that *you* are possessed?"

The man thought this was hilarious. "Oh, no, you got me! I'm faking it!"

"I knew it!" Valkyrie's mum laughed.

"How will I prove it? How could I possibly prove it to you? Oh, I know..." His smiling lips turned black and the veins rose beneath his skin. "How's that?"

Her mum paused a moment, then laughed again. "That's pretty convincing!"

"I thought it might be! Now your turn!"

"Now my turn!"

"Exactly!"

"Now it's my turn!"

"Let's be having you!"

Valkyrie's mum's laugh was becoming strained. "Are you ready? I don't think you're ready!"

"I'm ready!"

"I don't think you are!"

Her mum laughed and laughed, but the man's laugh turned to a mere chuckle. "So let's see," he said.

Her mum doubled over with laughter. "OK then! Here it comes! Ready? I hope you're ready! Three, two... one!"

Her mum straightened up. She blinked at the man.

"You're not one of us," he said, all laughter gone.

"No," Valkyrie's mum admitted.

"I'm... confused. What exactly did you think would happen when you counted down?"

"I'm not sure. I'm not very good at thinking on my feet."

"Apparently not." He looked around. "Are you Valkyrie Cain's mother? We were told that you might be on your way. Where's your daughter?"

"I don't know."

"You may as well tell me. She'll come running anyway when you start screaming."

"If you lay one finger on me..."

The man slowly pressed a finger into her chest. "Yes?"

Valkyrie's mum hesitated.

"Sorry?" the man said, leaning in. "What was that?"

Valkyrie burst from cover, but the man heard her coming and smacked the shock stick from her grasp even as she swung. She cried out, pain shooting up her arm, and he hit her on the shoulder and she fell to her knees, fireworks going off behind her eyes. She heard a mad scramble, her dad charging into the man from behind, looked up in time to see her father get punched in the face. He stumbled back, sat down heavily with a dazed expression. Valkyrie grimaced, forced herself up as the man returned his attention to her mother.

"Now then," he said, "what was that you were saying?"

Valkyrie's mum jabbed her fingers into his eyes and he howled in pain and staggered away. He tripped over his own feet, fell to his hands and knees, and Valkyrie ran up and kicked him in the chin. His hands lifted off the ground for an instant and folded beneath him when he collapsed.

Ignoring the pain in her arm, Valkyrie turned to her mother. "Are you OK? Mum?"

"I'm... I..."

"Mum, are you OK?"

Her mother looked at her. "Everyone has eyes," she mumbled.

65

THE SECOND TEST

Fletcher watched Skulduggery move through the dead city. The glass on the balcony, whatever it was, was better than any computer screen Fletcher had ever seen. At a gesture, Wreath could change their viewpoint whenever Skulduggery disappeared behind a building. He could zoom in close, swivel round to the side, tilt up and down – it was a fully controllable camera with perfect resolution. Something like this could change the face of movie-making forever.

"Has any sorcerer ever tried selling magic as technology?" Fletcher asked.

Wreath shrugged. "Sure. The Sanctuaries are usually very good at preventing it, but now and then they miss something, and some little slice of magic slips through."

"Like what? Smartphones? Bluetooth?"

"Glow-in-the-dark fridge magnets."

"Seriously?"

"Oh, yes. How do you think they stick to the fridge?"

"Magnetism."

"Magic."

"And what about the glow-in-the-dark bit?"

"Also magic."

"That's amazing."

Wreath nodded. "Practically unbelievable." His eyes narrowed. "Did you see that? Something—"

In the Necropolis, another porcelain-faced man stepped out into the middle of the street.

"And who might you be?" Skulduggery asked.

Wreath repositioned their viewpoint.

"I have many names," said the man, "and none. I am who I am. As are we all. You may call me the Validator, since that would appear to be my purpose." His accent was French.

"Right. Can we skip the talking in riddles part and go straight to the bit where you tell me what this test is?"

"This test is about you," the Validator said. "This is a test only you can take, only you can pass... and only you can fail."

"Is it maths?"

"You use humour to avoid taking your situation seriously."

"On the contrary, I use humour because it's really, really funny. I'm curious, though – do you live here? Do you ever leave? If you never leave and all you do is hang out with the last guy I was talking to, I can see why you're so ponderous."

"The City Below is my home. Why would I ever want to leave?"

"You make an excellent point. It's calm, it's peaceful, it's charming in a disquieting sort of way... Lonely, though."

"Oh, no," said the Validator. "It is anything but lonely. Sometimes, though, its citizens need some coaxing to emerge. The dead are such shy creatures."

"I've not found that to be the case."

A woman's voice spoke up. "Then you need to surround yourself with a better class of dead."

Wreath frowned, pulled the viewing angle back as a shape, a ghost, drifted from one of the darkened doorways. It was female, Fletcher could see that much. There was a face, hazy though it may have been. He saw eyes, and a mouth.

"Hello, my love," the woman said.

Skulduggery watched the ghost without speaking.

"I have missed you."

Skulduggery turned to the Validator. "How are you doing this?"

"This is not trickery, I assure you."

"It is really me," said the ghost.

"You're not allowed to talk," Skulduggery said, anger snapping at his voice. "However you're doing this, I'm going to give you one warning. Stop it before I lose my temper."

The Validator took a single step back, allowing the ghost to drift closer to Skulduggery.

"I have been waiting for you," she said.

"You are not my wife."

"And you are not my husband," said the ghost. "He was kind, and gentle, and loving, and he did all he could to avoid violence and bloodshed. But you... you are dark and twisted, and your soul is tormented by the things you have done. You have lost who you once were."

"That man is dead. I'm the man who's taken his place."

"You should be here, with me," said the ghost. "With us."

Fletcher saw another smaller blur, the size of a child. It ran, in that indistinct way, in and out of doorways, like it was playing.

Skulduggery stepped back suddenly, as if he'd been struck. His shoulders sagged.

"When that madman killed us," the ghost continued, "we stood on the other side of life and we watched. We watched you fall. We watched what he did to you, in the days after. We saw you scream and weep and beg. We prayed for you to die, for your suffering to come to an end. When he finally released you from your agony, we reached out, tried to pull you to us. To be together in peace. But you resisted. You fled back to the living world. Now the time has come again for you to join us."

The child ran to its mother, and Skulduggery took another step back. "I'm not going anywhere."

"You have taken your vengeance," the ghost said. "You have killed the man who murdered us. What else is keeping you here?"

"I have debts that need repaying."

He was speaking to the woman, but his head was down, looking directly at the child. As Fletcher watched, Skulduggery took one step forward. He started to reach down to the child, then stopped himself, and stepped back. He stood there, trembling.

Suddenly Fletcher didn't want to be seeing this. He didn't want to be seeing this at all.

"My love," said the woman's ghost, "my sweet, you have done terrible things, things that have marked your soul. You carry that mark with you wherever you go, and because of it you have worked so hard to redeem yourself. You have saved the world. You have done so much. Surely it is time for you to be at peace?"

"Maybe some day. But not today."

"My darling, you belong dead."

And then another voice, as a third blurred figure stepped into view. A familiar voice.

"You belong dead," said Ghastly Bespoke.

Skulduggery jerked away, raising a hand as if to ward him off. "Ghastly?"

"We're waiting for you," Ghastly said. "In the cold and the dark. We're waiting. We're watching. We see... everything."

"What are you?" Skulduggery asked. "Who are you?"

"You killed my mother," Ghastly said, and Skulduggery went quiet. "We see the past and the present and the future. I know the things you've done. I know the lies you've told. To me. To your oldest friend."

"If you truly see into my past," Skulduggery said, "then you know what happened. You know I wasn't myself."

"I don't care," Ghastly said. "Being dead means you don't

care. You don't hold grudges. You only need. We need you, my friend. Your time is up."

"No," said Skulduggery.

"We never got to say goodbye. We never got to shake each other's hand. I'm offering it now. Join us."

Ghastly held out his hand. Skulduggery observed it for a moment, then shook his head. "I'm sorry. I can't do that."

Another figure emerged from a side street.

"Told you," said Anton Shudder.

More blurred shapes stepped into view.

"You belong dead," said Shudder. "You deserve to rest. While I was living, I was never at peace. Now? Now I'm content. Now I can smile."

Skulduggery took another step back. "What is this?"

"We are the people you have left behind," his wife said. "We are the people you have let die. We are the people who have died around you. We are the people you have killed."

More figures, thickening the crowd. Fletcher saw Mr Bliss, and Kenspeckle Grouse, and the assassin Tesseract, and the Necromancer Craven. He searched the faces, eyes flickering from one blurred visage to the next, until he found her. She turned in that instant, as if looking back at him. Stephanie.

Fletcher grabbed Wreath's arm. "Is it real? Is it really them?"

"I don't know," Wreath said, disentangling himself without taking his eyes off the scene below. "I don't know how the Necropolis operates. I don't know what they're capable of."

"But it's a trick," said Fletcher. "They're drawing all these memories from Skulduggery's mind or something, right?"

"Skulduggery Pleasant does not have a mind that can be read," said Wreath. "But it may still be a trick. Some kind of subterfuge. Or..."

"Or what?"

"Or it could really be them, plucked from the Great Stream of life and death. Like fish."

One of the figures, the ghosts, reached for Skulduggery, snagging his sleeve.

He yanked his arm back. "What do you want?"

"You belong here," said Ghastly.

"Stay with us," said Skulduggery's wife.

A hole was opening in the ground, widening till it filled the narrow street. Some of the figures slipped down into it without alarm. Others saw it, and willingly let themselves fall.

Skulduggery looked back at the Validator. "How is this part of the test? What does this prove? People I've known have died? I've lived for over four hundred years. A lot of people die in four hundred years."

"These are your dead," said the Validator.

"Did you bring them here? What gives you the right to hold them in this place?"

"We're not just here," said Ghastly, "we're everywhere. At all times. We're with you when you are a boy. We're with you on your wedding day. The day you die. The day you die again. We see you laughing, and screaming. We see you whole and we see you broken. We see you when the worlds collide and when the darkness falls. We see you surrounded by blood, and fire, and rotting flesh."

"You see my future," Skulduggery said, "so you know I have one. I don't go with you today, Ghastly. But if you want to help me, if you really want to help me, you can tell me how to beat Darquesse."

"She can't be beaten," said Shudder.

"I don't believe that."

"It does not matter what you believe," his wife said.

Her hand closed round his arm, and Ghastly seized his hand. Skulduggery tried pulling back, but now Shudder was gripping him, and someone else, and then another, and they were pulling him towards the hole, and they were losing their faces, their forms merging into one blurred mass that was sinking beneath the surface. Skulduggery cursed and twisted, but could do little as more hands emerged to grab hold. One pulled at his ankle and he went down, and they dragged him, kept dragging him, and he lost his hat and now it was just him, clinging on while dozens of hands reached for him, gripped him, and all of a sudden he slid under and the hole closed up.

Skulduggery was gone.

Fletcher stared. "What... what does that mean?"

"I don't know," said Wreath. He sounded genuinely stunned.

"Is he OK?" Fletcher asked. "Where is he?"

Wreath shook his head. "I'm not entirely sure what just happened."

Fletcher watched the Validator step forward, looking down at Skulduggery's hat. He reached down to pick it up but froze.

The hole opened and Skulduggery lunged upwards, his jacket torn, his tie wrenched to one side. An unholy chorus of anguished cries followed him, and all at once there were a hundred hands reaching up from the darkness. Skulduggery rolled, got to his feet so he was standing beside the Validator.

"So this test is about facing your personal demons or something?" he asked. "Well, how about you face them instead?"

And he pushed the Validator, and the Validator toppled and the hands grabbed him and he vanished into the hole.

The hole closed up once again, and silence descended.

Skulduggery fixed his tie and buttoned his jacket, then he picked up his hat, dusted it off, put it on.

66

TABLE MANNERS

ventually, Valkyrie stopped hiding.

The Remnants knew they were there. Of course they knew. They couldn't not know. So with her parents behind her, Valkyrie walked to the town square, where all the people were. Black lips. Black veins. They stood silently, watching her. Hundreds of them. Above their heads, more Remnants flitted. Thousands. But they didn't swoop. They didn't attack.

The crowd parted. Valkyrie and her parents walked right through. The path led to a restaurant. The door was held open by Dai Maybury. He didn't say anything as they passed him.

Vex sat at a table in the corner, cutting into a bloody steak. The strap of the Sceptre bag crossed his chest. On the table beside him, within easy arm's reach, was Alice, sleeping in her car seat.

Valkyrie's parents started forward immediately, but Vex glanced up, black veins rising beneath his skin, and they froze. The veins faded, and Vex went back to his dinner. He speared a ragged bit of steak with his fork, popped it into his mouth, and chewed with his eyes closed.

"I was a vegetarian once," he said, "for about two years, back in the late sixties. I'd met this girl, Sally, who you'd probably—"

"Give us Alice back," Valkyrie said.

Vex opened his eyes. "Let me finish," he said. He took a sip of wine, put the glass down, and continued.

"So, Sally – she was a nice girl, what you'd probably call a hippy. This was in San Francisco during the Vietnam War – and I went on peace marches with her and I grew my hair and I thought, this might be it. She got me into eating rice and lentils and green beans and for a while, hey, life was good. But we went to the airport this one time, to pick up some friends of hers flying in from New York, and there was this GI walking past, this soldier back from the war in his army greens with his bag over his shoulder, searching the crowd for his wife or his girlfriend or his folks... and Sally doesn't even think, she doesn't even hesitate, she just spits on him. Spits on him and calls him a baby-killer.

"Now let's be clear, I did not agree with what the Americans did in Vietnam, but even if you object to the war, you respect the warrior. That's always been my feeling on the subject. So I cut my hair, and two days later I was in the Congo, tracking down the head of a death cult. You don't stay vegetarian for very long when you're hiking through the jungle."

He chewed another piece of steak, savoured it, and swallowed.

Valkyrie looked him dead in the eye. "What do you want?"

"Well, that's the thing, you see. I am a mess of conflicting desires. The man in me wants to help you. The Remnant in me wants to tear you apart. But the two together simply want a compromise."

"Give Alice back and we'll compromise," Valkyrie's dad said.

Vex held up a finger to silence him. "Hush now, Desmond, the adults are talking. When we first heard about the glimpse into the future, where Darquesse would decimate the world, we were positively giddy with delight. That's the world for us, we said. What we'd like, what we'd really love, is a future with, maybe, a tenth of the world's current population left alive. Enough for us to play with, but not enough to cause us any problems."

"Darquesse is not going to leave *anyone* alive," said Valkyrie.

"Exactly," said Vex. "When we started to realise the full extent of her plans, our giddiness faded. Only Foe and his crazy bunch of nihilists would find Darquesse's ultimate aim attractive, because not only do they want to die, but they want the world to die with them. And, to be honest, we also saw how she treats Remnants when they've served their purpose. Let's just say that they hold no special place in her heart."

"So now you're scared of her."

Vex smiled. "The same as everybody else."

"So I'll ask again. What do you want?"

"We wish to offer you our support. Sorcerers and Remnants, working together in perfect harmony. Can you think of anything more beautiful?"

"Problem is, Remnants can't be trusted."

"Normally I'd agree with you," said Vex. "In fact, even now I agree with you. But we promise to be good."

"How exactly do you see this working? Are you going to join our army? So you'll either possess hundreds of sorcerers or thousands of mortals? Do you really think anyone would agree to that?"

"Do you really think you can pass up this opportunity?" Vex asked. "As you say, there are thousands of us, each with a vast personal collection of knowledge and talents just waiting to be shared."

Valkyrie pulled up a chair, and sat. "If your accumulated wisdom is so great, then how come you haven't figured out a way to stop Darquesse without our help?"

Vex smiled at her. "Darquesse is tricky."

"There's no way China will agree to this. But if you let us leave with Alice, I'll do my best to convince her."

"Why are you so worried about the baby?" Vex asked. "Look at her. She's fine. She cried a bit earlier, but I changed her nappy, fed her, and she went right back to sleep."

"Then I'll stay," said Valkyrie. "Let my parents take her and you can keep me."

"That won't do, I'm afraid. I'll need Alice if I want to activate the Sceptre."

"What do you mean?" Valkyrie's mum asked, and Valkyrie went pale.

But Vex looked at her mum, and instead of opting for the cruel option, instead of explaining that Alice would have to die, he simply said, "For reasons too complicated to go into, your baby is the only one who can charge a very powerful weapon. I need her close to me if I have to use it." Then he looked back at Valkyrie. "Do we have an understanding?"

The truth would damage her parents. It wouldn't just shock them, wouldn't just horrify them, it would actually damage their ability to move forward. To be useful. If they were insisting on accompanying her, Valkyrie needed them to at least be able to function. Which meant the full truth would have to be kept from them.

"Just you," she said at last. "Your friends can stay here. I'll take you into Roarhaven and ask China to hear you out. That's the best I can do."

"I reluctantly agree to your conditions," Vex said, smiling, and Valkyrie knew this was what he had wanted all along. He dabbed at the corners of his mouth with a napkin, and stood. "Shall we leave? I assume your parents will be coming with us?"

"We're not letting Alice out of our sight," Valkyrie's mum said.

"That's the spirit." He picked up Alice's seat and went to carry it past Valkyrie, but she blocked his way, and looked over her shoulder at her parents.

"Can you give us a second?" she asked. "Please?"

Her mum frowned at her, concerned, but allowed Valkyrie's dad to move her back a few steps.

Valkyrie turned back to Vex and lowered her voice to a whisper. "Doctor Nye had a warehouse," she said. "You go in there, you're dead. Living bodies die, but they're still... aware. They can still move and think. Let me take Alice in. She'll be dead, technically she'll be dead, and you can take ownership of the Sceptre and then I take Alice back outside and she'll be alive again. I don't want to do it, I don't want to expose Alice to that horrible, cold feeling, I don't want her to experience that, but if it'll make you let her go..."

"Nye's warehouse was raided," Vex answered softly. "All enchantments, such as they were, have been dismantled. It's just an ordinary building now."

"Then the coach," said Valkyrie. "The coach the banshee calls, with the headless driver—"

"The Dullahan doesn't do favours, Valkyrie. If he takes your sister, you'll never get her back." He put a hand on her shoulder. "Besides, as long as I have her, you'll do exactly as I say. Because if you try anything, I'll kill her without a second thought."

He moved by her, exposing his back, leaving himself open and vulnerable, daring her to test his resolve.

But Valkyrie sagged, and simply followed Vex and her parents outside, where the crowd of black-veined people parted to reveal a sky-blue minivan.

"Behold our battle wagon," Vex said as the side door slid open. There were two rows of seats, plus the two seats up front. Vex climbed into the very back, clicking Alice's seat into place beside him. "Melissa," he said, "you can sit in the middle there, and Desmond, you drive. Valkyrie can sit up front with you. She knows where we're going. If anyone needs to pee before we leave, you better go now. We've got an hour's drive ahead of us and we won't be stopping."

67

LIGHTNING

They drove to Roarhaven.

Valkyrie was all out of leaves and the pain from her broken hand was making her sweat. She wiped her forehead and looked back. In the rear of the minivan, Vex sat with his head down. It was too dark to see his eyes, but his breathing was regular. She was sure he was sleeping. Even so, she didn't make a move. She'd been around the Dead Men enough by now to know that they never sank into deep sleep. If she tried anything, he'd be wide awake, fully alert and back in control in an instant.

She glanced at her mum, making sure she wasn't about to do anything desperate, but for once her mum's attention wasn't on Alice. She was frowning, looking out of the window.

"Mum?" Valkyrie said softly.

Her mum's frown deepened. "Do you hear something?"

Valkyrie peered out into the darkness, where the black shapes of trees and hedgerows blurred and melted together. She listened to the minivan's engine, to the rock and roll of the tyres over the poorly maintained road, to the sound of the heater blasting out warm air... and behind all that, what? What was that? Another engine?

"I see something," her dad said, his eyes on the rear-view mirror. "I think there's someone—"

Headlights flicked on, singular beams that cut through the gloom on either side of the minivan. There was a loud bang, like a gunshot or a small explosion, and the minivan wobbled violently. Her dad cursed, but Vex's eyes were open and calm.

"Everyone hold on," Valkyrie's dad said, and Valkyrie braced herself right before he braked. The minivan skidded to a shuddering, juddering halt, and two motorbikes sped into the yellow glare of his headlights and rode onwards, vanishing into the dark.

"Alice," Melissa Edgley said, starting to scramble into the rear seats as her husband flicked on the interior light.

"She's fine," said Vex, holding up his hand to block her way. It glowed briefly, but it was enough to make Valkyrie's mum freeze.

"Put your hand down," Valkyrie's dad said. "Melissa, stay where you are. Mr Vex, do not threaten my wife. Put your hand down."

Vex gave a little smile, and lowered his hand.

"Who was that?" Valkyrie's dad asked. "Steph, did you know those people? They blew out a tyre or something."

It was Vex who answered. "A man named Vincent Foe and his gang ride motorcycles, Desmond, and they happen to be working with Darquesse."

"You think she's here?" Valkyrie asked.

"No," said Vex. "She sends Foe out to do the little jobs she can't be bothered with. The only people out there are Foe and Samuel."

"We can take them," Valkyrie said, without much conviction.

"I'm sure you can."

She frowned. "You're not coming? I don't have my magic back yet."

"You'll be fine," said Vex.

"You have to go with her," Valkyrie's mum said. "She can't go out there alone."

"She's got her stick, hasn't she? She won't need me. Besides, I'm babysitting. Hurry now, Valkyrie. We don't want Alice waking up."

She could have argued, but she knew it'd be a waste of time. She unbuckled her seatbelt.

"I'm coming with you," her dad said.

"You can't," Valkyrie responded. "I may not be able to do magic, but my clothes are armoured. Yours aren't. Everyone stay here. I'll see if I can talk our way out."

She got out, closing the door behind her. The road was narrow, with trees on either side. Quiet. She stood in front of the minivan. Her shadow stretched before her, joining the darkness ahead.

The motorbikes were coming back. They stopped just out of reach of the minivan's headlights, and the engines cut off. A moment later, Foe and Samuel stepped into view, and her heartbeat quickened once more. Samuel was sweating. His hands were clenched. He was coming down off his serum. He was a hair's breadth away from turning.

"If things had gone differently," said Foe, "we'd just take the Sceptre. That's all we want, after all. Anyone else who wants the Sceptre also wants your sister so they can kill her and take control of it. But we have no intention of taking control of it. Darquesse doesn't want to use it. She just doesn't want anyone *else* to use it. So, as I said, if things had gone differently, we would have asked for the Sceptre, and ridden off into the night. But things didn't go differently. Things went exactly as they went."

Samuel walked to the edge of the light, and vanished into the darkness.

"Obloquy is dead," Foe continued. "That's not your fault. Darquesse did that, and Obloquy was fine with it. But Mercy... Mercy was killed to protect you. And I have to say, I have to say it, I kind of had a soft spot for Mercy. Call me an old romantic if you want, but I had dreams of dying with her. There'd be blood and screaming and fire and pain, and we'd be there... together."

Foe passed into Valkyrie's shadow, and was lost to sight.

"But I can't have that now," he said. "Because of you. And so, even though we're just here for the Sceptre, and we have strict orders not to kill you, we're going to anyway. We're going to kill everyone with you, too. We're going to kill your family. Your mammy and your daddy and your little baby sister. We're going to beat you to a pulp, we're going to make you scream and cry and beg, and we're going to kill them in front of you. Then we'll take the Sceptre and throw it in a ditch somewhere." He emerged into the light. "That sound good to you?"

"Dexter Vex is with me," Valkyrie said.

Foe nodded. "We'll kill him, too."

"You think you have a chance?" she asked. "Against me, yeah, of course you do. But him? This is Dexter Vex we're talking about. One of the Dead Men. And with that Remnant he's stronger and faster and doesn't possess one shred of pity. If I were you, I'd get back on my bike and I'd ride away. Fast."

"I like you," said Foe. "Despite it all, I like you. You're in a no-win situation that you're treating like a fair fight. You've got guts. But I have a vampire."

Something moved in the corner of her eye and then Samuel was on her, his body crushing her broken hand. She cried out and he snarled and launched her into the air. She landed and rolled, shrieking in pain as she got to her feet, but Samuel was there again to grab her.

"Beat her to a pulp," Foe said, walking to the minivan. "I'm going to kill her family."

Samuel hit her and Valkyrie dropped to one knee, her head swimming. Her jacket absorbed most of the kick that followed, but it still sent her tumbling. Holding her broken hand close to her chest, she whipped the shock stick from her back and leaped up. Samuel ducked under her first swipe and leaned back to avoid the second. Then he grabbed her wrist and twisted and the stick fell and his fist ploughed into her exposed belly and she staggered back, whooping and gasping.

Through teary eyes, she saw Foe reach the minivan.

Samuel grabbed her hair and yanked her head back. She twisted and fell and got up as he pulled her from one side of the road to the other. With her right hand, she tried pushing the air. She tried clicking her fingers. Nothing worked. The magic was inside her, it was bubbling and boiling and churning, but nothing was happening, nothing was working, nothing was—

White lightning danced from the tips of her fingers and Samuel jerked away.

Valkyrie scrambled backwards. Her hand. Her right hand was glowing.

Samuel doubled over. His snarls turned guttural. He straightened up suddenly, talons tearing into his clothes and skin, shredding it from the vampire's body beneath. White skin like alabaster. Bald. Big black eyes. The vampire sprang at her, claws ready for ripping, fangs ready for tearing. Valkyrie fell on to her back, her glowing hand held up, and it was through her hand that she poured her magic.

Lightning burst from her fingers. It caught the vampire in mid-air, snapping it back like it had hit a wall. It fell to the road as a charred, smoking carcass.

"What did you do?"

She looked round. Foe came forward, staring at the vampire's corpse, his face slack.

"*What did you do?*" he asked again. There was something in his face. Something Valkyrie recognised. Anger, of course. Surprise. Confusion.

But also fear.

It was dark, there on the roadside. But as Valkyrie stared at

Samuel's body, the patch of darkness she stood in seemed to brighten. At first, she thought she was caught in a beam of moonlight, but it just got brighter, and brighter.

Her hand. It was glowing again. Lit up from the inside with a silver light. Both her hands. And her face. Her neck. Beneath her clothes, her entire body was glowing. She stood up, fingertips burning. The magic churned inside her. Her hair stood on end. Energy crackled around her, forming a barrier that lifted her off the ground. Hissing in panic, she drifted sideways. The energy barrier kept her from colliding with a tree beyond the grassy verge. She didn't know how to stand like this. She fell, but didn't hit the ground. She turned over. Rolled. Tried to straighten up.

"What the hell are you doing?" asked Foe.

She turned, falling backwards again in this cocoon of energy. Foe stood there, staring, the confusion on his face beautifully illuminated by the light Valkyrie was giving out.

She managed to stand. She was unsteady, but she did it.

Foe threw a stream of energy. It hit the cocoon and flowed round it. It didn't hurt her. It didn't even touch her.

He threw another, and another.

Something was happening. Valkyrie could feel it. The magic thrashed inside her. It was building up to something.

"Run," she said.

Foe poured all his strength into another energy stream. It proved just as useless as the others.

"*Run*," she said again, but it was too late. The magic burst from her in a wave that turned the trees to splinters. It hit Foe and he was gone. Obliterated. She could feel the wave expand in all directions. She could feel it nearing the minivan. She grimaced, reached out with her mind, searching for control. She reached to the edge of the wave and snagged it, grabbed it, pulled it back, pulled it all the way back, and the magic returned to her and she dropped to her knees in the crater that had formed around her.

She was no longer glowing.

She stood up on shaky legs. She was exhausted. The roadside was dark again.

"Stephanie!"

Her mum ran to her, and Valkyrie slumped into her arms.

"Oh, God, Steph, are you OK? Please tell me you're OK."

"I'm good," Valkyrie mumbled.

"Oh, thank God. Oh, thank God. What was that? You were glowing and it was hard to look at you, it was all so bright. What was that lightning? Where's that man? Where is he?"

Valkyrie forced her eyes open. "Mum, I need you to help me into the van. Too tired to..."

Her mother pulled her up. "Shh. Don't talk. You don't have to talk."

They got back into the minivan and Valkyrie fell asleep while her dad changed the tyre.

68

THE HOURGLASS

Up in the balcony, Fletcher and Wreath watched Skulduggery walk into the square at the exact centre of the Necropolis. There, another man in a black Necromancer robe stood waiting. Beneath his hood, like the others, his face was porcelain.

Skulduggery approached. "Do you have a name, or are names beneath you?"

That porcelain face smiled. "I am known as the Guardian. I am the final test."

Skulduggery nodded, looked around, then back to the Guardian. "I go through you to activate the sigil, is that it?"

"In essence. But of course there is more to it than that."

"Well, of course there is." Skulduggery tilted his head. "Don't suppose you're going to tell me exactly what's in store for me, are you?"

"True understanding comes later."

"True understanding usually does."

The Guardian smiled again. "You are a warrior."

"When I need to be."

"You are a violent man."

"When I have to be."

"Is it, do you think, an appropriate response to the world around you?"

"Violence?" Skulduggery asked. "Violence is never the answer, until it's the only answer."

Another porcelain smile. "Your words are weary."

"They're just well travelled. If I could save the world with words, I would. I'd lay down my gun and I'd talk until my bones turned to dust. But words are for reasonable people. And too often, the people I meet are far from reasonable."

"You have blood on your hands."

"I do, so other people don't have to," said Skulduggery.

"But that is not why you fight. You fight because the fight is all you have. You fight because you enjoy it."

"What are you looking for?" Skulduggery asked. "An insight into my soul? You want to shock me into admitting some dark little secret that I've been hiding away for all these years? I've just spoken to beings claiming to be the ghosts of my friends, the ghost of my wife... I saw my *child*. After all these years, I saw the face of my child again. I'm all shocked-out for today. If we're going to fight, let's get to it." Skulduggery raised his fists. "I've got living people to get back to."

"So be it," said the Guardian. "If you prevail, you may activate the Meryyn Sigil, and power grafted from the source of all magic shall endow the one who wears the sigil with great strength and protect them from harm, until the last grain of sand falls."

Skulduggery dropped his hands. "I'm sorry, what?"

The Guardian gestured to the middle of the square, as a plinth rose from the ground. When it settled, an hourglass rose from within the plinth. "Once you have activated the Meryyn Sigil, the hourglass will turn and the sands will run."

"For how long?" Skulduggery asked, stalking over to examine the plinth. "This amount of sand... it looks like it'll only run for, what, a little over twenty minutes?"

The Guardian nodded. "Twenty-three, actually."

Skulduggery looked back at him. "So, if I fight you now and I win, and the sigil is activated, Valkyrie will only be invulnerable for the twenty-three minutes after that moment?"

"Yes," said the Guardian, sounding surprised at the question. "Twenty-three minutes of invulnerability and strength is quite generous, we thought."

Skulduggery looked up, and Fletcher had the feeling he was glaring at Wreath. He switched his focus back to the Guardian. "There's no way to delay it? I activate the sigil and the invulnerability kicks in when we need it?"

"That is not possible, I am afraid. Is there a problem?"

"There is," Skulduggery said. "That's not going to work for us."

"I'm afraid there is no way around it."

Skulduggery observed him. "Do I have to fight you now? Right at this moment?"

Porcelain eyebrows rose slightly. "Well... No, I suppose not."

"Can I come back?"

"It is most unusual," said the Guardian, "but yes. The tests will only be reset after I am engaged in combat."

"So I can walk straight here and there'll be no one to stop me?"

"Precisely."

"Then that's what I'll do."

The Guardian bowed. "I shall await your return."

Skulduggery turned, looked up at the balcony. "We're going back to Roarhaven."

69

STRANGE BEDFELLOWS

"There's someone up ahead," her dad said.

Valkyrie woke, launched from a troubled sleep like she'd been shot from a cannon. Her body ached. Her broken hand alone made her want to cry. The minivan was slowing as it approached an elderly man, smiling in the headlights. When they came to a stop, he walked to the driver's side as the window wound down.

"Afraid the road's closed, folks," he said. "A few trees down. Where you headed?" But when the elderly man saw Valkyrie, his expression changed. "Ah, excuse me, I didn't realise. Carry on."

He nodded to them and stepped back, vanishing into the darkness.

"He's with the Sanctuary," Valkyrie said. "We can keep going."

Valkyrie's dad put the minivan in gear and they started moving again.

"Slight change of plan," Vex said, like he'd been waiting for her to catch his eye. "China would throw me in a cell as soon as look at me, so I'll be fading into the shadows once we've arrived. If any of you try to signal to the guards up ahead that something isn't right, I kill Alice. That's the first thing I do. We all clear?"

"We are," said Valkyrie.

Vex smiled straight at her. "And as for you and your sparkly new powers, if you even *think* about using them against me, I'll kill Alice and then kill you before you've even learned how to aim properly."

Valkyrie's mum shifted in her seat. "Could you please stop threatening my children, Mr Vex? I would very much appreciate it."

Vex smiled. "But of course, Melissa. My apologies."

"I don't see anything," her dad muttered. "You said there was a huge wall and a gate. You said there was a city."

"Give it a few more seconds," Valkyrie said.

And then, suddenly, Roarhaven. One moment there was the road the headlights picked out, long and narrowing, hedged in on both sides by thin trees. The next, a brightly-lit wall, high enough to fill the windscreen and block out the stars.

Her dad went to brake when it materialised, but stopped himself. They drove on to the open gate.

Cleavers and sorcerers stood guard, and a man named Krull waved them to a stop. He went round to the passenger side, and Valkyrie lowered the window.

"Welcome back," said Krull, his eyes flickering over the people in the minivan. Valkyrie doubted he could make out Vex, sitting in the dark in the back.

"Thanks," she said. "We're just headed to the Sanctuary."

Krull nodded, but made no sign he was going to let them through. "Interesting times we're living in," he said.

Valkyrie gave him a nod. "Yes they are."

"Mind stepping out for a moment?"

"All of us?"

"Just you, if you wouldn't mind."

"Sure," she said, hesitating only a little. She glanced back at Vex, wondering how tense he was, wondering if he'd react to this. But he just sat there, an outline in the dark.

Valkyrie undid her seatbelt, opened the door and went to get out. When she was halfway out, Krull grabbed her wrist, yanked her forward. She hit the ground and tears sprang to her eyes and there was suddenly a lot of movement and a lot of shouting. Her folks were telling Krull to leave her alone, the sorcerers around her were telling them to stay in the minivan, and Krull was commanding her to lie still. Cold steel closed round her right wrist and she felt her magic dwindle. It snapped shut round her left wrist and jarred her broken bones.

"I'm Valkyrie Cain!" she cried, Krull's knee in her back.

"For all I know you're Darquesse," Krull said, grabbing the back of her collar. He hauled her to her feet, slammed her against the minivan. "You move and we kill you, you understand me?"

Her face was squashed against the glass. Her mum stared at her from the other side, horrified. On the seat behind, Vex was inching towards the far door.

"You killed my son," Krull said into Valkyrie's ear.

Her insides went cold, and began to churn. "I'm sorry," she said. "But that was Darquesse, that wasn't—"

"You killed him here, during the battle. Four weeks ago. Back when you *were* Darquesse."

"I wasn't in control. Krull, I'm sorry, I am, but—"

He grabbed her broken hand and squeezed and Valkyrie screamed.

"A few of us have been wondering why exactly Sorrows let you back into the fold," Krull said in her ear. "We think it's because she likes you. You and the Skeleton Detective. You're her favourites. Makes us wonder why the hell she's in charge anyway. Who the hell elected her? Who voted her in? I certainly didn't."

"Please, you're hurting me."

"You're damn right I am."

"You know I'm not Darquesse," Valkyrie said through gritted teeth.

"I know no such thing."

She tried to turn into him, but he slammed his whole body weight into her and she cried out again. That was too much for her dad to take, and he threw open his door. The Cleavers grabbed him when he got out. Now that they were distracted, Vex reached forward, slid open the side door to make his escape with Alice. He clearly figured his plan was falling apart. But Valkyrie's mum dived on him, and they tumbled out of the minivan and then Valkyrie was pulled away from the window.

She twisted, rammed her shoulder into Krull's chest. She kicked at his knee, got his shin instead. She heard him growl in pain and he hit her and bright lights flashed and she fell to her knees. Then he grabbed her hair, started dragging her backwards, and through the tears in her eyes she glimpsed something on the wall overhead, and it was dropping and spinning, and Tanith landed beside her.

She didn't even see the strike, but she heard it connect, and Krull went stumbling against the minivan. Tanith stalked up to him, her hand closing round his throat, her fingertips digging in behind his windpipe. She pinned his head against the corner of the vehicle and he gagged.

"Key," she said.

Krull fumbled in his pocket, fished out a small key. Tanith snatched it from him, smacked him in the jaw and he dropped. Tanith helped Valkyrie stand, and unlocked the shackles.

"See to your folks," Tanith said. "I'll take this little charmer to cool off in the cells."

Valkyrie nodded, not even waiting around to watch Tanith drag Krull off by the ear. Clutching her left hand, she hurried round to the other side of the minivan. The Cleavers were just allowing her father back to his feet. A pretty lady, Korb, was with them, apologising profusely.

Her mum was on her knees, her back to Valkyrie.

'Vex," said Valkyrie. "Where is he?"

"Ran off," said Korb, looking round. "There was a bit of a scramble but he hightailed it when he saw us closing in."

"No," Valkyrie breathed. "Alice."

Her mum stood, and turned, tears in her eyes and Alice in her arms. "Still asleep," she said, laughing. "Can you believe that? Still asleep after all that? What an amazing sister you have."

"What an amazing mum," Valkyrie said, running forward and hugging them both.

Wiping the healing mud from her hand, Valkyrie entered the Room of Prisms by Skulduggery's side. Synecdoche had patched her up, eased her bruises and mended her broken fingers, and now she felt great. She felt refreshed, strong, and she had a cool new array of magic powers she hadn't even explored yet.

China was resplendent in red. She sat atop her throne like an ice queen, gazing down at her loyal subjects – the Monster Hunters, Saracen, Fletcher, Wreath and Tanith. Standing within arm's reach of the throne was the Black Cleaver.

"Thank you for joining us," China said, in a tone that made it impossible to gauge whether or not she was being sarcastic. "Has everyone been briefed on the latest developments? We all know what's been going on? Valkyrie, where are your parents?"

"In the Dining Hall," she said. "The chef's making them something special and Alice is bringing the roof down with her crying."

"So I've heard," said China. "Have you told them that it's not safe for them to leave the Sanctuary?"

"I told them. They don't know the truth about Alice and the Sceptre, but I doubt they're planning on going for a walk anyway. They already asked a Cleaver to go out and bring back baby food and nappies. It had never occurred to me that you could buy nappies in Roarhaven."

"It truly is a wonderful place," China said. "To business, then, and before we begin, I'd like to introduce you to a new guest.

Though, of course, I use the word 'like' in its loosest possible sense."

The door opened, and Tanith muttered something as Billy-Ray Sanguine walked in. He flashed a smile of perfect white teeth, a smile that faltered slightly when his eyeless gaze fell upon Tanith.

"Folks," he said in greeting. "Once more we appear to be on the same side. This is getting to be a habit."

"Mr Sanguine," China said, "please tell the room what you told Mr Tipstaff."

"Darquesse is preparing," he said. "She's had to take some time for her power to soak through her new body. She also said something about needing to absorb Valkyrie's essence in order to be whole."

"Gross," said Valkyrie.

Skulduggery tilted his head. "Darquesse is not at full power?"

"That's what it sounds like. But she will be soon. I'm talking a day or two – tops."

"We need to draw her in now," said Saracen. "Before she's ready to face us."

"But *we* need to be ready to face *her*," China said. "Skulduggery, do we have any kind of a time frame?"

"The city will never be ready," he answered, "but we can make a decent stab at it. We'll need the night. Tomorrow morning, we'll take Ravel out of the circle that's keeping him hidden. Once Darquesse senses him, she *should* be drawn straight here."

"She will be," said Sanguine, nodding. "I reckon punishing him was her last act that's even remotely human, and there's a part of her that's clinging to that."

"When she gets here, what do we do with Ravel?" Donegan asked.

China sat back. "We arm him."

Saracen frowned. "We what?"

"It's in his best interests to help us," China explained.

"I am not fighting beside that man," said Saracen. "He murdered Ghastly, for God's sake. Shudder is dead because of him. Skulduggery, come on, talk some sense into her."

"Actually," China said, "it was Skulduggery's idea."

Valkyrie's eyebrows shot up. "What?"

"Ravel will fight alongside us or he'll spend the rest of his life in agony," Skulduggery said. "He doesn't have a choice. I don't like it any more than you, but we're going up against an enemy the likes of which we've never faced. We need everyone we can get – and at least we know how Ravel fights."

"This is unbelievable," Saracen muttered, but said no more.

"We have three God-Killer weapons," said China. "Mr Sanguine here has a fourth, but I doubt we'd get that off him without a fight."

Sanguine grinned. "Not a chance."

"Three God-Killers, then. Skulduggery, Saracen and Ravel will wield them. There is another out there, of course, the most powerful, but Dexter Vex has run off with it. If anyone encounters him over the next few hours, feel free to liberate the Sceptre from his person."

"What good will that do?" Valkyrie asked. "It's bonded to my sister. No one here is laying a finger on her, even if we *do* get the Sceptre back."

"I wasn't suggesting that at all," China said, but failed to elaborate on what she *was* suggesting. "And speaking of secret weapons," she continued, "we have one last weapon to take into account." She produced the Deathtouch Gauntlet from somewhere behind her, and put it on the arm of the throne.

"I told you," Valkyrie said, "I'm not wearing that. I don't even need it now that I've got my freaky new powers."

"New powers that we've never seen before," China said. "White lightning, a type of energy we have yet to identify... We don't even know what to classify your discipline as."

"*Freak* sounds good to me," said Sanguine.

China glanced at him. "And yet nobody asked you. Valkyrie, without knowing what you can do or how to control it, I'm afraid you need every advantage you can get. Take the gauntlet. Please."

Valkyrie shook her head. "I've seen myself wear it in the vision, just before Darquesse kills my family. My family is here *now*, China. Because of Vex, we have to keep them close. We can't even let them leave. The vision is coming true. If I wear that, I'm allowing that future to happen."

"And if you don't wear it," China said, "you might be allowing it to happen that much sooner."

Valkyrie glared, her heat matched by the cool of those ice-blue eyes. Finally, she looked away, and turned to Skulduggery. "I can't wear it..."

"You have to," he said. "China's right."

"That's Grand Mage Sorrows," China corrected, "or I'll have you both flogged."

"The circumstances in the visions are coming true," Skulduggery said, ignoring China, "so you know you'll be called upon to fight. You owe it to yourself, to us, and to your family, to give yourself every advantage. The circumstances haven't changed, but the details have. We've seen clothes change. We've seen people in the early visions that aren't there in the later ones. Your family dying? That could be one more detail that we see changed. But only if you fight hard enough."

Valkyrie folded her arms. "Fine," she muttered.

Skulduggery waved his hand, and the gauntlet floated down to her. She took hold of it, and stuffed it in her jacket pocket. It was too big to fit in all the way.

"Tell us about your plan," China said to Skulduggery. "When Darquesse attacks, we'll need you here to lead the initial defence."

Skulduggery nodded. "If Sanguine is right, her targets will be Ravel and Valkyrie. Ravel will draw her in, but when she realises that Valkyrie is here, I fully expect her to forget about Ravel and focus on her. So our main objective in the opening stages is to protect Valkyrie Cain. Questions?"

"We have sorcerers and Cleavers and God-Killers on our side," said Gracious, "not to mention our own nutball Death Bringer, but unless we get lucky, we're not going to be able to contain Darquesse for long."

"That's where Fletcher comes in," Skulduggery said. "He'll teleport me to the Necropolis, where I'll face the Guardian in the final test. So, if and when Darquesse does reach Valkyrie, hopefully she'll get a nasty surprise."

"How long will the final test take?" asked Saracen.

"I have no idea."

"This is far from ideal."

"Of that, I am aware."

"Are we sure this is a wise course of action?" Donegan asked. "Skulduggery, like it or not, you're one of our heavy hitters. We can't afford to lose you in the middle of a pitched battle."

"We don't have much choice," Skulduggery said. "If Darquesse kills Valkyrie and absorbs her essence or her soul or her power or whatever it is she's after, then we're done for. We're beaten. Twenty-three minutes of invulnerability, plus Valkyrie's new powers and that gauntlet, may be all that stands in the way of Darquesse and the end of the world."

"But we can't lose you," said Saracen.

"There's no choice," said Skulduggery. "Only the dead can enter the Necropolis. I don't see a whole lot of dead people volunteering to take my place, do you?"

At that exact moment the door opened and everyone looked round as a beautiful, athletic redhead walked in, followed by a handsome, muscular man.

"I am Vaurien Scapegrace," the woman announced, "and I'm here to save the world."

70

RETURN OF THE LIVING DEAD

What followed was confusing.

Valkyrie stayed out of it. She watched the arguments and the debate and said nothing. She watched people change their minds, change them back, and change them again. Gradually an unlikely outcome began to rear its head – people were agreeing that Scapegrace should have his brain put back into his old, dead, zombie body in order to go into the Necropolis and face the Guardian in battle.

It was all very unsettling.

She accompanied Skulduggery, Scapegrace and Thrasher to the Medical Wing, and Synecdoche brought them to see the two original bodies in all their zombie glory.

They floated in green liquid in a big glass tank. They looked disgusting.

"Are you sure you want to do this?" Valkyrie asked. "I mean... they're falling apart. And the way you look now is... well, it's a lot more attractive."

Scapegrace looked at her. "I'm a woman."

"A woman is not a bad thing to be."

He nodded. "I accept that. I understand that. I have had my horizons broadened by my time in this body. Not broadened as much as some of my pub's patrons would have liked, but broadened nonetheless. But we *belong* in those decaying shells, Valkyrie, if it's at all possible to get us back into them." He turned to Synecdoche. "Give it to us straight, Doc – our brains may not survive the transplant, right?"

Synecdoche hesitated. "They... they won't survive. There is no maybe here. If we attempt it, your brains will fall apart. They're only held together by twine as it is."

Scapegrace frowned. "Twine?"

"Yes."

"Our brains are held together with *string*?"

"I'm afraid so."

He stared at her, and shook his head. "I hate Doctor Nye *so much* right now..."

"So what's the point of doing this if our brains are going to fall apart?" Thrasher asked.

"I've spoken with my colleagues," said Synecdoche, "and we've come to the conclusion that we don't need to transplant your brains. We just need to transplant your minds."

Valkyrie stood there and waited for her to start making sense.

"There is a vegetable-plant hybrid we've been working on, modifying the genes and receptors, mutating the proteins and acids so that they are, in effect, neurotransmitters. Our work on the synapses alone has been quite illuminating."

Valkyrie stood there and waited for her to start making sense.

"Anyway," Synecdoche said, blushing, "we think we can install these hybrids into your old bodies and, with the help of some skilled Sensitives, transfer your minds into them."

"That sounds great," Thrasher said, a huge smile breaking out.

"Wait a second," said Scapegrace. "You're saying you're going to... you're going to put our thoughts into... into vegetable-plant hybrids?"

"Yes."

"Are... are our brains going to be vegetables?"

Synecdoche hesitated again. "Kind of."

Valkyrie couldn't help it. She burst out laughing.

The operation took most of the night. Valkyrie spent that time sleeping or in the Ops Room, a brightly-lit space of monitors and weird-looking computers. In the centre was a long table displaying what appeared to be a highly detailed scale model of Roarhaven. It was only when it started to flicker slightly that Valkyrie realised it was a hologram. Little hologram people ran about on its streets. She even thought she recognised a few faces.

The room was buzzing with activity. No one needed her so she stayed at the back, in the dark. She took the Deathtouch Gauntlet from her jacket, and put it on a table no one was using. She left it there.

She was on her third cup of coffee when the doors opened and the two zombies walked in, grinning like conquering heroes.

One of Scapegrace's teeth fell out, and he kicked it under a chair.

Skulduggery walked over to them. "This is a surprisingly brave thing you're doing," he said.

"I know," said Scapegrace. "I've just been thinking that. I think I felt more heroic in the woman's body. She was stronger and fitter and better and I just felt a lot braver speaking in her voice. My own voice is kind of nasal. Have you noticed that? How can my voice be nasal if most of my nose fell off years ago?"

"Don't worry, Master," said Thrasher, "I'll be right behind you, every step of the—"

"Shut up," Scapegrace said.

Thrasher looked bizarrely pleased as he said, "Sorry, Master."

"This final test," said Scapegrace, "is there any way I'll be able to cheat?"

"Probably not," Skulduggery said. He handed him a folded piece of paper. "This is a map. When Fletcher teleports you in, you'll be at the bottom of stone stairs. Before you, the Necropolis. Follow these directions exactly and you'll get to the square, where the Guardian waits."

"Will he be expecting me?"

"He'll be expecting *me*. Explain to him that I won't be coming, and don't take no for an answer. Then combat will begin."

"I have been trained in the martial arts," Scapegrace said, bowing slightly. "Although that was when I had a stronger, fitter, more athletic body. But I'm sure I'll be fine."

"You're going to have to be more than sure. We're relying on you here, Vaurien, OK? The fate of the world may very well rest in your hands."

"You can count on me."

"And me," Thrasher said brightly.

"Less so on him," said Scapegrace.

"Stay in this room," Skulduggery said. "I have a feeling, when we need you, things will move very fast."

Thrasher nodded eagerly, but Scapegrace looked decidedly paler. Valkyrie wondered how that was possible.

Saracen approached. "We're ready," he said. "Or ready enough anyway. We can't afford to wait around any longer."

"OK then," Skulduggery said. "Let's go talk to Mr Ravel."

Ravel was standing in the protective circle. Two Cleavers guarded the door. Skulduggery walked into the room first, then Saracen. Valkyrie came last.

"We're going to need you to step out here," Skulduggery said.

Ravel shook his head. "Skulduggery, you can't ask me to do that."

"Step out, or we'll drag you out."

"She'll come for me. Please, if our friendship has ever meant anything to you—"

"Friendship?" Saracen interrupted. "You want to talk about friendship?"

"Saracen, I'm well aware of what I've done, but that's no—"

"You murdered Ghastly," Saracen said. "You had Anton *beheaded*. You plotted and planned behind our backs for God knows how long, and then you betrayed us all."

"I was trying to do the right thing."

"*You killed them.*"

"Sacrifices had to me made," Ravel said. He spoke with the air of someone who'd had this conversation a thousand times before. Which was probably close to the truth. "I don't expect you to understand, but I have seen what's coming, OK? Sooner or later, our little magical community is going to be revealed to the world, and they're going to come after us. And as powerful as we are, there are simply more of them than there are of us. They will hunt us down and kill us."

"We're meant to protect the mortals."

A look of annoyance crossed Ravel's face. "Says who? Really, Saracen, who says that? Who commands that? We make up our own minds. Just because we've decided in the past to protect them doesn't mean we can't decide now to rule them. It's for their own good anyway. They can't be trusted to run this world. Look what they've done to the environment alone in the last—"

"We're not debating this," said Saracen. "You can come up with all the excuses you want, but nothing changes what you've done."

"I know," said Ravel quietly. "But Saracen, Skulduggery... Valkyrie... if I leave this circle, Darquesse will come for me. You don't know what it was like. Please. Don't ask me to go through that again."

"You're bait," Skulduggery said. "You've known for days now that you were going to be bait. You knew this was coming."

"So that's it? You're just going to leave me alone and defenceless against her?"

"No. Because we're not like you. We prefer to give people a

fighting chance. She'll be coming for you, and we're going to be ready. You'll be with us."

Ravel looked shocked. "You want me fighting beside you? After... after what I've done?"

"Do we *want* you beside us?" Skulduggery said. "No. But that's where you'll be. We don't know how long it'll take her to get here, but we're as ready as we're going to be. Let's go."

For a moment, Ravel seemed pinned to the spot. Then he took a shuddering breath, and stepped out of the circle.

71

Ravel.

He came through loud and clear, lit up in her mind like a star in the night sky. She turned, her eyes closed, until the star burned bright enough for her to follow.

South. Towards Roarhaven. He was in the Sanctuary.

It was a trap. It was so obviously a trap.

Darquesse opened her eyes and smiled.

Good.

72

The mission was a go.

Scapegrace had never felt anything like this before. While his stomach was incapable of producing the butterflies effect he felt sure should have accompanied such a moment, he nonetheless felt thrilled beyond measure at the thought of doing something so important. Of doing something so worthy.

Thrasher was unusually quiet, which was a good thing, and they stood quietly in the Ops Room while people around them talked really fast to each other.

"She's coming," Saracen Rue said.

China Sorrows, the most beautiful woman Scapegrace had ever seen, walked quickly to the hologram of the city. "She's been seen?"

"Our Sensitives are blacking out," said Rue. "The ones we've had searching for her. Finbar says their minds are being overloaded the closer she gets."

"Get Finbar isolated," China said. "Cassandra, too. Where are Geoffrey Scrutinous and Philomena Random? We need them all isolated."

"I've sent for them," said Skulduggery. "They'll be ready when we need them, you can count on that. Where's the Black Cleaver?"

China scowled. "I have no idea."

Skulduggery nodded, and looked at Tanith Low. "Tanith, you've just been assigned bodyguard duty."

"Me?" said Tanith, appalled.

"Her?" said China, appalled.

"Deal with it and move on," Skulduggery said. "How long do we have before Darquesse gets here?"

"We estimate no longer than half an hour," Rue answered.

Skulduggery turned to Scapegrace. "Are you ready to go?"

"We are," said Scapegrace. He found himself unbelievably thankful that Thrasher was coming with him. He didn't want to embark on this alone, no matter how tough he talked. He looked at Thrasher, and said, "You're an idiot."

"Thank you, sir," Thrasher replied.

"Fletcher will take you to the Necropolis now," Skulduggery said. "If you run, you can make it to the Guardian in a little over twenty minutes. No matter what, he has to agree to fight you. And no matter what, Vaurien, you have to win. Do you understand?"

"I do."

"We're going to be putting all our efforts into keeping Darquesse away from Valkyrie for approximately twenty-five minutes. If you take any longer than that, if you get lost or you take too long with the fight, or if you lose, then it'll all be for nothing."

"I won't let you down."

"We're counting on you. The world is counting on you."

Skulduggery held out his hand. Scapegrace shook it.

Clarabelle burst through the doors and ran up to him. "Scapey! Gerald! Take me with you! I can help!"

"Clarabelle, no," said Scapegrace.

Skulduggery stepped away, gesturing to Fletcher.

"I can mend you if you get hurt," Clarabelle said. "If bits fall off, I can stick them back on. I'll be useful!"

"You're alive," Scapegrace said softly. "No one living can enter the Necropotus."

"Necropolis," Thrasher whispered.

"But you're my only friends," Clarabelle said. She was crying. Scapegrace's heart was a rotten piece of meat in his chest, but even so it broke at the sight of her tears.

He hugged her. "We're doing this to save you," he said.

"Please don't go."

"You have other friends here."

"They think I'm weird."

"I think you're weird."

"But you're weird, too, so that doesn't matter. Gerald, please."

"I'm sorry," said Thrasher. "But if we can come back, we will. Because we're a family, Clarabelle. We'll always come back to family."

Clarabelle hid her face in her hands. "Don't leave me..."

Scapegrace stepped back. He took hold of Thrasher's wrist and then Fletcher took hold of his.

"Goodbye," Scapegrace said, and he didn't even have time to blink and they were somewhere else, somewhere new. In a cavern, at the bottom of marble steps, facing a city.

"Enter there," Fletcher said. "You have the map, right?"

Thrasher held it up. "Yes we do."

Fletcher nodded. "If I survive this, and if you survive this, I'll see you again. Good luck, the both of you."

He disappeared.

Scapegrace and Thrasher. Alone, in the City of the Dead.

"I feel sad," said Thrasher.

"Shut up," Scapegrace growled. He started running.

They got lost four times, thanks to Thrasher's inability to read the map. Even so, they made better time than expected, and reached the square in the middle of the Necropolis in nineteen minutes.

There was a tall man in a black robe waiting for them. His face looked like a living porcelain mask.

"You are not who I was expecting," the Guardian said.

"Skulduggery couldn't make it," Scapegrace. "He sent me in his place."

"And me," said Thrasher.

"He didn't send him," Scapegrace clarified. "But I am here to face the final test. Will you battle me?"

"And me," said Thrasher.

"I cannot," said the Guardian. "You are brave, the both of you, for coming here. But he who begins the trials must end the trials."

"He told me not to take no for an answer," Scapegrace said.

The Guardian gave a little smile. "You must be a great hero for him to pass this responsibility on to you."

"I'm no hero," said Scapegrace. "I'm just a man, who used to be a woman, who used to be a man. My name is Vaurien Scapegrace, and I have come here to—"

"The Zombie King?"

Scapegrace froze. Finally, he said, "Uh... you've heard of me?"

"This is the Necropolis," said the Guardian, "the City of the Dead. Of course I have heard of you. There hasn't been a Zombie King in centuries. It is an honour to have you here."

Scapegrace waited for the punchline.

Thrasher nudged him, and whispered, "I think he's serious."

"If the skeleton has asked you to come here in his place," the Guardian said, "then it would be a privilege to engage you in combat."

Scapegrace blinked. "So... so we can fight?"

"The both of us?" Thrasher asked. "Against you?"

The Guardian bowed. "If that is what you wish. Please, choose your weapons."

A pillar rose up, rumbling, from the ground. Hanging from it were swords and knives and maces and spears. Scapegrace looked at the Guardian, standing there with a peaceful expression on his porcelain face, unarmed and courteous, and he chose a curved, gleaming sword. Thrasher chose two smaller swords. The pillar rumbled again, and sank into the ground.

Brandishing his weapon, Scapegrace stepped towards the Guardian. "Shall we begin?"

"By all means," the Guardian said, and the biggest sword Scapegrace had ever seen materialised in his hands.

"Oh," Thrasher muttered. "Oh, dear."

73

The radio has been on for the last hour. Eighties pop. Gant has probably had enough of listening to Jeremiah. Now 'Don't You Want Me' by the Human League plays. Danny listens to it in the darkness over the Cadillac's engine. His mom loved eighties pop. The Human League, Duran Duran, Erasure. His dad preferred seventies rock. Led Zeppelin, Rush, Sabbath. They both had an appreciation for music, though, which is probably where Danny gets it from.

The Cadillac stops. The engine cuts off, taking the music with it. Car doors open. Danny waits. There's some muffled talking, then footsteps. A rattle and click and the trunk opens. Danny curls up tighter, like a flower shrinking from sudden cold, hands over his eyes to shield them from the light. Metal tightens over his wrists. Handcuffs.

"Out," says Jeremiah.

Blinking madly, Danny moves his aching bones. He's sore and tired and cold and he reeks. His left shoulder is throbbing and his right ankle is swollen. He's thirsty and his stomach is empty. He manages to get one leg out and clambers awkwardly from the trunk. They're on a residential street. It's the middle of the day, but it's quiet. No one around to see him. He could shout for help, but he doesn't bother. Gant would have thought of that. Jeremiah would be ready for it.

One side of the street is practically identical to the other. All big colonial houses, with lots of space in between. Jeremiah marches Danny ahead of him, and they follow Gant up the steps to number 4. Gant twists a key in the lock and walks through, then Jeremiah pushes Danny so that he stumbles in after him, and Danny pitches straight into hell.

The heat is the first thing to hit – so powerful it makes Danny close his eyes and turn his head. He tries to back out, but Jeremiah is behind him, already shutting the door. He can hear water, flowing and boiling, and behind that he hears screams. People are screaming. He cracks his eyes open, and fright tears through him.

He's on a metal walkway, a bridge suspended by chains above a lake of liquid fire. His surroundings are impossible. The inside of this colonial house is a church so vast he can't see the top. There are bridges above him, and ceilings and walkways, but they are impossibly high, and the twisted architecture vanishes into darkness, punctuated only by small patches of distant light.

Gant is halfway across the bridge. Jeremiah gives Danny a shove. Danny reaches out for the thin railing to stop himself from going over, but it burns his fingers and he hisses, clutching his hands close to his chest. He limps quickly after Gant, away from Jeremiah. The heat is oppressive. His shirt is already drenched with sweat. The screaming continues.

They get to a platform that sways under their weight. Danny walks with his knees bent, waves of dizziness roiling around his head. The heat doesn't affect Gant, but Danny can still find it within himself to be pleased that Jeremiah is finding this as uncomfortable as he is. Large patches of sweat have already soaked through the big man's jacket. His fat cheeks are red and he's puffing like it's hard to breathe. Jeremiah doesn't complain, though, and he doesn't walk like he's scared of falling.

They climb iron stairs. Danny keeps his hands to himself. He can feel the heat through his shoes. The stairs are steep, and there are a lot of them, and Danny's legs are trembling by the time they reach the top. He glances down at Jeremiah, who is finding the climb tough going. Good.

There's a hut ahead. Gant walks in. With no other route open to him, Danny follows.

This hut, at least, has a solid floor. Nothing to lurch beneath him, and no grille to allow the steam from the liquid fire to billow and scald his skin. Solid walls, too. Chains hang from the high ceiling. Gant turns to him.

"What did you give me?" Danny asks.

Gant smiles. "You think you've been drugged. You think this place is some ghastly hallucination. You think it couldn't possibly exist."

"I know it can't."

"And yet it does," says Gant, "so what does that say about the things you know? Does it, perhaps, say that there's a lot more to this world than you've seen so far in your limited little life? *There are more things in heaven and earth, Horatio, than are dreamt of in your philosophy.* Do you know where that is from?"

"*Hamlet,*" says Danny. "Everyone knows that line."

Gant chuckles. "Not so. There are still those to whom Shakespeare is a mystery they have no interest in solving."

Jeremiah joins them, sucking in mouthfuls of hot air like he's going to have a heart attack at any moment. Gant observes him with a look of distaste.

"Where are we?" Danny asks.

"My home," answers Gant. "A man's home is his castle, is it not? And a man must be master of his domain. This is my domain, Danny my boy, and I am master over it."

"But how can it exist? It's not right. It's not possible."

Gant pulls on one of the chains, one with a hook on the end. "There are many names for it," he says. "The easiest for you to understand would be, simply, magic." He attaches the hook to Danny's handcuffs, looks over to Jeremiah, who is still trying to get his breath back.

"Jeremiah," Gant says sharply.

Jeremiah nods and staggers over to a wheel on the wall. He takes a handkerchief from his pocket, wipes it uselessly across his forehead, then wraps it round his hand. He takes hold of the wheel, and, with every turn, the chain draws towards the ceiling, dragging Danny's arms up over his head. Jeremiah puffs and grunts and Gant waits, but finally Danny's feet leave the floor and he dangles there, the handcuffs cutting into his skin. Jeremiah locks off the wheel and comes to stand beside his master.

"Are you the devil?" Danny asks.

Gant laughs. "No, my boy, no I am not. Though you wouldn't be the first to make that mistake."

"And you think Stephanie's just going to come rushing in here to save me? She barely knows me."

"She's coming," Gant says, and gives another smile. "And when she gets here we'll be ready for her, won't we, Jeremiah?"

"Oh, yes," says Jeremiah. "We'll be ready, all right."

"Then we'll see," Gant continues. "We'll see who she is and what she is. Is she noble, like we've heard? Or is she evil incarnate, like others have said? Which do you think, Danny my boy? Which one do you think is coming to your rescue right at this moment? The angel... or the demon?"

74

Valkyrie and Skulduggery were on a rooftop when Darquesse drifted into view.

They watched her float down, a vision in burnished red, until she was standing on the shield that enveloped the city. She put her hand to it, and bright colours began to ripple outwards from that point. The shield darkened, and an overcast greyness fell upon Roarhaven.

"It won't hold her for much longer," Valkyrie said, and Skulduggery jabbed a button on his phone and spoke into it.

"Now," he said.

Valkyrie realised that, despite everything, she was actually looking forward to what happened next.

The shield faltered and sputtered and failed, and Darquesse hovered there, watching it retract, unaware that a helicopter gunship – recently liberated from an unscrupulous private army operating out of the Middle East – had just appeared behind her.

A *helicopter gunship*. This was *awesome*.

There was a streak of light and a sudden plume of smoke and before Darquesse even had a chance to turn the rocket hit her.

The explosion sent her spinning out of the sky, trailing smoke and fire, and she vanished behind a building. Skulduggery wrapped his arm round Valkyrie's waist and they flew to a roof that overlooked the square. Darquesse was on her hands and knees, trying to rise. The helicopter – an AH-64 Apache, according to the pilot Fletcher had been partnered with – opened up with its minigun. Bullets chewed up the ground around Darquesse, pummelling her and driving her back to her knees. The pilot, a sorcerer who could fly anything but preferred aircraft with fun weapons, let loose another rocket, and the explosion lifted Darquesse up and threw her like a rag doll. She rolled, her body limp. She'd been hurt, but there was no blood. No burns.

Darquesse rose suddenly, stumbling away from the minigun's angry bullets, raising her hand towards the Apache. The minigun altered its aim and loosed another barrage that thundered into her chest. She fell to a sitting position, but Valkyrie glanced up in time to see the helicopter's rotor blades disintegrating. The Apache whined and dropped, and she saw Fletcher grab the pilot and they jumped, disappearing the instant they cleared the stricken aircraft. The Apache had time to flip halfway over before it hit the ground – right on top of Darquesse.

"My turn," Skulduggery said, stepping away from Valkyrie. He hefted the God-Killer sword as Ravel and Saracen appeared on the rooftop opposite. Saracen already had an arrow nocked in the bow. Skulduggery and Ravel jumped down into the square.

There was a squeal of protesting metal, and then Darquesse stumbled from the smoking wreckage. Saracen let loose the arrow, but Darquesse whirled, snatched it from the air before it hit her. Saracen sent two more after it, keeping her busy while Skulduggery ran up behind her. She snatched both arrows and broke them, then ducked the swing that would have taken her head from her shoulders. Skulduggery spun, the blade going low for her legs, but again Darquesse moved just out of range, almost stepping straight towards Ravel's spear. At the last moment, though, she seemed to sense he was there, and she slipped sideways and backed away from them both.

"Ravel?" she said, in a voice so loud Valkyrie could hear her from where she stood. "You're working with *Ravel*, after what he did to Ghastly?"

"Until you're dealt with," Skulduggery said, "I'd make a deal with Mevolent himself."

Saracen sent another arrow her way, but she caught it, stopping it millimetres from her eye.

"God-Killers," she said. "And there I thought Tanith had destroyed them all."

Valkyrie frowned. Darquesse was getting her cockiness back. She was being given time to recover.

"Let me guess," Darquesse continued, "Billy-Ray, wasn't it? He did something? Switched them? Oooh, that Billy-Ray. He is in *so* much trouble."

"We're giving you one last chance to surrender," said Skulduggery.

Ravel hefted the spear and closed in. Skulduggery approached from the left. Darquesse smiled as she watched them come, moving slightly to avoid giving Saracen a clean shot.

"No you're not," she said. "If I surrender, you're going to kill me immediately. I'm far too dangerous to be kept alive. Where would you put me? Not even the Cube could contain me now. No, you're going to kill me. You just want me to make it easy on you by allowing you to get in close enough to do it. Sneaky, Skulduggery. Very sneaky."

"Thought it was worth a try," Skulduggery said. "I like this suit and I'd hate to see it crumpled."

"Oh, yes, that's the one you die in, isn't it? In Cassandra's vision? It's a nice one, I have to admit. You look good in black. Dashing, even. I'm glad you didn't try something silly like wearing the navy pinstripe. As if putting on different clothes would alter what's going to happen. We've both seen it. We both know how you're going to die. Out here, in the streets. Erskine and Saracen, though... now your deaths remain a mystery. Do I kill you here?

Do I kill you now, or later? How badly injured are you? How long does it take you to die? Is it quick and merciful or slow and protracted? Questions, questions... And speaking of questions – Saracen, are you going to take this opportunity to finally tell us what your power is?"

"You'll die wondering," said Saracen from above.

"I like your optimism," Darquesse responded. "But you all know I can kill you with a click of my fingers."

"So click," said Skulduggery.

Darquesse smiled.

Figures blurred past Valkyrie, forcing a startled cry from her lips. She hadn't even heard them run up, and here they were, leaping off the edge of the building, diving gracefully into the square, spinning to land silently on their feet.

The vampires fell upon Darquesse. They may not have been as savagely powerful as their night-time selves, but they were strong and agile, and proved enough of a distraction to make Darquesse forget about clicking her fingers. There were twelve of them, twelve or fifteen, it was hard to count they were moving so fast. Darquesse lashed out, caught two of them by pure chance, but the others weren't giving her time to get her bearings. She backed off, the vampires a constant whirling threat, avoiding her grabs and smacking her hands down when she raised them. Skulduggery went with them, jabbing at her with the sword whenever a space opened up.

Valkyrie's attention was diverted by the cracks in the ground behind Darquesse, cracks that hadn't been there a moment ago.

Darquesse took another step backwards and Billy-Ray Sanguine reached up, grabbed her ankles, pulled her into the ground, down to her knees. The vampires broke off on cue and Skulduggery brought the sword down in an overhead swing—

—and Darquesse raised a hand and the sword hit an invisible barrier, centimetres from her skull.

Valkyrie's eyes widened. Suddenly she could *see* the magic. Everyone in that square had an aura around them.

The vampires shone with a dull, pale blue. Saracen was surrounded by a deep purple, and Ravel by a strong shade of orange. Darquesse had a silver light that shone from deep within her, and it was this silver light that the sword was pressing against, trying to break through.

Skulduggery Pleasant burned with a brilliant red.

As Valkyrie watched, entranced by this new facet of her power, the silver light wrapped round the sword and she was about to cry out, to warn Skulduggery, when the blade shattered. Darquesse grabbed him, threw him into Saracen just as he was about to let loose another arrow. The vampires renewed their attack, but Darquesse was ready for them. The silver light pulsed and three vampires exploded into nothingness.

No, that wasn't quite right. Valkyrie could still see their swirling colours, now without physical forms to inhabit – their magic, their energy, feeding back into the world in a continuous stream of life and death. She looked at her own hand, turning it, mesmerised by the new brilliance that shone through her skin from within. She could almost see her veins, her capillaries, the bones of her fingers... and then Darquesse flew by and knocked her off her feet. She went rolling across the roof, and when she stopped her hand was normal and the brilliant colours were gone.

She looked up as Darquesse flew in great loops and steep dives, trying to outrun the two arrows that chased her. Skulduggery lifted Saracen, dropped him to the roof and he nocked an arrow and let it fly. This arrow went at Darquesse from another angle and she barely avoided it. It swerved when it missed, joined the other two in pursuit. Darquesse flew straight up, into the clouds. The arrows followed.

Ravel landed nearby in a gust of wind, helped Valkyrie to her feet before she even knew what was happening. She shook his hand off, but she doubted he noticed. He stood with Skulduggery and Saracen, peering up, as if he were still part of the team.

Skulduggery looked back at her. "Your turn's coming up."

Valkyrie nodded. The fear she felt was not just in anticipation of the conflict with Darquesse, it was also about the fact that her life now lay in the hands of the two most incompetent zombies who had ever died.

75

Scapegrace fought well.

In his imagination, he fought well. He ducked and whirled and countered and parried and thrust. In his imagination, the sword was an extension of his arm, and he was magnificent.

In reality, things weren't quite so impressive.

He swung his sword a hundred times and a hundred times the Guardian wasn't there any more. A step to the side or a step backwards or a step forward, and Scapegrace would miss and go stumbling and the Guardian would then turn to Thrasher and fend off his ridiculous attacks. Compared to this porcelain-faced stranger, they were clumsy idiots who didn't know what the hell they were doing.

But then, compared to anyone, they were clumsy idiots who didn't know what the hell they were doing.

But Scapegrace didn't give up. He couldn't. His sword clanged against the Guardian's. This wasn't about him any more. He knew how pathetic he was. He could see through all of his past delusions. He was a joke. A punchline. But so what? None of it mattered. What mattered was winning. What mattered was helping Valkyrie Cain save the world.

He turned again as Thrasher distracted the Guardian. Maybe

this was his chance. Now, while the Guardian's back was turned, while he was busy fighting Thrasher. Was it heroic, to stab an opponent in the back? Not in the slightest, but then Scapegrace wasn't a hero. He was just a man, doing what he could to help others. He started forward, and then the Guardian plunged his sword through Thrasher's head.

"No!" Scapegrace shrieked as Thrasher crumpled, the sword still lodged in his skull. Blind rage seized Scapegrace's mind and suddenly he was throwing his own sword down and diving at the Guardian.

They rolled across the ground, but Scapegrace was the first up, his teeth gritted, hatred burning in his eyes. Again and again, his fist came down on the Guardian's unbreakable face. He tried to keep the anger going, tried to draw strength from it, but he was weak and getting weaker. It was as if Thrasher, that idiot Thrasher, had been his strength all along, and now that he was lost...

Scapegrace fell back into a sitting position. The Guardian lay there, looking at him. Then he sat up.

"You have passed the final test," he said.

Scapegrace didn't care.

"The skeleton began the trials," the Guardian continued. "He was told the first test was a test of purity. But all the tests have been tests of purity. You have passed the most important test of all. You are pure of heart, Vaurien Scapegrace."

"Thrasher was pure of heart. Not me. I'm selfish, and mean, and stupid. What about me is pure, eh? If you think you can see something pure in me, you tell me what it is."

"I can see into your soul," said the Guardian. "The things you say about yourself are true. But the pure of heart rise from humble beginnings. Sometimes all you need is one single moment to redeem yourself."

"And I had that, did I?"

"You had. You had a moment of pure compassion. It was

flecting. In fact, I almost missed it. But it was there. In that moment, thinking about your friend, you were pure of heart. And now the sigil is yours to activate."

The Guardian opened his robes. A light burned where his heart should have been. Without even being told, Scapegrace knew what to do. He reached for that light, felt the warmth on his dead skin, and seized it. The light flared, spreading through hidden veins in the Guardian's face, and got so bright Scapegrace had to look away. When it faded, and he looked back, his hand was empty and the Guardian was gone. The hourglass turned slowly, and sand began to flow.

"I did it," Scapegrace said. "I... I did it."

From behind him, the weakest of voices. "I always... knew you would, Master..."

Scapegrace spun round to his hands and knees, crawled quickly over to where Thrasher lay. He took Thrasher's hand, held it tightly.

"It has been an... honour... serving you, sir," Thrasher said.

"Oh, you idiot, what have you done?"

"I seem to have a... a sword stuck through my brain, sir. That's... that's not good, is it?"

"It isn't."

"I thought as much. Master... there are some things I wish to say..."

"Call me Vaurien."

Thrasher's eyes blinked back tears that would never fall. "Vaurien," he breathed. "What a beautiful name."

"Thank you, Gerald."

A peaceful smile blossomed. "Vaurien, until I met you, my life was... unexceptional. I was a lonely man. I had no friends. I had no... one."

"Hush, Gerald," said Scapegrace. "Save your strength."

"I must speak, Vaurien. I have so much to say, so little... time. I met you and my life... ended. And yet... it began."

"Oh, God..."

"I've never been a brave person," said Thrasher. "I've never seen myself as being worthy of the things other people take for... for granted. Of being liked. Of being loved. But Vaurien, you... you make me brave."

"I treated you terribly."

A soft chuckle. "You did."

"I insulted you, I treated you like a fool. I should have valued every moment with you."

"I valued our moments enough... for both of us. I... oh, Vaurien, I feel myself slipping..."

"Hold on, Gerald. I'll get help, I'll—"

"It's too late for me, my master. But I want you to know that I will always be with you... I will always be right..." – he raised his hand, and his finger tapped against Scapegrace's chest – "... here..."

Despite himself, Scapegrace smiled. "You're quoting from *ET* at a time like this?"

"I love that movie," Thrasher said, his voice no more than a whisper. "But I love you... more."

And then his eyes closed, and he went limp.

Scapegrace's body was incapable of producing tears, but he cried nonetheless. He cried for his friend, his companion, for the one person who always stuck by him, no matter what. He cried for the man Gerald had been, the man he had become, and the man he would now never be. And he cried for himself, for the loneliness that was now gripping what was left of his heart, a heart that didn't beat, suddenly realising that if by some miracle it started to pump blood once again, it would have probably beaten for Gerald.

Scapegrace got up slowly, seized the hilt of the Guardian's sword, and with great effort he pulled the blade from the head of his friend.

Immediately, Thrasher opened his eyes. "Oh. I think that did it."

Scapegrace yelped, dropping the blade as he jumped back.

Thrasher sat up. "These new brains are remarkable," he said. "I suppose there's something to be said for having the brain of a vegetable after all, eh?"

Scapegrace stared as Thrasher got to his feet. The idiot grinned at him.

"Those were some pretty nice things you were saying to me. Maybe we needed this. From this moment on, Vaurien, maybe we can be equals? If we're careful, we have a hundred lifetimes to look forward—"

"Shut up."

Thrasher blinked. "Vaurien?"

"You call me Master. I was just being nice to you because I thought you were dying."

"I was dying."

"You're not any more. Now you're just an idiot with a hole through his head."

"But... all those things you said to me... You called me Gerald."

"Gerald is a stupid name for a zombie. Your name is Thrasher. Your name will always be Thrasher."

Thrasher slumped. "Yes, sir."

"Now give me the map. I'm getting out of here."

"Uh... sir?"

Scapegrace looked up, and froze. They were surrounded by blurred figures, their faces indistinct and their shapes hazy. Ghosts.

Two people, two solid people, stepped to the front. They were dressed like the Guardian, with robes and porcelain masks.

"We have been waiting for you," said the first of them. He spoke with a Scottish accent. "I am the Inquisitor. You have proved yourself worthy and you are, of course, entitled to leave Meryyn ta Uul at your discretion. Before you do, however, I beg a moment of your time."

Scapegrace glanced at Thrasher. "OK. Sure. What can I do for you?"

The Inquisitor's porcelain face appeared hopeful. "You are a Zombie King, are you not?"

"I used to be," said Scapegrace.

"He still is," said Thrasher.

"I gave that up," Scapegrace insisted. "Now I'm just me again. Just normal old me. I'm no Zombie King. Not really. I don't think I ever was."

"But we need you to be," said the Inquisitor. "We have been waiting for one such as you. We have been waiting centuries."

Scapegrace frowned. "For me? Why?"

The Inquisitor spread his arms wide. "This is Meryyn ta Uul. The City Below. The Necropolis. The City of the Dead. Down here, the dead number in their hundreds of thousands. The others are watching us even now, waiting for me to ask."

"To ask what?"

"To ask you to be our King."

Scapegrace blinked. "I'm sorry?"

"A Zombie King is but one name for a King of the Dead. We need you here, my lord. I beseech you. Rule over us. We are yours to command."

"Seriously?"

Thrasher stepped closer. "What about Clarabelle?" he whispered in Scapegrace's ear. "We told her we'd go back for her. She's waiting for us."

Scapegrace nodded. "That's right. Listen, Mr Inquisitor, we have a friend, and she needs us right now."

"We need you more."

"We made a promise, though."

"A promise to the living is a meaningless thing," the Inquisitor said. "Our oath of servitude to you, however, would be eternal."

Scapegrace hesitated. Eternity was a mighty long time. And to rule down here, to take on something as important as the mantle of King of the Dead... that was something he'd never even considered possible.

But to do so would be to abandon Clarabelle, and he could no more do that than he could cut off his own arm. Although he could probably have cut off his own arm relatively easily.

"Some day," he said. "When my work in the world of the living is done, when they need me no longer, I will return here. This I vow to you."

The Inquisitor bowed. All the ghosts bowed.

"As you command, my lord."

Scapegrace nodded to them all and, with Thrasher at his heels, he walked away with as much imperial majesty as he could muster.

76

Darquesse had gone through them like they weren't even there.

She'd taken out Saracen first. Those arrows had been getting too close, so she'd dumped a wall on him. He lay there now, his bones broken. Valkyrie didn't know if he were alive or dead.

Darquesse had killed or injured whatever sorcerers, vampires and Cleavers leaped at her next, and then she'd gone after Skulduggery. Valkyrie had watched it from her hiding place. He'd jabbed, swung and thrust with what remained of the sword, and Darquesse played with him long enough for her own amusement, then she'd torn the sword from his grip and hit him so hard Valkyrie hadn't even seen where he'd landed. Darquesse used the sword to kill a few Cleavers, then Solomon Wreath sprang at her from the shadows.

Darquesse had slashed him diagonally from the hip to the shoulder, and his body came apart in a violent display of blood and innards. Valkyrie's hand had gone to her mouth to stop herself from crying out. When Solomon's remains had settled on the ground, Darquesse discarded the sword and had gone after Ravel. And what had Ravel done?

He had thrown down the spear, and he had run.

Darquesse's laughter reached Valkyrie, and it beckoned her.

She couldn't stand by any longer. She didn't think the Meryyn Sigil had activated yet – she certainly didn't feel any different anyway – but she couldn't keep hiding, not when there were so many people risking and giving their lives to buy her time. She watched a lone Cleaver attack Darquesse. She watched his scythe burst apart and his legs snap. He fell into the dirt and the rubble of the street and Darquesse walked over to him to finish the job with her bare hands.

Screw this.

Valkyrie slipped out of her hiding place, ran across the rooftop. It was a long way down and she jumped.

While she fell, she focused on her magic, focused on the energy inside her, tried to summon the barrier that would protect her when she landed, the cushion of light that had made her bounce off the tree by the roadside.

But nothing happened.

She could feel the magic, it crackled between her fingertips, but she didn't know how to summon it or control it and now she was dropping towards certain, stupid death and she was going to die and her tattoo began to burn—

And she landed on her feet and her bones didn't break.

She straightened up, peeked inside her jacket. The sigil glowed on her arm. She was invulnerable. Cool.

She reached out with her hand and then reached out with her magic, and white lightning sprang from her fingers and hit Darquesse, made her stumble.

The injured Cleaver forgotten about, Darquesse whirled, and her look of anger became a look of curiosity.

"Well now," she said. "Look who's got herself a whole new bag of tricks."

"Damn right," said Valkyrie, striding towards her.

"What are you, an energy thrower? Your magic is bubbling and boiling inside you. I can see it from here. It's impressive. It's... different. You're not just an energy thrower, are you? There's something else. Your magic is purer than..." Darquesse frowned. "What *are* you?"

"I'm stronger than you."

"Well," Darquesse said, smiling, "we'll see about that."

She hit Valkyrie full force and a thousand suns exploded behind her eyes, and when Valkyric's brain came back online a moment later she was tumbling backwards down the street. She came to a sprawling, ungraceful stop beside a parked car, and waited for her head to clear. Apparently being invulnerable didn't mean that she couldn't feel pain. Good to know.

Valkyrie stood, rubbing her jaw.

"You're not this powerful," Darquesse said, walking after her. "You may have got your fancy new magic, but you can't be *this* strong. They've done something to you, haven't they? Have they boosted you? Did you finally step into the Accelerator? Did it drive you insane?"

Strength tingled through Valkyrie's veins. She waited until Darquesse was a little closer, then punched her hands through the car beside her and stepped back to fling it. But the doors tore off and she ended up throwing them instead. And they missed.

Darquesse laughed. "Super strength isn't as easy as it looks, is it? See, you've got to think about these things. If you want to throw a car, you've got to grab the body."

She darted to a little Volvo, got one hand on its underside while the other gripped the frame, and then flung it like a discus at the Olympics. Valkyrie tried to get out of the way, but it clipped her shoulder and spun her round. She stumbled, tripping over the pavement, and Darquesse flew at her. They collided, hit the wall and lurched away, hands clutching at each other's throats. The little Volvo had just come to a rocking stop beside them and Valkyrie slammed her forehead into Darquesse's face, and the back of Darquesse's head hit the Volvo. Valkyrie did it again, and again, doing her best to turn Darquesse's head to pulp, but it was the Volvo that gave way first.

Darquesse fell sideways, and she grabbed Valkyrie's hair, pulling her head down into a knee that would have caved in her face were it not for the sigil on her arm. Before she could recover, Darquesse's eyes lit up and twin streams of energy exploded against Valkyrie's chest, sending her crashing through a window. There were people in here, a family, and they screamed and ran out of the back as Valkyrie struggled to get up.

The front door burst into a million splinters and Darquesse came at her like a bullet train, driving her through the wall and into the kitchen in a shower of plaster. They rolled across the floor, punching and biting and scratching and gouging. Valkyrie scrambled up and heaved, swinging Darquesse into the fridge by her hair. She moved back quickly, dragging Darquesse the length of the room, then let go and kicked her head so hard she heard the spine snap. But even as Darquesse rolled away, Valkyrie heard the clicks as the vertebrae repaired themselves.

Darquesse got up and Valkyrie hit her with a chair that smashed on impact. She grabbed one of the legs as they fell and plunged it through Darquesse's throat, then punched her as she gagged. Darquesse spun, staggered, but spun again with a back fist that sent Valkyrie crashing into the hall. Darquesse pulled the chair leg out and dropped it, healed herself and spat blood. She was grinning. Valkyrie ran at her, but Darquesse flew upwards through the ceiling.

Valkyrie hurried out into the street, looking up.

She saw Darquesse as a speck in the sky, swooping around, coming back down at an alarming speed. Power crackled in Valkyrie's hands while she waited for her to get near, and then she let loose, and the lightning hit Darquesse, making her veer off course and crash into the ground.

Valkyrie sprinted over just as Darquesse was getting to her hands and knees. She lashed a kick into her side, kicked her again while she rolled. Darquesse caught the third kick, tried to twist Valkyrie's leg off, but Valkyrie just blasted her at close range.

They clung to each other, and there were hair pulls and eye gouges and headbutts and bites, and then they were lifting off the ground, rising high above the city, still scrapping, still fighting, still snarling. And then Darquesse let go, and Valkyrie fell.

And oh, how she fell.

Straight down, with the wind rushing in her ears and her hair whipping about her face. She was glad she didn't have her stick with her. It probably wouldn't have survived what came next.

She hit the ground.

It was painful.

Valkyrie rolled on to her back and lay there, panting.

Darquesse flew down to the ornate concrete fountain beside her and stood on the edge. "Is that it? Is this the full extent of your plan? Please, Valkyrie, tell me you have something more up your sleeve. It was a good tussle, it was, but let's face it – all I have to do is keep hitting you until whatever is boosting your power wears off. I can't imagine that'll be very much longer."

Something moved in the shadows behind Darquesse. Valkyrie said nothing.

"If you were as smart as you like to think you are," Darquesse continued, "you'd be trying to hide from me right now. I mean, it's you I'm after. You get that, right? I came here so that we can be whole again."

"Is that your way of surrendering?" Valkyrie asked.

Darquesse smiled. "I'm not the one who'll surrender. And it won't be like it was, either. There'll be no more of your annoying little voice in my head. But when you're gone, what you are – behind all the thoughts and the snarky comments – will remain. That's what I want, Valkyrie. You're a part of me. We belong together. You feel it, too, right? You feel that a part of you is missing?"

She did. She couldn't deny it. There was an emptiness to her now, a loneliness she hadn't felt before. Not even the new magic, whatever it was, could fill that gap.

"Come on," Darquesse said, holding out her hand. "Why are you fighting? All you ever do is fight. Why? Who says you have to? There are other ways, Valkyrie. Try acceptance. Accept that we belong together, that we're stronger when we are one. That we're better. Stop fighting. Stop hurting. I don't want to hurt anyone any more. Not even Ravel. I'm tired of that. I'm tired of this. Come on. Take my hand. You never have to be lonely again."

"Well, maybe that's the difference between us," Valkyrie said, getting to her feet. "I don't mind the loneliness. Not really. You know why? Because I know I have friends. And they're standing right behind you."

Skulduggery and Melancholia emerged from an archway. Shadows writhed round Melancholia's body like angry snakes, and more shadows seeped from beneath Skulduggery's shirt as he walked. They covered his body, forming armour, and when he rose up on a tide of darkness it was not Skulduggery Pleasant who crested that wave, but Lord Vile, in all his terrible glory.

77

Lord Vile and Melancholia attacked.

They were relentless. Two of the most powerful Necromancers of the last thousand years, and they drove Darquesse back between them.

Shadows were knives and whips and hammers and chains. They cut, tore, ripped and bludgeoned. Darquesse was given not one moment to recover, not one second to heal. Valkyrie watched in numb astonishment as her adversary, as *the* adversary, was sent to the ground again and again.

She watched as Darquesse got up, for maybe the tenth time, took a step and faltered.

Frowning, Darquesse looked down at her left foot. It was badly broken, twisted at an unnatural angle. She glared at it, and finally the foot moved, mending itself. But the frown on her face remained.

Vile and Melancholia closed in.

Twin beams of sizzling energy burst from Darquesse's eyes, but Vile was already shadow-walking away. Melancholia seized her chance, leaped high into the air and sent down a thousand thorns of darkness. They ripped through Darquesse, tearing through her armored clothes and shredding her flesh, and Valkyrie caught an unmistakable grimace of pain.

Darquesse was hurt.

The shadows coiled and Vile emerged, taking Darquesse's head in his hands and wrenching it to one side. Her neck broke and immediately mended, but the cry of pain that accompanied her wild swing was enough to spur Melancholia on even while Vile fell back. The shadows lashed again and again, cutting through Darquesse's defences. She was spending so much power healing her body that she could no longer dampen her pain. She was feeling every strike now, and her wounds were taking longer to repair.

She darted suddenly, closing the gap between herself and Melancholia. Caught off guard, Melancholia tripped and Darquesse landed on top of her. She rained down punches. Melancholia's shadow armour convulsed in panicked response. She wasn't used to physical confrontations.

Valkyrie ran in, slipped her arm round Darquesse's throat, hauled her off. Melancholia rolled over on to her hands and knees, regaining her bearings. Darquesse twisted, managed to hook a foot between Valkyrie's. They fell, Valkyrie on the bottom. Darquesse turned into her, hit her with everything she had, but Valkyrie grabbed her wrist, threw her left leg over Darquesse's head and straightened. Darquesse fell on to her back and Valkyrie yanked down on her arm as she raised her hips, and she heard the elbow break.

Darquesse screamed.

Valkyrie lost her grip and Darquesse rolled away, still screaming as she got up, clutching her dangling arm. Before she could heal, Vile sent a shard of darkness right through her torso.

Darquesse dangled there, off her feet, her eyes wide and blood running from her open mouth. The shard retracted and Darquesse stood, swaying. She was in shock.

They were going to win.

Darkness reared up around her, forming a Venus flytrap of shadows. It sprang closed, two dozen razored barbs skewering her body. The shadows started to melt and Darquesse stumbled through them, falling to her knees. She started to flicker. She was trying to shunt.

Valkyrie raised both her hands, white lightning flowing from her fingertips. The lightning hit Darquesse and she cried out and fell sideways. She stopped flickering.

Melancholia and Vile walked up behind her as she tried to crawl away.

Say this for her – she's not going down without a fight.

Melancholia reached down, grabbed a fistful of hair, and she pulled Darquesse back up to her knees. Darquesse gasped, her face splattered with her own blood. Melancholia allowed her shadow armour to retract, and it lashed at the ground wildly, like a petulant child denied its plaything.

"This has been invigorating," Melancholia said. "Truly invigorating. Finally, I'm realising my own potential. I can... I can sense life and death. I can see it. I can see it all around us. I see it in you, Darquesse. I see your life. I see how easy it would be to just... pluck it out."

Darquesse reached up, tried to free herself, but the effort was feeble, and Melancholia slapped the hand down.

"I am the Death Bringer," Melancholia continued. "I am the ultimate Necromancer. Who are you? You're Valkyrie Cain's dark side in the body of her reflection. You're nothing but a collection of spare parts. And they were all scared of you? Really?" Melancholia laughed. Her eyes were black, and black steam rose off her. "It's me they should have been afraid of. You thought you were a god? Maybe you are. But even gods can die. And I? I am death."

"Melancholia," Valkyrie said.

Melancholia looked up, blinking those black eyes. "Valkyrie," she said, sounding dazed. She sharpened. "Yes. Sorry. Getting carried away with the whole power thing. Are my eyes black? They feel black."

"They're black."

"Cool." Melancholia glanced at Vile. "Let's do what we came here to do."

Their shadows moved like a thousand tiny snakes, burrowing slowly into Darquesse's body. Darquesse screamed as blood ran. This time there would be no healing. This time there would be no surviving. They were going to kill her slowly, and make sure there was not even a sliver of life left behind.

Valkyrie's hands started to tingle. She unzipped her jacket, pulled it halfway down her arm. The tattoo was pulsing. Not long now. She could almost feel her invulnerability about to slip away. It didn't matter. Darquesse was done. Defeated. All they needed was another few seconds and then those shadows would split her apart, and it'd all be over.

Darquesse clasped her hands before her. Vile and Melancholia didn't notice. Darquesse's arms started to tremble. Silver light spilled from between her fingers.

Very, very bright light.

Valkyrie ran forward. "Stop her!" she screamed. "Don't let her—"

But it was too late.

Darquesse opened her hands.

78

The silver light exploded outwards and consumed the world.

79

It swallowed Vile and Melancholia.

80

a deafening rush of air

                              the world filled with fragments
              bricks and masonry
                          and glass and
                                    wood and metal
Valkyrie thrown

                          tossed
                              and
                                    spun
buildings torn down.

                              folded
                    like
                    paper.
streets cr   d.
          um   e
              pl
                          lamp posts snap
                                    p
                                        e
                                        d

81

And then everything was silent.

82

There was a wind.

Valkyrie didn't know where it had come from. Just a moment ago it had been a still day.

A moment?
A minute?
An hour?

But now there was a wind, a strong wind, catching the clouds of dust and spinning them into little tornadoes.

She turned over

83

on to her back. Dust in her eyes. Dust in her mouth.

She was cold. She'd lost her jacket. The shockwave had yanked it away from her. Was she hurt? She wriggled her toes. Wriggled her fingers. No broken bones. Was she bleeding? She didn't think so. She was OK. She was unhurt. Invulnerable? No, not any more. The tattoo had dulled. It had probably used up the last of its strength keeping her alive during the... what? What was that? That was more than an explosion. It had been like a small nuclear bomb going off.

Groaning, Valkyrie sat up.

84

Roarhaven was in ruins.

The eastern quarter had been obliterated. It was a flat, smoking landscape of rubble and wreckage. Fires raged in the southern districts. Some of the northern section still stood, from what she could see. Car alarms travelled to her on the wind. They sounded like people dying.

Valkyrie started walking. When she was sure her legs weren't going to fail her, she ran.

Finding her way around Roarhaven when it stood tall and proud had been hard enough, but now the landmarks she'd used were flattened or gone altogether. She took a few wrong turns, had to double back, often climbing through demolished buildings to save time. She passed bodies and ignored them.

And then a rock flew at her, struck her across the temple, and she went tumbling down a small hill of debris.

She sprawled in a heap at the bottom, her elbows cut and bleeding, blood running from her forehead into her eye. There were footsteps, slipping and sliding through the broken mess in their eagerness to get to her. Valkyrie managed to get to her knees, her vision blurry. Figures approached. She saw hate in their faces.

"We hurt her," one of them said.

"We can finish her," said another.

Valkyrie raised her hands. "I'm not her," she said. Her voice sounded weird. She sounded drunk. "I'm not Darquesse."

She didn't even see what struck her, but she felt the pain across her ribs and she cried out, fell on to her side. The figures crowded round, their boots seeking her, finding her, crunching against her. She covered up, yelled at them to stop. A rib broke jaggedly. A kick to her kidney sent new flashes of pain arcing through her. Someone tried kicking her skull and broke the fingers of her left hand. Again. They screamed and cursed and she heard their words. They knew who she was and they didn't care. In their eyes, Valkyrie Cain was as much to blame for all this as Darquesse.

A kick found the side of her head and rolled her over, her body limp. Funny how this seemed to clear her eyesight.

She saw in perfect clarity the foot coming for her face. It was clad in a heavy, steel-capped work boot. Good, she decided. She would have hated to be killed by a soft little running shoe.

But the work boot never reached her. At the last moment, it vanished. There was another pair of boots there now. Brown boots. Well-made. Familiar. They stepped and pivoted and spun, and then all the other feet ran away. The brown boots bent, and a leather-clad knee came down, and gentle hands touched her face.

"Val," Tanith said. "Val, can you hear me?"

Valkyrie felt her head being moved, and she tried focusing on Tanith's worried face, but she couldn't. Then she was being lifted, hoisted up over Tanith's shoulder. A fireman's lift, it was called.

Tanith started running.

She crossed the rubble smoothly, like she was skating on ice. She ran up the sides of broken buildings so that Valkyrie was looking straight down at the far-below ground. Tanith's balance was impeccable. She crossed narrow beams in ruined houses, leaped from rooftop to rooftop, landing so gracefully Valkyrie could have been floating on a cloud. She blacked out a few times, but that wasn't Tanith's fault. That was just her approaching death.

And then they were inside, in the Sanctuary, and she was being laid out on a bed in the Medical Wing and a light was being shone in her eyes.

"Multiple fractures," Synecdoche was saying. "Concussion. Valkyrie, can you hear me?"

There were people screaming. The Medical Wing was full of injured people. On the bed beside her, Valkyrie saw Saracen Rue hooked up to a respirator. She tried to sit up, but a pair of strong hands held her down. Tanith's face swam into view.

"Steady on, OK? They're helping you. Just stay there. Val, that explosion. Were you there? What was it? Is Darquesse dead?"

Synecdoche came back, shouldered Tanith out of the way and jabbed a needle into Valkyrie's arm. Warmth flooded her body so suddenly it made her gasp, and the pain fell away.

"I need an X-ray," Synecdoche shouted to one of her assistants as she lifted Valkyrie's shirt. "We've got internal bleeding here."

There was movement all around and someone was holding a scanner and there was a bright blue light, and Valkyrie lay there and looked up at the ceiling. She coughed suddenly, but it didn't hurt. It didn't even alarm her when she tasted blood. It should have, though. Coughing blood should have alarmed her.

She frowned. The warm feeling was nice. It was too nice. It wanted her to sink into it, to surrender completely. But she had things to do. She couldn't lie here and bleed. What was it that guy said in that movie?

"I ain't got time to bleed," Valkyrie muttered, sitting up.

Synecdoche looked horrified. "Valkyrie, lie down, you have serious injuries."

Now that she was sitting up, her head was starting to clear. She held out her left hand. Her fingers were swollen and purple. "Bandage me."

"Lie down."

"I'll lie down when I'm done."

Synecdoche clenched her jaw, but nodded to an assistant who hurried forward with a roll of bandages. While he wrapped, Synecdoche busied herself with applying a clear gel to the cut on Valkyrie's forehead. Valkyrie looked around as best she could. Donegan Bane lay three beds away. She couldn't see Gracious.

The door opened and China strode in. She was dressed in black. Her eyes were alive with worry. "What happened?"

"The explosion was Darquesse's doing," Valkyrie said. "There was a light, she was holding it, and then... I don't know. I don't know what it was. I didn't see what happened to her."

"I've heard reports that Lord Vile was seen in the area," China said.

Valkyrie nodded. "He was working with Melancholia."

"What about Skulduggery?" Tanith asked.

"I... I don't know," Valkyrie answered.

China's face was anxious. "Vile," she insisted. "What happened to Vile?"

Valkyrie looked at her. She knew. Somehow she knew.

"I don't know that, either," Valkyrie said. "He was closer to the explosion than I was. I don't know what happened to him."

China hesitated, her face no longer betraying any emotion, then nodded and walked out.

Valkyrie slipped off the bed as gingerly as she was able. She couldn't move her left hand in its bandage, her right leg was stiff for some reason, and when she prodded her side, it felt rigid. She stifled another cough, tasting blood again.

"Chew these when the pain returns," Synecdoche said, passing her a packet of leaves. Valkyrie nodded, stuffed them in her pocket and left before the doctor could find a reason to keep her here. With Tanith following behind, she glimpsed China talking with Cassandra and Finbar, and ran to join them, ignoring the ugly jolts that rang throughout her body with each step.

Cassandra had her eyes closed when Valkyrie reached them. "Darquesse is alive," she said. "She's weak, but recovering. At this rate she'll be back to full strength in twenty minutes."

"Fifteen," Finbar corrected.

"What about Skulduggery?" Valkyrie asked before China could.

Cassandra shook her head. "We can't sense him, but then we have *never* been able to sense him. His thoughts are constructed differently to ours, and this difference hides him from us. We were able to take a glimpse at Melancholia as the event took place, however – but I'm sorry to say that she didn't make it."

"She's *dead*?"

"The girl means nothing," China said. "Can you see Vile?"

Cassandra frowned. "Lord Vile is there? We've seen no sign of him. Are you sure?"

"What about anyone else?" China said, ignoring the question. "Any survivors?"

Cassandra nodded. "Some injured. Many scared. They're running from the blast site... apart from..." She tilted her head, stayed quiet for a few moments, then, "Your parents, Valkyrie. Your parents and your sister."

Valkyrie went cold. "They're outside?"

"They're running *towards* the blast site," Cassandra said. Her frown deepened. "They're looking for you. Someone's... someone's behind them, hunting them... It's hard to see who it is, it's hard to... a Remnant. It's a Remnant."

"Vex," Valkyrie said. "He's chasing them right into Darquesse's hands. We need to go. I have to..."

She trailed off as an idea came to her, and the full weight of what she had to do made itself known. It dragged at her soul, leaving her empty inside.

"Val?" Tanith said.

Valkyrie turned to China. "The gauntlet," she said. "The

Deathtouch Gauntlet. I left it in the Ops Room. Get it for me. Please. I have to go back to the Medical Wing."

Tanith gripped Valkyrie's arm, as if she were afraid she might collapse. "What's wrong? Are you OK?"

"I'm fine," Valkyrie insisted, disentangling herself. "I have to get something. I'll meet you back in the Ops Room." She ran, retracing her steps, holding her side as it began to ache dully. When she re-entered the Medical Wing, the staff were too busy to notice her, so she searched without being seen, found what she was looking for and pocketed it. A wail of pain caught her attention and she looked over. A woman having a broken bone reset. Nasty. But behind that woman, someone moving, someone slipping out of one of the smaller doors. Ravel.

She didn't have time for this. She really didn't. But she went after him anyway.

The moment the door shut behind her, the sounds of the Medical Wing dimmed to almost nothing. Valkyrie followed the corridor into a part of the Sanctuary she wasn't familiar with. She passed libraries with bookcases that stretched to the ceiling. She passed a room of swords, and another of masks, and another of glass cases containing old, wrinkled body parts suspended in solution.

She saw a flickering orange light on the walls, and she turned very, very slowly.

Ravel stood, leaning against the wall. His right hand, level with her belly, glowed with energy. He looked tired.

"What are you doing?" he asked. He sounded weary. "Don't you have enough to be worrying about without coming after me? I'm not a threat to you."

"You're a prisoner."

He shook his head. "Not any more. I thought I'd be OK with it. When I made my plans, all that time ago, I knew I'd end up either dead or in shackles. I'd made my peace with that. But after what Darquesse did to me... you have no idea what it was like."

"So you've said."

"I'm leaving, Valkyrie. You'll never see me again. I'm going to spend the rest of my life alone. That's enough punishment, isn't it? Exile?"

"Enough punishment? You had Shudder killed. You murdered Ghastly with your own hands. You started a war that killed hundreds of sorcerers. You're seriously telling me that a just punishment for all that is you feeling lonely?"

"I'm not going to stand here and justify my actions to you."

"Good."

"But you're not going to stop me. Darquesse is still out there, isn't she? She's your concern. Worry about her, not me. I'm not your enemy."

"Your hand is lit up. Are you going to fire? How will I fight Darquesse if you kill me? What if we fail, and she goes after you?"

A glimmer of cold determination flashed in Ravel's eyes. "I'll be ready for her. If she comes after me, she's going to have to finish the job. No more torture. No more taking her time." He raised his hand. "Go on, Valkyrie. You're not wearing your jacket. If I fire, you're dead."

She didn't have time for this. Didn't have time for him. "OK," she said. "But when we're done with Darquesse, we're coming after you."

Ravel smiled sadly. "You'll never find me."

His hand stopped glowing and he stepped back, and Valkyrie hurried back the way she'd come.

She got to the Ops Room just as Fletcher teleported the Sensitives away. China stood with Tanith and Sanguine at the table. Apart from them, the room was empty, the monitors abandoned.

"Valkyrie," Sanguine said. "You look dead."

She ignored him. The badly-flickering Roarhaven hologram showed the devastation the explosion had caused. Smoke rose from rubble. She could even see little bodies lying in the streets.

China gave her the Deathtouch Gauntlet and she pulled it on. It felt heavy and cold.

"Use the sigil to activate and deactivate," China said, indicating the symbol burnt into the black steel. "When it's activated, whatever you do, do not scratch your nose."

Valkyrie flexed her fingers. "It kills without pain?"

China nodded. "Instant, painless death, whatever you touch. Are you sure you'll be able to get close enough to use it?"

"Shouldn't be a problem," Valkyrie murmured. A cough rose in her chest and burst painfully. She wiped blood from her mouth.

"Jesus, Val," Tanith whispered.

"I saw Ravel," Valkyrie said. "He's running. He said if Darquesse finds him he'll be ready for her. I think he's going to use the Accelerator."

China's eyes narrowed. "One more use could overload it. Very well. Tanith, Mr Sanguine, you go with Valkyrie. We can't detect Darquesse on the map, but the odds are she's still in the blast area. I'll head down to the Accelerator and deal with—"

She stopped, frowning over Valkyrie's shoulder. "Where the hell have you been?"

The Black Cleaver stood in the doorway.

"How can you be my bodyguard if you're never around?" China continued.

The Cleaver took out his scythe.

"Now what are you doing? There's no one to guard me against now, you moron. Wait till our enemies show up before taking that thing out."

Valkyrie's hand closed round China's wrist. "Wait."

"Don't worry about it, Valkyrie. He's defective. Always has been."

"No," said Valkyrie. "What he's always done is obey orders. A Necromancy technique brought him back to life, so he started off by obeying the Necromancers. But then Nye stitched him back together, so it stands to reason that now he'd obey Nye's orders..."

"Yes? So?"

"So Nye was just broken out of prison."

China stopped trying to pull her wrist free. "With suspicious ease. A prison run by a secret member of the Church of the Faceless."

"And Eliza hasn't exactly been happy with you, has she?"

China observed the Black Cleaver. "Have you been sent here to assassinate me, you treacherous little toad?"

The scythe whirled, and the Black Cleaver started forward.

Valkyrie and the others immediately began backing away.

"Billy-Ray," Tanith said, her sword already in her hands, "take Val where she needs to go."

"I ain't leaving you," Sanguine said, his hand reaching into his jacket.

Tanith's eyes never left the Cleaver. "Yes you are, goddamn it."

"But get back here immediately after," said China.

Tanith nodded quickly. "Immediately."

Sanguine's face was a mass of conflicting emotions. Finally, he grabbed Valkyrie. "Fine," he snarled. "But don't die while I'm gone."

The ground cracked and swallowed them.

85

The fear that gripped Tanith's heart as she fought the Black Cleaver was not new. She had felt it before, in corridors very similar to this one, deep in the bowels of the old Sanctuary, back in Dublin. There she had faced this same man, back when he was clad in white, and a supposed pawn of Nefarian Serpine. Every move he had countered, every attack he had parried, and even when she thought she'd had him beaten, he had answered with a strike that very nearly ended her life.

And here she was again.

Tanith ducked the scythe and darted close, but the ever-spinning staff blocked her own sword swipe and sent her reeling. A snaith, the wooden handle was called. She'd learned that much since the last time they'd tangled, at least. She liked to know the name of things that hurt her. It was handy to have something upon which to focus her frustration.

The scythe whistled for her face and she jerked back, almost stumbled, managed to keep her feet beneath her while the Black Cleaver advanced. China was behind her, moving out of the Ops Room into the corridor, and Tanith followed. The Black Cleaver came last, his blade catching the light when it blurred by at a particular angle. It was pretty, in its way. Tanith's sword caught the light, too, but there was no rhythm to it. Against such an opponent her skills seemed to dull, and the grace and fluidity she was used to displaying abandoned her, replaced by clumsy movements and wild, desperate lunges. Fear made her stiff and uncoordinated, and filled her head with thoughts and strategies when it needed to be clear. The Black Cleaver let his body do the thinking. Tanith had forgotten how.

The Cleaver spun and caught her with a kick.

China flung her arms out, unleashing a wave of blue energy that cracked the ceiling and the floor, but which the Black Cleaver moved through like it was nothing more than a strong wind. China stepped back, tapping hidden tattoos around her body that glowed briefly beneath her clothes. Sigils on her legs made her faster, not only in movement but also in reaction. Even so, she barely stayed more than a hand's length from the blade that sought her out.

Tanith leaped. The Black Cleaver spun at the last moment, deflected her blade, but as Tanith landed she sprang again, twisted in mid-air and caught him with a kick. At the same time, China tapped her chest with both index fingers and a stream of energy burst from her sternum. It hit the Cleaver square in the back and he went staggering to his knees.

The energy stream cut off and China sagged, suddenly very pale. Trails of smoke rose from the Cleaver's coat as he stood. He turned to them, the scythe twirling in his hands.

86

Valkyrie hung on as Sanguine burrowed through the earth, the rumbling filling her ears. She kept her eyes closed against the constant spray of dirt, rocks and stones scraping painfully against her T-shirt and her bare arms. They changed direction a few times, then went up, bursting free of the darkness, into the daylight.

Sanguine let her go without a word, and he sank back into the ground.

In this part of Roarhaven, the streets were smoking ruins.

She heard her name being called – her mortal name – and scrambled up on to a hill of rubble. The wind was deceptive, carrying sounds through the ruined streets and whipping them away again before Valkyrie had time to pinpoint their source. All she could see was desolation and smoke. She hugged herself, shivering against the cold. She wished she had her jacket.

"Don't take this the wrong way," Darquesse said from behind her, "but you look terrible."

Valkyrie turned, and Darquesse's gaze dropped to her arms.

"You're wearing it," Darquesse said, almost excitedly. "The gauntlet thing! And you have the tattoo! You know what that means, don't you? The vision is about to come true."

"Not necessarily," said Valkyrie, coming back down the pile

of rubble carefully. She narrowed her eyes, trying to see the aura that would alert her to Darquesse's intent to use magic. "Already little things are different. There's no Ghastly, for a start. And you're wearing different clothes."

"But you're not, so not everything has to be different. I'm still going to take your family away from you."

"Why? You came from me – in a way, they're your family, too." Valkyrie picked up a faint silver light emanating from within Darquesse. "You said you wouldn't hurt them."

"I have no intention of hurting them," Darquesse said. "In fact, this *will* be different from the vision, because instead of burning them right out of existence, I'm going to allow them to live on as energy. You see? You're not the only one to have learned a few things from seeing the future." Her eyes flickered to the gauntlet, and her smile widened. "So come on. What does it do? Does it make you strong? I was punching you with everything I had and you didn't even bleed. You looked indestructible. You don't look indestructible now. What's the matter? Did you break it?"

"Why don't you come over here and find out?"

Darquesse laughed, and suddenly Valkyrie could see the aura surrounding her, like a light being switched from dim to full. "Oh, I would, but you're a sneaky little thing. I should know, right? I think it'd probably be best to take care of you from over here."

She raised her hand and the silver light pulsed, and Valkyrie held out her left hand, which was glowing white beneath the bandages. The white energy pushed against the silver, keeping it back.

Darquesse frowned, and the silver retreated, and Valkyrie lowered her hand.

"How did you do that?" Darquesse asked.

Valkyrie tried to reply, but her legs were shaking and her mouth was dry. That one act of self-defence had drained her.

Darquesse approached slowly and Valkyrie concentrated on not falling down. If Darquesse knew how weak she was, it'd be all over. Instead, she watched her come with what she hoped was a calm expression on her face. She couldn't even run if she'd wanted to. Darquesse got closer and Valkyrie found herself wishing she'd move faster. Valkyrie's legs weren't going to be able to keep her up for very much—

Valkyrie's legs gave out and she fell to her knees.

87

The scythe opened up Tanith's arm and China had to cover her as she stumbled away from the return swipe. Blood ran freely down to her hand, turning her grip on her sword slick. Another cut to add to her growing collection. Her left leg and her back shared similar wounds.

The Cleaver's boot heel smacked against China's jaw. She spun, her legs folding beneath her. Tanith charged, gritting her teeth as she pressed the attack. The Cleaver met her coolly and then, almost like he was proving that he could, he caught Tanith with the exact same kick that had felled China.

She hit the ground. She'd lost her sword.

Running footsteps. Someone had called for help. Finally. The Cleavers closed in, grey surrounding black. No time was spent on questions, and no breath wasted on negotiations. The greys had their enemy, and they attacked. They worked as a team, feinting when another slashed, moving forward when another dropped back. Their scythes went high and low and the Black Cleaver spun and dodged and parried and blocked. The sharp clang of blade upon blade and the dull whack of snaith upon snaith filled the corridor in a rapid rhythm, never slowing. Few openings appeared during the furious exchange, but when they did, scythe blades slid uselessly across armoured uniforms. Unless someone took the initiative, they'd fight themselves to a standstill.

The Black Cleaver dropped his scythe.

He moved between two swipes and grabbed the head of the nearest Cleaver, twisting it as he spun behind him. He shoved the dead man into the path of his comrades and lunged at the one who darted clear. They traded elbows and knees while they grappled for the scythe, and then the Black Cleaver whirled with a kick that snapped his opponent's head round so fast that Tanith heard the vertebrae pop.

But the two remaining Cleavers were already too close to avoid. One of them kicked the fallen scythe out of the Black Cleaver's reach while the other swung his own scythe down. With frightening accuracy, the blade slid between the Black Cleaver's helmet and collar, pierced his neck and buried itself deep within his torso.

The Black Cleaver dropped to his knees.

"His head!" Tanith shouted. "Take his head!"

The grey kept both hands on his scythe, pinning the Black Cleaver down, while his partner took an executioner's stance in front. The executioner swung without ceremony, without wasting a moment to gloat or ponder, but he was still too slow. The Black Cleaver ducked and the scythe cut through the snaith holding him down. Still with a blade lodged within him, the Black Cleaver sprang at the executioner, got his hands on that helmet and wrenched it to one side.

Three Cleavers. Three broken necks.

The remaining grey attacked with fists and feet and elbows and knees. The Black Cleaver was a blur. He never tired, he never faltered. The grey made one mistake, responded to a feint when he should have backed off, and the Black Cleaver got his hands on him and added another broken neck to his tally.

He took hold of the blade sticking out of his neck, and pulled it from him. Black blood dripped, and he let it clatter to the ground as he picked up another scythe.

"Where's Fletcher Renn when you need him?" China muttered as she helped Tanith to her feet.

"Go," Tanith said, grabbing her sword. "I'll hold him off."

China stared at her. "You?"

"I'm your bodyguard, aren't I? Besides, Ravel needs to be stopped and I don't know the way down to the Accelerator Room. So it looks like a grand and noble gesture is called for."

China raised an eyebrow. "I'm almost impressed."

"Yeah, well, I'm not doing this for..."

She stopped. Someone was whistling. Ennio Morricone – the theme from *The Good, the Bad and the Ugly*. The Black Cleaver looked round.

Billy-Ray Sanguine stood beneath the flickering light, whistling, one hand in his pocket, the other dangling by his leg, holding the God-Killer dagger.

China squeezed Tanith's arm, and ran.

Sanguine came to the end of his little tune, and he raised his head slightly, and Tanith reckoned he knew damn well that he'd never looked so cool as he did right at that moment.

"You have one chance to walk away," Sanguine said. "I were you, I'd take it."

The Black Cleaver faced him, his scythe ready.

Sanguine shrugged, like he was disappointed, and started forward.

88

Darquesse didn't laugh when Valkyrie fell. She didn't mention it at all. In fact, she wasn't even looking. Her eyes were on the man who was emerging from a broken doorway.

"Here he is at last," she said. "My little traitor."

"Oh, I'm no traitor," Dexter Vex said, smiling. "I'm just someone who wasn't seduced by the carnage you promised. I'm just someone who understands that our goals aren't exactly... compatible."

Darquesse shrugged. "Your fellow Remnants believed what they wanted to believe."

"Yes they did," said Vex, "and they almost doomed us all."

Valkyrie forced herself up. Her legs were weak, but her strength was returning. Slowly.

"And you think you can save the day?" Darquesse said to Vex, strolling towards him.

"Me," Vex said, nodding, "and a few friends."

A Remnant swooped down, attaching itself to Darquesse's face. She grabbed it, pulled it away, and another latched on to her back. She reached behind her and a third was suddenly in her hair, its little claws tearing at her scalp. A fourth Remnant flew at her, and a fifth, and they were at her face and prising open her mouth and Darquesse stumbled and cursed...

And when her mouth opened, the first Remnant slipped in. Then the second. Then the third.

And then a stream of Remnants flowed down from above, straight into her open mouth, and her hands were at her bulging throat and her eyes were wide, but there was nothing she could do to stop the flow. Hundreds of Remnants – no, *thousands* – flying into her, faster and faster, overpowering her, taking control even as black veins started to rise beneath her skin.

Then the flow ended, and Darquesse gasped, staggered, and Vex watched the whole thing with his hands in his pockets.

"You're going to deliver what you promised," he said. "You're going to give us a playground that will be ours forever."

The black veins faded slightly. "You think you can... you think..."

She gasped again and the black veins rose. Her lips darkened.

"You're one of us now," said Vex. "It took practically all of us to do it, but I think it's been worth it, don't you? Now it's time for you to do what you do best. Kill. Destroy. Have fun."

Darquesse smiled, but the smile turned sour, and she frowned. The veins faded again before rising. She was fighting it.

"Practically all of you?" she rasped. "Should've brought more."

She stood up straight, eyes locked on Vex. "I'm killing your brothers and sisters."

For the first time, Vex lost his confidence. "Impossible."

"I'm killing," Darquesse said slowly, "every last one of them. I'm burning them inside me. They want to... they want to get out..."

"Stop," said Vex. "Stop!" Energy burst from his hand, but Darquesse caught it in her palm. Her skin sizzled, and healed.

"They're making me stronger," she said. "Every one of them I kill makes me that little bit... stronger." The last of the veins faded. Her lips returned to their full, natural colour, and she smiled.

Vex launched himself at her and she batted his hands away and grabbed him by the throat. She forced her hand into his mouth, shoving it down his gullet.

"Come on now," she said, "where are you? Don't bother trying to hide. I can put you back together. You know I can. I can make you solid again. Ah, there you are... Come on out. Come on..."

She yanked the Remnant free and Vex sagged, and she threw him away. He hurtled through the air, landed and rolled. Dead or unconscious, with all that blood Valkyrie didn't know. All she knew was that he'd landed in the street beside her.

The Remnant wriggled in Darquesse's grip, but its struggles only made her widen her smile.

"Scared, are you? I bet you are. When you're like this, you can't form thoughts, can you? Not really. All you are is instinct. Emotion. Right now, all you are is fear."

Valkyrie reached Vex without Darquesse looking round, and she tugged the backpack from over his shoulder. She wanted to check his pulse, to check he was still alive, but she couldn't, she had to move, and so she sprinted for the other side of the street. Once safely behind a half-demolished wall, she put the bag on her back, fixing the strap across her chest, feeling the reassuring weight of the Sceptre. She peeked out as Darquesse let the Remnant go, and watched her laugh at the speed with which it flew off.

Valkyrie cut through the remains of an alley, started running.

89

She had to admit, she was impressed.

Sanguine wasn't taking any chances fighting the Black Cleaver, but neither was he missing opportunities. The God-Killer dagger gave him confidence, but he wasn't letting that spill over into cockiness. He attacked with skill, and timing, and patience, and he came close a few times. The Black Cleaver obviously knew what the dagger was, because he twisted and spun and danced just out of reach. There was a healthy respect at work here from both men.

Sanguine stumbled away from a swiping blade, into the wall. And he smiled.

The wall crumbled and he sank into it. The Black Cleaver turned, wary, stepping lightly and quickly.

Sanguine lunged from the opposite wall and the Black Cleaver blocked the slash, but the dagger cut through the scythe blade like it was paper. The Cleaver abandoned his weapon and flipped backwards, to the door of the Ops Room. He snatched a fallen scythe from the ground and whirled, but Sanguine was already gone.

The Black Cleaver was outmatched.

He turned his visored helmet towards Tanith, then broke into a sprint, and she readied herself.

As the Cleaver sprinted down the corridor, Sanguine leaped out of one wall and into the other, criss-crossing his path, slashing at every chance he got. The Cleaver flipped or jumped or whirled away from every cut. The closer he got to Tanith, the more desperate Sanguine seemed to become. Tanith tightened her grip on her sword, and bared her teeth.

The Cleaver was five strides from her when Sanguine tackled him. The dagger fell and the Cleaver's elbow smacked into the Texan's jaw, and he spun, ended up facing Tanith, the Black Cleaver right behind him, scythe whirling in his hands.

Tanith opened her mouth to shout a warning.

The scythe swung for Sanguine's neck, but he was already turning, launching himself into a dive. Tanith had seen walls and floors crack before him, but never had she seen clothes and flesh. This was the moment where that changed. The Black Cleaver's armoured coat frayed and the pale skin beneath split, almost too fast for it to register, and Sanguine dived through the Cleaver. He hit the ground behind and rolled to his feet, dripping with black blood. The Cleaver looked down at his ruined torso. Now Sanguine grinned, his cockiness returning to him. And he had a right to be cocky. Diving through the body would have killed just about any living creature.

But, of course, the Black Cleaver wasn't living.

Sanguine was still grinning when the Black Cleaver twisted round, and the tip of the scythe blade whispered across his throat.

For a moment, he stood there, frowning. Then a thin line of red opened up above his collar. He coughed, and the wound opened further, and wider, and he stepped back, gagging, his hands up, trying to close the cut, to keep the blood in. He dropped to his knees, the front of his shirt turning red, his tie becoming sodden. Blood splashed on to the floor, soaking into his trousers. He toppled over sideways, dislodging his sunglasses. He lay there, mouth open, gasping for breath that wouldn't come, choking on blood he couldn't spit.

And then he died.

Something wrenched deep within Tanith's chest.

The Black Cleaver turned to her.

He attacked and she blocked. Blades clashed. He was fast and so was she. Something burned inside her. Sanguine was dead. Did she care?

Some part of her did.

The burning gave her strength. Her wounds still bled and her head still spun, but she had found her centre now, and she sank into it and let her body do what it wanted to do. No longer was fear clouding her judgement. No longer were frightened thoughts obstructing her flow. She was an extension of her weapon, and her weapon was an extension of her.

She thrust her sword through the Cleaver's ruined coat, then retracted it and spun away before the scythe reached her. She found an odd, detached satisfaction in noting the black blood she had drawn. But she could stab him in the chest all day and it wouldn't make the slightest bit of difference. He was a zombie. The only way to stop him was to take his head – but there was no way she was going to be able to do that while he wore that uniform.

She was reminded of something she'd once told Valkyrie, years ago, and she smiled thinly as they broke off.

The Black Cleaver watched her get her breath back, the way a lion would watch an injured gazelle.

"I suppose it's fitting," she said, "that it comes down to you and me, after all this time. Sometimes I feel like I should have died that day we fought in the Dublin Sanctuary. I think that blade of yours was meant to kill me six years ago. Now, maybe Fate was looking the other way, or maybe it just changed its mind, but I survived. I always survive. And I always will."

Then she turned and she ran.

The Black Cleaver stayed where he was for a moment, probably expecting some cunning new attack. When he realised she wasn't turning round, he gave chase. But instead of leading him towards people, towards sorcerers and Cleavers, she led him to the quieter parts of the Sanctuary.

He caught up to her outside the Cleaver Barracks. Blades clashed once more. She backed up through the doorway into the training arena. Whether or not the Black Cleaver guessed her plan, she had no way of knowing. Similarly unknown to her was whether or not her plan even had the slightest chance of working. She was about to pit the Black Cleaver's training against his new master's orders.

Tanith edged her way into the Combat Circle, defending all the while. Her arms were tired. Her muscles screamed. Her sword got heavier with each parry.

She broke off, skipped back a few steps, giving herself room, and the Black Cleaver looked down, noticing where they now stood. He looked at her, and she took one hand from the sword and started to pull off her coat. It was just like she'd told Valkyrie, and like Darquesse had repeated to her. When someone steps into the circle, the challenge has to be met. No armour. No clothes. That's the rule.

Yet the Black Cleaver stayed where he was.

When the coat was off, she dropped it outside the circle. Then she knelt on one knee, slowly put the sword on the ground beside her, and started on her boots. When they were off, she stood, looked at the Black Cleaver, and said, "Come and have a go. If you think you're hard enough."

The Black Cleaver watched her for a moment, then laid down his scythe and opened his coat.

90

Valkyrie heard them. She crossed a ruined street, then another. Saw them coming. They looked tired. Frantic, scared, and tired. Her mum held out her arms, and her dad passed Alice to her. They were taking turns carrying her.

Valkyrie stepped back, out of sight. Her insides were cold. Her thoughts were jagged and awkward, and they fumbled around the options in her head, unable to come up with anything new, with anything better. She was locked on a course and for once she couldn't think her way out of it.

She heard her parents call her given name. She looked at her hands. Her left hand, wrapped in dirty bandages. Her right, wearing that gauntlet. She frowned, and peered down at herself, her mind suddenly swimming with a tremendous sense of déjà vu.

"I've seen this," she muttered. "I was watching from... there."

Her eyes fixed on the space beside her. It was empty, save for some swirling dust. But she knew it wasn't. In Cassandra Pharos's basement, she was standing there watching this happen with Skulduggery at her side.

"Hi," she said, because she could think of nothing else to say to her younger self. She remembered hearing the words she was to speak next, and the overpowering sense of guilt that came with them. "This is where it happens, but then you know that, right? At least you think you do. You think this is where I let them die."

Her dad called her name. They were getting closer.

She remembered what was set to come next, Darquesse waving her hand and her family being consumed by black flames. She shook her head at the image. "I don't want to see this," she said. "Please. I don't want this to happen. Let me stop it. Please let me stop it."

From her pocket, Valkyrie took the device she'd stolen from the Medical Wing, and looked at it through her tears. "Please work," she whispered. "Please let me save them."

She stuffed it back in her pocket, wiped her eyes, and ran out to the middle of the street.

"Steph!" her mum cried, grabbing her and hugging her. Her dad rushed in, embracing them both. Valkyrie fought to free herself.

"Mum, Dad, you have to get out of here."

"Not without you," her dad said. "We heard the explosion and we thought... we thought you might have been in the middle of it."

"I was on the other side of the city," Valkyrie lied. "You have to go, OK? It's too dangerous."

Her mum grabbed Valkyrie's left arm. "What happened to your hand? Is it broken? Oh my God, Steph, you're covered in cuts."

"I'm fine," Valkyrie said, pulling her arm away.

"We found your friend," said her dad. "The poor girl."

Valkyrie looked at him. "Melancholia?"

"She was lying in the street. She... Steph, she's dead. I'm sorry."

"I know. She... she didn't deserve that."

"Come back with us," said her mum. "Please, let's just forget about all this and leave. Stephanie, this is insane. You're going to get yourself killed. Please, honey, please come back with us."

"I can't, Mum. You know I can't."

"I don't know that. You have no reason to stay."

"I have the only reason to stay. Darquesse is part of me."

"Steph, please, I'm begging you..."

"Mum. Listen to me. I might be the only person who can stop her. I have to do it. Nothing you say will make me change my mind. I'm doing this for you, and I'm doing this for Alice, and I'm doing this for everyone. Everyone, Mum. If I don't, they all die."

Her mother's face crumpled. "But we can't stay with you. We have to protect Alice."

"I know," Valkyrie said softly. "That's what I'm counting on you to do." Bile rose in her throat as she held out her hands. "Let me have her. Just for a minute. I have a charm I can put on her."

"Like a magic spell? To keep her safe?"

Valkyrie nodded, not trusting her voice.

Her mother passed Alice over. She felt incredibly heavy in her blanket.

"I have to do this alone," Valkyrie mumbled. "If you're nearby, it won't work."

Her dad wrapped his arm round her mum. "We'll wait here. Don't be long."

Valkyrie turned, hurried away as fast as she could so they wouldn't see her face.

She turned a corner, found a building still standing and went inside. The living-room table had a bowl of fruit on it. She swept it on to the ground, and put Alice lying in its place.

She stared at her little sister.

"I'm so sorry," she said. "I'm so sorry, sweetie."

Tears sprang and she sagged against the table. Great racking sobs sent new spirals of pain running through her. She barely noticed.

"Please forgive me. I love you so much, Alice. I love you so much, sweetheart."

Her face was wet with tears. Her nose ran and spittle flew with every word. Her crying became a roar. She curled her right fist, slammed it against her own head. The edges of the gauntlet drew blood. But it wasn't enough. It wasn't enough pain. It wasn't enough suffering. It wasn't enough punishment. She put her injured left hand flat on the table and slammed her right fist down on to it. She screamed, fell back, curled up on the floor and screamed until her screams became long, anguished wails. A part of her was aware of how pathetic she sounded. This part of her was *glad* she sounded pathetic. She *deserved* to sound pathetic. For what she was about to do she deserved everything bad that was coming to her.

It was only Alice's crying that brought her back.

She got up, her whole body trembling.

"I'm sorry, honey, I'm so sorry, I didn't mean to scare you, please don't cry..."

She didn't mean to scare you, but hold on, because she's about to do something much worse.

"Shut up," said Valkyrie.

Arguing with yourself, eh? First sign of madness, that.

"Shut up, I said." She leaned over Alice, soothing her cries.

Thought this whole thing was in the past, did you? This little voice in your head? You thought just because Darquesse was gone you were alone in here? Or maybe you thought she left and took all your badness with her.

Seriously?

That's what you thought?

If she did take all your badness with her, then why the hell are you doing what you're about to do?

Valkyrie stuffed some leaves in her mouth, chewing quickly, forcing herself to swallow. The pain in her hand lessened. She used her torn, dirty, bloody T-shirt to wipe her eyes and nose.

filthy dirty filthy dirty filthy dirty filthy

She took the Sunburst from her pocket, laid it carefully on the table. Then she took the Sceptre from the bag, and put it beside it.

Tell her you love her. Go on. Tell her.

"I love you," Valkyrie said.

Hypocrite.

"I love you, Alice. I have never loved anyone as much as I love you. What I'm... what I'm about to do, it... it kills me."

Yeah?

Not as much as it's going to kill her.

With her left forefinger – broken and crooked – she pressed down on the sigil on the back of the gauntlet. Gritting her teeth, she dragged her finger clockwise, and the sigil lit up.

Then she held her right hand over Alice's little body.

She realised she was speaking, repeating *I'm so sorry* so fast it almost became one long word.

She had to do it. She could not think of anything else to do. Darquesse needed to be stopped. Skulduggery's plan was too uncertain. The Sceptre was the only thing that was guaranteed to work.

So do it. Kill her. Kill your sister.

Alice babbled away in her own private baby language, her bout of crying completely forgotten. She blinked up at Valkyrie and smiled, showing dimples. The most beautiful child in the world. She reached for the gauntlet and Valkyrie snatched her hand away instinctively.

"No touch!" Valkyrie heard herself say.

Somewhere in her mind, she heard mocking laughter.

She lowered her hand again.

"I love you," she said, and pressed her finger to Alice's forehead.

91

There was a *crack*, and her heart lurched as her baby sister went limp. Valkyrie's mind turned to ice. She almost ripped the gauntlet off without deactivating it. She pressed her broken finger into the sigil until it stopped glowing, then dropped the gauntlet on to the table and grabbed the Sceptre.

Her powers were acting up again. She saw the Sceptre anew. She saw the magic inside it suddenly churn as it recognised its new mistress.

Then she dropped it, grabbed the Sunburst star and pressed it to Alice's chest.

"Please work please work please work please—"

The star gave a little beep as a pulse went through Alice's body.

And nothing happened.

"NO!" Valkyrie screamed. "NO! PLEASE!"

She reset it, her hands shaking, the world moving much too fast and much too slow. Reset it and the sigils started lighting up.

Come on. Come on.

You've killed her.

Come on. Work. Please.

You've killed her.

The star pulsed.

And those beautiful eyes snapped open and Alice let out a wail.

Valkyrie grabbed her, hugging her so, so tight. "I'm sorry, I'm so sorry, I'm so sorry, baby, please forgive me, please."

Alice just cried and cried, scared and hurt, and Valkyrie cried with her, relieved but distraught. She'd killed her sister. No matter what else she did with her life from this moment on, she could never escape the fact that she had knowingly and voluntarily killed her own sister. And she didn't even have Darquesse to blame it on.

92

Fighting naked was an extremely liberating experience.

Tanith dodged back, deep into the Combat Circle, her bare feet sure on the ground, and the Black Cleaver came at her again. She blocked his slash and kicked at his leg for the fourth time. He lurched left, kept her at bay with his scythe. She glanced down, saw his swollen knee repair itself. It was still an uneven battle, but it was no longer so weighted against her. One good swipe was all Tanith needed to separate his head from his body, and with this renewed optimism, fresh strength poured into her arms.

She pressed the attack. Now that she could see his face she was no longer in any danger of being gripped by the same kind of fear that had turned her into a clumsy, awkward fighter. His face was unremarkable. His head was shaved, as all Cleavers were. His eyes were dull. His skin was pale. His head, like his body, was an intricate jigsaw of scarring. Tanith had heard that Doctor Nye had put him back together, piece by tiny piece, and it hadn't been overly concerned about the aesthetic quality of what it was doing.

Tanith's sword drew a line of black blood across the Cleaver's chest, adding a new scar to his collection. She hoped he liked it. She batted his blade to one side and slashed again, caught his leg, then went up high, angling for his neck. At the last moment, he snapped his head away and she found herself overextended. He whirled, the snaith taking her feet from under her.

Tanith hit the ground, tried to roll to absorb the impact, but she wasn't quick enough. He stabbed downwards and she turned over, tried to get up, got a knee in the face. She landed on her ass, stunned, the sword almost slipping from her hand. The Black Cleaver brought the scythe down and she tumbled backwards and immediately cartwheeled to her left. But she was still dizzy, and she wobbled. He could have ended the fight there and then, could have got behind her and killed her before she had a chance to get her bearings, but he kicked out, and instead of getting a blade in the back she got a foot in the ribs.

Breath heaved from her, and something sharp and nasty dug into her side, but at least she wasn't dead. Not like Sanguine.

Billy-Ray's face swam into her mind.

What the hell?

She blocked the scythe and tried to reply, but her strength was leaving her again. The Cleaver was relentless, and he drove her back. He broke through her defence, cut her. It was a shallow wound across her arm and she barely felt it, but it was there. And blood called to blood, and one wound led to another, and within moments her right leg was bleeding.

She limped sideways, holding her sword in one hand. The Black Cleaver moved parallel with her, then came forward. At first, Tanith didn't think anything of it – she was getting too tired to think at all – but then she noticed that he had come up against the edge of the Combat Circle. That's why he hadn't gone for the killing blow. The first rule of the Combat Circle was no clothes, no armour. The second rule was that nobody leaves until the victor stands over the vanquished.

The Black Cleaver's training had allowed her the chance to even the playing field. Now it seemed like it would allow her the chance to win – providing she was willing to cheat.

Which, of course, she was.

She got both hands back on the sword, and met his attack with a parry and a thrust and she moved right, as quick as her injured legs would let her. She started to follow the curve of the circle, and he anticipated the move and went to close off her retreat.

And then she cheated.

She stepped sideways, out of the circle, went low and spun, her sword slicing through the Cleaver's knee.

He fell awkwardly and she slashed upwards, taking the fingers from his right hand. She didn't stop there, though. She took his left hand off at the wrist, noting the black blood that leaked from the stump as his scythe fell. He rolled backwards, giving himself space. She was fairly sure he wasn't going to be able to kick her to death, but she didn't intend to put that theory to the test. She closed in, cutting off his avenues of escape, and he backed up, his bare feet on the edge of the circle.

She smiled at him. "I like your shoes."

He looked at her strangely.

Then he launched himself at her and she swung. She was aiming for his neck, but her foot slipped in all that blood and so her blade carved his skull in two instead. His body fell to the ground, suddenly graceless.

She took off the rest of his head, and then went to gather up her clothes.

If the world was about to end, she might as well be dressed for the occasion.

93

Alice finally stopped crying, and Valkyrie carried her back to her parents. But as she neared, there was a deep, low rumble and the building beside them, weakened by the explosion, started to lean sideways. Valkyrie yelled out a warning that was swallowed by the noise, but saw her dad grab her mum's hand and break into a sprint as the building fell around them.

Clouds of dust rolled up the street and Valkyrie ducked into a doorway, covering Alice's head with her blanket. The dust followed them and Valkyrie kept moving, running through two connecting rooms and out through a ruined wall into the next street over.

She bent double, coughing, and made sure Alice was OK before straightening up.

"Stephanie!" she heard her father shout from somewhere nearby. "We're here! Steph!"

She climbed another pile of debris, saw her folks dusting themselves off. She went to wave, to shout back, when Darquesse landed behind them.

Valkyrie ducked down. This was it. This was the moment in the vision. She placed Alice between two pieces of rubble and took the bag off her back – an empty bag with a jagged hole in the bottom.

Her eyes widened.

She stumbled, retracing her steps. The Sceptre had fallen out when she was running. She would have noticed otherwise.

And there it was, lying on the floor in the building she'd just come through.

She ran to it and grabbed it, sprinted back, passed Alice and got to the top of the pile of rubble just as Darquesse waved her hand and Valkyrie's parents exploded into nothing.

"No!" she screamed.

Darquesse looked at her, the surprise on her face quickly replaced by a smile, and the smile quickly replaced by a frown when she saw the Sceptre being raised as Valkyrie ran at her.

Black lightning flashed, turning the wall behind Darquesse to dust.

Darquesse darted sideways, but Valkyrie fired again, sending her reeling. Everywhere she moved, every direction, Valkyrie cut off with a streak of lightning, until Darquesse was scrambling backwards and Valkyrie was standing over her, breathing hard, the black crystal pointed right into her face.

The Sceptre trembled. Inconsolable, unknowable rage scraped its fingers through Valkyrie's mind.

"Bring them back," she said.

Darquesse looked up at her, licking her lips to wet them. Valkyrie recognised the mannerism. She did that sometimes. When she was nervous. Even Darquesse was scared of the Sceptre.

"Bring them back."

"They're energy," said Darquesse. "Don't think of them as dead, think of them—"

"I will kill you," Valkyrie told her, "if you do not bring them back to me right now. I know you can do it."

Darquesse shook her head. "Before, maybe. When I was whole. When we were together. But I'm not as strong as I was. If you join with me, if you let me absorb your energy, I'll be able—"

"I will kill you," Valkyrie said dully. "Bring them back. You have three seconds."

"Valkyrie, come on."

"Three."

"I'm not strong enough any more!"

"Two."

"Please! I'll bring them back when I have more—"

"One."

"OK!" Darquesse said. "OK! I'll do it."

Valkyrie didn't lower the Sceptre.

Darquesse raised her hand, very slowly, to the space where Valkyrie's mum and dad had been standing. She narrowed her eyes, bit her lip...

... and then, with a soft *whump*, Valkyrie's parents were standing there, blinking.

"What the hell just happened?" her dad said.

Valkyrie looked round, made sure they were all in one piece, and a vice closed round her throat and the Sceptre was ripped from her grasp.

"You stupid girl," Darquesse said, lifting her off her feet. She kicked uselessly as her parents ran to help. "You had a chance to kill me. You had the *only* chance to kill me. And you wasted it."

With a flick of the wrist, Darquesse threw Valkyrie into her parents. They went down in a heap.

Darquesse examined the Sceptre. "This was your one remaining weapon. I am disappointed. I thought you were smarter than that. You take your chance when you can, Valkyrie. Haven't you learned anything from Skulduggery? You have to be ruthless. You just have to be. Because what have you achieved here? You made me return your parents to you at the expense of controlling the situation."

She cocked her hand back and hurled the Sceptre into the air. In an instant, it was a speck in the distance. Then it was gone.

"And I'm just going to kill them again. Along with you. And everyone else. So congratulations, Valkyrie. You've doomed the world."

Valkyrie got up slowly, painfully, and her dad tried to pull her back down. No, not pull. He was tugging at her shirt. She glanced at him, saw he was looking behind Darquesse. She followed his gaze, saw Fletcher standing in a doorway across the street. He was holding up his hand, five fingers splayed. He started counting down.

Four fingers.

Three fingers.

He vanished, and Valkyrie turned her attention back to Darquesse, continuing the countdown in her own head—

Two.

One.

She lunged, energy erupting from her hand, blasting Darquesse right in the face. Darquesse screeched, staggered, managed to grab Valkyrie as she went and she twisted, hurling Valkyrie off her feet. Before she hit the wall, the impact snapping her bones like they were dry twigs, Valkyrie glimpsed Fletcher again, teleporting in right behind Darquesse. And he wasn't alone.

94

They were all around Darquesse before she knew what was happening. Fletcher's work. So that's why they'd been keeping him out of the fight until now. Sneaky. She saw hazy outlines, heard voices, felt hands on her. Valkyrie's blast – whatever it had been – had disorientated her for a moment.

But just for a moment.

Darquesse healed her eyes first so she could see what the hell was happening. She was on her knees. Four people formed a circle around her. Cassandra Pharos stood in front with her eyes closed, one hand on Darquesse's head. Finbar Wrong and Geoffrey Scrutinous were on either side, a hand each on Cassandra's shoulders. They held hands with Philomena Random, standing behind Darquesse and closing off the circle.

Darquesse didn't know what the hell these crazy old hippies were trying to do. Probably kill her with love, or something.

As the rest of her face healed, she reached up, wrapping her fingers round Cassandra's wrist. That hand on her head was annoying her. She crushed the wrist as she stood and Cassandra's eyes popped open in astonishment, like she hadn't expected something so pedestrian as pain to interrupt her meditations.

Darquesse's own eyes lit up and she let Cassandra have it full blast. The old woman's head blew apart.

Geoffrey tried to run, but Darquesse grabbed him, twisted his head round, let his lifeless body crumple. Finbar, fair play to him, at least tried to attack. In his last few moments, he realised that a pacifist's life was not for him, and he launched himself at Darquesse with a war cry. She killed him easily, of course, and wondered if Sharon would mourn the loss.

Philomena shot her point blank in the head. Darquesse gave her a smile, took the gun from her trembling hand and used it to cave in her skull.

Fletcher was kneeling by Valkyrie's side, next to Desmond and Melissa. They hadn't even noticed that the circle of love had spectacularly failed. Melissa was sobbing. Valkyrie wasn't moving.

"Fletcher," Darquesse said.

Teleporters were the most dangerous of sorcerers, she had decided. Fletcher's was not a power designed to hurt or kill, but all it would take was one sinister motivation and no one could stand against him. She had figured that out a while ago, and she'd made a decision to kill Fletcher without warning the first chance she got.

True, calling his name didn't exactly qualify as 'without warning', but he deserved to at least see her face as she killed him.

He turned his head to her. In that moment, she examined his power, poked and prodded at it, saw how it worked. Then she flicked her fingers and his heart burst inside his chest. He made a small sound and keeled over, and Desmond and Melissa both jumped to their feet.

"Mum," Darquesse said. "Dad. It's time for our tearful farewell."

Desmond stood in front of his wife, protecting her. Darquesse had expected no less.

"You're not our daughter," Desmond said. Tears ran down his face. "You *killed* our daughter."

"We're all just..." Darquesse began, then laughed, and shook her head. "I was going to say we're all just energy. I was going to say there is no death. This, what I'm doing? In the grand scheme of things, it means nothing. Only... only if I really and truly didn't get some little bit of pleasure from doing this, then why take the physical approach? Why blast Cassandra's head off? Why get my hands dirty?"

"Because you're sick," Melissa said, hatred ablaze in her eyes.

"I think you might be right," Darquesse responded. "I think I'm sick. I reckon I'm evil. I must be, right? To have fun doing this?"

She laughed again. The wind carried her laugh who knows where.

"What a relief," she said, "to admit that. Not just to you, either, but to myself. To admit that I like doing this. Fighting. Killing. Destroying. It's just... it's just so satisfying, you know? I must be evil. That's the only explanation I can find. But then... but then I came from your daughter. So does that mean your daughter was evil?"

"She's a hero," said Desmond.

"Was," Darquesse corrected. "Better get used to referring to her in the past tense. Or, hey, forget it. You don't have to get used to anything. You'll be dead soon, too, right? But that's interesting, isn't it? All this time I thought I was doing something nice for the universe and actually... actually no, I just wanted to tear it all down.

"Do you think we're all like that, maybe? People, I mean. Behind all their ideas about themselves and who they are, do you think they're all just... bad? Hmm. Not in the mood for a philosophical debate, eh? Yeah, I get that. That's OK. I think... I think Valkyrie, though, because I knew her so well, much better than either of you ever did, I think Valkyrie would agree with me on this one. She had a dark heart, deep down. Dark and twisted. I just thought you ought to know that about your own daughter before you died."

Darquesse brought her hands together and then splayed them out to either side, and Desmond and Melissa Edgley came apart in such an outrageous display of blood and innards that it actually made Darquesse queasy. She laughed at the absurdity of her reaction, and walked over to Valkyrie, careful not to step in the puddles of her parents.

The body of Valkyrie Cain lay broken and battered at her feet, and the energy inside her was gone. Darquesse could taste it in the air, it lingered faintly, but her essence had dissipated in the moments after her death. That energy was now lost, flowing as it had back into the stream of existence. She hadn't meant to kill her like that. She hadn't meant to throw her so hard. She'd thought that after everyone else was dead it would just be her and Valkyrie, exchanging words at the end of the world. Then Valkyrie would finally surrender and Darquesse could become whole again.

But life, being life, had a funny way of disappointing you.

Darquesse brushed her hair back, trying to get rid of that awful feeling of Cassandra's hand on her scalp. She tucked a few strands behind her ear, looking up as she did so. At the end of the street there was a black hat, blowing along in the wind. It tumbled behind a corner, out of sight, and Darquesse allowed herself a sad smile.

95

"Is it working? Tell me it's working."

96

She took what she had learned from Fletcher's magic, and teleported to the corner. She watched the hat blow into the middle of the street and then settle like a slowly spinning coin. Skulduggery emerged from a side alley. He stood over the hat for a moment, then reached down, picked it up and brushed it off. He returned it to his head, angling the brim.

He'd seen the vision. He knew what was coming.

Darquesse walked up behind him. He turned to her slowly, dumping spent shells from his revolver. She watched him take bullets from his waistcoat pocket and slip them into the empty chambers. One by one. One to six. Enjoying the ritual of it.

"My favourite little toy," said Darquesse.

"Are you referring to my gun or to me?" Skulduggery was supposed to say. But of course he didn't. He stood there in silence and she waited for him to speak.

He finished loading the gun, and he clicked it shut, held it down by his leg.

"She's dead," Darquesse told him, breaking the silence. "I didn't mean to kill her so soon, but... well."

He stayed quiet.

"Anything you want to know before you die?" she asked. "Any

last questions? Ask me anything about Valkyrie and I'll answer, as honestly as I'm able. Anything you've always wondered?"

Not a sound.

She smiled. "You're an impressive man, Skulduggery. There will never be another like you. And if you don't want to talk, I understand that. You want to get to it, I suppose. I'm... I'm going to miss you. Please know that." She took a breath, and gave him a sad smile. "I know you made a promise," she said. "Until the—"

He was so fast she never even saw him raise the gun. The first bullet hit her throat, the second burrowed through her cheek, and the third blew the back of her head open. They didn't worry her, of course. The entry wounds were already healing before the exit wounds had even formed. The fourth and fifth bullets caused her a little concern, however, smashing through her brain the way they did, and the sixth tore through her breastbone and punctured her heart. That one was probably symbolic.

Six bullets, though. He'd got off six bullets. In the vision, he'd only fired three.

She reached out to him with her magic, started plucking at the energy holding him together. His fingers went first, and the gun and the glove fell, the finger bones rattling on the street. She kept pushing, skewering his magic, and she watched his arm fall, his sleeve flapping in the wind.

His other arm now. And then she went low, to stop him from getting any closer. She sliced at the magic around his feet and then his ankles fell apart and he dropped to his knees and his hips went and he toppled backwards and now he was just a skeleton in a suit that was quickly deflating around him.

He tried to sit up, tried to raise his head, but she finished him off and his bones clattered. The only magic remained in his skull, and she plucked it from his spine and held it up, made sure he could see her, and then she kissed him, with all the love she could muster. She kissed him goodbye, and when she let the skull fall the last of who he was disappeared into the ether, and the skull broke and the jawbone spun away.

She stood there, looking down at him, suddenly aware that this was being watched by some past version of Valkyrie and Skulduggery himself, and she turned to look into the space where they would be standing, and she forced herself to give them a smile.

97

"Get ready," said Skulduggery, as

98

Darquesse lifted off the ground, rose high into the air, where the wind dried her tears. Roarhaven spread out below her like a wounded animal, waiting to be put down. She drifted to its weakly beating heart, touched her feet to the ground and walked right through the front doors of the Sanctuary. Cleavers came at her and she waved them out of existence. The sorcerers who tried to fight exploded into nothingness. Those who tried to run she killed with a little more brutality. She wasn't as strong as she once was, but the extra effort made it all the more rewarding.

Tanith sprang at her from the shadows. Darquesse allowed the sword to almost reach her neck, but teleported before it scratched her. Tanith's cry of surprise was amusing. Darquesse punched through her from behind, her fist bursting from Tanith's chest.

Tanith Low had time to look down at her own heart before she died.

Darquesse went from room to room. Killing. Black flames and blood. No one could stand against her. No one could reason with her. China Sorrows tried. China Sorrows died.

When the Sanctuary was clear of the living, when Synecdoche and Clarabelle were resting in peace and when Erskine Ravel had screamed his last, Darquesse reached her magic into the very foundations of the building and shook them. The walls cracked and the floors crumbled and the world was filled with a thousand roars, and the Sanctuary fell.

Roarhaven fell soon after. She left it in her wake, a flat and smoking ruin. By the time she reached Dublin, her heart was heavy. She carved up the streets and threw cars into buildings and she thought about what she had done. Not even the screams and the sirens could pierce her grey mood.

At first, she wanted to take the cities of the world one at a time. So she took London, and New York, and Moscow and Paris and Berlin and Beijing. She turned missiles to flowers and bullets to rain. She breathed in nerve gas and it cleared her sinuses. She survived the first three nuclear strikes aimed at her by enclosing herself in a little bubble. By the fourth one, she'd figured out how to survive it without the bubble. She may not have been as strong as she once was, but she was still becoming indestructible. And while she may have had the odd headache now and then, she was still a god.

But Beijing annoyed her. The mortals were still fighting her and the sorcerers were helping them. All over the world, they refused to accept the fact that their silly little meaningless lives were over. It was insulting, if she were to be honest. They thought they still had a

99

chance with this, and one only." Skulduggery grabbed Fletcher, pulled him to his feet, and pointed at Valkyrie and her parents. "Get Alice and get them the hell out of

100

here she was, destruction incarnate, and these mortals dared to hope that somehow, maybe, with the help of all these sorcerers, they could find a way to beat her.

It was aggravating.

She went away for a week, thought about her next move, and decided to just kill them all, absorb as much of their energy as she could, and move on. She had itchy feet. She wanted to explore the universe. To seek out new life and new civilisations. Then to kill them, too.

So she killed the world, burned it to a husk, and flew off into space.

She set foot on the moon. She teleported to Mars. The gases of Neptune made her eyes water. By the time she breached the galaxy, she didn't need her body to travel any more. Her body became her mind, and she travelled at the speed of thought, and upon discovering life her physical form would take shape once again.

She appeared as a vast alien god to these otherworldly species. And she was not a nice god.

There were challenges that she had to overcome. Weapons she was unfamiliar with. Life cycles she was ignorant of. A constant pressure on her head, like a hand pressing down on her. But her biggest challenge was boredom. When she had had her fill of this universe, she returned to what remained of Earth. She began to long for something new. Something different.

Using everything she had learned from all those thousands of Remnants she had absorbed, she solved the mechanics of reality, and lifted off the ground and

101

rose high into the air. Fletcher watched, sure that she would snap out of it, fix her gaze on them, but she didn't, she kept rising, a peculiar look on her face. She reached out with her hands and pulled

102

the empty space apart. Darquesse felt her fingers buzz. This was a new way of doing it, a new way of creating a portal, a doorway to a world with a

103

red sky, there was a red sky, and Fletcher's heart thundered in his chest when he heard that noise, that awful, sickening

104

mourning call of the Faceless Ones, beautiful in its way, and Darquesse smiled at last. She hadn't smiled since she'd killed Skulduggery Pleasant, all those years ago.

She stepped through the portal, leaving the lifeless universe of her home, and the portal closed behind her.

105

Fletcher blinked. "It worked?"

Cassandra sagged and Skulduggery caught her. Finbar collapsed and Fletcher only noticed when he heard the thump beside him.

"Oh," he said. "Sorry."

Finbar mumbled something, and waved his hand weakly.

Fletcher looked up again, at where the portal had just been. At where Darquesse had vanished. "We beat her?"

"We didn't beat her," Skulduggery said. "We fooled her. There's a difference. Everyone link up."

Geoffrey and Philomena held out their hands. They were pale. Weak. What they had just done had taken a lot out of them. Fletcher made sure everyone was touching, then teleported back to the Medical Wing.

Valkyrie was the first to see them – of course she was – and she sat up in bed and tried to move her parents and Synecdoche out of the way, but the doctor was having none of it.

"You do not move," she said sternly.

Fletcher and Skulduggery walked over. Valkyrie's neck was in a brace and her face was swollen and cut. Her left hand sported new bandages which matched the bandages on her elbows.

"She's gone," Skulduggery said.

Valkyrie tried to nod, and winced. "I know," she said. "I felt her somehow. She seemed happy."

"She's got a whole new universe to conquer. I'm sure she's thrilled."

Fletcher spotted Tanith across the room, sitting on the edge of a bed with her head down. "Is Tanith OK?"

Valkyrie hesitated. "She's fine. But Billy-Ray Sanguine is dead. I... I told her about, you know... the two of them. When she had the Remnant. I couldn't *not* tell her. Not after he gave his life to save her. I figured she ought to know the whole story."

"How did she take it?"

Valkyrie shook her head. "I'm still not sure."

Synecdoche sat her up, lifted her shirt, and applied clear gel to her badly-bruised torso.

"We've got an assortment of broken ribs here that we'll have to mend later today," the doctor said, "along with the broken arm, the concussion, the fractured skull and the internal injuries. For now, though, we'll strap you up and move you on. We need the space and, astonishingly, you're not critical."

Synecdoche motioned to an assistant to finish the job, and hurried to a moaning patient elsewhere.

"Is that it?" Desmond asked. "Darquesse is gone? It's over?"

Skulduggery nodded. "Cassandra and Finbar and the others gave her the reality she wanted and then allowed her to leave it. As far as she knows, we're all dead. Our universe is dead. There's nothing for her to come back to."

"No more danger?" Melissa asked.

"Not from Darquesse."

Melissa sobbed, turned to Valkyrie and grabbed her good hand. "Sweetheart..."

"Mum..."

"Sweetheart, I am so proud of you. I am so... proud. No parent has ever been as proud of their daughter."

Valkyrie managed a strained smile that looked odd to Fletcher somehow. The assistant finished up and Skulduggery helped Valkyrie stand.

"You're coming home with us?" her mum asked.

"I will," Valkyrie said. "When I'm cleared here."

"Steph, please—"

"Mum. Fletcher will take you three home now and I'll be there as soon as Doctor Synecdoche says I can. I still have things to do here, and I want to check on a few people. I won't be getting hurt any more today, though, I promise."

Melissa hesitated, then nodded, and looked up at Skulduggery. "I owe you an apology."

"No," he said, "you don't."

"I said some pretty horrible things."

"Entirely justified."

"Oh, I know they were," Melissa said, "but I'm beginning to think that your good points outweigh your bad. Steph says it's because of you that she's alive today."

"That may be so. But I'm only here today because of her."

Melissa looked back at Valkyrie. "Can I hug you? Would it hurt too much?"

"You can hug me a little," Valkyrie said, an actual smile poking through. Both her parents gave her the lightest of hugs, but they both spent ages doing it. When her father was done, he stepped back.

"Gordon would be so proud of you," he said. "I know I am. You helped save the world today, sweetie. The kid I raised helped save the world. In a way... in a way, I suppose that means *I* saved the world."

"If anyone's still listening," Melissa said, "I would like to apologise for my husband."

"I'm going to get a T-shirt printed up. Maybe a mug."

Melissa turned to Fletcher. "When you take us home, are we going to throw up again?"

He couldn't lie. "Probably," he said.

She sighed.

Desmond poked his finger at Alice. "And don't think I'm forgetting about you, young lady. Your big sister saved the world today. What the hell have you done?"

Alice giggled, and Fletcher took them home.

106

Valkyrie and Skulduggery left the Medical Wing. The Sanctuary was in chaos. People ran, shouted at each other. Emergency crews took over. Valkyrie and Skulduggery ignored it all. Valkyrie and Skulduggery had had enough.

"Are you sure you're OK?" he asked when they entered the peace and quiet of the Old Sanctuary.

"I'm fine," she said.

"You're bleeding internally."

"A little internal bleeding never hurt anyone."

"That's not strictly true, though. Do you want me to carry you, or...?"

She gave him a look. "Am I slowing you down? Is that what it is? Would you rather be walking faster?"

"To be honest... yes."

"Well, tough."

They walked along in silence for a bit.

"Congratulations on saving the world," Skulduggery said. "Or helping to save it anyway. Being in the general vicinity. Cassandra and Finbar and the others *actually* saved it. But it was my plan, and you enabled it to happen, so... I think we're all winners here, really."

"Yay us."

"You don't sound overly delighted."

"Would you be? I didn't help save the world, Skulduggery – I helped cancel out the threat I posed to it. Those people, the ones who attacked me, they had it right. I'm to blame for all this."

"You know it's not as simple as that."

"Darquesse was part of me. That little fact is inescapable." Valkyrie paused. "I notice you haven't asked me yet how I could suddenly use the Sceptre."

"No I haven't. And I won't. We're called on to do things, again and again, that a person should never be asked to do. But we find a way, Valkyrie. And your family is safe and Darquesse is gone. It looks like we're going to have a happy ending on this one."

She grunted. "Since when do we ever get a happy ending?"

"It's rare," he said, "but it's possible."

They started down the steps.

"You think she stands a chance against the Faceless Ones?" Valkyrie asked.

"I don't know. Part of the reality the Sensitives constructed was to convince her that she'd accumulated more power than she had. But *she* opened that portal. It probably took everything she had to do it, but that part was no illusion. And if she could do that... she might stand a chance against a Faceless One. Maybe even two."

"But not an entire race of them?"

Skulduggery shook his head.

"Then she's gone," said Valkyrie. "My bad mood is gone. Odd, I don't feel any cheerier. I thought..."

"Yes?"

They got to the bottom of the steps, walked the cold corridor to the next set.

"I thought Darquesse was my bad side," she said. "But I did something so... so terrible..."

Skulduggery looked at her. "Long life can be a curse. The longer you live, the greater the chance that you're going to do things you regret. But long life is also a blessing – because you have a lot of time in which to set things right."

"And what if there *is* no setting it right?"

His voice was soft. "Punishment is not the answer. Punishment is easy. It's lazy. Redemption is hard. Redemption makes you work."

"You've been working for redemption for a while now. Are you any closer to it? Are you ready to pick up your family crest again?"

He tilted her head to her. "You remember."

"That you wouldn't carry the crest until you reckoned you were worthy of it? Yes, I remember. So are you ready to carry it now? How do you know when your redemption is complete?"

"I'm hoping you just... know."

"The scientific method."

His jaws opened, he was about to say something, probably something like "Precisely", but he didn't. He stopped. China lay very still in the corridor ahead of them.

Skulduggery sprinted to her. Valkyrie hobbled as fast she was able, reaching them just as China's eyes fluttered open. "I'm fine," she said, her voice a whisper. "Darquesse?"

"It's over," Skulduggery said, her head in his hands.

A slight smile. "Not yet." Her blue eyes flickered behind them. "Ravel. Trouble."

She dipped into unconciousness, and Skulduggery left her there and stood. Valkyrie followed him into the Accelerator Room.

The Accelerator itself was churning. The humming sound was coming from deep within its core. And it was getting louder.

The Engineer stood looking at them. Ravel was slumped on the ground, his hands shackled behind his back. He was conscious but clearly dazed.

"What happened?" Skulduggery said.

"Erskine Ravel demanded that his power be boosted by the Accelerator," the Engineer responded. "While I knew that the title of Grand Mage now rested with China Sorrows, I had never been given the specific instruction to disregard any orders from Mr Ravel."

Valkyrie glared. "So you said yes?"

"I am a robot," said the Engineer. "I obey my instructions to the letter. There is no room for personal interpretation."

"And did it work?" Skulduggery asked.

"Yes. But when Mr Ravel stepped out he was somewhat disorientated. Upon her arrival, Grand Mage Sorrows engaged him in what was a quite spectacular physical confrontation, during which she was able to secure these shackles upon his person."

Valkyrie frowned at the Accelerator. "It's overloading."

"I am afraid so," said the Engineer. "I warned Mr Ravel that his usage would hasten the countdown towards its end. He chose to ignore me."

"So how long do we have?"

"Twelve minutes, eleven seconds."

Valkyrie paled.

The circular platform within the Accelerator, the dais, lit up.

"One soul," the Engineer said, "willingly given. The individual steps on to the dais. Death is instant. Their energy, what my creator called their soul, is then used to deactivate the Accelerator."

"Well, OK," said Valkyrie. "OK, so there are loads of injured people upstairs. Loads of dying people. I'm sure we can get one of them to volunteer."

The Engineer held up one metal finger. "A clarification," it said. "When the soul is used to deactivate the Accelerator, it is used in its entirety. If there is a heaven or an afterlife, it will not journey onwards. Its energy will not rejoin the Great Stream, if such a thing exists. The soul will be used up, here and now. Never to return."

"But..." Valkyrie said. "But... wait... Erskine, you did this, so this is your chance to—"

Ravel looked up at them, and shook his head. "I've sacrificed enough," he said. "You're on your own."

She looked at Skulduggery. He tilted his head towards her.

Valkyrie bolted for the dais, but he caught her, yanked her back, and she cried out and pushed against him and he hit her, hard, in the side, and she folded, gasping.

"Sorry," he said.

Tears in her eyes, and not just tears of pain.

"Don't you dare," she gasped.

"I have, unfortunately, little choice in the matter." Skulduggery looked at the Engineer. "A soul, willingly given," he said. "That's it? That's your entire brief?"

"Correct," said the Engineer.

"No loopholes? No other way around it?"

"None."

"A soul, willingly given. That's what your creator programmed into you? Those words and no others? No stipulations? No qualifications? No exceptions?"

"None."

Skulduggery looked down at Valkyrie. "You heard the robot."

She ignored the pain, forced herself to stand. "Please don't do this. Let me go instead."

"Nonsense."

He went to turn away, but she grabbed his arm. "No! Listen to me! We can think of something else! We can figure it out!"

"We don't have time."

Valkyrie put herself in front of him, pressed both hands against his chest, felt his ribs. "For God's sake," she said, "please don't do this. Skulduggery, please. I can't lose you."

He tilted his head and, with a gloved finger, he brushed a tear from her cheek. "You'll never lose me, Valkyrie."

"But I need you with me," she said. "I've done awful things. I... Skulduggery, I killed Alice."

"Alice is alive."

"But I still killed her. It doesn't matter what I did after that moment. I killed my own baby sister. What kind of person would do that?"

"A person with no other choice."

"I need you here. Please. I've done terrible things. I hate... I hate myself. I have to go away. But I need someone to come back to. You can't leave me alone."

"Valkyrie—"

"Please don't go. Skulduggery, I'm begging you."

"You're really making quite a fuss over nothing."

She hit him, punched him right across the jaw, pain flashing through her fist, through her entire body. "You are not nothing, you bloody idiot! You changed my life! You made my life better! You made me better! What do you think I'm going to do when you're gone? You think I'm going to be happy? I swear to Christ, if you go, I go."

"Well," he said, "now you're just being silly."

"You have nine minutes, fourteen seconds," said the Engineer.

"Nine minutes," said Valkyrie. "Nine. We can think of something in nine minutes. We can find a volunteer in nine minutes. Please!"

Skulduggery put his hands on her shoulders. "Valkyrie, trust me on this one thing, and step out of my way. I have to do this."

She looked up at him. "I don't want you to leave me."

"And I never will."

"You said we'd be together until the end."

He nodded. "Yes I did."

A face flowed up over his skull, an unremarkable face with unremarkable features. He leaned in, and softly kissed her cheek. The face flowed away. He hugged her, then peeled her arms from around his neck, took off his hat and put it on her head. He spent a moment angling it just right.

"There," he said. "Looks good on you."

She couldn't speak as he stepped round her. He walked up to the Accelerator. The Engineer watched him impassively. Ravel looked away.

"I love you," Valkyrie blurted out.

Skulduggery didn't look back.

107

"Danny. *Danny.*"

Danny opens his eyes. Someone is behind him, holding him, their arms round his legs, taking his weight.

"Stephanie?" he mumbles.

"May as well call me Valkyrie," she says. "Can you lift your hands off the hook?"

Danny makes the mistake of looking up. A river of stinging sweat flows into his eyes, blinding him. He grits his teeth, tries freeing himself.

"Can't move my arms," he says.

She releases him, and his full body weight hangs from his wrists again. He swings a little, enough to see her hurrying to the wheel on the wall when he cracks one eye open. Stephanie, or Valkyrie, dressed in black, sweating in the heat, but not looking overly concerned about it.

"They're waiting for you," he says. Christ, he's thirsty. His words feel thick and slow. "This is a trap."

"Yep," she says, "bears all the hallmarks of one." She abandons the wheel, comes back over. "What a place, eh? Bigger on the inside. Like the TARDIS. Look away." She raises her hand. "This is going to be bright."

He closes his eyes but not all the way, and sees white lightning crackle from her fingertips. The lightning hits the chain and suddenly he's swinging wildly. He looks up. The chain is scorched. He can see a clear fracture in one of the links.

"Sorry," Valkyrie says, reaching out to steady him. "Haven't done this in a while. Another blast should—"

A large shape bursts from the door and Danny shouts a warning, but he's too late. Jeremiah swings a sledgehammer into Valkyrie's ribs. The impact lifts her sideways.

"Mr Gant!" Jeremiah screeches. "She's here! She's here!"

Valkyrie tries to get up. She's wheezing. Jeremiah doesn't give her the chance. The hammer comes down, right between her shoulder blades. Valkyrie flattens out.

"Mr Gant! I have her! I have her, Mr Gant!"

He goes quiet all of a sudden, and assumes the look of a man to whom an idea has just occurred. He leans the sledgehammer against the wall, takes hold of the collar of Valkyrie's jacket, and drags her from the room. Amazingly, Valkyrie is still half conscious, but she's in no fit state to fight back. The last Danny sees of her are her boots.

He starts swinging wildly, kicking out and twisting. The broken link bends a little. He torques, grunting with the effort.

He stops when he hears footsteps. Moments later, Gant walks in with a smile on his face, a smile that dims when he realises Danny is the only person here.

"Where are they?" he asks.

Danny swings from side to side, but doesn't answer. Gant fixes him with a stare. "She's here. Your usefulness is at an end. Allow yourself a few minutes more of life and tell me where they went."

"Jeremiah took her," says Danny. "Through there."

A troubling frown crosses Gant's face, and he strides from the hut.

Danny kicks his legs up in front, then swoops them behind. He starts swinging forward and back. With every swing, he kicks higher. The chain creaks. Kick in front, swoop behind. Kick and swoop. Higher and higher. He looks up as he swings. The broken link widens its jaws.

Kick and swoop. His shoulder is on fire. Kick and swoop. Kick and—

The world tilts, suddenly and without warning. The broken link gives way and he's crashing to the floor. He rolls over, gets to his knees, but he can't wait for his burning muscles to soothe. Up he gets, feeling returning to his arms. His hands are still cuffed, but his fingers are tingling. He flexes them until he's sure he can grip, and then he picks up the sledgehammer.

He leaves the hut, limping only slightly, and steps on to a bridge suspended by chains. It sways under his weight, almost tips him into the sea of fire. He crosses, doing his best not to look down. He can still hear the screaming.

Danny gets to the platform ahead and takes the metal steps down. He pauses to wipe the sweat from his eyes, then continues on to where the steps flatten and meet a grille floor. More stairways and bridges lead off it. He leans over the railing, glimpses Gant on the level below him. It takes a moment to figure out the best way down, but when he has it, he hurries after him.

Hefting the hammer, he approaches a hut suspended entirely by chains. He can hear voices inside.

"The audacity," Gant is saying. "The sheer *audacity* of you. I'd almost be impressed if I wasn't so disappointed."

Danny peers in. It's a small room, with a heavy, bloodstained work table against the far wall. Valkyrie is on the ground, not moving. Gant is standing over her, his hands on his hips. Jeremiah stands with his back to the door, his shoulders slumped.

"No," Jeremiah is saying, "I was just getting her ready for you, I was just—"

"I'll tell you what you were *just* doing," Gant snaps. "You were going to kill her. You were going to kill her and claim the credit all for yourself."

"Mr Gant, no, I would never do—"

"And yet here you are, Jeremiah. Here you are in your fetid little cubbyhole with your grubby hands round her throat. Do you think this is how she would want to die? Do you think this is how anyone would want to die?"

"No," says Jeremiah meekly.

"I thought you were better than this. I thought you respected me more."

"I'm – I'm sorry, Mr Gant. I was weak. I saw her, I put her down, I was going to give her over to you, I was. But... but Mr Gant, I haven't killed anyone like this in a long time."

"I let you kill ordinary people. Isn't that enough for you?"

There's a pause as Jeremiah hesitates. Danny wipes his hands on his trousers, and takes a grip on the sledgehammer. It isn't as wide as he'd like, because of the cuffs, but it's a firm grip nonetheless.

"What?" Gant says, irritated. "Out with it, for heaven's sake."

"You said you'd let me kill the next one," Jeremiah says quietly.

"You're not ready, Jeremiah."

"You always say that." He's almost whining now. "When will I be ready?"

Gant adopts the tone of a disappointed parent. "I don't know. Up until a few minutes ago, I would have said soon. Very, very soon. Maybe even today. I was so close to letting you do this one. But after this... after this, Jeremiah, I just don't know any more."

"Mr Gant," says Jeremiah, and he's crying, "Mr Gant, I'm sorry."

Danny takes another peek.

Gant is looking down at Valkyrie. "I need to know I can trust you, Jeremiah."

"You can," says Jeremiah. "I promise you can."

"I don't know. I don't think so."

Gant turns away a little more and Danny sees his chance. He

runs in, swinging. Jeremiah hears him and ducks under the sledgehammer, but all that does is clear a path right to Gant's face.

And it's like he's swung the hammer into a metal pillar.

The shock of the impact wrenches the sledgehammer from Danny's hands and he cries out and staggers back. The hammer clatters to the floor and Gant shoots Danny a smile.

Jeremiah roars, charges, takes Danny off his feet. They go down, the big man's weight on him. Danny barely has any fight left. Jeremiah brings out a knife from somewhere. Danny grabs Jeremiah's wrist with both hands, but not fast enough to stop his arm from being nicked. They struggle with the blade. Gant doesn't say anything. Doesn't even move.

They roll across the floor, Danny finding reserves of strength he never knew he had. Gant doesn't follow the fight. He's just standing there, smiling and not moving.

No, wait, he is moving. But very, very slowly.

As he struggles with Jeremiah, Danny remembers the people in the gas station – the dead bodies stacked up in the backroom. How had Jeremiah found the time to do all that, unless...

Gant said this house was magic. Danny doesn't know about magic, but this place definitely defies reason. Valkyrie shot that weird light from her hands and Gant himself hadn't even blinked just now when the sledgehammer hit him. OK, so if the house really is magic, and Gant and Valkyrie are magic, then maybe Jeremiah is, too. And by the looks of things his magic is the ability to draw out his kills while the world slows down around him. The perfect power for a serial killer.

Danny refocuses on the knife. Jeremiah's strength is leaving him with every breath he puffs out. He's relying on his weight now to keep the knife in position – saving the last of his energy for one final push. Sweat rolls off Jeremiah's forehead and drops on to Danny's face, on to his gritted teeth. Danny heaves, and they roll, and for a moment Danny is on top, but then Jeremiah flips them over again. Danny's head knocks against Valkyrie's leg. The tip of the knife scrapes his chest.

Danny lets the blade dig in. Sensing that his moment has arrived, Jeremiah grunts and snarls and drives downwards, but Danny surprises him by holding on, and they strain and struggle and strain again, and Jeremiah is the first to weaken.

Danny shoves him off, rolls on top, and Jeremiah gasps and cries, like he doesn't want to play any more. Danny knocks the knife from his hand and, just like that, normal time resumes around them.

Gant turns, his smile quickly becoming a scowl as Danny finds himself being lifted off the floor. Valkyrie has him.

"Run," she says.

He runs. She's right behind him. They run across a swaying bridge of chains and mesh. Twice Danny's foot slips through, dangles above the fire, and twice Valkyrie has to haul him up again. They reach a spiral staircase on the other side, and head up.

"I can't," Danny gasps.

"You have to," Valkyrie says.

He trips and he falls and he bangs his knees and scalds his hands on the hot metal, but he keeps going. He doesn't know how, but he keeps going. By the time they reach the top, his legs are jelly. Valkyrie wraps her arm round his waist, and she practically carries him onwards. Some distant part of his mind takes a moment to appreciate her strength.

"I'm all turned around," she says. "Any idea how we get out of here?"

He looks around, then points at a distant platform. "There, I think."

She scans the area, finding the quickest path through all the walkways and bridges. "Got it," she says, and they're off again.

Danny lets himself be led. He's too tired to do anything but follow blindly. Valkyrie is the expert here. She's the warrior. He's just some guy.

They cross another chain bridge, almost get to the platform when Gant clambers up a ladder on the other side.

Valkyrie holds out her hand. She grits her teeth, focusing, and that lightning bursts forth. It hits Gant square in the chest, burns right through his shirt, but he never stops smiling.

"I'm afraid you can't beat me," he calls to them as he nears. "But if you surrender now I promise to make your death relatively painless."

"Back," Valkyrie whispers.

Danny retraces his steps, the chain bridge swaying. He gets to the last platform and looks back. Valkyrie's hands are glowing white, but instead of firing that lightning at Gant, she grips the chains on the bridge. There's a snap as they break, and a lurch, and the bridge sags, and Valkyrie turns and leaps as it collapses. Danny catches her.

They look back at the other platform, at Gant who shakes his head in an amused fashion. Calmly, he takes another set of stairs.

"This used to be easy," Valkyrie mutters. "You shoot someone, they go down. Mostly. This guy... this guy can't be hurt."

"No," says Danny, "he can. I think. I heard it. They were going after this woman, there was a fight, I heard Gant, you know, in pain. Not much pain but... definitely hurt."

Valkyrie wipes her sleeve across her forehead. Her jacket looks crisp and dry – so unlike Danny's own sweat-soaked shirt. "Well, he's not feeling any pain in here."

"He says he's master of his domain."

Valkyrie looks at him. "Maybe that's it. In this house, we can't beat him."

"So what do we do?"

"We take it outside."

She has another look at the criss-crossing walkways and chooses a new route. Danny runs by himself to the next set of stairs, but she has to help him climb them. When they reach the top, they find themselves on the same level as the door out of here.

Valkyrie leads the way across a chain bridge. Danny comes after her – slow but steady, gripping the chains and making sure his feet don't slip off the edge. This is the longest of the chain bridges, and it sways dramatically as they traverse it.

"Huh," Valkyrie says. She has stopped walking, and she's scanning the area. "Can't see him."

Danny stops behind her, grateful for the chance to catch his breath.

"Can you see him?" Valkyrie asks.

Danny grunts, shakes his head, not really bothering to look. All they have to do is get to the platform on the other side, pass through the hut he'd been chained up in, and take the walkway to the door. They are almost there. Almost out.

Valkyrie curses and pushes him and Danny cries out and falls, almost slipping from the bridge as a dark shape swoops overhead, cackling with glee.

Cadaverous Gant, swinging from a chain like Tarzan, and coming back this way.

Valkyrie grabs Danny's hands, pulls him up. Gant passes again, his long fingers barely missing Danny's shirt. The swing takes him up high and he leaps like a circus acrobat, snagging another chain, and swings in at a different angle. This time when he passes he kicks at the railings and the bridge lurches and Valkyrie nearly falls. Danny lunges, his hands grabbing her jacket, steadying her. She fills the air with imaginative swear words, and Danny releases her. Then something snags his shirt collar and he's plucked off his feet.

Valkyrie spins, grabbing the chain of his handcuffs. The sudden stop is jarring, and above him, Gant grunts in surprise.

Danny hangs in the air between them. Below him is nothing but fire.

"I can hold on forever, young lady," Gant calls down, laughing. "Can you?"

Valkyrie's free hand glows. Lightning surges and bursts forth, rattling the chain Gant hangs from. He lets go and Danny drops. Valkyrie braces herself and Danny comes to a jarring stop once again, the pain in his shoulder sending bright flashes before his eyes. He hangs there, not even daring to scream. He sees Gant out of the corner of his eye, swinging gently above them.

Danny doesn't know how Valkyrie is holding him, but she is. And, incredibly, she starts to pull him up.

As they sweat and strain, Gant watches. When it becomes clear that Danny's going to be able to clamber back on to the bridge, he sighs, looks around, and starts climbing the chain into the darkness above.

Danny gets to his feet. Every part of him is trembling.

"Come on," Valkyrie says. He nods dumbly, and follows.

They get to the platform. Danny's legs give out. He tries to get up before Valkyrie notices, but she looks back.

"I'm fine," he says.

"We're almost there."

"I know. I'm fine." He gets up, gives her a smile to reassure her, and his eyes widen.

Valkyrie turns as Jeremiah runs at her.

He slashes at her with the knife. Once again, Danny is surprised by how fast he is, but Valkyrie doesn't try to duck or jump away. Instead, she meets him, moving right into him, wrapping her left arm round his knife arm and repeatedly slamming her right palm into his face. Jeremiah's nose splits and his lips burst and there's blood everywhere. The knife clatters to the metal floor. Valkyrie sweeps his leg and he lands heavily, mewling like a spoiled child. He reaches up, grabs her hair, yanks her down on top of him. His hands encircle her throat. They start to blur.

The act of killing, this time seen from the outside. To Danny, a blur of movement. To Valkyrie, a struggle that is going on forever.

Danny lunges forward to help, but the blurred images are no longer there. There's a screech behind him and he whirls. Valkyrie lies on the edge of the platform, clutching Jeremiah's hand as he dangles over the sea of liquid fire.

"Help me!" Jeremiah screams.

But his weight, plus all the sweat, prove too much, and he slips from Valkyrie's grip and disappears, screaming, into the flames below.

Valkyrie stays where she is for a moment, then gets up. She wipes her hand on her trousers.

"No!"

They both look round at the scream. Cadaverous Gant stands on a higher platform, a hanging chain in his hand.

"Danny," says Valkyrie. "We have to go—"

She doesn't even get the chance to say "now". Gant leaps into a deep swing. At its apex he lets go, and for a moment Danny thinks he's going to miss the hut, but he slams into it, scrabbling for purchase before he slips. His fingers dig in. He climbs on to the hut's roof, then drops on to the walkway, and strides to the platform.

"The first chance you get," Valkyrie whispers to Danny, "you get out of here."

Danny shakes his head. "I'm not leaving you."

"Get out of here and get help," Valkyrie says, and walks towards Gant, her hands glowing.

She fires that lightning and Gant just walks through it like it's nothing. He hits her and she goes spinning.

"I'm going to rip your heart out," says Gant.

108

Gant picks her up only to slam her down again. Then he kicks her and Valkyrie goes rolling across the platform, gasping.

"I've known that boy since before either of you were born," he says, his voice little more than a guttural snarl. "I practically raised him. He had his flaws, of course he did, but he was a good boy, and he worked hard, and all he ever wanted to do was make me happy. And you... you come to my home and you..." Gant grabs her by the collar, lifts her off her feet. "What gives you the right? What gives you the right to kill that poor boy?"

Valkyrie struggles to breathe. "How many... people has he... killed?"

"They don't count!" Gant screams. "They don't count!" He headbutts her and lets her drop, and Valkyrie staggers and stumbles away from him, blood running down her face.

"They're cattle!" he continues to scream. "They're practice! Their lives meant nothing!"

Danny sees his chance. The walkway is clear. But he hesitates, his feet stuck.

Valkyrie glances at him, waves. "Go," she says, spitting blood. "Go."

"Yes, Danny," Gant says, kicking Valkyrie's legs out from under her, "go. Run. I'll hunt you down soon enough." He stomps on Valkyrie's back. She cries out.

Limping, staggering, throwing one foot in front of the other and willing his knees not to buckle, Danny crosses the walkway. He almost falls at the hut, but manages to keep himself standing. He doesn't look back. He doesn't turn at every cry of pain. He lurches into the hut, clinging to the hanging chains for support. The broken link dangles above him and he looks at it for a moment before reaching up to slip it from the chain. He pockets it, then stumbles to the doorway on the other side. He rests there for a moment. He's almost out. He just has to keep it together for another few minutes. Just one more little bridge, and then the front door, and fresh air and freedom. That's all.

He leaves the hut. One foot in front of the other. Hands on the railing. Easy does it. Don't get distracted. Don't look over at what's happening to Valkyrie. Don't look over at what Gant is doing.

One foot in front of the other.

One foot in front of the—

Danny falls against the door. He grabs the latch. It's slippery beneath his fingers. For the first time the thought occurs to him that it might be locked, that it won't open, that some kind of magic will deny him his escape, but when he finally gets a grip and turns the latch the door does indeed open, and he pulls it wide and cold air blasts his whole body.

He sobs with relief and throws himself forward, the steps taking him by surprise. He falls to the sidewalk, skinning the palms of his hands but not feeling it. He crawls on, tries calling for help, but the street is as empty now as when he first got here.

He reaches the Cadillac, fumbles for the handle, uses it to pull himself to his feet. Valkyrie's pickup is parked right behind it. He hears her yell in pain.

He looks back, into the house. He can still see the top of Gant's head, bobbing up and down as he continues to beat Valkyrie to death. Danny takes a deep, deep breath, and wipes some of the sweat from his eyes. Then he stands, and takes the broken link of chain from his pocket. It's heavy and big.

He turns to the Cadillac, and smashes the driver's window.

Next to go is the wing mirror. That smashes easily, making plenty of noise.

"Hey!" Gant yells from inside the house.

Danny ignores him, goes round to the front of the car. He swings the broken link into the left headlight.

"Hey!" Gant screams. "You leave that car alone!"

Danny moves slowly over to the other headlight, making deep dents in the hood as he goes. *Clang. Clang. Clang.*

Then there's a *smash.* And no more headlights.

"Hey!"

Danny looks up. Cadaverous Gant stands in the doorway, lips pulled back from his teeth. He looks livid. He looks, with the sunlight hitting his liver spots, like a really angry corpse. Danny laughs. This only makes Gant angrier.

"First you kill Jeremiah and then you attack my car?"

Danny brings the chain link down on the hood. *Clang.*

"Stop that! Jeremiah took great pride in maintaining this car. He would wax it every day until I could see my—"

Clang.

"Stop!" Gant screeches. "Stop it!"

"Make me," says Danny. His throat is so dry it hurts to speak. "Come on out of there. Face me like a man."

"What is this?" Gant sneers. "You think you're the hero? You think you can—"

Danny doesn't think anything of the sort. Danny just smashes the passenger side window.

Gant lets out a cry of anger and horror and jumps down the steps. Danny backs off into the middle of the street, giving himself room. Gant stalks right up to him and Danny raises his fists, thinking maybe he can use the broken link to knock out a few of Gant's yellowing teeth now that he no longer has the house to make him unstoppable. But even out here, the old man surprises him with his speed and his strength. Danny barely glimpses the punch that rocks his head back. He completely misses the one that knocks him on his ass.

Dazed, he can only look up as Gant takes Jeremiah Wallow's knife from his pocket. He closes his eyes. He doesn't want to see the end coming, and he has no strength left in him to fight.

Then suddenly he's being pulled to his feet and spun. Gant holds him from behind and digs the knife into his throat. Danny opens his eyes.

Valkyrie stands on the steps of the house. Her face is a mask of blood and she's holding her ribs with her left hand. Her right hand is outstretched, and it's glowing white.

"Your aim is off," Gant snarls, almost directly into Danny's ear. "You'll hit your friend here. Might even kill him."

"My aim's improving," Valkyrie says. "I'm just out of practice, that's all."

"Then go ahead," says Gant. "Fire. If you think you can do it. Go on. Tell you what, I'll make it easy on you. I'll count down from three. If you haven't fired by then, I'll cut his throat. Does that sound fair?"

"I have a counter-proposal," says Valkyrie, coming down the steps. Her eyes burn. "You let him go and drop the knife. You surrender and I arrest you. You tell me why you came after me and who wants me dead. That sounds pretty fair to me."

Danny can hear Gant's smile in his voice as Valkyrie joins them on the street. "Three."

Valkyrie's hand glows brighter. "Two," she says.

The knife digs a little deeper into Danny's throat. "One," says Gant.

"OK!" Valkyrie says, the glow immediately fading from her hand. "OK, you win."

"Naturally," says Gant. "You have shackles, I take it? Put them on."

Valkyrie's face turns to stone.

Gant's laugh is not a happy one. "You think me stupid, girl? You think I'm going to leave you even the slightest chance to gain the upper hand?"

She hesitates. "The shackles are in my pickup," she says, and starts forward. She freezes when Gant presses the blade deep enough into Danny's throat to draw blood.

"Do not take one more step, you insolent little whelp."

Valkyrie narrows her eyes. "You want me to get the shackles, I'm getting the—"

"You're not doing anything," Gant says. He drags Danny back towards the pickup. "I've heard all about you," he says as they go. "I've been told about the things you've done. Up until now, I wondered which version of you we were going to get – the angel or the demon. Jeremiah and I, we were prepared for both."

Valkyrie actually smiles. "You'd never be prepared for Darquesse."

"You'd be surprised," says Gant. "I've killed all sorts of people in the course of my work."

"And what work would that be, exactly?"

"Killing people like you." They come to a stop at the door of the pickup. "Angel or demon, we wondered. Now I know."

"No," says Valkyrie. "You only think you do."

Danny feels Gant's grip loosen as he reaches for the door handle. "Is that so? Well then, you tell me, young lady. Which are you? Angel or demon?"

Valkyrie smiles again. "I'm like anybody," she says. "I'm a little bit of both."

Gant opens the door and all Danny sees is a flash of brown and black as Xena leaps from the seat. Danny recoils and Gant falls, the big German shepherd snarling as she rolls off his chest. She goes for him again, jaws clamping down on his forearm.

Gant screams and Xena shakes her head furiously. The old man staggers to his feet, kicks the dog in the side. Xena yelps, dances back, dives again, closing her teeth round his ankle.

Hollering, Gant swipes at her with the knife. This time Xena gives a yelp of real pain and lets go. Gant swipes again, misses, and then Valkyrie is barrelling into him. The knife falls. Valkyrie catches him with an elbow that cracks against his chin. He tries to make a space between them, but she has a hold of him now and she won't let go. She digs her fingers into his face, shredding across his features. He panics, tries to push her off. She's like a limpet. There's no dislodging her. Gant's eyes are squeezed shut. His face is bleeding. Danny watches as Valkyrie's fury is let loose. It's terrifying.

They fall and Valkyrie is on top. Xena dances nearby, barking her rage and thirst for blood. Valkyrie crouches over Gant, starts slamming her right palm into his face.

He tries to push her off and she grabs his wrist, wrenches it and Gant hollers in pain.

Valkyrie leans in, and snarls. "Not so much fun when you're on the receiving end, is it?"

"Please!" Gant squeals. "I'm an old man!"

"Damn right you are," she says, and drops with an elbow to the jaw. Gant goes limp.

Valkyrie puts both hands on his face, shifting her weight to jump to her feet. Then she stands, well out of the way of his limbs.

"Xena," she says, "hush."

Immediately, Xena quiets down. But her tail doesn't stop wagging as she keeps her eyes fixed on Gant.

Valkyrie walks over to Danny and helps him stand. He hadn't even realised he'd collapsed. "You OK?"

He nods. It's a blatant lie, but Valkyrie doesn't seem to mind.

Once he's on his feet, she leaves him, walks back to the front door. She shuts it.

The dog barks and Danny looks back and Gant is halfway to the Cadillac with Xena biting into his already bloody leg. He curses in pain and throws himself through the broken window, shaking Xena off as he drags his legs in after him. Valkyrie's hands glow and white lightning catches Gant in the shoulder as he squirms behind the wheel. The engine roars to life and the car lurches forward. Valkyrie fires again, burning a deep scorch mark into the Cadillac's body, but she's too late to stop it. They watch it speed away, swerving dangerously.

Once it's out of sight, Xena stops barking.

"Dammit," Valkyrie mutters. She looks back at Danny. "You in any mood for a car chase?"

"You can have one if you want," he says. "I'll wait here."

Valkyrie shakes her head. "Naw. I reckon we've done enough these last few days, what do you say?"

Her hand wraps around the chain of his handcuffs and glows white, and a moment later the chain breaks. "Get in the pickup there," she says. "I'll make a few calls and then we'll head back to Meek Ridge."

He gets in, groaning a little when Xena jumps in on top of him. She settles herself in the middle, then reaches back to lick her bloodied fur. Every so often, she licks Danny's face. He is too tired to stop her.

Valkyrie talks on the phone for a bit, then gets in behind the wheel. "Some people are on their way here," she says. "They'll seal off the place, make sure Gant doesn't get back in. Hopefully, they'll pick him up on the road. If not, you'll get round-the-clock protection until he's arrested."

Danny nods. "OK," he says.

She reaches into her jacket, takes out a slim packet of dried leaves. She folds one, offers it to the dog. Xena swallows it and Valkyrie scratches behind her ears.

"Who's a good doggy, huh? Who's a good doggy?"

Xena wags her tail in a steady, happy rhythm.

Valkyrie pops one of the leaves in her own mouth, chewing it, and holds one out for Danny. "For the pain," she says.

He takes it without asking what it is. It tastes exactly like he expects it to – like a leaf. But the feeling that floods his body takes him completely by surprise.

"Wow," he says.

Valkyrie starts up the pickup and pulls away from the kerb. "Long drive back to Meek Ridge," she says. "You want the radio on?"

He'd wanted to sleep, but now that the leaf is working wonders, he's got more important things on his mind. "No," he says. "I want to know what's going on. Stephanie, Valkyrie, whatever your name is... please. Who *are* you?"

She gives him a smile. "Well, OK. You deserve it, I suppose. I'll start at the beginning, how about that?"

"Sounds good," he says.

She fixes her eyes on the road. "It all started with the death of my uncle."

By the time Valkyrie has finished the story, told him all about Skulduggery and Tanith and Ghastly and Darquesse and the Accelerator, they have reached Meek Ridge and are driving past the grocery store.

It hasn't burned down, which is a good sign. They take the road up to Valkyrie's place. They pass Danny's car, but they don't stop until they get to the house.

They get out. Xena disappears immediately. Valkyrie stretches. Danny looks at her, says nothing. He follows her up the steps, into the house. It's cold in here.

"Make yourself some coffee," she says, and that's what he does while she busies herself in another room.

When he's done, he sits at the kitchen table, looking at his reflection in the window. They'd cleaned up at a gas station, but his face is a swollen mess and his clothes are stained with dried sweat and blood. His eyes dip to the mug of coffee he's set aside for her. Steam rises from the brim.

A few minutes later, Xena comes in. She goes right up to Danny, nuzzling her snout into his hand until he pets her.

Elsewhere, he hears water running.

Xena wanders over to her bed, circles it a few times, and lies down. She rests her head on her paws, then looks up at him with wet brown eyes.

Valkyrie is standing there, in blue jeans and a jacket. Her hair is freshly washed. He hadn't heard her come in.

"Now I know why you're ninja-quiet," he says. There are two bags by her feet. "You going somewhere?"

"Home," she says.

This surprises him. "After... after everything that's happened?"

"It's time." She comes forward, picks up her coffee, tastes it. "This is cold."

"You've been gone a while."

"I suppose I have."

"Why did you leave?" he asks. "I mean, I know, the trauma must have been... unimaginable, but..."

"We won," she says. "But the things I did when I was Darquesse, and the things I did later, in order to beat her... I had to leave. I couldn't stay. Not after what I'd done to..."

"Alice."

She nods. "I didn't deserve a sister or a family. Stephanie... now Stephanie deserved a family. Everything she did, she did out of love for them."

"But so did you. You said it yourself, protecting them was the reason you did *everything*."

"I did it wrong, though. I did it badly."

"You did what you had to do. I can't believe you've been living up here alone for the past five years, blaming yourself, hating yourself for the things you had to do. You saved us all."

"No. I didn't save us. Not that time."

Danny finishes his coffee. It's lukewarm. "Skulduggery sounds like... an amazing person."

Valkyrie gives one of those soft smiles. "Yeah."

"He was a true hero, to give his life like that."

"Hmm?" says Valkyrie. "Oh, no, he didn't give his life."

Danny frowns. "He didn't? But you said he walked into the Accelerator."

She shakes her head. "I said he walked *towards* the Accelerator. He told me later, when he was taking his hat back, that a world without him would scarcely be worth living in. No, he hauled Ravel up off the floor and pushed him in instead."

Danny blinks. "But... but the soul had to be given willingly."

"It was," Valkyrie says. "But there was nothing in the rules that said the soul you willingly gave had to be your own."

"And that... worked?"

"Yep. The Engineer shrugged, said Skulduggery made a fair point, it allowed the soul to shut down the Accelerator, and Skulduggery turned round and made fun of me."

There's a knock on the door, and Valkyrie glances at her watch. "That'll be him now."

Danny jumps to his feet. "Skulduggery? That's Skulduggery Pleasant?"

"Probably, yeah. I called him, told him it was time I came home. It's like he said, years ago – punishment is the easy option. If I really want to make up for the things I've done, I've got to help people. If I want to make up for what I did to my sister, I have to be around her. I have to be a part of her life. She's six now, for God's sake. *Six*. She barely knows me. It's... it's time that changed." She picks up her bags. "You can let yourself out, can't you?"

"Uh... yeah..."

Valkyrie smiles. "I'll get the rest of my stuff shipped over to me and then, I don't know..." She looks around. "I'd sell the place, but I kind of like it."

"Will I ever see you again?" Danny asks.

"You might."

"But I might be an old man, yeah? And you'll look exactly the same?"

She gives him a sad smile. "Yeah. Maybe. There'll be some people calling round to talk to you. Sorcerers. Good people. They'll make sure everything is all right."

"Yeah. Cool."

She raises an eyebrow. "*Is* everything going to be all right?"

"I... I don't know. You're asking me to return to my boring life after... after all this. After you. I don't know if I can do that."

"So don't. You have dreams, right? You don't want to spend the rest of your life running a grocery store in Meek Ridge, do you?"

"No. I... I used to have a record deal."

Valkyrie tilts her head. "Seriously? Wow. Well, there you go. Get your record deal back. Become a rock star. Live an extraordinary life. You don't have to save the world to change it."

She taps her leg and Xena trots over. Danny goes as far as the hall with them. Through the frosted glass in the front door, he can see the dark outline of a tall, thin man, wearing a hat.

He remembers, as a kid, being scared of Santa Claus. He remembers lying in bed on Christmas Eve, curled in a ball, eyes wide, jumping at every creak the house made, waiting for this ghostly presence to visit. He feels that same kind of fear now – fear of the supernatural, mixed with pure, undiluted excitement.

Valkyrie stops with her hand on the latch, and looks back. "You want to meet him?"

Danny hesitates – hesitates for a long time – then shakes his head. "My mind is already blown enough, thank you very much. I think actually seeing a talking skeleton in person would just... I think my head would literally explode."

Her smile turns to a grin. "Yeah, fair enough. Hey, you have a good life, Danny, you hear me?"

"Same to you, Valkyrie." He gives her a little wave, feels the twinge in his injured shoulder, and winces. "What'll I tell people about all this?"

"They won't believe you anyway," says Valkyrie, "so tell them the truth."

Now it's his turn to raise an eyebrow. "What, tell them about sorcerers and lunatics and kidnappings and murder?"

"Naw," she says. "Tell them the real truth. Tell them about what's really important."

"And what, if you don't mind me asking, *is* really important?"

Valkyrie holds her hand palm upwards, and it starts to glow from within. She smiles at him.

"Magic," she says.

In 2007,
Derek Landy
introduced you to a world of
murder, magic and monsters

In 2015,
he's going to do
it all over again

**Brave New World
Brand New Story
Same Old Derek**